The Stevenson Plan

The Stevenson Plan

A Novel of the
Monterey Peninsula

M. Bryce
Ternet

To my wife, Renata.

Russian River

Sacramento River

SAN FRANCISCO
SOLANO DE SONOMA

SAN RAFAEL
ARCANGEL

SAN FRANCISCO
DE ASIS
(DOLORES)

SAN JOSÉ DE GUADALUPE

SANTA CLARA DE ASIS

SANTA CRUZ

San Joaquin River

SAN JUAN BAUTISTA

SAN CARLOS DE BORROMEO DEL RIO CARMELO

NUESTRA SEÑORA DE LA SOLEDAD

Carmel River

Salinas

SAN ANTONIO DE PADUA

SAN MIGUEL ARCANGEL

SAN LUIS OBISPO DE TOLOSA

PURISIMA CONCEPCIÓN

SANTA INÉS

SANTA BARBARA

Santa Barbara Islands

SAN BUENAVENTURA

SAN FERNANDO REY DE ESPAÑA

San Nicholas Is.

Santa Catalina Is.

SAN GABRIEL ARCANGEL

San Clemente Is.

SAN JUAN CAPISTRANO

SAN LUIS REY DE FRANCIA

N

SAN DIEGO DE ALCALÁ

W   E

SCALE OF MILES

S

BAJA CAL

CALIFORNIA

Colorado River

Prologue

It is the year of our Lord 1818 as I write this confession at the Mission San Antonio de Padua. Once this confession is complete, I will continue to the Mission San Carlos Borromeo de Carmelo and complete my mission.

I do not seek absolution, as I would not ask for forgiveness after having committed a heinous act of such a grievous nature. By the grace of God, I was brought to this land of Alta California to perform my duty to the Holy Church. I was left with no choice but to sin or fail my mission. I chose to sin.

His name was Diego Alvarez, and I confess that I, Father Dominique Margil of the Dominican Order, did take his life.

I accept the consequences awaiting my eternal soul. I can now only hope that my mission will achieve the results expected of it.

Father Dominique Margil

Year of our Lord 2009.

ISIDRO DE LA VEGA dropped the nearly two-hundred-year-old letter and stared at it on the uneven wooden table in front of him. He had only read the first paragraph and a flurry of questions was already swirling through his mind. The primary question concerned the authenticity of the letter. *Could this letter really be legitimate?* Isidro had examined enough letters from the late 1700s and early 1800s to be able to recognize the apparent authenticity of the cracking, thick parchment paper typical of the era and thus to preliminarily discern that the letter certainly appeared, at least initially, to be legitimate. Adding to this assumption was the fact that the letter had been written in a style of Spanish that he knew from his extensive studies was used in Spanish California during the earliest years of its establishment, long before it became a state of the United States. But the content of the letter itself bothered him most.

Legends and myths of the days of the early settlement of California by the Spanish were consistently intermingled with actual historical events of the time, and anyone studying California's early days had to learn to be skeptical of any new *story* they might come across. If what he was reading were true, though, then Isidro de la Vega had stumbled across a previously unknown piece of history.

Isidro suddenly felt an urge to reinsure that he was indeed alone in the abandoned room of the Mission San Antonio de Padua. He stepped slowly to the doorway, which had a wooden beam over it that looked as if it would collapse if struck, and peered down the darkened hallway leading back to the building segment of the mission complex, which nowadays served as a Sunday school area for children.

The mission had been elegantly restored in the 1950s, but the sprawling buildings of the mission, which had at the mission's heyday been even more sprawling, posed too great a challenge to restore every dilapidated piece. Thus, rooms such as the one where he stood were cordoned off from access and Isidro had to request special permission to wander through them, which he did more in an attempt to connect to the past than to seek to discover artifacts. It would be unlikely that anyone would be in the vicinity, as the San Antonio Mission received a tiny percentage of the annual visitors received at the Mission San Carlos Borromeo de Carmelo and, unlike the Carmel Mission, the church of the mission itself was rarely used, but he wanted to be sure.

Once he was certain that no one had followed him, he continued reading the letter on the table before him…

Part I

I.

Year of our Lord 2009.

I T WAS AS IF THE HEIST had already been recorded in California history books. Everything had been executed according to the meticulous plan Number Two had made the three other members of the group memorize months before, including the alternatives he crafted, which would be called upon on the off chance that something did not happen as planned. Number Two, however, was a very intelligent man who knew how to analyze a situation strategically from a complex multiple-system approach and then carefully design a solution. His plan had been flawlessly conceived and it was perfectly executed.

In appreciation of his genius, God had seemingly approved and enshrouded the entire city of San Francisco in a dark, thick blanket of fog on the July afternoon when they caught the United States Federal Reserve Bank of San Francisco with its pants down. It was so easy that Number Two considered adding that they had caught it not only with its pants down, but also peeing into the wind. Within less than ten minutes, the federal bank branch found itself missing a hundred million dollars.

Number Four steered the small fishing boat southward along the concealed California coastline while the other three men, referring to one another as Numbers One, Two and Three, stood along the rail of the boat, gazing into the unknown reaches of the darkness around them as the fog drenched their slickers. Number One, who no one would dare disagree with on any issue, ordered them to remain calm and quiet on the boat ride south as they pretended to be fisherman readying themselves for a night out at sea. Except for Number Two, they silently reflected on the day's events and the possibilities that awaited them now that they would each have millions of dollars coming their way.

Number Two continued to muse on how impeccable his logistical planning had been. It was, like many other accomplishments in his young life, flawless. Everything is related to a system, he thought, and the means of mastering any system were available to those able to calculate and dismiss potential solutions before committing to any attempt. His plan had been meticulous.

It began with Number Two arriving in San Francisco a day before the others and installing himself in a hotel room across from the Federal Reserve Bank building at 101 Market Street. Number Two considered *hacking* to be for degenerates that disgraced the name of computer science. Number Two didn't *hack*; he turned math and science into art. Number Two had grown accustomed to being called a computer geek. Although he despised the term, he did not deny his genius. He used his elaborate knowledge of computers to break into the Reserve Bank's system, no easy task even for the most gifted of computer geeks. It took him a few hours, rusty as he was, but he found his way through and accessed the file he sought.

Number Two researched the Reserve Bank building's system beforehand, and thus knew exactly where to find information concerning the weight scale of the exclusive-access freight elevators once he was inside the system. These elevators, located in the rear of the building, descended from ground level to a floor below, where vaults keeping the branch's currency reserve holdings were kept. The subfloor possessed a security system that was as tight as anything in Fort Knox. There may have been a ton of computer geeks in the area, but the upper tier of computer geniuses was a select group. Number Two was considered a lifetime member.

He discovered the level of sophistication of the Reserve Bank's system by casually discussing computer-automated security systems in the Bay Area with colleagues and contacts in Silicon Valley. He was sure he would have some professional connection to whoever designed the system. His reputation alone enabled him to remain discreet as he gathered information on the Reserve Bank's security system by pretending to be in the market for a highly advanced security system for his own home, which raised no eyebrows. With multimillionaire computer geeks, it's considered normal to desire a ridiculously unnecessary technology at home.

After limited subtle inquiry, Number Two located the technician who had overseen installation of the Reserve Bank's system. The two met for chai lattes in Palo Alto one sunny afternoon and Number Two, after inflating this fellow's exceptional computer genius with praise, received a nearly full description of the Reserve Bank's system. A small amount of additional research was all that was needed to fill in the blanks, and by the end of investigation, Number Two deduced that the Reserve Bank's system was close to impenetrable. But Number Two envisioned a solution to the problem.

Only two people at any one time during the day had direct access to the vault. These individuals were required to pass retinal, speech, and fingerprint scans to enter the vault, which, from the way the technician had described it, was a long hallway lined with individual vaults. Each vault contained an additional personnel scan and required a different eleven-digit numerical code. Light, sound, pressure, and heat sensors were activated when the corridor room was not in use, while a multitude of cameras surveyed the room as well. When Number Two described the system and the odds of being able to conquer it, and calculated less than one percent probability of success, Number One nearly snapped into convulsions at having his dream dismantled before it could move beyond a conceptual phase.

Number Two, after selfishly enjoying watching the grief-stricken Number One look as if he were going to choke, quickly added that he had not finished his assessment and that he believed they could overcome the system. Number One asked how this would be possible facing such insurmountable odds; Number Two replied that they would simply leave one equation unsolved and move to another where a solution could be attained. Number Two savored the anticipation and relief encompassing Number One's face until he thought Number One might strangle him, then added that he had found a solution: The solution was the vault room's elevator.

What he discovered was that the vault room's elevator operated on a system that configured the exact weight accounting for every currency deposit or withdrawal while also accounting for the weight of the two guards accompanying any shipment down into the vault room. Each shipment in or out would take into account the weight of the currency being moved, the weight of a specially designed dolly for moving loads in and out of the vault room, and the exact daily weight of the two guards moving the currency shipments, who had to stand on a precise scale before entering the vault room's elevator. Even a fraction of a pound off what the system configured for the total weight would reflect a compromise in the system and the elevator would automatically lock while a series of alarms would be triggered.

Number Two's initial explanation did nothing to relieve Number One's boiling tension. He stared at Number Two in disbelief until Number Two added that he would be able to hack into the system for a brief moment before a delivery in order to install a smaller weight total for the currency delivery than what was being moved. By doing so, the system would not calculate an error upon delivery, as it would have no way of knowing that a portion of a shipment was missing.

Number One declared Number Two a genius, which Number Two did not dissuade. Then Number One's mind cleared of money signs in order to reveal the obvious question: How would they be able to extract the unaccounted currency from the transfer room of the Reserve Bank's building? Their plan from the beginning was to involve no firearms whatsoever. In fact, they agreed that they would not even carry firearms. Armed robbery was for amateurs and speed freaks; they would be something different, an altogether new breed of thieves. They would be well-financed nerdy thieves that would rob the federal government without firing a shot or injuring a soul. This proclamation, though, seemed ever more daunting as Number One and Number Two reflected upon the challenges of their proposed heist.

Number Two took a delicate sip from his glass of Chardonnay, a hundred-dollar-a-bottle vintage from the Santa Lucia Highlands, and again provided a solution to the equation at hand. "We have money at our disposal, lots of money," he offered.

Number Two's comment was intended to convey that with money, they had an array of options to consider. For instance, in addition to the two guards in charge of accessing the vault room, the transfer room of the Reserve Bank building was occupied by government employees, government employees who never saw the light of day during work hours, government employees likely paid low salaries to do the majority of the heavy lifting in the transfer area while they watched the two highly paid guards do what would appear to be minimal work compared to theirs, yet the guards received the entirety of the praise for the facility's security. These individuals would perhaps be disgruntled government employees, people susceptible to outside influences, especially top-dollar offers.

This was where Number One's expertise became important. Number Two may have been the tech guy, but Number One was the people guy. If there was any convincing to be done, Number One could do it. Despite having done minimal careerwise, Number One was a natural salesman, and a natural salesman with financial backing, or at least perceived financial backing, such as a gigantic plush estate in Pebble Beach, was a lethal combination. Number One immediately tasked himself with identifying their target person. He spent hours on the phone talking with anyone and everyone he knew in San Francisco and he took numerous trips to the city to focus his efforts, which proved successful when he identified a young man named Claude.

Claude had grown up in Oakland in one of the less-than-fashionable enclaves of the city regarded by many as a stepchild to its glamorous neighbor across the bay. Perhaps it would be better to say that Claude had spent his early life in inner Oakland rather than to say he had grown up there with a proper upbringing, as by the tender age of ten, Claude had grown accustomed to things that no little boy should grow accustomed to, such as drive-by shootings in front of him as he walked home from school, such as friends his age getting roped into carrying drugs and guns for their older brothers, such as his father leaving for prison and never returning. Claude's memories of his childhood were mostly of fear and desperation, rather than of the magical moments most people hold onto from their days of innocence while they forge their way into the unforgiving world of adults.

Claude never dreamed of going off to college; the insurmountable odds of it happening had become reality while he struggled through high school with barely above-average grades. Unlike some of his friends, he didn't have superior athletic skills to offer. The federal government rescued him, however, from an otherwise unpredictable existence by accepting him as a security guard for federal buildings in San Francisco. Unlike many of his friends who were also applying for the coveted federal jobs throughout the San Francisco Bay Area, Claude had never touched drugs in his life; this amounted to a huge asset for those applying for positions requiring pre-employment drug screening. Further, Claude had no record of crime. He was constantly surrounded by it while sprouting to maturity on the streets of Oakland, but he somehow managed to keep it at a distance.

His job with the government gave him an opportunity to shine. It provided him with the means to move out of his mother's house within two years of graduating from high school and allowed him to rent his own studio in South San Francisco. It wasn't the nicest apartment. It wasn't the nicest neighborhood. But Claude enjoyed being able to look at Oakland from across the bay and know he had escaped a seemingly predestined life of misery. For many years he blamed the world for his troubles, for the lack of opportunities it sent his way. He hated the world, as he felt it hated him. The government job initially changed this. For a time, he stopped despising everything around him. It even made him see white people in a different light. Claude didn't consider himself racist, but coming of age in inner-city Oakland and receiving the impression that there were more poor dark-skinned people than white people did take its toll on his overall views. *Perhaps they aren't all so bad after all*, he began to think.

This new way of thinking, though, did not endure long after he was reassigned to a position at the San Francisco Federal Reserve Bank building. Claude recognized that he was not a highly intelligent person and he was able to accept such a humbling self-revelation. His boss, Frank Matherly, however, was not able to accept Claude's occasional lapses of mild ineptitude. Matherly began tormenting Claude from the first day of his reassignment and never ceased. At first, Claude was able to brush aside Matherly's disgusted glances and insensitive comments, but after months and then years of abuse, Claude grew incapable of hiding from Matherly's comments. He grew incapable of escaping from Matherly's glances. What bothered Claude most was that Matherly's attitude toward him gradually spread to others who were a part of the building's security group.

Before long, Claude felt the uncomfortable sense that everyone he worked with was against him and he began to feel as he had growing up in Oakland, a second-class citizen that no one cared about. His hatred toward the world began to burn again. His distrust of white people also resurfaced. Among the group of standard security guards working security detail shifts for the building, he was the only non-white person, which Matherly took pleasure in reminding everyone not so subtly with his staple comment referring to affirmative action whenever Claude committed the tiniest of mistakes.

Claude was single, black, in his late 20s, unhappy with his job, and enraged. He was a perfect target for Number One, although Number One being a white man gave little comfort to Claude at their first prearranged meeting. Number One arranged the meeting through a friend with a contact within the Human Resources Department of the Federal Reserve Bank's branch. The white man was obviously extremely wealthy and willing to pay Claude tons of money for simply leaving a door open for thirty seconds longer than he was supposed to; which would indirectly induce revenge for the many wrongs perpetrated against him. Claude may not have cared for white people, but he had no problem taking a white man's money and the deal was attractive, especially knowing that he would get back at all the bastards who had talked down to him his entire life. *I'm finally going to show them how smart I can be.*

Claude agreed to do as he instructed for a fee far lower than Number One was prepared to offer, and displayed more enthusiasm about it than expected. It was an easy sale for Number One, although, when recounting the exchange to his crew, he exaggerated the complexity of the negotiation.

Number One may have been responsible for getting Claude on board with their scheme, and therefore responsible for securing the paramount thirty-second door delay, but it would be for nothing without Number Two's further engagement. Number Two's genius continued its noteworthy display when he was able to crack into the

City of San Francisco's traffic network and disrupt traffic on Market Street by reordering the timing and sequencing of stoplights.

Number Four arranged for an Arab-looking delivery vehicle to be parked directly in front of the Federal Reserve Bank in an attempt to arouse suspicion in the post-9-11 era, when every person of Middle Eastern decent could be blatantly accused of having ties to terrorism and being related to Osama Bin Laden. It had been a job well done; however, without the traffic light disruption, Number Two doubted that the delivery man, actually born in Freemont, California, would have attracted the attention of the federal officers streaming out of the front of the building. With the majority of the attention focused on the front of the building and the Middle Eastern-looking delivery man in a parked, unlabeled white van on the side of the road, Market Street was in momentary chaos, while the rear of the building, just as a currency transfer was being delivered, received little attention.

The armored vehicle delivering currency arrived on schedule, as always. Claude did his duty of opening the rear door of the building after having been given the okay from the two security officers responsible for escorting the crates of currency from the delivery room into the vault chamber below. Claude had witnessed the same routine so often over the years that he knew the mannerisms of every person involved in the deliveries, from the two men delivering the shipments from the rear of the armored tank-like vehicle to the two men that took the shipments below, taking each delivery into a precise vault identified to them beforehand. The two men even repeated the same stupid jokes to one another with every delivery. Typically Claude would feel the brunt of some sort of joke about dumb people, and he would also be reminded of his general lack of intelligence. Claude imagined that even if he did every detail of his job correctly, he would still be called stupid. But he was going to show the world how stupid he was not.

The day of the heist, Claude used the fat white security officers to his advantage. He let them call him stupid for leaving the door open seconds longer than he was supposed to after the crates had been unloaded into the delivery area and the armored vehicle had departed. They were so used to calling him names and making fun of him that they didn't question the action as anything more than what it appeared to be: Claude was just being an idiot again. However, the idiot secretly won the day and did so without letting a huge smile cross his face that he felt bursting inside of him. A few seconds were all that were needed for two men, Numbers Three and Four, who had tirelessly practiced the situation for months, to step from a specially constructed van parked next to the loading dock.

The two men entered the loading area through the lingering-open door, while the two guards descended into the vault chamber. They carried a specifically designed hand cart, loaded one of the crates of treasury bills onto it, and were back in the van long before the two guards returned from their first delivery to the vault chamber. Claude assured Number Four that the two security guards responsible for accessing the vault chamber would never notice if one of the crates in the shipment stock was missing as they lazily took their time to move the delivered shipment. *Claude was right.*

The avalanche of security cameras in and around the entire area would spot them surely, if it were not for Number Two's brilliance at programming the cameras to skip at a precise time for a matter of seconds. Seconds were all that was needed to steal four hundred million dollars from the U.S. Government.

Numbers Three and Four were often lumped together in the crew's discussions, a bitter reality that left both displeased, but was an arrangement Number Three despised. They disliked the categorization for differing reasons. Number Three hated not being considered an individual component of the team. Numbers One and Two didn't bother to conceal their high-and-mighty impressions of themselves. By being tied to Number Four, though, Number Three felt even less appreciated. Number Four, on the other hand, didn't mind doing whatever he was told by Number One or Two; it was just that he was scared of Number Three.

Number Three loathed being linked with Number Four. Number Three did not care much for Number Two, either, but at least Number Two brought something to the table in their crew, unlike his opinion of Number Four. In his view, Number Four was nothing but a fat, pompous, kiss-ass, wannabe follower with no creativity or imagination.

Despite the palpable tension emanating between the two, they were paired to work together to pull off a vital component of the job. Number One had inflated their egos during their practice sessions and more thoroughly the morning of the heist by stating that their portion of the score would be the most physical and most dangerous. Without them, all of them would go to jail and none of them would get any richer. They were essential, he praised to them.

At the moment when they needed to excel, they did. The inside man came through, as when Number Three stopped the van behind the building's loading doors at the exact planned time, the doors were still slightly ajar, just as concocted. Number Four did as they had practiced, springing quickly from the rear of the van, astonishingly quickly for a man of his belly girth, Number Three thought, at the moment they came to a full stop. Number Four had the electronic dolly unloaded and was moving into the open doors of the dock by the time Number Three had exited the van to join him.

They ran into the darkened interior of the loading area and instinctively guided the dolly underneath one of the crates waiting for them in the center of the loading area, just where they were supposed to be. From the moment the electronic dolly that Number Two had engineered for the heist was underneath the crate, it was smooth rolling. They exited the doors, and with the loading apparatus already waiting for them in the rear of the van, it required mere seconds to load the crate onto the van. They both hopped in and drove north, towards Chinatown. They had not seen a soul while inside the Reserve Bank building.

Of course, even though people were panicked about the disruption on Market Street and were scurrying past the back of the Reserve Bank at the time, someone might have noticed two men quickly loading something into the back of a van from the unmarked and discreet delivery area of the building's rear. In that case, Number One had made them wear latex masks an associate of his had designed for each of them. The masks were just enough to alter their features sufficiently to make them appear as different people from a distance.

Although effective, the masks were terribly itchy and the men could not wait to remove them, especially Number Four. He also felt an urge to defecate, as in times when he felt nervous — it comforted him to be sitting on a toilet seat, but he would not dare utter any mention of his stress level to Number Three. Number Four knew that he had done his task as instructed, and Number Three had to know it as well, and would therefore have no reason to rag on him as he did other times. Number Four wanted to savor the moment.

Neither of them spoke, fearing that by doing so they would ruin the perfection of what they were experiencing. Number Four wanted to smile, but suppressed the urge. They both sighed in silent relief as they noticed they were approaching the alleyway where they would turn, bring the van to a stop, remove their masks, and casually walk away from the four millions dollars in gold they had just helped steal from the U.S. Government.

Although Number Two felt complete elation at having been responsible for what was undoubtedly the most difficult, precise, and challenging segment of the entire operation, he sadly acknowledged that his portion was completed. He felt the passing fog leave cold droplets of water upon his face. From this point onward, he would no longer have any real involvement and the thought of having no control over *their own system* irked him severely. In fact, it bothered him to the point that he could only compare it to the sensation of having flies incessantly buzzing around one's head.

Number One was trustworthy, and so were the others, but something about Number One's addition to the plan had always seemed slightly miscalculated to Number Two. It left too much open to failure without providing sufficient alternatives should any unpredictable element enter into the equation. It bothered him relentlessly, but Number Two kept quiet and tried to steer his thoughts toward the demonstrated success of his plan.

Numbers Three and Four had completed their task with profound precision, leading to the next component of the plan, which had been accomplished with an equal amount of precision. Number Two could not imagine how, with what possible connections, Number One had been able to hire a group of Chinese laborers to move their crate from the van parked in an alley in Chinatown and deliver it to the fishing boat on the wharf that was now slightly bouncing along in the Pacific as it headed south toward the Monterey Peninsula, carrying them home; but the son-of-a-bitch had pulled it off.

Number One had been exceptionally quiet on this portion of the plan, only revealing that he had hired a group of Chinese immigrant laborers working at a construction site on the edge of Chinatown to unload the van, move the crate through the construction site from the back alley to its front entrance, load the crate into one of the dump trucks carrying debris away from the site, deliver the crate to a fishing boat docked at the wharf, and then make the van disappear. Number One described it with frivolity, as if it were as natural a scenario as a family taking a Sunday stroll through Golden Gate Park.

Regardless of its described frivolousness, it had been pure brilliance. Not only did it remove their men from the theft vehicle, which of course had fake tags for extra precaution, but it also added a new layer of complexity for anyone trying to follow from the scene of the crime. Not only would the van they used be destroyed, but the delivery path of the crate would be indistinguishable from any number of truck loads of debris being removed from the construction site.

Number One had also relinquished to Number Two, after Number Two's disbelief in the reliability of the plan, that it had been arranged for the dump truck carrying their delivery to visit another construction site near the wharf in order to further dissuade suspicion … just another stop at another construction site before crossing over the Golden Gate Bridge, destined for Marin's landfill. And while at the construction site, the crate was covertly unloaded, with the contents removed and repackaged. When Number Two questioned whether they would be able to trust the delivery men, as one of them was sure to, given the curiosity prone to human nature, peek inside and discover the contents of their shipment, Number One only replied that in his opinion Asians were the most efficient businessmen in the world. They were interested in money and honor. Pay them enough, and they would be loyal. Number One ensured his group of delivery men were satisfied with the payment for their services, payment that Number One transferred in advance — fully in advance.

The thick fog bank clinging to the California coastline rescinded at times as the small fishing vessel charted south, but as it passed Santa Cruz and approached the southern end of Monterey Bay, all on board of the vessel felt the density of the fog encompass them. Everything had gone as planned, but Number One, even more so than the rest of the group, could not relax, and the thickening fog only added a new level of tension on his frayed nerves. He felt confident that hiding the gold off the coast of Point Lobos was a brilliant addition to the overall plan — his plan that the others had merely supplemented.

The addition was his idea, of course, and the fog arrived as perfectly as he could have hoped for, as it would add another layer of protection and they would likely pass Monterey, Pacific Grove, Pebble Beach, and Carmel undetected. Further, once they reached the shores of Point Lobos, the fog would conceal the boat when they anchored it and conducted their night dive with the jet-propelled underwater equipment he had procured. Something, however, didn't feel right to him. He questioned if one his crew was planning to betray him. Number One sneered in anger at the thought as he paced the deck of the boat, staring out into the halo of light that the boat's lights produced in the fog in front of them as it moved southward.

"Number Two, I'd like to talk to you for a moment," he said, motioning for Number Two to approach him.

"Yes?"

Number One responded in a veiled, quiet voice. "Did you notice any of the others acting strangely today?"

"No. I don't know what you mean." The chill in the moist air brought a shiver to Number Two and he stiffened in his fisherman's slicker overcoat. He waited for Number One to continue.

It took a few moments for Number One to respond, and when he did, he abandoned his previous line of questioning, apparently having decided to begin a new discussion. His voice rose again to its usually domineering level. "Get the other two to start moving the gold into the boxes and have them bring up the jet movers onto the top deck. Once they have that done, tell them to get into their wetsuits and you do the same. I want us to be prepared to dive once we get to Point Lobos. I don't think we're going to run into any trouble, as fishing boats troll in these waters at night often and there's only one Coast Guard patrol boat for this entire stretch of coast, but just in case, we don't want to linger off-shore any longer than we have to."

Number Two considered Number One's words before replying. It had been rather clever of Number One to come up with "burying their treasure" for a few months while the heat from the robbery subsided. Number One found the highly resilient, airtight steel boxes to store the gold in and the jet-propelled underwater transporters through a defense contracting firm that designed equipment for the U.S. Navy and told him the equipment wasn't available to civilians, but that he was able to purchase it in an untraceable transaction.

It sounded legitimate enough to Number Two and he began to feel giddy, with nostalgic feelings jumping inside him. He couldn't help but feel like they were pirates about to stash their treasure on an island and then have a treasure map of sorts to return to it. What was it again that Number One had labeled their venture …? He racked his brain momentarily to uncover the answer to his question.

"The plan, the *Stevenson Plan*, is going to work," he said in a proud and cheerful voice.

2.

Year of our Lord 1818.

FATHER DOMINIQUE MARGIL LOVED this new land known as Alta California, but he did not love those who had followed a calling to colonize it for the glory of God and the Kingdom of Spain. Father Margil didn't know who he considered worse, though, the soldiers or the upper class individuals that the King himself had personally appointed with the promise of affluence in the far-off new world of Alta California. On one hand, the soldiers were undisciplined, vile men and were prone to sin whenever he or another man of the cloth was not in their presence, while on the other, the ordained aristocrats began their pompous, distinguished displays long before their departure from Spanish soil from the port of Mazagan.

The indigenous peoples of Alta California, however, were the very angels of heaven descended to Earth. In his brief time in the mission system, he had relished in their innocence, purity, and willingness to understand the word of the Lord. Father Margil had dreamed his entire life of teaching God's will in such a place as the New World. Undoubtedly, life in the New World and the work it entailed would be difficult for a man of God; and it had been in the months since their arrival. However, Father Margil cherished every moment of his existence and did not for one moment regret having pleaded to his superiors to be allowed to venture to Alta California to fulfill his destiny. It was a destiny he had accepted by his eighth birthday.

∞

Father Margil was born Dominique Margil in a village outside of Seville. Memories of his childhood before the monastery were not pleasant. His father was a blacksmith, a drunken and vicious man who beat his mother and took her by force in front of him whenever the temptation overwhelmed him. His mother cried often when her husband was not within sight. At the tender age of six, Dominique tried to stop his father from pinning his mother to the ground and hurting her, as his father so often did, only to receive a blow so severe from the back of his father's hand that his jaw remained subtly crooked into adulthood.

Two years later, after the death of his mother, Dominique was visited by an angel. The angel told him to run away, away from his father and away from the house where his mother had died. The angel told him that there was a better place for him. The boy waited for a moment when his father's drunken snores seemed to shake even the earthen ground of their hovel, and then he ran. He ran and ran into the unknown of the night. The boy did not know where he was running and the darkness of the night quickly swallowed him whole. He quickly passed into the forest bordering their village and realized he had passed beyond the farthest point he had ever ventured. It didn't bother him. The angel had been beautiful and would lead him to a better place as promised.

The boy ran as fast as his little legs would carry him. He felt as if he were flying through the forest. When the sun rose in the east, he imagined he was in the sky and flying by it. He waved to it and smiled. Soon he would find the better place that the angel promised him he would eventually find. Soon he would find the state of peace he had never glimpsed in his young life.

Without rest or nourishment, the boy's legs eventually tired beyond his control or acceptance. The boy was stubborn and he resisted the urge to rest, or to try to find food or water. He leaped over downed trees, imagining a force had overcome him that gave him the strength to run forever.

Forever arrived in the form of a miscalculated jump over a log in his path that resulted in his foot getting caught and his left leg snapping loudly as the rest of his body fell heavily forward. The boy was spared the anguish of having a fractured leg wedged within a log by his head slamming into a small tree, knocking him blissfully unconscious.

The boy awoke to find himself in the arms of a large man wearing a thick, brown robe with a wide, clean-shaven face who spoke softly to him of angels. After that day, the Monasterio de Santa Maria de las Cuevas became Dominique's home.

3.

Year of our Lord 2009.

SAMUEL P. BECKWITH knew from childhood that he was destined to be a wealthy man. His privileged upbringing confirmed his belief. Even his name rang with an affluent tone as it passed from one's lips. The stock market crash may have nearly wiped him out, but he still had his family name and there's a lot to a name, especially a name like his. He was distantly related to the inventor of a breakthrough global communications code; however, he was more proud of another notable man in his family tree, his grandfather, F.B. Beckwith. F.B. Beckwith was a vital figure in the founding and establishment of one of the most expensive pieces of real estate in the world: Pebble Beach.

Having been raised in Pebble Beach, Samuel quickly learned to understand and appreciate that his family's history of being so intertwined to the origins of Pebble Beach embellished on him a distinction of modern-day royalty. However, his family's origins were rooted even deeper in the history of the area. The first of his descendants to arrive, not too long after Monterey's founding by the Spanish, was an Englishman by the name of John Beckwith. Beckwith had married the daughter of the governor of the time, a man of great importance. As was customary in those days for an Englishman marrying into a Spanish family, the young Beckwith was required to convert to Catholicism and adopt the last name of his wife. Samuel's ancestor had done both, but the Catholic tradition in his family died out long ago and the family eventually dropped the second half of the name of Beckwith-Fages.

One characteristic of his family's heritage was that they always knew how to acquire wealth, and the family joke was that John Beckwith himself had started this tradition by marrying into a wealthy family. It was family legend that John Beckwith's only son dreamed of finding the mythical treasure that the pirate Bouchard, had buried somewhere along the Monterey or Big Sur coastline. This son never found the treasure, but discovered a talent for expanding cattle ranches and added to the family fortune in this manner. His family's history was quite a tale, Samuel had to admit.

Of course, all the old families of the Peninsula, including the old Spanish families in Monterey and the artists in Carmel, considered themselves as distinguished as any Beacon Hill family with ties to the Mayflower, but the families of Pebble Beach were different. Pebble Beach had been separated from the rest of the Peninsula from the time of its origin and it had remained so not only tangibly, as access was restricted, complete with guarded gates at each of its four entrances, but also figuratively, as residents of Pebble Beach viewed themselves and were viewed by others as distinct from the rest of the Monterey Peninsula. But Samuel's combined familial history, tied both to the founding of Monterey and the establishment of Pebble Beach, put his family into top-tier distinction.

As for Pebble Beach, it made Samuel laugh that there were those who lived in the unimpressive houses in the upper-hill neighborhoods of Pebble Beach thought they were just as privileged as the upper-echelon residents of the community because they happened to live or rent a house located in Pebble Beach. They were lucky they were even granted the small steel placard reading "Del Monte Forest" that residents placed on the front of their vehicles so they would not be badgered by the gatemen.

The square mile of wealth and influence in Pebble Beach was unsurpassed anywhere he had ever been, and Samuel P. Beckwith had traveled the States and the world extensively. Having been born and raised within the protective grasp of an exclusive Pebble Beach family, Samuel had spent summer vacations on sailboats touring the gleaming Cape Cod, or on the white beaches of Cannes, while enduring winter ski vacations on the glamorous slopes of Aspen or Gastaad. Aside from those fortunate enough to never leave its borders were those of excessive influence from New York or LA who kept second homes in Pebble Beach, so Samuel often found himself playing golf next to investment wizards and movie producers.

Samuel sat on the extended balcony of his gargantuan villa and gazed out at the vastness of the ocean stretching from one end of the horizon to the other. He had a modest frame that he managed to keep in fairly good shape, a full head of dark hair, and dark brown eyes. A copy of his favorite book, *Treasure Island*, by the great Robert Louis Stevenson, rested on the wide armrest of the oversized wooden patio chair he sat in. Samuel often took the book onto the patio with him. Sometimes he would pick it up and read a few pages, sometimes not; he just liked having the book in his presence.

He heard his wife, Bridgette, parking her Mercedes in the driveway, having arrived home from her weekly massage at the spa. She often annoyed him, but she was twenty-five years younger and had warmly accepted his gift of a sizeable breast augmentation; so it wasn't too bad having her around when he wanted female attention. He sipped slowly from his tumbler of scotch, reflecting on how he deserved this life and needed to preserve it. He needed to regain the millions he had lost in the crash. On top of his dwindling inheritance, if he didn't supplant his fortune entrusted by his parents, he would be forced to relinquish his life of luxury. That was something Samuel P. Beckwith could not do.

He supposed it was destiny knocking at his front door; he had been planning the robbery for years; the crash had only accelerated his plans. It was amazing what one could plan and coordinate with an overabundance of free time and money. One could even pull off stealing millions from the federal government and get away with it.

He felt his young wife's breasts press against his back as she leaned in to grasp her arms around him. She kissed the back of his neck and told him that she had ordered dinner delivered from their favorite Italian restaurant in Carmel. She kissed his neck again, this time a little more forcefully, while playfully running a hand down the front of his chest. She mentioned how relaxed she felt after her massage. Samuel needed no more invitation. No, he definitely could not give up this life.

Everything had so far gone according to plan, his plan, the

Stevenson Plan. In another week they would return to the stashed *buried treasure* off the jagged coast of Point Lobos and would be able to move the stolen gold overseas and turn an incredible profit.

A mountain range of fog was building in the distance over the water, and he figured by sundown it would be settled upon them like a moist, gray blanket.

Victor Mathews was a brilliant man. He first conquered a degree from Stanford at the impressive age of nineteen. He next conquered Silicon Valley by becoming one of its top software designers. He had most recently calculated and orchestrated how his team would beat the U.S. Government and execute the greatest heist that the State of California had seen since the final days of the Old West. An image of the money resting safely at the bottom of the ocean in its secured cases flashed across his mind as he perfectly executed his putt on the 9th green of the elite golf club in his private enclave known as the Santa Lucia Preserve.

Victor watched with delight as the white golf ball slowly carried itself over the sloping, perfectly maintained carpet of trimmed grass and finally dropped into the hole with a slightly echoing *thunk*. He had just sunk an incredible fifteen-foot putt and he felt joy jolt through him with the sound. He didn't even hear the rest of his threesome let out a gasp of deserving approval, not even the overexaggerated one proclaimed by Dick Lombardo, who was constantly trying to kiss Victor's ass for some reason or another. No, Victor only heard the sound of his golf ball falling into the hole, and it represented more than a brilliant putt to him: it represented victory.

And indeed, victorious they had been. The plan had been implemented smoothly and without any difficulties, just as Victor had predicted. The money didn't overly concern him, as unlike Samuel, he had survived the recent stock market crash, as he had invested his millions into low-risk investments that were only lightly impacted by the financial crisis. Unlike other millionaires he was acquainted with, such as Samuel P. Beckwith, Victor had steered away from excessive investments in real estate and stocks. Others had called him foolish for years, but Victor no longer heard jeers at his investment schemes. Victor bent his tall, thin body over to grab his golf ball from the hole. As he did, a few strands of hair slipped out of his dark blonde ponytail.

Although Victor was aware that he was a genius, as without a doubt he was concerning anything to do with software and computers, he could not take credit for what had proven to be a wise investment strategy and gloat in his superior investment skills. Victor was simply not a man prone to taking risks. Samuel may have been able to talk him into the robbery, but Victor conceded for a far different reason than the others.

Victor joined the crew and masterminded the logistics for the sole reason that he had become bored in recent years. After retiring at the ripe age of twenty-eight from his career in Silicon Valley, he had been searching for something, anything to fill the void he felt sinking deeper into his soul every day. He started by purchasing a ridiculously large chateau in the Rancho San Carlos, later renamed the Santa Lucia Preserve, which was followed by devoting himself religiously to the game of golf. As he continued to loathe the boredom, he tried an internet-order bride from Thailand, who, after signing a prenuptial agreement, failed to keep him interested, even if she seemed content at displaying her affection for him and pleasing him. The little woman even wanted to throw herself on him when he tried to take a shower!

Victor appreciated the efforts of his celestial wife, but he had never been entirely interested in the opposite sex. School had been a time to prove himself and to not let himself get distracted, although it had not been difficult for him to remain focused on his studies, as girls never seemed to find him attractive, which he never understood. He realized he may have been slightly nerdy-looking, but he didn't believe he was a bad-looking guy. Computers, however, had always been easier for him to understand than females.

Working eighty hours a week in Silicon Valley after Stanford had left no time to socialize, and he satisfied any male calling he felt with an occasional trip to Vegas and its offering of tantalizing, and obedient, women for hire. He always preferred Asian girls on his visits and had established a relationship with a particular outfit that specialized in such women. After his wife arrived with her one suitcase from Bangkok, he tried to be happy with his life, but the tiny, hot, young — she was ten years younger than him — wife, the gigantic house in one of the most exclusive neighborhoods in the country, and playing five times a week on one of the most pristine golf courses in the world were not enough. Victor needed something different, and Samuel P. Beckwith offered this with his idea to rob the San Francisco Federal Reserve Bank.

Samuel liked to think of himself as a leader and even more so as *their* leader, but Victor considered himself the real force behind their endeavor. Samuel could call himself Number One as much as he liked and label Victor as Number Two, but Victor knew that without his involvement, the job would never have happened. He didn't need the money, but he increasingly began to think of it in a new light, as an unexpected opportunity. Maybe he would take his wife and travel the world for a few years, stopping as long as they wanted wherever they wanted. It was a thought. Although he would have to convey that she didn't need to constantly feel as if she had to toss herself sexually toward him. He was a man who needed a challenge, and obedience could come after the contest was won — won by him, of course.

It was getting late in the afternoon and a band of thick fog was creeping into the valley from the coast. Dick Lombardo watched as Victor Mathews sunk his incredible putt on the 9th green with utter envy. Victor had everything Dick wanted and he hoped that with his share of the loot from the heist, he would finally be able to have a life more like Victor's, the life Dick always wanted. He admired how intelligent and successful Victor had been in his life. He admired how Victor had a house in the Santa Lucia Preserve. Samuel always talked about how much more superior a Pebble Beach address was than anywhere else in the county, but Dick secretly admitted to himself that he would rather live on a spacious valley estate such as Victor's rather than anywhere in Pebble Beach. Dick also admired how Victor had a hot, young wife who seemed to worship him. *If only I had that!* Dick said to himself every time he saw Victor's wife. Dick even admired Victor's frame over his; Victor was thin and tall with healthy long hair, while Dick was on the shorter side, persistently battling a bulge to his belly, and had an obviously receding hairline.

Dick could only pretend to be on the same social level as Victor. He lived in a modest house in the Monterey hills and was only able to play on the Preserve course once a week through Victor's good graces. Victor was initially disappointed when Dick informed him that he would not be able to join Victor's group as a regular for their daily golf outings, and it was mere luck that Dick had been able to get on it once a week when one member of the foursome mentioned that he could only play four times a week due to his need to be in San Jose for Tuesday board meetings. Unlike the others, though, Dick held a full-time job.

Dick was a senior underwriter for Redwood Insurance Company, which was headquartered outside of Monterey on the Monterey-Salinas Highway, and although he was able to work in the time to take one afternoon a week off for golf, five was not remotely possible. Victor Mathews, on the other hand, had achieved the envious goal of retiring young; he was fifteen years younger than Dick. Dick had no attractive wife to return home to. After three divorces, he concluded that women could not stand to be with him. At first, this realization bothered him, but after watching his old Stanford roommate achieve what appeared to be marital bliss, he knew that he should follow Victor's lead. Victor never discussed how he met Areva, and in fact refused to discuss any particulars of their marriage; but Dick assumed it had been some sort of internet-order bride situation. Not that Dick judged Victor negatively for it, if it were indeed true. As far as Dick saw it, American women had become too damn independent, and as soon as he was on his feet he planned to go internet bride shopping himself. He dreamed of soon having a tight Ukrainian woman lying next to him, or more appropriately — *lying on top of him*. First thing, though, was that he needed to get rich.

Thus, when Victor first broached the subject of joining himself and a few others for what sounded like a sure way to get filthy rich, Dick didn't hesitate. He would be Number Four, and although he would have preferred to be at least Number Three in order to be closer to Victor, he could live with being Number Four without complaint.

Big Sur was the only place for Zande Allen, otherwise known as

Number Three. Zande was born in Big Sur and would die in Big Sur. Growing up in a rustic forest setting had resulted in Zande's developing an imposing physique. He was well under six feet in height, but his wide shoulders and padded chest revealed his dexterous frame. He rarely had a full beard, but it was equally rare for him to be clean-shaven. His sharp blue eyes appeared constantly narrowed by a furrowed brow.

His ultimate fantasy was to load Bixby Bridge with enough explosives to blow the damn bridge apart so badly that the federal government, the federal government that had allocated the funds for Route 1 that had ruined Big Sur by connecting it to the rest of the dirty world, would never be able to garner the support to rebuild it. Big Sur would survive. In the early 80s, when the blessed mudslide shut down Route 1 for weeks, Big Sur was just fine. Big Sur would always survive.

Most would think the glorious fantasy of one so noble as him would be to demolish Garrapata Bridge, farther north than Bixby, as it would allow more of the historic Sur area to be disconnected. But as anyone educated on the history of Big Sur knew, it was Bixby Bridge that had placed a tombstone on old Big Sur. Before it, the Old Coast Road was the only passage to the Sur from the north. The grand old road had fallen into the realm of nostalgia and history books and the once-thriving roadside businesses along it had been forced to close after traffic was diverted to Route 1. *That bridge had put the finality on the death of old Big Sur.* It would be a shame to not include Palo Colorado Road, as it was located north of Bixby Bridge. That famed former logging route once had a landing at its mouth on the coast that was as wild as any place in the Old West, but it was a sacrifice Zande was willing to accept.

Zande was the founder of the group "Return the Sur to Big Sur" and had even paid for a computer geek to create a website and a blog for the cause. The outside world was evil, but it offered useful tools. The website, for instance, had twenty thousand people visit a year, and the number had been steadily growing. Also steadily growing was attendance at the annual rally Zande organized deep in the Los Padres National Forest, east of the Sur's coast. The rally consistently provided pro-old Big Sur and anti-federal government sentiment, roaring campfires, countless kegs of beer, indistinguishable men with pot bellies, unkempt facial hair, caps, dark sunglasses, head-to-toe camouflage, and lots of guns. Zande didn't advertise the event on the webpage for fear of government suspicion and instead only emailed individual people who contributed comments to the blog. They, in turn, would be encouraged to invite others. Zande took an extra precaution by labeling the event as a fundraiser.

When a notorious contributor submitted the largest contribution ever received by the organization, Zande contacted the individual to personally convey his appreciation. To his surprise, the notorious individual replied that he desired to meet Zande in private to discuss his own views on old Big Sur and what could be done to assist the mission of Return the Sur to Big Sur. Zande was delighted to accept. He and the individual arranged to meet at an appropriate destination: the dining cabin of Deetjin's Inn. As they toasted their after-dinner glasses of scotch, Zande Allen looked into the eyes of Samuel P. Beckwith and decided to trust the man before him.

4.

Year of our Lord 2009.

SPECIAL AGENT JOHN GIBSON liked San Francisco. Something about it reminded him of being in a European city. He had been transferred from FBI headquarters in DC to the bureau's San Francisco field office on an assignment within the Counterterrorism Division to monitor and investigate potential infiltrations of the Basque separatist organization, Euskadi Ta Askatasuna, better known as ETA, in California and other western states. This task also involved tracking funds from any groups in the U.S. that were destined to reach ETA's efforts. The FBI had grown increasingly interested in the group's presence in California in particular after the murder of José Aldarossa Arana, a prominent San Francisco city councilman, was linked to the organization. Although there was a requirement for the posting, Gibson assisted in the creation of the position. After having spent his entire adult life in DC, he figured it was time for a change of scenery. His supervisor, Division Director Robert Smith, initially opposed the idea of Gibson's transfer; however, he eventually came to accept that his trusted friend needed something different.

Gibson had been on the assignment for six months and felt that he was finally seeing tangible results of his efforts. He identified a list of groups and organizations that had any Basque affiliation whatsoever. He then identified a targeted list of contacts within each group, with some unofficial assistance, and personalized his list of contacts by traveling to visit each individual. Some resistance to talking with an FBI agent had been experienced, as expected, but Gibson encountered less hostility than he feared. He considered that perhaps his demeanor had changed and he had become friendlier than earlier in his career.

The day after the Reserve Bank's heist, he received a call from Director Smith.

"Hello, John. How's life out there in crazy liberal land treating you?" Smith asked.

"Hello, Bob. I'm doing very well, thank you. I'm even beginning to enjoy all the *crazy liberals*." Smith laughed in response. Gibson continued, "And as you have no doubt noticed from my weekly status reports, I'm making some progress on my assignment."

"Oh yes, yes. I've seen your progress, and great job, of course. I would expect nothing less from you." Smith paused noticeably. "However, I'm afraid I'm going to have to ask you to put that assignment temporarily on hold." As Bob spoke, Gibson foresaw what would be said. With recent budget cuts, the bureau's staffing had become stretched thin in certain areas, especially in field office operations, and reassignments were becoming fairly standard. "I'm sure you noticed what happened at the San Francisco Federal Reserve Bank yesterday," Smith continued.

"It would have been difficult for anyone to miss. It's been all over the news since the Bank figured out what happened." Gibson paused. "I suppose this is my reassignment?"

"*Bingo*," Smith replied.

"As you know, bank robberies are not really my skill-set, Bob." Gibson curtly replied.

"Indeed, I do realize that. However, you haven't given me time to explain the situation."

"Sorry, please continue, then."

"You're not to head the investigation; Agent Alan Shapiro out there will be lead. Do you know him?" Smith asked.

"We've crossed paths some. He has a solid reputation."

"Good, glad to hear. He's already been made aware of your involvement on this case."

"Which will be?" Gibson inquired.

"You are to serve as his investigator and follow-up on any leads he may have, or any you develop on your own. Shapiro already has a team and has more than enough junior agents to help him with grunt work; what you'll be doing is supplemental to his efforts. Shapiro has agreed to give you complete independence and field support if and when you need it. I've discussed the situation at length with him and he's aware of your background and abilities and pleased to have you on his team. Shapiro is a straight shooter and will give you space, but I want you to keep him aware of your activities and any leads you may come across." Smith paused again.

"Now I know you might be feeling a little apprehensive about having to report to someone so frequently after your relative flexibility, but I promise this guy is going to give you space. I hope you believe me on this." Another brief pause. "Everything clear and understood?"

"Yes, sir. I understand. I'll report to Agent Shapiro right after I finish my shawarma."

"Finish what?"

"I just picked up a shawarma pita sandwich and you caught me on my lunch stroll. You should try one sometime."

"No, thanks. I think I'll stick to burgers. Sorry to disturb your lunch *stroll*," Smith replied. "Listen, John. I'm sorry to take you off your assignment. I know how personally vested you are."

"It's okay. I understand it's out of your hands."

"Trust me, it is. This is coming from the Bureau's director himself, who, it's rumored, received a call from the President after the robbery. This heist is no small deal. This is a hundred million dollars from a district branch of the Federal Reserve Bank. We haven't seen anything like this in decades, and the Administration is determined that the perpetrators be apprehended as quickly as possible. If not, there's a worry that this affair, occurring in this blasted recession of ours, or whatever they're calling it these days, could inspire others, and we could be plunged back into the days when we were up against mobsters and bank robbers."

"That's certainly motivational. I'll see what I can do."

"Where are you planning to start?" Smith asked.

John Gibson looked out at San Francisco Bay, his attention briefly caught by a passing boat. "I think I'll take a boat ride. Good talking with you, Bob."

5.

Year of our Lord 2009.

I SIDRO DE LA VEGA'S name was announced, introducing him for his luncheon presentation. As usual, Isidro laughed inwardly at hearing this name. It blended a surname traceable back to the original Spanish families that settled in California when it was known as Alta California and was a part of the Spanish Empire with a name created by an eccentric woman who wrote stories while sitting in her tree house in the pine trees of Carmel.

Isidro felt the group of mostly elderly and mostly male faces of the Monterey Rotary Club watching him intently. The room was still noisily finishing its fish entrée; this annoyed Isidro, as given the median age of the members of his audience, he was already aware that he would have to remember to raise his voice. As he approached the podium he wondered how many of the faces would be showing signs of nodding-off over dessert and coffee while he gave his memorized presentation on the history of Monterey from its days as a provincial capital of Spanish California until its incorporation, along with the rest of California, into the borders of the United States of America. Presenting to groups such as the Rotary Club was a major task of his position as Senior Historian at the Monterey Historical Society. He used the remote control to turn on his PowerPoint presentation, which would project images on the large screen behind him.

First PowerPoint slide: A panoramic photograph of modern-day Monterey as seen from a vantage point on Monterey Bay.

Isidro began his presentation as he always did, with a question. "How many of you are aware that Monterey was once the capital of California?" He asked his audience.

Nearly every person in the room raised a hand in response, and those who couldn't be bothered to raise their hands nodded their heads in acknowledgement. Isidro expected such a response from a group of well-educated individuals who lived in the Monterey Peninsula area; however, he would not have expected such a favorable response if he had asked the same question to a similar group of individuals in any other location in the State of California. Society has committed a crime by letting history be forgotten, he thought; and California has forgotten Monterey.

"Okay, great," Isidro continued, pressing the remote control button in order to change the slide.

"Now how many of you know that Monterey was the capital and most important settlement of Upper Spanish California, which was called Alta California, and later of all Spanish California?" Only a few hands were raised in response.

"I'm not surprised, but I believe it to be unfortunate that even those who live in this beautiful area are unaware of its historical significance." He noticed a few faces in the audience near him turn reproachful and realized his tone had likely come across as scornful, as it did often on such occasions.

"But, that also means that my job here today has even more importance, as I'm going to help educate you all on the historical significance of this area." The reproachful faces returned to expressions of mild interest.

"Now, due to the absence of available time allotted for this presentation, I'm going to have to bypass part of the Monterey area's history by skipping to European exploration and colonization."

PowerPoint slide change: A painting of a small Native American village located next to a calm river in a valley lined on both sides by low hills.

"By doing this, I'll be skipping over addressing the area's history before the arrival of Europeans, and I want to recognize that there were Native American tribes living here, most notably the Rumsen Ohlone, that had their own complex cultures; and although we don't know as much about these tribes as other Native American tribes, partially because the tribes became assimilated into the European population or were wiped out by illnesses brought by the Europeans, I do want to show them due respect by mentioning their existence.

"An odd, inaccurate historical portrayal I come across often in my studies on the Monterey Peninsula area is that the Spaniard, Sebastian Vizcaino, is often credited as the first European explorer to discover Monterey Bay, when, in fact, it had been discovered fifty years earlier by another in the service of the Spanish Empire, a Portuguese explorer named Juan Rodriguez Cabrillo. There is also substantial evidence that Sir Francis Drake, Elizabeth's glorious pirate, made it to the Monterey Peninsula before Vizcaino."

PowerPoint slide change: A painting with Spanish galleons passing by a wild and rugged coastline.

"Perhaps, however, Vizcaino is given credit as it was only after his voyage that the Spanish made a serious effort to colonize Alta California. The date Vizcaino landed on our shore was December 15, 1602."

"The region of present day Baja California was first expanded into by the Spanish from the power base in the capital of Mexico City. But the northern portion of the territory, what is today the State of California and also included other areas of the southwestern United States, was for the most part left untouched. This is quite interesting, because if the Spanish Empire had acted more quickly, the entire history of California, and indeed of the United States, may have been altered. At the time of Vizcaino's voyage, the Spanish Empire was considered the most powerful European nation, albeit in its days of decline, and English dominance was spreading. The Spanish, in fact, were growing increasingly nervous about their enormous wild territory of Alta California.

"A serious effort had been made to colonize Mexico, as can still be seen today in Mexico's culture, history, architecture, et cetera; however, Alta California was either seen as too distant, or uninteresting. Or perhaps the Spanish were too full on paella and vino, and were groggy from partying all night and taking long afternoon siestas to do any more colonizing." Although Isidro did not consider himself to be a humorous person, and no one who met him would accuse him of being so, his dry, intellectual humor was occasionally recognized. A few laughs around the room responded to his stab at the ambrosial excesses of Spanish culture. Isidro allowed himself a small smile.

"I don't feel badly about making fun of the Spanish sometimes, as my family heritage is Spanish," he offered in explanation.

"But, my point is this: The Spanish only made a serious effort to settle and populate California after it was learned that Englishmen such as Drake and Cavendish were having a look at the territory. And they were not alone. It was well known that French explorers were in the area as well. These threats prompted the Spanish Empire to get moving, but it was too late, as you will see shortly — threats of encroachment upon California were not to subside. And, in fact, the Spanish Empire didn't even move quickly after the voyage of Vizcaino. It would be another 150 years before the Spanish Empire seriously moved on Vizcaino's discoveries.

An interesting side note here related to the perceived remoteness of the Monterey Peninsula — the first overland expedition sent into Alta California, led by Gaspar de Portola, managed to completely miss the gloriously described Peninsula and ended up somewhere to the north. My personal opinion of how this occurred is that Portola reached Monterey Bay somewhere near the mouth of the Salinas River, and it was probably a day of either thick fog hiding the Peninsula or a day of rain and rough waters in the bay. In either scenario, it would not have appeared like the paradise described by Vizcaino in the report of his voyage.

"All said, I do believe the later-to-form United States would have expanded into California one way or another. This would have occurred whether the territory of California was Spanish, Mexican, French, or *Russian*." Isidro anticipated the response he received.

"Oh yes, I can see from the surprised looks on some of your faces that the mention of this last global power of the time surprises you, but I can assure you, elements within the Russian Empire were extremely interested in what is now the western coast of the United States. Like the

Spanish, though, they moved too slowly and missed an initial opportunity to settle in what is now Oregon at the mouth of the Columbia River, which would have spread their holdings significantly down from Alaska and made California much more in reach ... but I'm getting far from my point and I apologize. We historians love to talk about history, but not about much else." Isidro received a few more laughs in response to his introspective comment.

"My point is that if the Spanish had moved more quickly and confidently into California, the effects of Spanish culture would have been more profound and it would have taken longer for America's mounting pressure to penetrate. Sure, one can respond to such a statement by claiming that Spanish culture is palpable in California today; however, I'll disagree with such an observation. What we have in California is predominantly Mexican heritage, not Spanish heritage. I would go so far as to say that California has nearly forgotten its Spanish heritage, but I would then also add that this is unequivocally due to the lethargic efforts of the Spanish empire to colonize California to begin with."

Isidro paused in order to gauge his audience. A good majority of the older men in the group were predictably dozing off. "But perhaps this debate is only interesting to Spanish Californian historians." There were a couple of laughs in the room. Isidro thought he noticed a few previously closed eyelids open and a few previously downed heads rise up. Isidro took a drink of water from the glass sitting on the podium.

PowerPoint slide change: A picture of the Mission San Carlos Borromeo de Carmelo, or the Carmel Mission, in the late 1700s with Native Americans working in the agricultural fields surrounding it and Franciscan friars walking among them.

"Now when the Spanish Empire did finally decide to colonize California, it primarily turned to the church to do its bidding. The Jesuit Order would likely have been enthused to carry the torch and spearhead the settlement of Alta California; however, at about the time the Spanish Empire decided to colonize California, it also decided that it no longer desired Jesuit involvement, and the order was expelled from the Americas. This left an opening that the Franciscans were happy to fill. One man in particular, Father Junipero Serra, should actually be considered the Father of California. It can easily be argued that it was through his resilience, fortitude, and determination that California was successfully settled by the Spanish."

PowerPoint slide change: A painting of Monterey in the late 1700s. The painting depicts a wide bay and a pine-covered peninsula extending into it, with a white mission and its fenced walls set back from the water. The dark hills jutting up behind the mission form an apparent wall around the mission, which was vulnerable to its surroundings, conveying the remoteness of the outpost at the time.

"Now, after the Spanish enlisted the assistance of the good friars to help convert the native populations and convince them that working in the fields or making tallow or tanning hides were better ways to live than the lifestyle these populations enjoyed before the arrival of Europeans, there was a need to expand outward from the protected walls of the missions. Monterey's original mission church, the Royal Presidio Chapel, which still stands today, is a reminder of the richness of the history surrounding us." He paused to take a deep breath.

Isidro took another drink of water from the glass in front of him. "So, what we have next in the historical line-up is the aforementioned outward expansion from the missions, which also included the relocation of the mission from Monterey to its permanent site on the Carmel River. Although a goal was spreading influence, this move of the mission was mostly likely based on Father Serra not fully appreciating the Spanish Empire's administrative arm meddling in the affairs of his mission.

"Another mission was established in southern Monterey County, called Mission San Antonio de Padua, which still exists today, but it is remote and surrounded by a desolate area of rugged lands that are also primarily owned by the U.S. military." As he mentioned the San Antonio Mission, Isidro thought of what he recently discovered there. He forced himself to stop thinking of it.

PowerPoint slide change: An image of Monterey with numerous white adobe houses scattered outside the area of the original mission; it is clear from the previous picture that a great deal of trees have been cleared from the landscape.

"Gradually, adobe houses began to be constructed outside of the settlement's walls. The walls also housed the military garrison, and this made it a strange combination of a religious and military compound, as even though Father Serra moved to his new Carmel Mission, other men of the cloth stayed at the Royal Presidio Chapel in Monterey. And so, as these houses were constructed, gradually farther and farther outside of the walls, the village of Monterey began to take form.

"Monterey was growing, and growing quickly. Explorers and traders began to share stories of the wealth just waiting to be had in Monterey. They spoke of the wealthy citizens in the Spanish Empire's newest darling colonial settlement. All of this attention, however, was noticed by everyone … even *pirates*. This was a time when pirates roamed the open seas, looking for ships to capture and settlements to plunder. Oftentimes such pirating activities were sanctioned, either transparently or through a veil by empires around the globe. Pirates, after all, could create difficulties for a competitor's trading capacity.

"Such was the case with Hippolyte de Bouchard."

PowerPoint slide change: A portrait of a man of medium height, wearing a dazzling dark blue uniform, gazing from the deck of a 19th century ship. The man has dark hair, a noticeable midsection, and a creamy, expressionless face.

"Bouchard had the dubious title of a privateer working under the flag of the newly formed government of Argentina, although he was French by birth. The new country enlisted Bouchard and others like him to pillage vessels on the high seas; however, it can be assumed the primary target was Spanish vessels, as anger towards the former colonizer flowed deeply in South America.

"It can also be easily imagined that Bouchard, a man reputed to have a cruel disposition intermingled with powerful ambition, viewed raiding Monterey as the pinnacle strike against the Spanish Empire. Monterey was the crown jewel of Alta California, and tales of its riches crisscrossed the world."

PowerPoint slide change: Monterey as a small town of roads and adobe houses and buildings, with all of the buildings ablaze.

"Returning back to our man Hippolyte, in 1818 he and his two ships invaded Monterey and did their best to burn it to the ground, as depicted in the painting displayed behind me.

"No one really knows what triggered Bouchard's anger to the point of ordering the entire town put to the torch. There is no evidence that Bouchard received orders from his superiors in Argentina to inflict such damage in any conquest, even in Spanish Alta California. Further, Bouchard did not have a reputation for inflicting such damage. His M.O. was to invade, pillage, and leave before most knew he had even invaded. In the taking of Monterey, though, he stayed for a couple of days before ordering the town burned to the ground. It's almost as if his extended stay in Monterey was deliberate, although the reason remains a historical mystery.

PowerPoint slide change: A picture of a group of wooden buildings revealing a Slavic architectural style with an area bordered by a high wooden wall surrounding it.

"Interestingly enough, the foreign power that may have most recognized the potential of Alta California and the only one that made a concentrated effort to settle it aside from the Spanish was the Russian Empire. The Russians established a small settlement, as you can see in this picture, along the coast, roughly sixty miles north of San Francisco."

PowerPoint slide change: A painting of the small village of Monterey developing along Monterey Bay with a solid wall of pine-laden hills behind and a sizeable galleon anchored off-shore in the bay.

"As I mentioned at the beginning of this presentation, Monterey was made the capital of Spanish Alta California, all of it; but this didn't last long, as at the conclusion of the Mexican Revolution against the Spanish Empire, Spanish California became Mexican California.

During this time, Monterey flourished. It was not only a capital, it was a center of commerce, culture and life. With the change of ownership, the ports of California were opened to the world and the world came to see Monterey, much as it still does during the summer months."

PowerPoint slide change: A painting depicting a group of soldiers in navy blue uniforms standing at attention as an American flag is hoisted over the Monterey Customs House.

"Of course, during this time the United States was expanding and the idea of Manifest Destiny was reverberating throughout the young nation, and California had long been viewed as a desirable territory. Emissaries, both legitimate and non-legitimate, breached the California frontier during both the Spanish and Mexican periods of California. As troubles with Mexico began to brew, associated with the ongoing troubles in Texas, it became apparent that an all-out war between the U.S. and Mexico would be inevitable.

"Some in the U.S., even in its Navy, grew impatient awaiting the battle to commence, as displayed in this painting, when Commodore Jones of the U.S. Navy landed with an overwhelming force in Monterey's harbor in October of 1842, under false pretenses that war had been declared between the two countries; he invaded Monterey and claimed it for the U.S. Within twenty-four hours of the conquest, information gathering and careful diplomacy conducted by the sole U.S. Ambassador to Mexican California, Thomas Larkin, concluded that war had not been declared and that Jones had committed an embarrassing mistake. Apologies were issued and the American flag was replaced with the previously flown Mexican flag. Jones took his men and ships and left Monterey.

"Monterey celebrated the departure of the Yankees, but it is interesting that Jones received no resistance when he landed at Monterey. I think it had become clear to everyone in Monterey that its days as an old-world capital at the very edge of the New World were destined to come to an end, which they did four years later in July 1846, at the start of the Mexican-American War, when Commodore Sloat of the U.S. Navy landed and declared Monterey for the United States of America. During the war there were numerous battles in California, and a skirmish here between a hot-headed guy named Fremont, a group of his compatriots, and the local Mexican governor is attributed as an event leading to the war. Fremont and his men defied the local governor and put up a little fight as they held out on a ridge north of here, today known as Fremont Peak.

"There may have been some that did not believe the Mexican-American War had ended in 1848 with the Americans the victors, as it would take months for word from the East Coast to reach California, but even these last holdouts had to relinquish their hopes when over five months later, official proclamation finally reached Monterey, validating the outcome of the war."

PowerPoint slide change: A painting of a pair of gruff-looking men in tattered clothing pan-handling for gold in a mountain stream. One of the men is looking into his pan, which reveals golden sparkles. The man staring into his pan smiles genuinely. His counterpart, looking over the other's shoulder, revealed an expression of content.

"Interestingly enough, nine days before the end of the Mexican-American War, gold was discovered by prospectors, such as the two shown here," Isidro motioned to the screen behind him, "in the Sierra Nevada mountain range of California."

"The discovery of gold not only solidified the importance of the territory to the United States, with many convinced they were destined to find riches, and their onslaught earned them the nickname forty-niners, but it also represented the beginning of the end of Monterey's place of importance in history." Isidro noticed that he had once again lost his crowd; not necessarily their attention, but their comprehension.

"What I mean is: Sure, Monterey is still an important place in the minds of many. We are a tourist destination, a dreamlike relocation destination, and a golfer's paradise, amongst other things. Even after 1848, the Monterey Peninsula continued to have some importance, one way or another throughout the years, be that as a turn-of-the-century affluent tourist destination with the luxurious Hotel Del Monte, or a religious retreat center as seen in the founding of Pacific Grove; however, the Peninsula's place in economic and political importance all but died the day that gold was discovered in the Sierras.

"I can see that some of you are not following my point, so I'll elaborate on what happened in the late 1840s and early 1850s." Isidro sipped from his glass of water again. "Up until this time, Monterey was *the* place.

"However, after the discovery of gold in the Sierras, one thing became perfectly clear, as it remains clear to this day: Due to its geographic location, the Monterey Peninsula was too isolated to become a commercial center and major port-of-call once economic concerns expanded beyond the California coast. A later-to-become-famous author by the name of Robert Louis Stevenson stayed in Monterey after this fall from grace and aptly labeled it the *Old Pacific Capital*. Although Stevenson, after recovering from sickness, seems to have spent a good majority of the rest of his time in Monterey hunting for legendary buried pirate treasure."

"But let's return to geography... In truth, it was inevitable that Monterey would see its demise as California prospered. Geographically speaking, strictly from a transportation logistics perspective, the Monterey Peninsula could not be more challenged. As all of us know who live here, we have even today, one route north and one route east to choose from. Obviously there is no route west and the route south offers seventy or so miles of one of the curviest cliff-hanging roads on this continent. As you may recall, a few times in the 90s, there was flooding of all three major bridge crossings of the Salinas and Carmel Rivers, leaving those highways impassable, and the Peninsula was literally an island cut off from the rest of the world. The Monterey Peninsula is an island unto itself.

"Anyway, back to my point. Monterey's location was paramount to its demise as a place of importance. Once gold was discovered in the Sierras, it was evident that the natural landing port for anyone destined to seek their fortune would be San Francisco and not Monterey. Thus, Monterey lost its dominance as a commercial center.

"Thereafter, even though the State of California would be founded here in Monterey in 1849, Monterey would lose its political importance. The capital designation left Monterey and moved to San Jose, closer to the gold rush action and to a few other places, before ending up in the present-day capital of Sacramento."

PowerPoint slide change: A photograph of Monterey in the early 1900s. It's a black-and-white image clearly displaying the town's buildings crumbling and its desolate streets.

"Tourist guides around the Peninsula recount that one need only look around to see Old Monterey in this present-day place of ours;

however, I disagree. I believe one must go further. One must imagine what Alvarado Street looked like when it stretched all the way to the bay instead of being cut off by a giant hotel. One must imagine a grimy wooden tavern in the middle of Monterey's central square where there is now a bus stop. One must picture a place that offered a distinctive culture of its own.

"The vast majority of us who live in this amazing place don't fully appreciate the cultural and historical significance of the ground we daily walk upon. We walk past adobe houses hundreds of years old without a second glance, and now that the state has cut off the funding for keeping them open to the public, we are stuck with a city full of closed *museumesque* houses."

Isidro paused again, this time to wipe a band of sweat from his brow. Nothing riled him more than cultural and historical indifference. He noticed that his latest diatribe had indeed captured the audience's attention. He saw a group of elderly eyes staring widely at him as if he had threatened to cut dried prunes and apricots from their diets.

"Now, I know you are aware that I am here today on behalf of my organization, the Monterey Historical Society, and I would be remiss if I didn't say that I'm asking for your consideration, as we need all the help we can receive. We strive to do all that we can, but I need not tell you how federal, state, and local funds have been rescinded, and I am personally asking for any contribution you can make toward our cause."

Isidro hoped his words would settle into the aged hearts and souls of those seated throughout the room. He could come across intensely at times, but he hoped it at least displayed the passion he brought to his position.

PowerPoint slide change: A photograph of the renovated Casa Abrego on Pacific Street. The white adobe of the house's walls glows in the sunshine while its front garden spews indigenous plants from a terraced design.

"With assistance such as yours we will be able to maintain these marvelous historical and cultural edifices we are blessed with. We will continue to do all we can to educate the masses, especially those fortunate enough to live here, of the wonders of the ground they tread upon every day. With assistance from good people such as yourselves, we can continue to safeguard these wonderful places such as Casa Abrego shown behind me." Isidro bit his lower lip in concentration. He enjoyed giving his presentations, but he did not enjoy feeling as if he was a salesman for historical preservation.

He attempted to concentrate and closed his eyes for a quick moment. *I need to close this on a positive and cheerful note.* "Of course, there's much more to the story of the Peninsula. Even in this portion of my presentation, I didn't have time to delve into some of the colorful characters who have visited Monterey. Nor did I have time to go into the many legends of pirates and bandits or the tales of tragic love stories or the countless ghost stories that have been documented. If you would like to hear those, you'll have to ask your event organizers to request I join you again."

Isidro forced a smile, hoping his little attempt at an amusing close would at least draw a few smiles of appreciation. He saw a few smiles, and even a few checkbooks. Isidro relished in knowing he was helping to preserve what would otherwise be forgotten.

It has been a good effort, Isidro congratulated himself.

6.

Year of our Lord 2009.

S AMUEL P. BECKWITH SIPPED from his glass of wine that had been poured from the five-hundred dollar bottle of Chateauneuf-du-Pape that the sommelier left on the table in between Samuel and his wife. He gazed across the table at his wife. Bridgette was wearing a plunging dress that displayed her perfectly-sculpted breasts. She was glowing in excitement from his decision to order the exclusive fifteen year old bottle from the restaurant's extensive wine list. He noticed the familiar blush that enraptured her as she tasted the wine. Samuel figured she would show her appreciation by going down on him later; it was just a question of whether or not she would wait until they were back at their house or if she would lean over into his lap on the drive home after dinner.

"How do you like the wine?" he asked her, trying to conceal the smile he felt emerging on his face at the thought of later events.

"It's divine. This is probably the most amazing wine that I've ever tasted." Samuel's inward smile grew exponentially … it would absolutely happen on the car ride home. "Thank you so much, honey, for getting this for us," Bridgette added.

"I thought we should celebrate tonight," Samuel responded.

"Oh, what are we celebrating, baby?" his wife asked.

Samuel's bulging pride wanted to tell her that they were celebrating his having orchestrated a heist of four hundred million dollars from the U.S. Government. "We're here to celebrate our love for one another." Speaking the words nearly made him gag, but he hoped this proclamation may even result in her pulling down the top of her dress while she went down on him in the car. He liked seeing her marvelous bare breasts, the marvelous breasts he had paid for.

The spacious, open atrium dining room of the restaurant was nice, in an opulent, over-done way, he thought. Although he preferred restaurants that had table arrangements that allowed for greater privacy. Bridgette suggested the restaurant, and Samuel considered that her primary motive was the restaurant's famed wine cellar.

As he sipped from his wine glass, he pictured the stash hiding safely waiting for his return. In a few days it would be time to re-convene with the team and make arrangements to move on to the next stage of their plan. Like pirates from hundreds of years before, they had left buried treasure behind, and it was time to plan for the return of their booty. It supremely pleased Samuel that only he knew the exact location of the *buried treasure*. He was careful to not reveal the exact GPS coordinates of the crevice where they had hide the loot in the underwater kelp forest. Considering that they completed the task on a night dive, and as the rest of his crew were nowhere near as good of a diver as himself, he could not imagine that any of them would be able to find the locate on their own. No, only he knew the exact whereabouts of the treasure; only he knew the exact coordinates of the "X" on the treasure map.

The bay, the same bay that he had gazed upon for months and had appeared to be calm, was not so calm once Agent John Gibson found himself on a small boat that departed from Pier 33 loaded with tourists. The tour was to circle Alcatraz Island and then pass underneath the Golden Gate Bridge and briefly enter the Pacific Ocean before turning back to pass once again through the Golden Gate, which was the actual name for the entrance to San Francisco Bay.

The waters churned below and small waves, that looked so minimal from the shore, persistently pounded against the side of the vessel. An overweight middle-aged couple wearing matching "Property of the University of Nebraska" sweatshirts hung their heads over the boat's deck railing, anticipating a deluge of vomit to spew forth at any moment. The cold, rough, and shark-infested waters of San Francisco Bay had deterred or claimed many a victim attempting to escape from Alcatraz when it was a high security prison, and now it was adding to its list of victims by torturing a pair of Nebraskan tourists.

Gibson never considered himself to have any potential to become a seaman, but being on the choppy water didn't bother him too much. He leaned back in the hard plastic seat on the boat's bow and took in the fantastic view of the San Francisco skyline from its bay. A sizeable wave pounded against the front of the boat, providing a fine spray of frigid water which covered the first two rows of seats and the tourists seating in them to a chorus of cries and shrieks.

How could someone have pulled-off stealing from a federal reserve bank building in broad daylight? Gibson pondered. As the boat inched increasingly closer to the towering edifice of red-colored steel expanding across the bay, he sorted through possibilities, but, somehow he was unable to move beyond the memories of his first trip to San Francisco. *What was it?* He struggled to clear his mind, but began to feel frustrated with himself. Another jolting of the boat confronting an oncoming wave head on sharpened his focus and he congratulated himself on having solved the puzzle configuring in his thoughts. He had indeed been attempting to remind himself of his previous visit to San Francisco: He needed to talk to Detective David Chiles.

Gibson periodically saw Chiles since his relocation to San Francisco, although never on a professional San Francisco Police Force-Federal Bureau of Investigation basis. Their previous visits had been to meet for coffee and polite conversation, normally at the same dive diner in Soma where they had initially conversed after analyzing the DB site of the murdered politician, José Aldarossa Arana.

Chiles was seated at a table near the front entrance of the diner when Gibson arrived after his boat tour. As usual, Chiles was dressed like a police detective straight out of a television show: taupe trench coat, a plain indiscriminate suit, and a white shirt with a cheap-looking tie that was crooked.

"Gibson. Great to see you again. I got down here as soon as you called," Chiles said as he rose to shake Gibson's hand.

Chiles was one of those law enforcement officers that would never let their guard down, would never consider themselves to not be on duty. Thankfully there were still some like him, Gibson thought. "Chiles, great to see you again as well," he replied as the two firmly shook hands and seated themselves opposite from one another at the table. Gibson was pleased that the diner, apart from a couple of patrons at the counter, was empty.

A cup of steaming coffee appeared on the table in front of him as soon as soon as he was seated. He looked up to find the restaurant's seemingly only employee looking down at him. "Can I get you a menu?" The waitress quickly asked.

"Just coffee for now. Thank you." She methodically topped-off Chiles' cup and slowly ambled away to return to her perch behind the restaurant's discolored counter.

"You sounded like you were on a boat when you called me earlier," Chiles said.

"Yes. I was actually. I was on one of those touristy boat tours that circles Alcatraz and then passes underneath the Golden Gate Bridge."

"Wow," Chiles exclaimed.

"What?"

"Well, I've just never heard of someone who lives here actually going out on one of those things."

"Remember I'm still relatively new here," Gibson said and the two shared a slight laugh. "Actually, I was out there for a reason; the same reason I asked to talk with you today."

Chiles raised his eyes from the white coffee mug to meet Gibson's gaze. He set his steaming mug down on the table. "Would it have anything to do with what happened at the reserve bank downtown?"

"It would," Gibson honestly replied.

"Well, you know I'm always here to help, Gibson." Chiles proudly responded.

Gibson smiled in response. *Ever a boy scout.* Chiles actually reminded Gibson of himself, although the similarity was of him at the debut of his law enforcement career. "Here's the deal, Chiles. As before, this is a federal investigation and, as you know, this all stays between us." Gibson regretted saying the words before he even finished the sentence. David Chiles was likely the most trustworthy person he knew and he could see from the change of expression on Chiles' face that he also felt slightly chided by Gibson's remark. Gibson decided to act quickly to reinsure his young friend. "Listen, David, you know I have to say that sort of thing out of habit with the job--it's absolutely nothing at all personal. In fact, I regret the obligation to have to say it."

The recovery attempt had an immediate positive impact, as the expression on Chiles' face turned from slightly downcast to elated. He finished his coffee in one quick gulp and sprung from his seat, so quickly and abruptly that it startled Gibson, and moved towards the counter to request a refill of his coffee, no doubt wanting to energize himself with caffeine as much as possible before taking on a new assignment, Gibson thought. "What can I do to help?" Chiles asked gleefully after he returned to his seat.

Gibson smiled inwardly at the display of enthusiasm. *This guy is going to be Police Chief of the San Francisco PD someday.* "Okay, for now, I would just like to talk through some things with you. I'm still not entirely familiar with the city and could use your opinions and expertise." Gibson took a long drink from his coffee mug. Chiles remained as before, appearing enthused, interested, and attentive. "It seems to me that if one were to rob a bank, any bank, in the financial district of San Francisco, one would have limited options on how to escape quickly from the city."

Chiles, eager to contribute, added: "Yes, that's absolutely correct. As you've no doubt come to realize even in your short time living here, San Francisco is extremely limited in its accessibility. We are almost like an island here, such as Manhattan, but due to the geography, population density, or perhaps just overall appearance--SF could even be considered more inaccessible than downtown NYC."

"From the financial district, the options are relatively minimal if one were trying to get out of town in a hurry. Yes, the Bay Bridge and the highways heading south are in the vicinity; however, during times of traffic, such as when the robbery occurred, getting a few blocks just to get to those highways can be a nightmare. Cutting west through the city would be an equal nightmare and that leaves north, which would likely lead directly through Chinatown and that would be even more horrific. Unless…"

Gibson had been staring into his now empty coffee mug, but looked up at the abrupt halt in Chiles' deliberation. "Unless what, Chiles?"

"Unless we are dealing with one of the worst kind of thieves."

"Which are?" Gibson expectantly inquired.

"Patient ones. Sure, the ones that are willing to kill are worse, but I'm talking about being able to catch them. We are obviously dealing with someone with patience, combined with the fact that we already can assume that they are well-financed, well-informed, and intelligent. I believe it is safe for us to assume that no common criminal would have been able to pull this off, agreed?"

"Unfortunately, I agree," Gibson replied.

"Then, we could be dealing with someone who's going to be very difficult to track. If they have patience, on top of those other attributes, we have our work cut out for us." Chiles concluded.

Gibson was undeterred. "Why do you say so?"

Chiles looked surprised at the question. "Surely you realize after what I've just said that if we have someone who is a meticulous planner that they could have segmented their entire operation--they could have transferred what they stole to one location initially and then somehow moved it to another place later and subsequently moved it out of the city." Chiles stopped when he saw a slight smile developing on Gibson's face. "You thought this all along and just let me keep going," he ventured.

"I suspected it, but I needed confirmation from a bright young mind such as yours. I'm sorry if you think I was playing with you; I just needed you to derive the possible conclusion on your own without my influence," Gibson added.

"Okay, okay. I forgive you." Chiles shook off the embarrassment he felt and let his eyes linger around the diner until they fell upon a yellowed picture of the bay hanging on the wall next to their table. "That's why you went out on that tourist boat? You think that perhaps they moved their cargo out of here on a boat?"

"Well, it certainly would be something that most people would not expect, and after so many years of doing this job, it seems like people are constantly trying to envision new ways to commit crimes that will keep people like you and I mystified."

"Hmm, that's definitely an interesting theory." Chiles slammed his hand down on the table, forcefully enough that the two old men perched on bar stools at the diner's counter turned to cast ungrateful glances at the youngster making too much noise. "You know what, I have a contact at the port authority here that could look into any abnormalities that he may have noticed in recent weeks."

Gibson nodded in agreement. "That would greatly appreciated and thank you for your help. I see a bright future for you." Chiles blushed and looked away like a ten-year-old being told he had done a good job.

"Now, I've got a more personal question to ask you." Chiles returned to expressing his undivided attention. Gibson swallowed and cleared his throat. "I've been, well, *dating* a woman I met here for a couple of months now and I've been meaning to invite her for a weekend away and, since I'm not really familiar yet with this part of California, I was wondering if you could recommend somewhere. I was thinking somewhere along the coast within a couple of hours drive from here."

Expressing romantic sentiment was not something John Gibson was accustomed to, but he was trying to get more used to it. It was true that he had been planning to get out of the city for a few days, but he also saw an opportunity to combine business with pleasure; a thought occurred to him while on the boat earlier that if there had been an escape via a water route, it would be logical not to go too far along the coast in one direction before docking.

Although Gibson's question clearly surprised him, there was no need for Chiles to ponder the question. "I have the perfect place to recommend for you."

"Where's that?" Gibson asked.

"*The Monterey Peninsula.* I think it'll be perfect," Chiles added with a smile. "I also have an old college buddy that lives there that knows everything about its history and culture and I'm sure he'd give you a little tour if you head down there." Chiles then paused, looking slightly embarrassed. "I'm sorry to ask, but with such an important investigation beginning for you, do you really have time for a weekend trip?" Chiles delicately inquired.

Gibson considered how only a couple of years earlier he would have asked the same question. "It's true that it is not the best timing, I agree. But something I've learned, Chiles, after all my years is that work and play can at times be combined." From the expressionless change on the face of Chiles, Gibson assumed it would be many years before the eager young detective would comprehend Gibson's words, *if ever*.

"What do you mean?" Chiles asked.

"Let's just say I have a hunch that I want to explore further," he added.

Gibson then pondered Chiles' recommendation for a further moment before responding. *"Monterey, huh*? I have heard it's a nice place."

"Trust me--You'll love it." Chiles responded, pleased to have the subject changed.

"So what's your friend's name?" Gibson asked.

"Isidro. His name is Isidro de la Vega." Chiles answered.

7.

Year of our Lord 1818.

GOD'S PLAN REMAINED A MYSTERY, even to a devoted believer such as Father Dominique Margil. Father Margil had long before concluded that he could spend his days questioning the Great Father's motives in a futile attempt of understanding, or he could spend them trying to better mankind's existence on earth by preaching salvation through the Lord's path. The first option would result in his complete isolation, either in a monastery in some isolated mountain range, or on his own in a desert cave; while the other option would result in tireless days of preaching His word and in loving mankind. Of the two, there was little choice for Father Margil. The Church had saved his life and it was his duty to devote his life to it, which, as far as he could see, was not to selfishly lock oneself away in isolated contemplation. His mission was to be with the people of the world. He could not abandon them; *he would not abandon them.*

However, his purpose became clouded when he was directed by the superiors of his Order on his recent voyage to Mexico City to lead a group of people and supplies from his home of the Mission San Vicente to the distant post of Monterey in the vast and wild lands to the north. Father Margil did not doubt nor fear the quest of the Church to spearhead the Spanish Empire's colonial desires; in fact, he relished in the thought of being among the first of the Church to penetrate into the vast mysterious lands of northern Alta California.

Yet he did question the motivations of those around him. He was ordered, or politely "instructed" as they referred to it, to travel with a heavy contingent of soldiers. Father Margil believed that soldiers could have their uses; however, more often than not, in his humble opinion, they tended to complicate situations rather than offer assistance. The soldiers talked down to the natives and Father Margil was certain that without his presence and constant reminding the soldiers that the natives were people just as they were and should be treated as such that there would be rampant beatings or worse occurring. He didn't know if other friars at other missions in the New World were as strict on their assigned soldiers as he was with his, but it was not important to him how others conducted themselves.

He would do everything he could to protect the natives; in his eyes, they were God's lost children and they were beautiful. He not only saw it as his duty to protect them, but to also teach them the word of the Lord and to enlighten them on the ways of Spanish society, which would soon overwhelm them if they were not prepared. Father Margil empathized with their plight at having foreigners come to their lands and tell them that they were not living the way people should live and therefore should adopt a new way of living; but although Father Margil held romantic ideals dear to his heart, as a man of God watching over the fallen grace of mankind, he also grasped strongly to some realist views.

In light of this, he knew the natives had no choice. They could either leave their villages, pagan worshiping, and hunting and gathering lifestyles and assimilate themselves into the agricultural production systems of the missions and accept Christ in their hearts, or their existence would be erased forever from the coming onslaught of imperialism. It was indeed not much of a choice for them, and, realizing this fully, he found a new level of compassion for his fellow man that he had never recognized before. They had become *his* children. And if the Crown kept its promise, once the lands of Alta California were eventually divided for private ownership, the converted natives would be included in those who would be given land entitlement.

Father Margil would lead the group, which would include the soldiers along with men, women, and a few children, northward to join the great Father Junipero Serra at the Mission San Carlos Borromeo de Carmelo, located near Monterey. It saddened Margil to be leaving the group of natives he had instructed for years at the San

Vicente Mission, and he regretted admitting that he would miss their faces and company. Although he met his replacement, a Father Cruz, in Mexico City and he believed the father to be a noble man of God who would watch over the converted natives at the mission.

The prospect of having his new home at the Carmel Mission assisting Father Serra was exciting to Margil and he felt a level of shame for feeling so prideful. He disregarded these prideful feelings by telling himself that it was not a sin to want to further spread God's word by traveling to new lands where there was still resistance to conversion among native populations. Monterey, although an established outpost of the Empire, was still considered a wild place.

It was in Mexico City that he was informed of his new assignment and consequently, of his destiny. In Mexico City he learned that he would not only be leading a group of settlers, accompanied by a division of soldiers, but also escorting a large chest of gold from the Church's treasury that would accompany them to Monterey.

The political motivations and objectives of the gold were delicately shared with Father Margil. Its designated purpose was simple: to bribe a Russian, who through his ambitious drive was urging the Russian Empire to extend its holdings south into Alta California. Russian incursion into Spanish lands was highly anticipated and the Spanish military forces in Alta California were still weak.

With no known passage crossing the American continents, the voyage to Alta California required voyaging around the tip of South America by water or an overland journey through Mexico after landing at Veracruz. Each alternative posed risk, difficulty, and time; which, combined with other factors, deterred placing a rushed emphasis on the strengthening of Alta California.

As Father Margil was aware, the Russian was considered extremely dangerous, as he represented the Russian Empire's collective interests in the New World; many attributed the Empire's efforts in the cold lands far to the north of California to this man. But the man was also extremely self-interested and was above all an ambitious merchant with a desire to enrich *himself* as much as possible.

The chest of gold was, therefore, to be given to the Russian in exchange for his word that his ventures would not extend southward beyond the great river mouth to the north of Alta California. He would thereafter report to Saint Petersburg that he did not believe it to be feasible for the Russians to expand their holdings south in the New World. Margil was informed that a secret meeting between the Russian and the governor in Monterey had occurred, in which the arrangements had been made and the Russian had agreed to the terms, as long as the promised payment of gold would be waiting for him upon his next visit.

Father Margil thus realized his new posting involved the transportation of a small fortune destined to be used for bribery. The arrangement for the Russian's payment of the gold had been agreed upon by both the governor and Father Serra, despite the reputed disdain they shared for each other, and that this was undeniable proof of the grand purpose of the cause. Father Margil did not approve of bribery, even less with the involvement of gold, but he could not deny that a good intention, that of keeping Alta California out of the hands of the ruthless Russians, would result from the deed. Stories of the Russian's vile treatment of the natives of their colony in the north had filtered throughout the world, and Margil would not let the same fierce rule overtake any more of God's children if he could do anything to help prevent it. Notwithstanding, traveling through the unknown north brought fear and doubt into Father Margil's heart. He spent the days before the expedition's departure from the Mission San Vicente deep in prayer, hoping the voyage to Monterey would be successful.

8.

Year of our Lord 2009.

I SIDRO DE LA VEGA took care of himself in all aspects of life, be they physical, emotional, or spiritual. He rarely got involved with people. His parents died when he was young, leaving him to be raised by his grandmother, and he had never had any serious girlfriends; in fact, he found it difficult to approach women.

Spiritually, Isidro considered himself a devout Catholic who never missed Sunday mass at Monterey's cathedral, known as the Royal Presidio Chapel or San Carlos Cathedral, the oldest surviving stone building in California and the oldest cathedral in the western United States. He loved how this gift of a cathedral remained "hidden" in Monterey even though it was next to major roads and intersections. The cathedral was rarely more than a quarter full during mass, and most attendees were of Monterey's older generations, yet in general, Monterey still honored some Catholic traditions. An example was how every deli or sandwich shop around Monterey offered a Friday fish sandwich lunch special ... with a fried calamari sandwich being a favorite. Isidro assumed that the "calamari" part of the equation was derived from Catholic tradition, while the "fried" part could be attributed to an Italian influence.

Isidro was also physically maintained. He had never seen the purpose of seeking vanity through building his muscles beyond normal proportions, but he did keep a sharp, trim physique. Isidro watched what he ate, never smoked, rarely drank, and never touched drugs.

A brisk, damp morning breeze blew in from the ocean, crashing against his left side as he ascended the front face of the mountain in Garrapata State Park, located along Highway 1. He could feel moisture building on his clothing. A group of sea lions was barking loudly far below on an outcropping of rocks in the treacherous waters off the Big Sur coast. Their cries carried with the wind, even to 1,000 feet above sea level, which Isidro estimated was his current elevation.

He was hiking the trail that he conquered weekly. He considered it his personal hike, despite numerous "hiking clubs" from the Bay Area having recently discovered the poorly marked trail off the coast and made it a favorite daytrip destination. Isidro wished they would stay in their congested, air-polluted, crime-ridden places and leave the Peninsula and Big Sur uncontaminated with their big-city ways. They didn't even know the proper hiking etiquette of giving right of way to an ascending hiker.

As he steadily hiked up the steep, rocky incline, he cleared his thoughts of distaste for the intruders on his trail. Locals were fine with him; in fact, he looked forward to passing the same faces, but the others … He was aware that his thoughts were not compassionate for his fellow mankind, as the Church and Bible taught. But he could not resist temptation to harbor personal feelings, especially as he considered the trail a church-like experience, and they were trying to ruin it for him and anyone else who understood its true value. This was how Isidro justified negative intentions towards outsiders on his trail. He didn't go out of his way to be rude to anyone he deemed an interloper, but he refrained from being kind to any non-local.

A group of loose rocks crumbled beneath his left foot, and he stumbled to regain his footing. He looked toward the wide expanse of the dark blue ocean and felt a presence. Isidro accepted that he needed to attempt to be more accepting. Perhaps he should be more forgiving, he considered; just as he did, a group of three pot-bellied middle-aged men he guessed were from the East Coast, given their obnoxious accents, came barreling down the trail with no regard to their surroundings, nearly ramming into Isidro, and having equally no regard for the tranquility surrounding them, as they were gabbing in voices loud enough to hear from a fishing boat out in the ocean. Isidro shook his head in disgust and continued his ascent.

The vibrant smell of sage overwhelmed his senses as he passed a bench overlooking the ocean from around 1,200 feet above. The view was amazing, stretching from Monterey Bay to the north and to the rugged Big Sur coast to the south. Isidro often considered stopping to savor the fantastic scenery, but he never did, partly as he didn't enjoy interrupting his hike and workout, but because the one time he had sat on the bench on his first ascent up the trail, he felt an overwhelming sense of loneliness. He didn't mind having no significant other in his life, but he preferred to avoid reminders of his solitude.

Isidro crested the last stretch of trail that led to the peak's summit. He deeply inhaled the enticing blend of sage, wildflowers, and ocean. He closed his eyes for a moment as he strode across the relatively flat summit; when he opened them, he was startled to find a young woman in front of him. Isidro noticed that she was attractive, slender but athletically built. She had light brown eyes and dark hair pulled into a ponytail. She was wearing convertible hiking pants, as he was, and had on a light jacket that clung to her body.

She smiled as they closed the few remaining paces between them and Isidro felt anxiety rise. He liked women, but had never felt entirely comfortable around them; they made him nervous. He felt his grip on his trekking poles slipping as his hands began to perspire.

She stopped and smiled even wider. "Hi. Great day to be on the trail, isn't it?" the young woman said as she turned her head slightly, causing her ponytail to swing.

Tension took over Isidro as he forced himself to stop. He struggled to formulate words in response. "Yeah, yeah, it is."

She looked at him expectantly. When it became apparent after a few awkward seconds that he was going to utter nothing more, she attempted again to initiate conversation. "How do you like using trekking poles?" she asked with another smile.

"Uh, they're okay," he managed to say, although he wanted to say how much he preferred using the poles when hiking, as they not only added another element to the exercise one received with an additional arm workout but also provided more balance when one had a heavy backpack. Isidro wanted to say more but couldn't think of anything to say.

"So, do you hike here very often?" she asked.

Isidro desired to truthfully respond that he made a point to go hiking on his trail once a week, usually early on Saturday mornings, but at times on Friday afternoons, as on that day. "Sometimes," he replied instead. His inner voice told him to ask her name, but she lost interest in the bumbling guy in front of her and moved around him to continue along the trail.

"Well, have a good day," she said as she brushed past him.

Isidro watched her walk away. He yelped a meek "see you around." However, if she did hear him, she didn't turn to acknowledge it. He kicked the ground in frustration. She had obviously been interested in him and he blew his chance. It was nothing out of the ordinary, though. Women often tried to talk to him, as he was considered to be attractive — tall, dark-haired, with defined cheekbones he could thank his Spanish ancestry for, but he had not inherited any of the famed Spanish charm. Isidro watched the woman stride away until she began a downhill stretch and disappeared from sight. He sighed and returned to hiking the trail.

As Isidro carefully made his way down the steep slope, he gazed into the thick redwood forest that extended throughout the crevice in between the ridges and peaks in the area and he reflected on how the Big Sur pioneers must have felt that they had discovered an earthly paradise.

At the base of the mountain's face, he followed the trail as it gently wound into a forested glen area. A giant redwood had long before fallen in the center of a small, cleared area of the forest and had thereafter reinvented itself as a bench for exhausted hikers to rest on or for nature observers to sit and enjoy the tranquil calm of the forest surrounding them. Redwoods towered above and a small creek meandered through the canyon on its course toward the ocean. Isidro could not imagine a more peaceful setting and he often thought that it would be an incredible spot to meet someone for the first time as he passed by it.

At times, he would take a seat on the log and enjoy the forest, but this day a group of twenty or so people, likely from the Bay Area, had converged there in the midst of a mid-hike snack. It aggravated him that he had to ask a pair of men standing in the middle of the trail to move so he could pass by.

Isidro breathed deeply and shook off his frustration as he finished the relatively flat two-mile stretch returning to the trailhead.

9.

Year of our Lord 1818.

THE GOVERNOR OF ALTA CALIFORNIA should not have the added stress of worrying about the behavior of his young daughter, Governor Pedro Fages considered as he sipped a steaming cup of chocolate with added pepper spice that he saved for special occasions. Some chocolate stuck to the sides of his thin mustache, and he wiped his mouth with a napkin. This morning was no special occasion, but he saved the limited chocolate supply he had brought from Mexico City for occasions when he felt he needed to keep himself calm.

He sighed deeply at the complications swirling around him. *What if the Russian returned for his promised gold before it arrived from the south? Would the Spanish Empire lose Alta California?* If this would be the case, he would undoubtedly be blamed for the loss. *And where was the priest that was supposed to be bringing the gold with a contingent of soldiers?* The delivery was already weeks overdue. Fages imagined that the priest, whoever it was, was encountering unexpected difficulties crossing the coastal mountain ranges and this was the explanation for the delayed arrival. Whatever the explanation, it was unacceptable to the governor. The future of Alta California was at stake.

He took a long sip of the hot chocolate and let the rich liquid linger in his mouth before swallowing. The governor closed his eyes momentarily and breathed in deeply, now smelling the blooming flowers of his house's garden. A slight breeze then introduced the smell of the horse stable on the far side of the garden, breaking his relaxing reverie and returning him to the harshness of reality.

Another worry he had to consider was that the French pirate, Hippolyte de Bouchard, was known to be scouring the Californian coast, planning an attack on one or more of the still relatively young settlements.

Bouchard had thus far limited his activities to raiding trading vessels and Spanish supply ships sailing south on their return journeys to the east coast of the United States or to Europe, but the persistent rumors of his shifted focus to invade the settlements was too disturbing to be ignored. If Bouchard were to invade Monterey, Governor Fages feared the results would be disastrous.

In addition he had his lovely daughter, Isabella, to oversee. Isabella was his only child and he cherished her. Her dear mother had succumbed to a fever soon after her birth and thus, Fages raised the child on his own. A second marriage was never an option to him. His love for his wife would remain with him to his grave and he would never fathom marriage to another. He was distraught, however, at the thought that perhaps the absence of a motherly figure in Isabella's life had led to an undeterred stubbornness within her that only a mother's careful touch would have been able to tame.

He often wondered how well he had raised his child. Most of the time, she was wonderful, obedient and devoted, eager to learn and to be helpful. However, there were times when she decided to show an alternate side of her personality, and such times displaying her flaming insolence were a testament to her father's patience. Combined with the undeniable fact that his daughter had, in what seemed like mere months, been transformed from an inquisitive, soft-spoken girl into a daring, outspoken young woman. Her body had equally transformed quickly from that of a scrawny girl into that of a beautiful young woman, and it unnerved the governor to notice so many of the young soldiers of his garrison stealing glances of her as she passed by them. And then there was the young Englishman.

William Beckwith was his name. Much to the governor's chagrin, he could not describe many, if any, negative qualities of the young man. He was a fine-looking lad, healthy and strong, with a handsome face and a full head of hair. Beckwith consistently managed to appear clean and neat in his suits, even after disembarking from long voyages at sea. He had pointedly learned how to speak the Spanish language before his arrival to Alta California and he presented himself as cordial, respectful, intelligent, and charming. It had been his charm, in fact, that had first secured permission from the governor for Beckwith's ship to dock in Monterey Bay for a few days of illegal trading with the residents of Monterey.

The governor was uneasy with his defiance of Spanish law that distinctly forbade any trade activities with foreign parties in Alta California; but he could not deny, as Beckwith cleverly highlighted at their first encounter, that his vessel contained items the residents of Monterey would not easily obtain otherwise. Some of these items were necessities, such as cooking utensils; others were not, such as the newest fashions of women's dresses. Nevertheless, the governor justified his actions by recognizing that allowing this limited trading to occur assisted in the overall sustainability of Monterey.

Even the non-necessities introduced cheer and life to his citizens. The women relished in wearing the new dresses and the men gushed in seeing the women display their new clothing. Governor Fages was cognizant that those who lead should be careful to attend to the sentiment of those they oversee, and the situation in Monterey and all of Alta California was already precarious enough without any added discomforts or restrictions.

Resupply ships from Spain were routinely late and persistently under-stocked, which equaled a troubling situation for the governor. A few pans and a few dresses would not harm the Spanish Empire, he deduced.

The aging governor sipped deeply on his warmed chocolate. On one hand, he could not imagine a better suitor for his daughter's hand. On the other, even though she was in her sixteenth year, older than many other young wives in Alta California, he still viewed her as his little girl. Without doubt, the two of them shared many a prolonged glance at one another at the fandango. Beckwith was even bold enough to request from Fages to ask Isabella to dance with him. That had been some months before, and Fages hoped the upstanding young man would continue to impress him by soon sharing his intentions with him and respectfully requesting he be allowed to court Isabella.

One of his workers, a young man named Esteban he had brought with him from Mexico City, meekly requested to speak to the governor. The governor motioned his approval.

"Excellency, I would like to inform you that the men have brought in the bear that was caught in the valley for the fight this afternoon," Esteban said, referring to the grizzly bear that had been caught in the Carmelo Valley where Father Serra had moved his mission.

Esteban's report reminded the governor of two items, the first being that he had forgotten that before the planned feast and fandango that evening, there was also to be a bear and bull fight. There was no ship docked off shore in the bay to welcome, but Fages liked to keep spirits high in his settlement, and having a fiesta always brought cheer to the people. The second item Esteban's comment reminded him was that he should invite Serra to the evening's festivities.

"Very good, Esteban. I have a task for you now. I would like you to ride over the hill to the mission and extend an invitation to the fandango this evening to Father Serra on my behalf. Please leave as soon as you are able." The governor considered adding for Esteban to not mention the bear and bull fight beforehand, as Serra would of course disapprove of such an event. The governor himself was not much of a supporter of the raw and bloody spectacle, yet his men loved the spectacles, so he allowed the fights to occur; but he guessed that Esteban would so nervous with his assignment that he would be lucky to convey any invitation to Serra once he was in the Father's presence.

Governor Fages was suddenly surprised to have not yet heard an affirmative response from Esteban. He turned in his chair to gaze at the young man and discovered that a genuine look of fear had overtaken Esteban's face. "Well, what is it, Esteban? I can assure you that no harm will come to you once you deliver the invitation to the good Father. We may have had our differences in the past and we may indeed still share many of the same differences, but the Father is a man of God and he would not dispel any harm on you in my name."

Esteban turned his eyes downward. "It's, it's not that, Excellency," he said in a broken voice. "It's just that, well, it's been said that there are *ghosts* on top of the hill on the way to the valley."

The governor acknowledged that there had been stories of strange occurrences on the road between the mission and Monterey; regardless, he believed the strange happenings were more likely the result of too much wine having been consumed at one end of the trail.

He attempted to accommodate Esteban's fear while trying to humor him as well. "Well, my dear Esteban, as far as I know, *ghosts* only emerge in the darkness, and as it is now only early morning, you shall be there and back long before nightfall." Esteban's expression remained fixated in fear, unchanged by the governor's assurance.

"I'll even let you take one of my better horses for the voyage. Would that ease your mind?" Esteban was unable to suppress a wide smile escaping on his face. *Riding one of the governor's horses ... it would be a rare honor!* He excitedly nodded his head in agreement. "Now, be quick with you and relate my wishes to the stable master."

Governor Fages finished the last of the chocolate in the cup and rose from the table. With the prospect of his future son-in-law and Father Serra attending the fiesta, he wanted to be sure that all arrangements had been made accordingly. He hoped it would be an evening to remember.

10.

Year of our Lord 2009.

I SIDRO DE LA VEGA ENTERED through the pub's thick doors and was reminded how his friend, Chris Walker, who was already seated at the bar, fit the stereotype of a typical American. Chris wore jeans that were too baggy, a long-sleeved T-shirt underneath an equally baggy bright blue T-shirt that had "Wrigley Field" sprawled across it in bright red letters, a San Francisco 49ers baseball cap turned backwards on his head, and, to top off the ensemble, a pair of dirty white gym shoes on his feet. At one time, Chris had been in decent shape, but over the years, he'd let fast food and beer pile on pounds to his midsection. They had met years earlier in a class at California State University Monterey Bay, where Isidro had transferred to finish his undergraduate degree after briefly moving away from the Peninsula.

Isidro, on the other hand, was wearing a smart outfit of gray slacks and a white fitted button-up shirt with black pinstripes, and shiny black oxford shoes. His dark hair was sleek and combed back. Isidro nodded as he noticed Chris gesturing to him from the bar. Chris was quite possibly his complete opposite, but something about the guy had always amused Isidro. Perhaps it was Chris's capability to make Isidro laugh.

"Whew, I don't think they're gonna have your favorite bottle of wine in here, monsieur," Chris joked as Isidro approached and the two shook hands.

"Well, that will be okay, Chris. I'll stick to a diet soda for now," Isidro replied as he sat himself on the stool next to Chris. The bartender, who had been engaged in a conversation with an elderly man at the other end of the bar, gradually made his way within earshot of Isidro, who promptly ordered a Diet Pepsi. Isidro guessed that the old man hunched at the bar spent many an afternoon in the sunken pub. It took only moments for Isidro to recognize the scents he had labeled as being components of this particular pub: stale beer, fried food, and mold.

"By the way, my family's heritage is Spanish and not French, so *señor* would be more appropriate of a jest to call me than *monsieur*."

Chris's expression changed and he looked amused. "Oh, so right off the bat, you're going to play that California superiority card on me like that?"

Isidro grinned in response before responding. "I didn't utter anything about superiority, *you did*." The bartender, in the process of placing a glass of sizzling Diet Coke in front of Isidro, overheard the conversation and chuckled at Isidro's response.

Chris responded by making an obvious exaggeration of narrowing his eyes at Isidro. "So, you're telling me that you really think this overcrowded, overhyped, overcongested, overpolluted, and overpriced place known as California is really that much better than the rest of these great United States? I mean, people always think of the beaches of southern California when they think of this state, yet most of it looks more like the Central Valley, which is really like a flatter, hotter, drier version of anywhere and it's so polluted that you can barely even see the mountains around it most of the time.

"And how about people here being so concerned to get home from work so they can go for their run or bike ride or get to their yoga class, yet they insist on driving everywhere and will look at a pedestrian in a crosswalk like they are circus animals … and at the same time, these people that drive everywhere also claim to be environmentalists!"

Isidro took a drink from his glass, considering a way to deflect the oncoming debate away from discussing the personality traits of Californians. Isidro noticed Chris ready to pounce, but beat him to it by continuing. "However, I do want to note for the record that I consider right here, here in the vicinity of the Monterey Peninsula, to be the superior location within the great State of California. And, before you cut me off again, let me add that even in the mid 1800s, an author by the name of Bayard Taylor recorded that although Monterey may be initially viewed as dull, anyone who spends any time here leaves loving the place."

"*This place?* Are you serious?" Chris replied loudly, catching the attention of the old man and bartender at the other end of the bar.

"Let's consider a few things we have here. *The weather*? It's foggy and cold in summer and then damp and freezing in winter. You would expect a place like Seattle to have a lot of depressed drunks with their cloudy winters, but down here could be worse, as in winter, one expects to endure foul weather, but here, one is also dealt gloom in summer!" Chris raised his glass in salute and took a long drink.

"People love to refer to 'May Gray' and 'June Gloom' all along the coast of California, but in Monterey there should be a couple of new expressions to describe July and August, as it doesn't clear up and get nice like nearly every place south of here. How about *Jittering July* and *Awful August*? I think those would work. And, before you start getting into the 'second summer' argument that everyone living here loves to bring up, even then, in those fall months when it does actually happen, it doesn't get sunny and *mildly* warm until after noon, and then it only lasts for a few hours before it gets chilly again. What's more, on the hottest days, if there's no breeze, it stinks like dead fish and sea lion piss everywhere on the Peninsula.

"*How about the scenery?* Sure, it's pretty, but you have to pay to get into most of the prettiest areas and many others are private havens for rich people.

"*The standard of living*? Most of us can barely afford to live here and even fewer of us can hope to ever be able to buy a house that's not in some bad neighborhood far away from desirable locations.

"*The history?* Cannery Row is a goddamn joke and only fills the area with dumbass tourists."

Isidro raised a mock threatening finger towards Chris. "Ah, ah … you know the 'history area' is off limits with me."

Chris conceded by clinking his glass against Isidro's. "Okay, okay, I'm sorry to go there." He paused to consider a new direction to argue. "But of course, let's not forget how much influence the military has had and still has on this place." Isidro attempted to conceal a grin. It was a sensitive subject with Chris, who felt truly that he had been personally wronged by the military and pledged himself to promote the departure of the armed forces from the area. Isidro leaned back on the barstool, preparing to hear Chris's usual diatribe against the military's presence.

"Why is there such a large military presence still in Monterey? Are the Japanese going to invade Monterey Bay one of these days? They'd rather sell us cars and electronics and even buy real estate in Pebble Beach than go to war with us again."

Chris took a long drink from his beer and a line of white, bubbly foam remained on his upper lip when he removed the glass. "Or maybe we're worried that the Russians are going to invade and that's why so much military presence remains," he continued, staring straightforward into nothing as if making a dire prediction. He remained in this pose of reflection for a few moments before a convulsion of laughter erupted from him. He laughed loudly, slamming a hand down on the wooden bar. "God, the Russians … now there's a good excuse. What do they have for a navy? A few rusted leftovers from the early days of the Cold War?"

"Well, your mentioning of Russian interest is in fact not so far off the mark, historically speaking, anyway," Isidro chimed.

"Damn it, Isidro," Chris said teasingly. "You've always got to ruin my intro," he added, turning to gaze at him with a blank stare. Isidro bowed his head in acknowledgement of his seemingly rude interruption, beckoning Chris to continue by raising and turning his palm. "Now, where was I?" Chris asked out loud.

"Monterey Bay's invasion!" the bartender uttered in slight mockery from the other end of the bar.

Chris smiled in his direction and raised his beer in salute with a wide grin, ignoring the mockery. "Well, thank you, good sir." He took another drink from his beer and continued with his well-rehearsed script. "So, we have all this military here really for no reason and we get to be reminded of it every afternoon with that trumpeter up at the Presidio playing taps."

Isidro took a moment to quickly glance around the room. The pub was, as the others on Alvarado Street in downtown Monterey, a regular hangout for military personnel from the Naval Postgraduate School or the Presidio, and Chris had more than once caused confrontations between himself and those enlisted men; however,

Chris's down-home Midwest friendliness was always able to get himself out of trouble after he explained that he had nothing against the soldiers themselves and then bought them a round of beers.

"Hey, what do you have against the military here, anyway?" the bartender, who had been pretending to not listen to Chris's speech, called over.

"Well, good sir, I don't have anything against any of the individuals, it's just that I think they are able to get away with a lot here."

"Like what?" the bartender inquired, moving closer to Chris and Isidro.

Chris pretended to reflect upon his response before saying a word. He took a slow drink from his beer, finishing it, before gently placing it on the bar in front of him. "As my friend Isidro here could tell you, they've been allowed to take over one of the more historic complexes on the Peninsula, the Del Monte Hotel, for the Naval Postgraduate School, which thereby places a restriction on access to the place. Or there's the land of the Presidio, now housing the Defense Language Institute, which is probably the most pristine real estate in Monterey and could easily be designated for a mixed-use purpose. And if you say that the Presidio could never be closed due to its historical presence, I will respond by telling you that this very thing was done in the not so distant past in San Francisco. And further, the biggest problem with the military presence here is in fact due to the Presidio."

The bartender shook his head in confusion. "You're not making any sense, guy. What are you talking about?"

Chris pointed at his empty beer glass and waited for the bartender to place a new freshly poured glass in front of him before continuing. *"Traffic,"* he calmly replied.

When his proclamation received only an utter look of confusion from the bartender, Chris continued. "The military gets away with causing traffic violations that no one else would be able get away with. Lighthouse Avenue over in New Monterey is the perfect example, as it causes a lot of traffic jams and accidents."

"Just wait right there, Sonny. Why is it you care so much?" The old man from the end of the bar, who had been staring into space after the departure of the bartender, asked in a voice passing through a throat that had withstood decades of alcohol and smoke.

"Because, good sir," Chris responded, "because I am going to do something about it! In fact, I'm already doing something about it. I'm suing the City of Monterey for not having forced the military to improve that intersection at the end of Lighthouse Avenue. The city may have enforced some fee upon the Army two decades ago, but my charge is that none of that did or does anything today ... It's an outrage!"

"So, let me guess: You were in an accident there?" The bartender asked with a smirk.

Chris glared at the bartender intently, narrowing his eyes slightly as he had done mockingly at Isidro earlier. He stood up from his bar stool, pulled out his wallet from his back jeans pocket, and patted a few bills on top of the bar with a smile in the direction of the bartender. "We'll see who laughs last when my case gets called. C'mon, Isidro, let's go somewhere more welcoming," he said as he brushed pass Isidro on his way to the door. Isidro dropped down from his own barstool and followed his friend out of the door into the overcast afternoon.

II.

Year of our Lord 2009.

ER NAME WAS RACHEL DOWLING and she was everything John Gibson's ex-wife was not. Instead of being a no-nonsense high profile saleswoman, she was a program manager of a non-profit group. Instead of being a tense, neurotic individual who worried incessantly about everything, as far as he could see, Rachel remained calm in every situation. Instead of being materialistic in any way, she showed no sign of serious attachment to material items. Instead of going through inner turmoil over her outfit or makeup for the day, Rachel dressed quickly and applied little if any makeup to her face. This is not to say that she presented herself as an unkempt woman in any manner; in fact, Gibson was consistently impressed with her simple yet elegant sense of style.

Rachel had long, almost silver-colored hair, which she would either let fall upon her shoulders or pull back into a ponytail. She had soft green eyes that he was beginning to enjoy witnessing soften even more when their eyes would meet. They had been dating for a month, and he didn't know if he had fallen in love with her, but it was undeniable that he was thoroughly enjoying their relationship and was beginning to feel hopeful that it would mature into something grander. She had not seemed the least surprised when he asked her to join him for a weekend getaway to the Monterey Peninsula. He didn't mention that he was mixing their little trip with an initial feeling he had regarding the heist in San Francisco, but he didn't think it was necessary; it was just a bit of intuition anyway.

As she walked beside him along Monterey's waterfront towards Fisherman's Wharf, he attempted to slyly steal glances of her from the side of his right eye. She looked stunning to him in her long, flowing brown dress and cream sweater.

"Hey, I see you checking me out," she whispered into his ear as they walked. Rachel playfully nudged her hip into his side.

Gibson blushed. He couldn't remember the last time someone had made him blush. "Um, no, ma'am. I was merely ensuring your safety by keeping an eye on your surroundings," he clumsily muttered.

She smiled in response as they continued walking along the path. There was definitely something about her that Gibson was growing addicted to. From his first arrival on the West Coast from DC he had felt more relaxed, but Rachel's presence amplified the easing of tension.

They had driven southward on Highway 1 from San Francisco, passing the redwood forests of the Santa Cruz Mountains, followed by the city of Santa Cruz itself, and then circling around Monterey Bay to Monterey and on to Cannery Row, where Gibson had booked a room in a hotel overlooking the water. He knew that Rachel was not the kind of person looking to be impressed, or even looking to have affection lavished upon her, but he wanted to try regardless.

They approached the pier known as Fisherman's Wharf and took a few minutes to walk to the end of it, passing by countless tourist eye-grabbing souvenir shops and a string of cheerful people offering free tastings of their clam chowder outside their respective restaurants. Rachel and Gibson agreed that they found the wharf to be a scaled-down replica of its big brother in San Francisco: overdone, overly crowded, and entirely unsubstantial. As they returned to the entrance of the wharf, Gibson suggested that they walk inland towards Monterey's downtown, taking in a few of the historic adobe buildings as they did. He had briefly read about Monterey's historic adobe homes the previous evening when trying to prepare some sort of agenda of activities for their weekend getaway.

First stop was the Old Custom House, appropriately located nearest the edge of the water, where merchants of prior days would have to register upon their arrival and provide a listing of the goods they wished to sell while docked in Monterey's harbor. When Gibson and Rachel approached the one-story building with its white adobe walls capturing the sun's rays, they found the doors to the building closed. They walked along the open porch covered with wooden planks and tried to peer into the windows. Inside they saw what appeared to be a replica of a trading center from hundreds of years ago: barrels aligned against one wall, boxes marked as commodity goods in another, piles of animal hides and woven garments, and a simple desk and chair in the center of the room ready to receive visitors on their entrance through the doorway.

Disappointed yet undeterred, the pair moved on to the next adobe building in sight, a two-story structure much longer than the Custom House, which Gibson remembered from his brief research being called the Pacific House, which presently housed a local museum. When they passed through the short and narrow doorway to the building, a woman leaning back in a chair with reading glasses dangling from the end of her nose stiffly awoke from a midafternoon nap. She looked surprised to see them.

The pair slowly toured the museum, comparing notes in whispers on how it was slightly cheesy, yet informative. While passing by a revolving book rack near the exit, a book caught Rachel's attention and she began to casually flip through its pages. The book was titled: *The Monterey Peninsula, Through the Eyes of Robert Louis Stevenson*. It was a mixture of text, photographs, and drawings depicting life on the Peninsula in the latter part of the 19th century. Gibson offered to buy the book for Rachel, and the elderly woman behind the front desk of the museum seemed equally surprised at Gibson's purchase as when they had entered the museum; she laboriously used a calculator to assess the sales tax on the book and then wrote out the order on a receipt pad.

As they had entered the museum building, they departed from a crystal blue sky and bright sunshine, only to emerge now into a landscape being quickly devoured by the mercilessly approaching fog. The fog had not yet totally overcome the coastline and it gleamed brightly in white magnificence as the sunshine from above bounced upon it. Rachel and Gibson decided to forego any more touring of downtown Monterey in favor of returning to their hotel room for a little afternoon break before they heading out for dinner.

The walk along the coastal recreational trail to the hotel was far colder than either of them would have wished for, with a cool, damp breeze blowing in from the bay in apparent partnership with the approaching fog. Within minutes, the sun and blue sky disappeared and all that remained was an ominous and dense blanket of fog surrounding them. They quickened their pace.

A biker nearly collided with them as they rounded a turn, appearing suddenly as if she were a phantom of the fog. They both noticed the lean biker's vibrantly bright red hair protruding out of the back of the cap she was wearing as she vanished in front of them.

The sounds of sea lions barking and yelping somewhere nearby increased in volume the more thickly the fog encased the coastline. They had not even seen a faint formation of fog on the horizon when they had left the hotel for their stroll an hour earlier. Despite the sudden chill the fog delivered, Gibson thought it also installed a sense of stillness, calm, and quiet when it made its grand entrance from the ocean … or, on the other hand, it introduced an unmistakable eeriness — it was all dependent on one's perception.

Shortly thereafter, Gibson was seated on their hotel room's terrace with a glass of the hotel's complimentary offering of a bottle of Monterey County Pinot Noir in his hand, staring off into the abyss of the fog surrounding everything on the Monterey Peninsula, as if the entire area was stuck in some sort of dreamlike state or altered reality.

He had called Agent Alan Shapiro before leaving San Francisco. He told Shapiro that he was going to be out of town for a couple of days, but that he was following a hunch he had on the heist. Shapiro sounded as understanding as Director Smith had described him; he merely replied by wishing Gibson a pleasant weekend and asking him to call him after he returned to the city. Gibson appreciated Shapiro's attitude toward him, and although he was trying to enjoy the moment, the case never left his mind.

The steady pounding of waves on the beach below the hotel, which he could barely make out through the fog, softened his senses. He had changed clothing and put on a thick gray sweater, and he was waiting for Rachel to emerge from a hot shower fully prepared to encounter the chilly late afternoon with him. The plan was to have a glass of wine on their terrace and then make their way down Cannery Row until they found a restaurant that interested them.

Rachel appeared wearing jeans and a loose turtleneck sweater. Her hair fell upon at her shoulders. She looked marvelous and comfortable at the same time. She cracked open the glass door separating the room from the balcony.

Gibson poured her a glass of wine and said, "Please, do me the honor of joining me for a fine glass of wine here on our beautiful terrace."

Rachel's response was initially to wrap her arms around herself, indicating that the thought of sitting in the damp air was not her favorite idea. "How about you toss on your jacket and that knit hat you brought as well, and then maybe you won't be bothered by this glorious fog greeting us," Gibson added, hoping his powers of persuasion were stronger than his attempt at charm.

Rachel momentarily disappeared, reappearing wearing the warm weather gear Gibson had suggested. She sat opposite him at the small table after kissing him on his left cheek. As she withdrew from the kiss, Gibson was refreshed with the scents that dangled with her.

"I don't know if I would call it *glorious*," Rachel said, referring to his previous comment on the fog that nearly enveloped them and made it difficult to see even the next room's balcony only feet away. She raised her wine glass to her nose, took in its aroma with a slight inhalation, and then slowly poured a small amount of the garnet wine into her mouth. She closed her eyes as she tasted the wine and let its after-effects linger throughout her senses. This was a woman that enjoyed and appreciated life, Gibson thought. She opened her eyes and stared directly into his from across the table. "But it is certainly *intriguing*."

They sat in the stillness of the coastal fog, listening to the sounds of the ocean: the persistent surf hitting the beach, a passing sea gull crying out, barking sea lions in the distance, the sound of a ringing buoy somewhere offshore.

As they finished their glasses, their eyes met across the table. Gibson smiled and Rachel smiled back at him. She was the first woman he had felt comfortable around since his divorce. He felt relaxed and content with life, even with the high profile case he had been assigned looming over him.

"Should we walk down Cannery Row so I can see what it's all about?" Gibson asked Rachel.

"Well, it doesn't much resemble the area as John Steinbeck and Doc Ricketts knew it, but let's indeed go check it out." She noticed a blank look on Gibson's face. "Never read Steinbeck's book *Cannery Row*, huh?"

Gibson didn't attempt to hide the slight level of embarrassment he felt. "Well, no. Literature has never really been one of my great interests," he said, fumbling to set his wine glass on the small patio table.

"But I have begun to appreciate reading more in recent years, as well as history. I did a little research on the area yesterday online, but I didn't have enough time to do as much as I would have liked." He paused before adding, "You know, work ..."

Rachel reached across the table and squeezed his hand. "It's okay, John. I know you've been busy and I like that you even found it possible to look into any of this; on that thought, I wanted to thank you for proposing this little trip to begin with. I thought it was a charmingly romantic idea and I'm very delighted to be here with you." As Rachel spoke, she gradually moved closer to him, culminating in pressing her lips against his in a firm embrace as she finished saying the word *you*.

12.

Year of our Lord 1818.

THE LATE AFTERNOON SUN was shining through the thick branches of the massive oak tree in the garden area behind the adobe house. The gentle light fell upon Isabella's face and shoulders and made her skin glow even more radiantly than normal. A smile beamed across her face as she spoke to the group of musicians she had assembled to perform at the evening's fandango.

The long solo horse ride the governor had taken earlier in the day into the thickly wooded hills peering over Monterey had done well to calm his spirit. William Beckwith may not have been his favorite choice of suitor for his only daughter, *he wasn't even Spanish for God's sake*, but he did present himself as a gentleman with a billowing prosperous career on his own personal horizon. Beckwith would likely convert to Catholicism, as other foreigners had done when seeking the hands of Spanish maidens in Monterey. One such gentleman was a close friend of the governor's named John Cooper-Molera. The festivities of the evening were to take place on Cooper-Molera's property, in the open space behind his general mercantile store. It was a grand place for a fiesta.

The thought reminded the governor that the bull and bear fight would be commencing soon and he ought to make his appearance. Even if it was not his favorite event, he was the sponsor of the activities of the day and evening.

∞

The governor heard the bloodthirsty yells of men long before reaching the makeshift arena in Cooper-Molera's garden where the bull and bear would be fighting one another. Fages found the spectacle to be crude, with nothing of the elegance and beauty of the bull fights he had witnessed in the great stadiums of Madrid as a young man before seeking his destiny in the New World.

Nonetheless, the bull and bear fights gave the men of the settlement something to look forward to and to talk about weeks after each contest. With a shortage of women and cantinas in Monterey, and the relative isolation of the location forcing all to remain relatively close to the town, as the frontier was still feared by many, the governor did not believe it a great sin to allow the men some level of comforting activity, even it was the brutal display of two confused large animals being forced to gore one another until one bled to death. The wounds inflicted during the battles were normally so severe that both animals died anyway, but one normally died first and then the other was declared the victor.

"Governor! So glad you could attend your own event," John Cooper-Molera said to him as he outstretched a hand to be shaken. Cooper-Molera was wearing one of his trademark hats, and his long hair protruded from the back of it.

Fages dismissed Cooper-Molera's comment instantly. A man such as himself didn't have time to consider taking offense to slightly snide comments. Furthermore, he was fairly certain that Cooper-Molera did not intend to convey disrespect when he uttered such comments. From what the governor knew of the man, he was honest, hard-working, devoted to his family, and highly respected by all within Monterey and those who arrived to trade. Cooper-Molera was originally from the eastern American city of Boston, and the governor came to assume that all who hailed from that area of the still young United States must have similar dispositions of coming across as slightly rude and condescending.

"I apologize for my late arrival, John, but I see that my workers have been busy preparing for the evening," Fages responded, waving a hand in the direction of the remaining expanse of Cooper-Molera's space, enclosed by a white adobe brick wall, where a flurry of Fages' workers were busily arranging tables, chairs, dishware, table centerpieces, and decorations. The group of four musicians arrived as well, after their conversation with Isabella. The musicians were adjusting their instruments as they anxiously awaited to begin performing.

Fages said to Cooper-Molera, "As they are already here and look ready to play, perhaps we could offer to let the musicians come closer to the ring and let them play during the *spectacle* we are about to endure."

"That's a splendid idea, Governor!" Cooper-Molera replied. He raised a hand and within a few seconds, a young boy named Juan, who Cooper-Molera had more or less adopted and referred to as his personal assistant, ran up to Cooper-Molera's side. Cooper-Molera instructed the lad to inform the musicians to approach and begin playing.

By the time the musicians situated themselves adjacent to the arena area, the spectacle was already underway. At one side of the circular fenced-in area was a large gleaming black bull, his nostrils flaring with agitation and his feet pounding the dirt beneath him as he struggled to free himself from the rope tied around his neck. At the other side of the circle was a medium-sized grizzly bear, ferociously growling and helplessly swinging its large arms at its sides in an attempt to free itself from the rope tied tightly around its neck. At the time of the governor's arrival some ten years before, there were captures of even larger and more aggressive bears in the vicinity of Monterey; however, Governor Fages noted that it was becoming very rare for the men to trap one of these other bears.

A contingent of men, with spears drawn, stood on the opposite side of the embankment from the bear, serving as precaution in case the bear opted to confront the group of spectators rather than the snorting bull in front of it. The rest of circular arena was lined with men, soldiers and civilians, standing two to three deep and peering over shoulders in order to view the fight. As often was done, the two animals were situated opposite from one another to allow the physical fight to be preceded with anticipation.

"Do you believe these two animals have any idea that they are supposed to be enemies?" Fages asked.

"Well, it seems to me that most of the time when we put them together like this, they do certainly go after one another without any encouragement," Cooper-Molera confidently replied.

"Yes, but they are put into a situation where they are forced to battle one another there in that arena. We, meaning those of us with European descent, introduced cows, and thus bulls, to this land. Before that, a bear here would never have even encountered a bull."

Cooper-Molera lit one of his small cigars. "You ought to not read into everything so much, Governor. After all, they are just a couple of dumb animals." He blew a puff of smoke from his mouth. "I often wonder about your education. It interests me."

For the second time within a few minutes, Fages had to dismiss the words of his friend. Cooper-Molera had a habit of wanting to discuss the education of others while noting his own distinguished education in Boston. "Yes, yes, John." The governor lightly capitulated. He considered that the discussion he was provoking was likely pointless to begin with, as it never made a difference which animal actually won the match. It was typically the bear, and usually by the time the bull had finally gone down, the opposing bear had a gaping wound or two in its chest where the bull would have driven its horn into the bear's flesh. Regardless, though, the victor was always brought down after the match was over.

The tension was mounting as the two animals stopped being distracted by their captivity and instead gazed directly across the arena at one another. The hollers of blood lust increased into a collective roar. The musicians, no doubt sensing the increased activity, began to play their instruments more loudly and fervently. After a few moments when every spectator remained clenched in anticipation, the bonds holding the animals in place were cut. Despite Governor Fages' contemplation of the two species as not being natural enemies, the natural instinct of survival was displayed as the two hulking animals were forced on one another in the small circular arena. The bull snorted loudly and pounded the ground hard with its front hooves. The bear growled with its large teeth exposed and stood tall on its hind legs, fully displaying its powerfully built body. The bull attacked first by charging full speed at the bear. The power of its shoulders and neck were demonstrated by its flexing muscles as it charged.

The bear took a few steps forward to confront the charging bull and for a moment appeared confused on how to defend itself from the attack of such an animal, as it quickly darted its eyes back and forth, but then swiftly moved sideward to avoid being directly punctured by the bull's horns, and while doing so, was able to land an effective swipe of its claws down the side of the bull's neck.

The bear then ran to the opposite side of the arena, creating space between it and the bull, as if it were carefully calculating the bull's next attack. A small patch of blood appeared on the fur covering its chest area where the bull's horns had grazed its side. The bull, however, had taken a direct hit from the bear, and a steady trickle of dark blood dripped from the side of its neck onto the light colored dirt of the arena.

After a few moments of the bull being distracted by lunging toward a group of men hanging over the makeshift wall of the arena who were taunting it by waving their arms wildly in front of it, the bull turned to see the bear waiting for it. The bull once again barreled forward at full speed. The bear did not look at all confused during this second attack and methodically repeated its previous performance of waiting until the bull was directly in front of it and then moving quickly to one side while swiping one of its large claws down the side of the bull's neck. Unlike the previous charge, this time the bear escaped completely unscathed by the bull's horns.

The bear backed away from the bull, roaring in triumph. The bull veered unsteadily into the side of the barricade of the arena, a deep wound gushing blood from the side of its neck. The music and the calls of the spectators erupted in unison. The bear strode triumphantly around the arena as it watched the bull slowly descend downward on its front legs, followed quickly by suddenly falling on its side. The bear roared once again, its growl overbearing the noise of the men's yells and the music.

Governor Fages turned away. Having to witness the brutality of the match was taxing for him, but having to watch the conclusion of the bear's slaughter would be too much. John Cooper-Molera turned away from the arena as well and commented, "At least the bull made it to two charges this time. In the last match, the bear brought it down after one pass."

"Yes, the charging bull always comes to a stop one way or another," the governor reflectively replied. "Now let us see that everything is being properly arranged for the remainder of the evening. Esteban returned from the Carmel Mission to inform me that Father Serra has accepted my invitation to attend the fiesta this evening and, as you know, it would please me to have a productive encounter with the good Father."

John Cooper-Molera considered saying something in response, but knowing the history between Fages and Serra and sensing the careful urgency in the governor's tone, he decided it would be wise to remain silent.

13.

Year of our Lord 2009.

T HE GLASSES OF wine Gibson and Rachel shared on the balcony of the room enticed their appetite, and Gibson inquired at the concierge desk if they had any suggestions as to where to walk for a nice glass of pre-dinner wine. The impeccably dressed man at the desk suggested a wine tasting room down Cannery Row that specialized in Monterey County wines.

Once they left the entrance of the hotel, Rachel began a summarized interpretation of the history of Cannery Row. Rachel had always been fascinated with the history of Cannery Row after reading Steinbeck's story in her late teens, and her interest had prompted her to learn more about its history. Gibson listened attentively, savoring the sound of Rachel's voice.

"The fishing industry on the Monterey Peninsula really began in the mid-1880s and stayed in the hands of Asian immigrants for awhile, evolving into a Chinese population mixing with the Japanese."

Although the layer of fog had brought darkness long before the normal time of sunset, Gibson was able to see that Rachel had stopped them in front of some sort of abandoned and decrepit wood building that he could discern through a tall wire-chain fence was located on the water, with vestiges of a pier extending into the bay. Rachel followed his gaze to the building, pausing in order for him to get a sense of his surroundings.

"The next era of the fishing industry here really came with the arrival of the Italians. They arrived and introduced their brand of fishing; it absolutely flourished, and they quickly discovered the vast multitude of sardines thriving out there. Monterey then skyrocketed into history, becoming the 'Sardine Capital of the World,' and places like this, right here where we are standing, were huge sardine processing and canning facilities."

"I remember seeing this old black and white film where they show a young Marilyn Monroe frolicking around as one of the cannery workers, all cute and perky, but it really was not so glamorous working down here. The hours were grueling, the conditions reproachable, and the smell, oh God, I can't even imagine how it must have smelled." She turned away from facing the idle decimated wooden building hiding in the fog like a forgotten tombstone. She motioned that their tour was continuing and they resumed walking along the sidewalk.

"So, any questions so far?" she asked.

"Well, *yes*, actually." Gibson came to a halt once again and Rachel stopped in response. He looked backward at the crumbling former cannery building they just passed. "Why is a building such as this not *still* an operating fish processing plant, but instead it's a vacant lot?"

Even in the dim light, Gibson could see a look of reflection cross Rachel's face as she quickly configured a response. "The reason why Monterey Bay and thus Cannery Row, which by the way was only named Cannery Row after Steinbeck cleverly gave Ocean View Avenue the title in his story, is no longer a fishing hub and more pointedly no longer the Sardine Capital of the World is because the sardines were overfished. They were decimated, in fact. It's been decades since the last cannery closed its doors down here and the sardine population has yet to return, if it ever will. And these canneries weren't just canning sardines; they were also processing sardines and other fish into various fish by-products such as oils and fertilizers, et cetera. Anyway, all of that died off eventually as well."

As they strolled down the sidewalk, passing by long interconnected buildings with gift shops and restaurants, carefully dodging the maniac stroller-pushers or sugar-hyped children charging toward them from the opposite direction, a young girl called to them. "Hey there, you two … How about trying some of Cannery Row's best clam chowder?" The girl, who didn't look a day over sixteen, held up a ladle from a steaming cauldron of creamy clam chowder. A few hearty dollops of chowder spilled over the side of the ladle and dropped back into the cauldron, causing small splashes. Gibson glanced at Rachel, who responded by giving him a "why not" face and shrug.

"The best on Cannery Row, eh?" Gibson said to the young girl, who was wearing a long, atrociously loud red and white checkered apron that Gibson pictured she was forced to wear, topped off with a baseball cap advertising the restaurant whose entrance was directly behind her.

The girl handed each of them what looked like a plastic shot glass of steaming chowder and they happily accepted. The fog, combined with the slight breeze blowing in from the water, made it an extremely chilly evening. "Yup, the best you'll find down here," the girl said in a monotone voice. Gibson and Rachel knocked back their shots of chowder and exchanged glances. In their relatively short time together, they had begun to quickly learn each other's expressions. The look they shared conveyed that although they thought the chowder was good, it was certainly nothing exquisite.

The chowder peddler picked up on their shared opinion; she leaned closer to them from behind her small counter. A few of her blonde hair strands fell from their place tucked behind her ears and hat as she did, and she added, "Actually, I think the Fish Hopper just down the way has the best chowder on the Row." She leaned back and quickly resumed her role as spokesperson for the best clam chowder on Cannery Row as she invited two Hispanic women, each with a few children trailing behind them, to come closer and try her restaurant's chowder.

Shortly after their first clam chowder tasting, the line of buildings blocking the coast disappeared and they were standing at the end of a small but quaint square area set above a beach and overlooking Monterey Bay. Rachel pointed to a small bronze memorial of a man's head set upon a stone pillar and said that it was the first tourism promoter of Cannery Row himself, John Steinbeck.

Gibson crept closer to the memorial, attempting to read the writing was inscribed on a placard below the bronzed head, but had difficulty reading the words in the dim light. When he relinquished to the fact that the low level of light, combined with his gradually diminishing eyesight, resulted in the endeavor being impossible, he turned away from the memorial and found a young man with dreadlocks running down his back and a foul-smelling cigarette dangling from his mouth thrusting a small coupon in front of him, muttering something about a half-off sale at a silver store somewhere down the way, gesturing towards the ocean and then quickly turning away to attack his next victim.

For a moment, Agent John Gibson felt a bit stunned as he glanced down at the small pink scrap of paper in his hand. He felt a little embarrassed as well. In his golden days, the punk would never have been able to get that close to him. In his golden days, he would have grabbed the punk's hand long before it ever got close to his body. In those days of his prime, he would have been more alert. He wondered if perhaps it was time for him to consider letting the golden days pass into history indefinitely.

Before he could slip any further into self-reflection, mixed at the moment with self-doubt, Rachel grabbed his hand and led him inward from the crowded sidewalk into the square area. It was the first time they had held hands, and Gibson wasn't sure if she had only done it to steer him away from the crowd and punk kid, but he definitely was not going to let go of her hand if she did not first. That constant contact with her, the dry and cracked skin of his hands pressed against the softness of hers, was very comforting.

"Look, there's that restaurant the chowder girl told us about. Let's go and see if she's right about their clam chowder." Rachel smiled widely.

She led Gibson through various groups of people who seemed to be standing around doing what tourists do in tourist places: taking pictures, some serious and some goofy; overindulging in sweets, from Ghirardelli chocolates to ice cream to fudge; drinking Starbucks coffee; gazing around at everything and wondering how much it costs to live in such a place and what people do for a living who live there; and finally, paying no attention whatsoever to where they are walking.

A plump woman greeted them as they approached the outstretched awning over the entrance to the restaurant that appeared to be hanging over the edge of the water and the rocky beach underneath. Flaming tiki torches lined the entrance to the restaurant, which although they could easily be considered out of place for the surrounding atmosphere, did exude a brilliant effect in the fog. She smiled broadly at the middle-aged couple holding hands like teenagers on a first date and handed them each a shot of steaming clam chowder in small plastic cups as before. Gibson and Rachel said "cheers" to one another and slowly poured the cups into their mouths. The expression they shared this time was as uniform of their respective opinions as the previous chowder tasting: they both found this chowder to be exceptional. Whereas the previous chowder had been slightly thin tasting, despite its appearance, and lacking in flavor, this chowder was as thick as chili and was packed with flavor, yet never quite losing the salty taste of the sea.

"Wow, this is excellent. Thank you very much," Rachel said to their greeter.

They were invited to enter the restaurant for dinner; the greeter even promised them a nice cozy table on the patio over the water, with a heat lamp directly overhead if they desired. Rachel told her that the idea sounded wonderful but that they had plans to taste some wines first and then they would be looking to have dinner somewhere. The greeter motioned that the place they were looking for was directly above her restaurant, on the second floor of the long building that stretched from the street all the way out over the bay, which Rachel later told Gibson was an old cannery building that had been refurbished.

They walked into the entrance and up a small flight of stairs and were surprised to find themselves walking into a giant room with a wall of glass overlooking the bay, which they knew, even though it was blanketed in fog, was still there. The entrance had separated tables covered in gift items, most of which were related to wine. After this area, the room opened up lengthwise with a double row of wooden bistro tables made out of sections of former wine barrels surrounded by chairs that abutted the wall of glass windows. At the far end of the windows was an angled granite bar complete with a couple of wine servers behind it attentively pouring tastings and glasses of wine to customers.

"This place is pretty amazing. The view from here is lovely even when it's foggy out there over the water; I can't imagine what it's like when it's clear," Rachel said to Gibson.

A wrinkled man in small round smudged glasses and disheveled salt and pepper hair seated by himself at a table next to the windows responded before Gibson had a chance. "Oh, believe me, *it is*. This place has one of the best views of Monterey Bay, period," he said as he raised a glass of white wine that looked nearly empty towards them. "And I should know better than anyone; I'm here once a week, every week." He finished his wine glass and rose from the chair. "Unfortunately, you're not able to see much out this evening," he observed as he pointed out the windows to the gray veil hiding the late afternoon. "On most days, you can see the sea otters tangled up in the kelp out there or the harbor seals lounging around the rocks. On days when the water is clear, you can even see starfish down there in the tidal pools below us." The man paused, as if lost in his own thoughts. "If you'll excuse me; it's time for my number three."

They watched as the man slowly drifted towards the bar area, where one of the servers had a glass of white wine poured and waiting for him by the time he reached the bar. "Guess he really does know this place well," Gibson commented as they watched the man set his old glass on the bar counter, remove the new glass, place a dollar bill on the counter, and utter some comment to the server that made the two of them chuckle. "Well, I think he has the right idea. Maybe we should go find a couple glasses of wine ourselves and return to one of these tables ."

Rachel nodded her head in eager approval and they walked towards the bar area, passing the disheveled hair man on their way. "Now you've got the right idea," he said to them as he passed by with the glass of wine looking dangerously as if it would spill in his slightly rocking hand.

As they walked up to the bar, they were welcomed by a server who looked to be in his late twenties with curly, brownish colored hair. Gibson noticed that he wore a thick brown leather bracelet on his right wrist of the sort that had been popular in the early 1970s.

"Hi folks, welcome to A Taste of Monterey," he said to them as set a sheet on the bar counter in front of them. He asked if they had been in the tasting room before and they replied that it was their first time, but that they were interested in doing a little wine tasting. "Well, you've come to the right place, then." He produced two wine glasses from somewhere under the bar and poured what he called a classic style of Monterey Chardonnay into the glasses and urged them to try the wine with a slight nod of his head. The server then continued by describing that the establishment was not a winery itself, but a representative of Monterey County wines and that over eighty different wineries were represented.

As the young man spoke, Rachel and Gibson noticed a large sea gull standing regally outside the window behind him on a wooden railing.

The young man, who somewhere in his rattling of facts and introduction to Monterey County wines mentioned that his name was Michael, suddenly stopped himself. "Oh, I'm sorry," he exclaimed, as if he had poured gasoline into their glasses instead of wine when he noticed the empty glasses on the bar in front of them. Michael shifted a few steps to their right and opened what appeared to be a refrigerated area, then produced a new bottle of Chardonnay, which he poured into their empty glasses.

Michael said something about this Chardonnay being more heavily oaked than the previous one, which had showcased slightly more tropical flavors. Gibson and Rachel nodded their heads and let him continue. They stole a glance at one another and pondered collectively if they should mention that they were only interested in ordering a glass of wine and being seated at one of the tables and not actually in wine tasting at that moment, but their server, Michael, was educating and amusing them.

They both noticed from the sheet of thick paper he had placed in front of them that they were expected to pick between one of two wine tasting flights, but neither of them minded whatever Michael decided upon for their fate. Not only did he seem to enjoy his job and be knowledgeable about it, but he also exuded confidence in his ability to engage his customers and keep them satisfied. However, they also both shared the thought that if he brought out one more bottle of white wine, they were going to stop him and politely request that they be moved on to tasting red wine, a preference they shared.

Next up for tasting arrived, a couple of pours of what Michael called an *elegant* Pinot Noir.

"Okay, so I've gathered that you two are not the biggest fans of white wines, or at least of Chardonnays." Gibson and Rachel quickly glanced at one another, silently marveling how he could have known. Michael watched the interaction between the two of them and remarked, "It's my job to notice such things."

"Anyway, back to *vino*," Michael briskly remarked, refilling their glasses with pours from another bottle of Pinot Noir he produced.

Michael handed them a small bowl of crackers. "You each should have a cracker; helps to clear the palate." Gibson and Rachel each grabbed one of the *saltinesque* wafer crackers.

Michael pulled out yet another bottle from somewhere behind the bar and poured wine into the three wine glasses on the bar. "Now this one, this is going to be as concentrated as one can get, as it's from a small and distinct vineyard in the county called Gary's Vineyard." Gibson and Rachel followed Michael's lead as he raised his glass towards the light and slightly swirled his glass before sticking his nose into the wine glass. "The fruit from this vineyard is one of the most sought after in the entire state these days, especially with this current Pinot Noir craze."

"What do you mean by *Pinot Noir craze*?" Rachel asked.

"Well, a certain movie definitely helped to promote Pinot Noir …"

"*A movie*?" Rachel questioned.

"Yeah, just don't do the 'I'm not drinking any Merlot' line. Those of us working in tasting rooms have heard it a few thousand times," Michael requested. Noticing the blank expressions staring at him, he continued, "*Never mind*," he said shaking his head.

Michael tasted his wine as well and responded with a contented smile crossing his face. "That's a beautiful wine," he observed.

Sensing that they had 'tasted' enough, Michael offered to pour them each a glass of wine. They both asked for the second Pinot Noir they tasted and, at his suggestion, also ordered one of the store's cheese platters. They thanked Michael for his time and attention and retreated with their wine to one of the bistro tables.

As soon as they were adjusted in their chairs, a young woman working at the store's front register delivered a platter with assorted cheeses and crackers. Gibson noted that the jolly man with glasses and messy hair who initially greeted them was no longer seated where he had been.

"We're going to have to get some food after this. All of this wine is starting to make me feel quite woozy and I don't think this lovely assortment of cheese is going to do it," Rachel commented.

"That sounds like a good idea. I'd head back up to the bar to ask his opinion on where we should go for dinner, but I think if I did, I'd be up there for quite awhile."

The two of them laughed, and, having overheard Gibson's comment, a couple sitting next to them at the next table laughed as well. "Yeah, he's a good one," the man said. The man had a wide, cheerful face and Rachel took advantage of the introduction, and after finding out that the couple lived locally, she asked them where they would recommend for dinner.

"It depends on what you're looking for," the woman, who had an equally joyful demeanor about her, replied. "There are many fantastic restaurants over in Carmel, but the prices are equally as fantastic. Are you planning on walking wherever you go?"

Rachel nodded in response.

"Okay, so that leaves us with what's here on Cannery Row." The woman looked at her husband, requesting his participation.

"Well, most of the restaurants down here are very tourist-oriented," the man commented.

"There's a place just a block up which is a little on the fancier side, even though it looks like a trailer from the outside, that is kind of a historic icon around here. After that, we also like this place just down from there that is actually more of a fresh seafood market than a restaurant, but they do have a little seating area and a respectable menu; it's very much a locals' place." The man's wife approved of his recommendations by patting his knee.

Their neighbors explained that on calm, sunny days there would be dozens of kayakers paddling directly off-shore, and that at times one could see whales breaching and pods of dolphins or sea lions moving in fluttering masses along the coastline.

"Wow, quite the place," Rachel observed. "Thank you for the recommendations."

"So, what do you think?" she asked Gibson.

"Do you have a preference?" he asked in return.

She slightly smiled as if she were devising something in her head. "I do, but I wanted to ask you first to see if we are on the same page."

"Well, let's see. I was thinking the locals' place sounds intriguing."

Rachel smiled broadly. "That is precisely what I was thinking as well."

14.

Year of our Lord 2009.

A HUMMINGBIRD DANGLED delicately in front of Isidro's face
and the sounds of rapidly fluttering tiny wings distracted his
attention from his book. He looked up to see the small eyes
looking directly at him. Isidro met the hummingbird's gaze and the
little bird remained in the same spot for a few seconds, as if it was just
as interested in staring at him.

He was seated at one of his favorite reading spots, within the
walled garden of the Larkin House historical adobe in Monterey. The
hummingbird darted slightly one direction and then zoomed away in a
flash of green past his face in the other direction. A slight breeze shifted
the leaves of the lemon tree in front of him and he noticed gleaming
shards of a white fog encroaching upon the blue sky overhead. As
anyone who spends a considerable time on the Peninsula knew, with
such an obvious threat from the fog, what had been a previously sunny
day on the Monterey Peninsula would assuredly turn into a day of gray
fog before long. It could happen in a couple of hours or in less than an
hour; no one really could estimate the unpredictable fog with complete
accuracy.

A popular joke on the Peninsula was that weather forecasters liked to
state there would be a chance of fog every day from March to November,
which made them more or less correct. The joke continues to state that
from December through February, the weather forecasters like to claim
that there's a chance of rain every day; and rain on the Peninsula, due to
its proximity to the ocean, is often accompanied by a fog-like mist.

Further, forecasts predict that when it's not foggy, nor raining, the sky will be crystal-clear blue, there will be abundant sunshine, and it will be warm and wonderful on the Monterey Peninsula. These predictions result in the weather forecasters consistently being more or less correct. Weather on the Monterey Peninsula is one of extremes; not necessarily extremes in terms of severity, as the temperature on any given day of the year is very likely to fall between fifty and seventy degrees Fahrenheit, but one of extremity in terms of either being gorgeous or gloomy, with little possibility of in-between.

Isidro looked down at the book in his lap. It was a historical account of the period of California's nascent statehood. He was nearly finished reading the book, although it would be his second time finishing it. Nevertheless, he felt a certain jubilation as he followed his tradition of reading certain books only in specifically related spots in and around Monterey.

Perhaps his most cherished of these location readings was his experience many years earlier, when he first read *Cannery Row*. He read the book near the street; however, Isidro purposefully chose a bench off the recreational trail, above the street itself, that was located near the few remaining artifacts of the Row's golden era, a couple of rusted-through large steel containers that once held rendered fish until they were transported away via the long department railway. Something about being able to periodically glance up from the pages of Steinbeck's quirky novel and see the crumbling remaining edifices of Monterey's former fishing center while sitting along the same right-of-way that used to be the preeminent rail line transporting products from Monterey to the outside world was fascinating and haunting.

Isidro closed the book, stood up, and walked towards the exit of the Larkin House garden, a doorway cut out of the stone wall surrounding the side of the house. For a brief moment, Isidro had a thought that there, sitting *there*, one could feel entirely disconnected with the surrounding city. Sitting there and only seeing the pale white stone walls through the lushly vegetated garden, filled with lemon trees and small oak trees and other shrubs, while only noticing the sky overhead, as the stone walls magically deflected the noises of passing cars in the vicinity — it was like being in a different world altogether. Lowering his head to pass through the doorway, Isidro felt the unpleasant sensation of having returned to the modern age, complete with cars screeching past one another on Pacific Street.

He planned to stop by his favorite local coffee shop, where he was sure to see the familiar group of elderly men seated around a table drinking small cup espressos near the entrance, talking loudly in Italian as they waved their arms wildly, or as *wildly* as their ages allowed them, while they conversed; these guys were a sampling of Monterey's former fishermen. Isidro would often see the same group of men arguing over a toss at the city-maintained bocce court behind the Custom House.

As he walked along the sidewalk back towards the offices of the Monterey Historical Society, he remembered that he still needed to call David Chiles' friend as he had promised. He stopped and dug into his leather shoulder bag before pulling out his cell phone. He found the piece of paper where he had written the man's name and telephone number and called John Gibson.

15.

Year of our Lord 2009.

IBSON'S CELL PHONE VIBRATED against his side where he kept it in a small holster. He pulled the phone out to look at the caller identification number on the front of the screen. It was an "831" number, which he knew was the local Monterey Peninsula area code, but he didn't recognize the number. He and Rachel had just pulled into the small parking lot of a winery for wine tasting. Rachel opened the door of the car and stepped outside, although she didn't walk into the tasting room without him; instead, she patiently stood outside the car, allowing him to take his phone call without her being present.

At the beginning of their relationship, Gibson had felt forced to lay out a few standard, possibly inconvenient, ground rules that apply when dating an agent of the Federal Bureau of Investigation. One of these was that he would need to answer his phone, whenever it rang, or *buzzed,* as he usually left his cell phone on vibrate mode, despite any circumstances he would find himself in and with no questions asked. At the time, he wanted to add that she need not worry much, as he had recently reached an epiphany that he was going to try his hardest to enjoy life more, but he figured that if she got to know him better, she would figure this out. Thus far in their relationship, Rachel had proven to him that she was more than capable of accepting the responsibilities attached to his job. So far so good, he thought.

He opened the cell phone and brought it to his ear. "Agent Gibson here," he affirmatively spoke into the phone.

"Hello. My name is Isidro de la Vega. I'm a friend of David Chiles and he asked me to give you call when you got down here from the city."

It took Gibson a moment to catch his memory and remember that Chiles had said something about a friend of his being in Monterey. Gibson wasn't at all hung over, as after their experience at the wine tasting room the evening before, he withdrew himself from the red wine lure and stuck with water over their dinner of locally caught seafood. But the long day in general, followed by some late night activities once they got to their hotel room, left him feeling rather sluggish this morning.

They had slept in until nine o'clock, which was especially late for Gibson, who usually awoke, alarm clock or no alarm clock, at six. They had coffee together in the room. The thick layer of fog that had moved in from the ocean the night before had not dissipated and somehow even looked more ominous in the morning. As they sat in their hotel room sipping coffee and staring out into the fog, Gibson's thoughts returned to the heist. How far would it be to travel by boat from San Francisco to the Monterey area, he wondered?

Rachel's suggestion that they venture into Carmel Valley for a little wine tasting and lunch snapped him from his reverie. She claimed that the Valley had an almost unfailing characteristic of being warm and clear when the coast was cool and damp. Looking out of the sliding glass patio door of the hotel room at the wall of fog waiting to devour whatever it encountered, Gibson happily and enthusiastically agreed that a daytrip into Carmel Valley sounded like a great idea.

"Oh yes, that's right. Chiles did recommend we get in touch with you while we were down here. I almost forgot, so thank you for calling. What did you say your first name was again?"

Isidro," he flatly responded. He summarily questioned if he should have called in the first place. If the guy hadn't even thought about him, Isidro could have gone hiking for a second day in a row. But he had promised a friend, and he tried to always keep his promises, especially to the relatively few people he considered friends.

"*Isidro*," Gibson repeated. "That's certainly an original and interesting name. I'm sure you hear that often though."

"Yes."

Gibson pulled the phone away from his face and glared at it for a second. The voice on the other end wasn't exactly unfriendly in tone, but it definitely was not endearing either.

"Well, Isidro, Chiles mentioned that you were old friends from down here and that you may be interested in showing me and my ..." Gibson struggled momentarily on how to refer to Rachel and asked himself if old guys really referred to their lovers as *girlfriends*, "my *friend* Rachel around the area a bit?"

"Yes, David and I are old friends, and sure, I'd be happy to meet you and your friend for an outing."

Gibson waited for the voice to continue, perhaps with a recommendation on what exactly an outing would consist of; however, only the faint sound of distant vehicle traffic came through the phone. *This guy is not exactly the most engaging type.* "Great. What did you have in mind?" he managed to say in his most practiced, non-annoyed and joyous voice.

"What did you have in mind, Mr. Gibson?" Isidro promptly answered. Again, his tone was not unfriendly, but it was direct and without much, if any emotion.

"Well, we're down in Carmel Valley now for some wine tasting and then we're going to have lunch," Gibson commented, hoping to urge more life out of the young man on the other end of the line.

"Have you been to Point Lobos yet?" Isidro asked.

Gibson was pleased at having enticed the young man into making a recommendation, as he was not feeling adequate to face the day and was more than willing to let others make decisions, for a few hours, anyway. "No, but I do remember reading about it online and it looked very interesting."

"Indeed, it is. I have time available this afternoon and I could meet you there at three thirty and we can walk around the reserve together. From the mouth of Carmel Valley, back where you turned eastward off of Highway 1, the entrance to Point Lobos State Reserve is about a five minute drive southward towards Big Sur."

Rachel's backside, *and it was a nicely formed backside,* Gibson thought, was pressed against the car's passenger side window and he couldn't quickly get her attention. He would have liked to confirm that the Point Lobos idea was okay with her, but he assumed that he knew

Rachel well enough that she would consider any time a good time for a walk in a beautiful place. "Okay, Isidro, that sounds good. We'll meet you there at three thirty."

"Great. Park off the side of the road near the entrance to the reserve and I'll meet you there. I drive a navy Volkswagen and I imagine you will be able to spot me before I recognize you. Goodbye for now." The line went blank.

16.

Year of our Lord 1818.

E VERYTHING WAS IN PLACE for the evening. The arena was
disassembled and removed from the tract behind John Cooper-
Molera's general store, including the carcasses of the fallen bull
and the later slain grizzly bear. At Governor Fages' recommendation,
buckets of sand were produced in order for the blood splotches
soaked onto the light colored Monterey soil to be thoroughly covered,
hiding the remaining evidence of the brutal late afternoon exhibition.

Governor Fages approved of what he witnessed before him. In
addition to the arena having been entirely cleared, the long dining tables
were elaborately arranged, at his request, and a space was cleared near
where the band was playing that would serve more than adequately for
dancing once the meal was finished. Morale throughout the colonial
outpost of Monterey had been diminished in the previous months. He
could see it not only in the faces of the soldiers of the garrison, but in the
faces of every inhabitant of Monterey.

The landing of vessels had been sparse in the previous six months
and the arrival of a ship in Monterey's harbor was always a time of
celebration. The arrival of a vessel was more than an opportunity to be
provided with goods; it was a reminder that the world had not
forgotten Monterey.

The prolonged absence of a ship in its harbor thereby added to the
governor's fear that his citizens would consider having made too
quick of a decision to journey to Alta California. It was not that life in
Monterey was unpleasant. On the contrary, even the least wealthy

citizens of Monterey appeared to enjoy a better quality of life than their counterparts Fages had seen in places such as Mexico City, or even in Spain. Of course, some who had agreed to establish themselves at the settlement had already been wealthy, and they continued to expand their wealth with the vast land holdings they were allotted through the good graces of the Crown. However, many others had come to Monterey without wealth or prestige and had proliferated themselves into very comfortable positions. John Cooper-Molera was an excellent example of one such individual.

Yet, even with the primarily pleasant climate, the profitable opportunities, and the pleasures of the small yet diverse Monterey society — all was not well. Governor Fages was aware of the pending threat of Bouchard attacking, but he had not been aware that the people themselves had any awareness of it until after the bear and bull fight, when he and John Cooper-Molera shared a few moments of candid discussion. Cooper-Molera was more in sync with the people, and Fages benefited greatly from their occasional chats.

The town's nervousness at this possibility was justified. The governor admitted this to himself, but he would admit it to no other; not to Cooper-Molera and not even to his daughter, lest he frighten her. The fact was, however, that Monterey's garrison did not have enough soldiers or cannon to fend off a resourceful pirate such as Bouchard, much less an invasion by the Russians if they ever decided to extend their reach further southward. Fages repeatedly requested more soldiers, guns, and artillery from Mexico City, and even directly through letters to Madrid. The responses consistently stated that the Crown was unavailable at the current time to commit any additional resources to Alta California and that Fages would have to cope, just as every other settlement in the region, regardless of whether or not Monterey was the capital. Governor Fages was not a man to often lose his temper, yet his reading of each rejection letter produced enough disgust and anger in him to curse aloud. *They are fools*, he said to himself.

The lack of interest or even attention from the Crown left him with no choice but to grasp the situation firmly in his own hands, which is precisely what he had done on his last voyage to Mexico City. He carefully designed his plan, informing only those who absolutely needed to know of his intentions to make an arrangement with the Russians. He had no real solution for dealing with Bouchard, but he could at least plan how to hold off the Russians. Bouchard may be able to attack Monterey, but he would eventually leave. If the Russians attacked, they would never leave. And if the Spanish Empire was going to leave it in the governor's hands to save it, then he did not doubt that it was his duty to do so.

Governor Fages watched from a distance as the young Englishman, Beckwith, approached his daughter, Isabella, received her extended hand, and kissed it lightly as he bowed his head to her. It was a respectful and dignified greeting.

Beckwith and Isabella began talking. Even from a distance, the governor could see how his daughter's entire demeanor altered when in Beckwith's presence. Isabella possessed a natural beauty that radiated from her at any given time, but in Beckwith's presence, she emphatically glowed. The two of them smiled broadly and laughed. Fages then considered how he had not noticed Beckwith at the bull and bear fight. Surely he would have noticed the young Englishman if he had attended. The governor wondered if he and the young man shared a dislike for the event. The possibility of such a scenario increased the governor's liking of Beckwith.

Beckwith and Isabella looked complimentary together: Beckwith tall, strapping and handsome in a pale English way and Isabella as lovely as an elegant flower. Fages had difficulty considering that it was time for him to let go of his only daughter, but seeing the two of them together, he accepted the fact that he could not hold on to his daughter forever.

Seats had not been taken at the tables, as Fages was adamant that no one be seated until after Father Serra arrived. The governor hoped that this small act of consideration to the good Father, in addition to the invitation to the evening's festivities, would go far in softening the Father's occasionally difficult character. Fages respected Serra for his fortitude, determination, and tenacity; but not for the Father's renowned stubbornness. The relocation of Father Serra's order some years before over the hill to the mouth of the Carmel River continued to be a thorn in the side of the relationship between Fages and Serra, but as the governor grew increasingly anxious about the future, having improved relations between himself and the most revered religious authority figure in Alta California was paramount.

Fages sent Esteban, again allowing him take one of the governor's finest horses, to ride to the base of the hill where Serra would arrive, assuming the good Father remained true to the response he had given Esteban earlier in the day accepting the governor's invitation. Fages waited eagerly for news of the Father's arrival.

He greeted the couples who approached him to thank him for the invitation to the fiesta and the single men who thanked him for both the earlier bull and bear fight and the opportunity to associate with young maidens. Such occasions were especially good for an unmarried man to be introduced to señoritas, since families that lived on the large ranchos on the outskirts of Monterey and were not seen in the town often would be sure to attend a fiesta sponsored by the governor. He shook hands and extended his welcome to his guests, keeping watch of the gate with eager expectation to see Esteban's small figure emerge through it with a wide smile on his face.

Fages perceived that his guests were growing timidly impatient at not being allowed to be seated and begin dinner, but only John Cooper-Molera would be bold enough to say anything to him concerning the situation. "Maybe we could skip dinner and just get straight to the fandango," Cooper-Molera said as he came to halt at the governor's side.

The governor contemplated commenting on the distastefulness of the comment. Cooper-Molera's insolence was, at times, nearly intolerable. The governor once again questioned how such an altogether pleasant man could have such a sharp tongue. "I just ordered the servers to make another round through the crowd with wine to refill cups and to refill the platters of food they are carrying around, so hopefully that will keep the crowd satisfied a little longer while we wait for Father Serra."

"You really think Serra will come?"

The governor took a deep breath before responding. "I don't honestly know; I do honestly hope he does." Fages reflected upon how even though Cooper-Molera was an intelligent and well-informed man, he would have no way of understanding the dire predicament of the settlement; and although the governor trusted Cooper-Molera, even with his foul sense of humor, as much as any man in Monterey, if not more so, he could not risk sharing his concerns for the young capital with anyone. All of Monterey and its surrounding ranchos would undoubtedly erupt in panic if the true state of affairs were known by all. The anguish tore into him.

"By the way, John — let us refer to the good Father as 'Father Serra' in his presence, as we do not want to offend him in any way this evening, which is also why I remain insistent that we all remain standing until his arrival."

Cooper-Molera snorted a laugh. "If he arrives," he said, shaking his head.

Governor Fages smiled and turned to face Cooper-Molera, who was considerably shorter than him. "If that is indeed the case, we shall wait until Esteban's return at nightfall, as only then will we be able to be certain that the good Father is not going to arrive this evening."

It was only under the governor's good graces that Cooper-Molera had been able to establish a trading post in Monterey as a foreigner. After their friendship had sprouted, it had been at Fages' suggestion that John Cooper consider a marriage into a Spanish family, which would solidify and essentially legalize his presence in Monterey. John Cooper thus became John Cooper-Molera.

"Can I offer to bring you a glass of wine? Perhaps some of the brandy I traded for with that last French vessel that came to port?"

"No, thank you. I will wait for Father Serra for that as well, in order to toast to his health," Fages responded.

Cooper-Molera muttered something about checking with the kitchen staff, who were situated in a side room that he had constructed adjoining the original structure of his adobe house, which also functioned as his general store. Fages didn't acknowledge Cooper-Molera's comment. He was growing increasingly nervous at the possibility that Father Serra would prove to be by far the most stubborn man he had ever encountered in his life. His eyes fell downward. He noticed a dark patch in the sandy soil on the ground in front of his feet. All of the blood had apparently not been covered.

As he was about to succumb to despair, the wooden door to the east in the adobe brick gate surrounding Cooper-Molera's spacious courtyard opened and Esteban appeared. Even over the raucous noises of the chattering crowd and the music in the background, Governor Fages was able to hear the sound of the hinges of the door creaking as it was opened further. When Esteban's eyes located the governor, he grinned proudly. He then retreated from the doorway and was replaced by the stout figure of Father Junipero Serra.

Governor Fages strode across the courtyard to formally greet Father Serra. Serra awaited the governor's arrival with an unveiled expression that conveyed indecision on how he was going to respond to the evening's invitation. Fages, not missing Serra's mistrusting gaze, told himself to soften his demeanor. This greeting would set the stage for the evening. If the atmosphere between the two men could begin as hospitable and even friendly, there would be the possibility for Fages to make amends with Serra and the remainder of the guests, sensing a level of comfort, would relish in a splendid evening. If, however, the evening began with a spat of irritable and hostile words exchanged between the two men, the evening would begin and endure with an air of discomfort hanging thickly over Cooper-Molera's courtyard like a heavy fog bank. That is, assuming Serra would even stay for the evening's festivities if an initial exchange did not please him.

"Father Serra. I'm pleased and honored to have you as my guest this evening," Fages said as he extended a hand towards the friar, having to lean his tall frame slightly in order to reach the far shorter Serra.

Father Serra stared intently at Fages' hand in front of him. He didn't move a muscle and the governor remained rigid before him.

Neither man noticed, but every guest in the courtyard paused in their conversations and turned to witness the encounter occurring at the courtyard's eastern gate. Father Serra eased his stance and grabbed the governor's extended hand with his own.

Governor Fages graciously accepted Serra's extended hand. The two men even managed to smile at one another. Adversaries they may have been, but each held a certain regard for the man in front of him, and if they were to be permanently locked in some form of disagreement, each of them considered that they could at least collaborate when needed.

Fages turned to face the crowd of his guests with little attempt to conceal the grin displaying his appreciation at the recent turn of events. He lowered a hand in the direction of Father Serra in order to wordlessly announce the Father's arrival. Fages followed this action by raising a hand in the air in order to indicate to both the guests and the kitchen staff that the awaited time to be seated at the beautifully arranged tables, decorated with centerpieces of local wildflowers arranged by his own daughter, had arrived.

17.

Year of our Lord 2009.

S AMUEL WAS ANXIOUS FOR the first reunion with his fellow collaborators. Of course, he longed for the day when they would return to claim their *buried treasure*, but he also felt a yearning to meet with his crew. With all of the planning, anticipation, risk, and danger involved in their plan, he imagined that a bond had been sealed between the four men. Samuel did not consider himself to be an overly sentimental type, but something about the entire execution of the plan filled him with bubbling joy that he was not accustomed to feeling.

Samuel descended the staircase leading to the second floor of his house. He still wore a suit from a previous luncheon. He considered changing clothes, but decided against it. He enjoyed the feel of his five thousand dollar suit on him. Just as he was about to open the front door of the house, he heard Bridgette calling to him from the kitchen.

"Honey, if you're going out, can you pick up some ground coffee from Starbucks on your way back?"

It annoyed him that she had obviously forgotten their earlier conversation, when he clearly stated that after his luncheon he was going to meet with some friends. "Sure!" he called out, hoping his answer would allow him to slink out of the front door of the house without further delay.

Before he had the door closed behind him, Bridgette appeared and grabbed the door. He released the knob and she opened the door. "Honey, did you hear me about the Starbucks?" She turned her head to one side while talking, causing her high ponytail to sway.

Seeing Bridgette before him made Samuel forget about how she annoyed him on occasion. His wife was wearing one of her yoga outfits, which was always tight in all the right places on her. "Sure, sugar. I'll get your coffee for you on my way back." Samuel had to admit that her ground coffee kick was kind of cute. She had begun replacing her previously daily trips to Starbucks for nonfat lattes by making her own coffee at home after she learned from him of their financial distress. Bridgette had no clue as to how much his accounts had been hurt, as he never revealed specifics to her; he figured that she probably assumed he was overreacting, as Samuel would not allow his lifestyle to be degraded and he continued to exhibit an appearance that all was well ... *but all was definitely not well.*

"Which car are you going to take?" she asked him.

"The Bentley," Samuel replied. He hadn't driven his ultra show-off car in some time and felt an overwhelming urge to get behind its wheel. He briefly considered how much he would probably get from selling the car, but he didn't want to have to resort to pawning off his property in order to continue with his very exceptional standard of living. What he had done was a far better option. Samuel would rather go to prison than be forced to reveal to the world that his inherited fortune was no longer intact.

Normally Samuel kept his wife oblivious of their financial status, a relationship that she did not seem to mind. However, with the stock market crash, Samuel had taken to drinking one more glass of scotch on a regular basis. One night when he had particularly been depleting the crystal decanter after having had a phone conversation with his personal financial advisor, he admitted, at least partially, to Bridgette that their wealth had been severely depleted. At the time, Samuel could have punched through the phone if possible in order to smack his prick advisor, who had earlier convinced Samuel to pull out all of his low-risk investments. Instead, he let his gorgeous wife console him.

She obediently sat by his side while he drank himself to an incoherent level. She offered to do whatever he wanted that would make him feel better, and overly emphasized the word *anything* a few times in order to make her point unmistakable. At the time, Samuel wasn't interested in sex, though. He didn't want to do anything but sit and drink. At some point, he fell out of his chair. He awoke the next morning in their king-sized bed with a throbbing headache and to an additional throbbing between his legs as he felt his wife performing fellatio on him. *She wasn't so bad,* he had to admit.

"Thanks, baby," she said as she leaned inward to kiss him. Samuel raised a hand as she did and dropped another behind so that when her lips met his, he had one hand on her breasts and one on her ass. He squeezed both of his hands at the same time, causing her to lightly squeal. She smiled at him and gently slapped his shoulder. "Now you go have your guy time and I'll be waiting for you right here when you get back."

Samuel considered stepping back into the house and backing her onto the stairs while peeling off the yoga gear from her body, but then considered the importance of his pending meeting. As the leader, there was no possibility of him being late. Steamy sex with his hot young wife would have to wait.

"How about you wait for me in bed … wearing that black slinky nightie thing I like so much," he recommended.

Bridgette stepped backwards further into the house. "Just don't be too late." She winked, puckered her lips, and let the door slowly swing in front of her.

Samuel purposefully picked a touristy place for the meeting; he didn't want to draw too much attention. The place he had chosen, on Lover's Point in Pacific Grove, would be perfect, he thought.

The draw the restaurant had on tourists certainly wasn't its menu. He remembered the food being overpriced and bland, which, of course, would largely go unnoticed by the typical tourist from the East Coast or the Midwest. East coasters would find themselves too caught up in how much more laid back the California coast was than their own, and the inflated prices would not be any different from the high prices of Boston, NYC, or DC.

Midwesterners would be appalled by the prices on the menu, but would soon become entranced by the sweeping view of Monterey Bay through the restaurant's panoramic windows. They would notice how the bay slowly arched to the north of Monterey and then began to turn inward as a line of coastal mountains along the horizon all the way to the far tip of the bay at Santa Cruz. The calm waters of the bay in between caught the late afternoon sun and slowly released it in a resonating clam around the periphery of the bay. The foreground of the view also offered the charming road wrapping around the jagged tidal pool coast lined with a blend of Victorian houses, remodeled prior hovels that had served as lodgings for former fishermen, and new Spanish-influenced mini-mansions attempting to emulate their much larger cousins further south down the coast. The small peninsula of Lover's Point extended directly in front of the restaurant. Its grassy knoll and large coast live oak trees stood in stark contrast to the bay behind. Returning their gaze from the serene scene in front of them to the menu in their hands, the prices before them would be inconsequential.

Samuel parked his Bentley in front of the restaurant and took a moment to consider the view. He conceded that it was spectacular. It was even more impressive during April when Pacific Grove's famed ice plant flowers would magically explode from the dense green carpet lining the road and quite literally transform the coastline into a purple and pink display that almost appeared otherworldly, as if only conceivable in the mind of an abstract painter.

Samuel saw Dick Lombardo's portly frame seated in the restaurant's bar near the windows. Dick was so eager to impress the others, and anyone, for that matter. Dick likely got there a half hour early just to be the first to arrive. Dick smiled goofily and held out a half-wave as Samuel walked towards the restaurant's entrance. Dick was firmly Number Four in their outfit, the one nobody really cared about having on their team, but tolerated because the extra number and resources were needed.

Victor Mathews, his Number Two, appeared from around the side of the restaurant as Samuel reached the door. Samuel wondered if Victor had arrived at that same moment or purposefully sat outside waiting for Samuel's arrival. Victor may have also delayed his entrance, as he didn't wish to sit alone with Dick. Samuel knew that Victor liked Dick despite the man's obvious flaws, but Dick still managed to annoy Victor at times with his incessant quest for acceptance.

Samuel and Victor shook hands without uttering a word and entered the restaurant's bar area to be seated at the table with Dick. Dick eagerly shook their hands and hastily motioned for a waitress.

Samuel ordered a glass of a single malt scotch, neat; Victor ordered a cranberry juice and soda water, to be served in a white wine glass; and Dick ordered another microbrewed beer.

Once the drinks arrived, which took longer than it should have, Samuel thought, especially considering that the three men were the only patrons of the bar at the time, the three men toasted their drinks.

"Anyone hear from Zande?" Victor inquired.

Samuel took a slow drink of his scotch. "He'll be here. You know Zande, he'll show up late even if he's on time in his own mind. He's got his Big Sur reputation of not caring about the rest of the world."

Samuel was slightly perturbed that Zande was not there, despite his comment. He was doubtful that anyone could possibly be suspicious of them. The heist from the Reserve Bank building had been big news all along the Central Coast and throughout California, even making national news for a few days. However, America's love affair with a distracted attention span had once again proven its valor, and the front pages and top stories quickly turned to coverage of increased fighting in the war in Afghanistan and the U.S.'s mounting budget deficit. Four hundred million dollars was a penny left in a payphone change slot compared to how much the U.S. Government was borrowing from other countries. A few minutes later, Zande's mangled black Jeep appeared outside and Samuel sighed in relief, although he hid it from the other two men. He wasn't overly worried about anything regarding their plan; there was no reason to be, but he still felt anxiety building. If they did everything as planned, if everything kept propelling forward as it was supposed to, then they would all be wealthy enough to live out the rest of their days in total peace. If something went wrong, circumstances would get extremely volatile.

Seeing Zande Allen puffing on a cigarette hanging from his mouth as he parked his Jeep on the side of the road only exemplified his thoughts, as he knew Zande would never accept going to prison. Zande kept a handgun in the glove compartment of his Jeep, and he would not be surprised if Zande also carried a concealed gun on his person. Zande stepped into the restaurant and approached them.

Zande nodded to each man stiffly as he shook their hands and seated himself. The waitress soon appeared and another round of drinks was ordered, with Zande ordering a Budweiser.

Zande relaxed his shoulders. "Well, boys; it's good to see everybody."

"Good to see you, Zande." Samuel replied. The three other men glanced at each other, wondering what the other was thinking. Samuel had called for the meeting, but did not provide any details on its intended purpose, not even to Victor. After the drop-off night, they agreed that Samuel would arrange the next time when they would regroup, and they all knew that the plan included a return to the coast off of Point Lobos at some point in order to recover the hidden cargo and then *move* it elsewhere, but Samuel's details of the future order of events were vague from the point following the heist.

Samuel took a long sip of his scotch and savored the burn of it as the liquid descended his throat to the core of his body. "I thought it was about time for us all to get together to arrange a time to go diving together. I was thinking we should agree on a date sometime in a couple of weeks."

The other three men grinned in approval. "That sounds fantastic," Victor replied.

"Yeah, that would be great," Dick enthusiastically added.

Zande approved with a forward nod of his head.

"Fantastic." Samuel tilted his glass of scotch to his mouth again. He was more than aware that the others were eagerly awaiting the next steps, but he enjoyed making them wait. The sense of empowerment was as thrilling as the taste of the strong liquor at the back of his throat. "And afterwards, if it's okay with you, Zande, I was thinking we could all have a night away from wives and girlfriends and do a little drinking down at your cabin in Big Sur."

Zande's demeanor instantly turned suspicious. Now Zande understood why some time back Samuel inquired about his multiple residences in the Big Sur area, all of which Zande had inherited after his father died. Samuel seemed particularly interested in one of Zande's houses, really more of an isolated cabin without running water or electricity; it was located a ways inland from the highway near the ocean.

Zande's great-grandparents had built and lived in it. In that discussion, Zande assured Samuel, at Samuel's persistent questioning, that no houses or roadways had views of the cabin or the coastline next to it. In describing the property, Zande remarked that there was a break in the rocky coastline near the cabin. Two large outcroppings on either side of the break offered some reprieve from the pounding waves. Samuel asked Zande to confirm that the break would allow a small boat to dock at it, a question which Zande answered affirmatively, stating that he often left a boat docked there himself. At the time, Zande had not thought too much on Samuel's questions. After the discussion of the cabin, Samuel inquired about Zande's other properties and residences in Big Sur. Samuel had evidently only ever been interested in the cabin, yet he managed to conceal his true intentions for it by continuing an equal line of questioning on Zande's other assets.

Zande reflected upon this prior conversation as the three men looked to him for his response. Samuel should have better conveyed his intentions to him long before that moment, especially considering that the plan included utilizing *his* cabin, but Zande decided to hold his trust in Samuel P. Beckwith. He remained somewhat distrustful of the man, as he did of most people, but he found Samuel to be far more clever than most. After all, Samuel had even managed to slightly fool him.

Zande swirled his Budweiser bottle and set it down on the table in front of him. He looked each man in the face carefully and then nodded forward at the center of the table.

Samuel leaned back in his chair, pleased.

18.

Year of our Lord 1818.

FATHER MARGIL COUNTED each day as a blessing and witnessed the presence of God displayed before his eyes everywhere around him. Even in the vast, arid, sun-baked lands the caravan passed through as they marched north to their first stop at the Mission Basilica San Diego de Alcala, Father Margil felt the presence of God.

The caravan moved nimbly forward, much to the distaste of the commander of the soldiers, a stern man named Captain Juan Antonio Echevarria, who hailed from the Basque region of Spain. Father Margil's relationship with Echevarria had begun on a sour note on the day of the caravan's departure from the Mission San Vicente. Captain Echevarria desired to divide his soldiers into two groups, one that would remain to escort the civilian population being taken north to settle the upper reaches of Alta California, Monterey in particular, and the other half would march ahead on its own in order to scout the areas they would be passing through. Father Margil insisted that the soldiers be kept together, fearing not only for the safety of the civilians, but also for the loss of the gold in his care. Echevarria was clearly furious with Father Margil's demands, but to the man's credit, he managed to quell his anger and frustration and abide by Margil's wishes.

Echevarria did not force Father Margil to claim, as he rightfully could, that the interests of the Church were by Crown law to be considered before those of the military, as the military's primary purpose for its presence in Alta California was to protect the missions, colonial outposts, and serve the interests of the Church. The rule was often overturned by military interests, but in their confrontation, Father Margil considered the irony that although the Catholic Church and its savior was his primary interest, in the case of the Russian's gold, he was acting as his conscience dictated, which happened to be in the primary interests of the Spanish Empire. However, it was easily justified, as the success of the Spanish Empire was intricately connected to the successful expansion of the Church throughout the world.

An unspoken agreement was thereafter formed between Margil and Echevarria. Father Margil would say nothing to Echevarria when the man gave the orders for when the caravan would break from the march or when it would be stopped each day for the night's repose. The captain appeared to be as determined as Father Margil to reach Monterey and it was essential that they arrive in Monterey with the gold before the Russian changed his mind. Granting Echevarria authority in most affairs of the journey thus was agreeable to Father Margil.

The trail from San Vincente to San Diego was brutally hard on the feet and backs of the civilians and soldiers alike, but as it was still the beginning of their long voyage to Monterey, their spirits remained elated. Although Father Margil saw the strain on their faces, there was minimal complaining. Father Margil prayed that spirits remained high on the journey, especially among the armed soldiers; he would never entirely find comfort in their presence. And Father Margil had heard from others that while strenuous, with searing heat and unforgiving terrain, the first segment of the voyage to San Diego de Alcala would be miniscule in comparison of difficulty with the trail segments between the Mission San Gabriel Arcangel and the Mission Santa Barbara and then onward from Santa Barbara to the Mission San Antonio de Padua.

The Mission Trail in Alta California, as it had become known, connected all of the missions and was established by Father Junipero Serra when Serra had adjoined the first overland expedition of Alta California. On that first glorious trek, Serra's meticulous planning was defined. He hand-selected priests, civilians, and converted natives to accompany him with a sizeable contingent of soldiers, and they moved north into the unknown. Serra himself determined where future missions would be established along the trail. The missions of San Diego, Santa Barbara, Monterey, and later Carmel were supplied by way of the ocean, with Spanish ships delivering additional settlers and supplies. Once established, the missions relied on the labor of converted natives, neophytes, who worked with each mission's cattle herds, but also assisted in the growing of corn, peas, lentils, barley, beans, olives, oranges, lemons, pears, peaches, and apples. Each mission also planted grapevines for the production of sacrament wine.

Serra's original voyage was intended to lead a heavily supplied and heavily guarded expedition into the unfamiliar interior of Alta California in order to establish inland missions that would strengthen the trail system in the new lands. The Crown and the soldiers referred to the trail as the King's Trail, but those of the Church knew it by its true name: the Mission Trail.

Serra arrived in Monterey and quickly established a grand mission, the Mission San Carlos Borromeo, although another well-known fact in Spanish California was that Serra and the Governor of Monterey, Governor Fages, clashed with insurmountable differences of opinion, and Serra once again proved his dexterous nature by establishing a new mission, the Mission San Carlos Borromeo de Carmelo, outside of Monterey. Such a temperamental action was unfathomable and Father Margil could only imagine the personality of the man who could make such a decision while knowing that the action would be severely frowned upon, at least by both the Crown and the Church. Father Margil was anxious to meet Father Serra.

The Mission San Diego de Alcala was the first mission established by Fathers Serra and Portola on their journey into Alta California. For this reason, it was known as the Mother of the Alta California Missions. The mission and its surrounding area were named after Saint Didacus, but the more commonly known name of San Diego ensued from the time of the mission's inception.

A priest by the name of Father Perez was appointed by Serra himself to serve as the mission's head priest. Serra's decision had shocked many, as Perez's reputation held nothing of Serra's infamous compassion for native peoples. Perez had developed a far different reputation, one renowned for a lack of compassion. Rumors swirled throughout the empire of his harsh treatment of native populations in the lands that had come to be known as Peru. Many believed that he aided in fostering a dislike for the Spanish in general, and when the country had declared its independence from the Crown, Father Perez was singled out and forcibly removed.

Father Margil believed in mankind, but he also believed more in people's ability to speak for themselves and to display their true nature than in what others may say of them. Margil therefore dispelled all that he had heard concerning Father Perez as the caravan dragged their feet toward the mission's cathedral. It had been an enduring day of sun and heat. Every member of the band felt the dust that had caked onto the skin of their faces. Despite what he may have heard of Perez, Margil was thrilled to meet the fellow missionary. Perhaps he was a stern man of the cloth, but he was above all a friar such as himself, and Father Serra would not have vied for the man's posting if there had not been some endearing qualities about Father Perez.

Father Margil saw the shape of a tall man wearing a friar's robes appear through the tall doorway of the cathedral. As the priest approached, Father Margil took in the image of the man: bald on top of his head, but not on the sides or back of his head, where a dark ring of hair formed; firm-looking shoulders; small eyes; and a narrow face. The priest acknowledged the members of the exhibition as he passed them, but his attention was clearly focused on Father Margil.

The priest came to a full stop directly in front of him, but did not extend a hand. His arms remained crossed in front of his abdomen, inside of the sleeves of his gray habit, which was identical to Father Margil's in every manner except that Margil's habit was brown. The robe-like garment was the standard apparel of missionaries in both Alta and Baja California, but the varying colors indicated that Margil was of the Dominican Order and Perez of the Franciscan Order.

"Father Margil. I'm Father Perez. We have been expecting you."

"Thank you, Father." Margil glanced at his own hand, debating if he should offer it to Father Perez or not. Perez's unchanged expression, however, led him to the conclusion that the man did not wish to shake his hand, for whatever reason. "It's been a long road, but God has been with us." The bells of the church were ringing, which could have been in response to the arrival of the convoy or the daily call to the end of labor for those of the mission. Regardless of the true purpose of the bells, the neophyte men Margil noticed working in the fields surrounding the mission responded by discontinuing their work and turning to saunter towards the mission.

"The Lord is always with us in our hearts," Perez resolutely replied. "He's even with those of this land that chose to remain as savages," he added coolly as he suspiciously eyed two neophyte men returning from their daily labors. "These two here, for example," he said, nodding his head in the direction of the two men passing by, "are suspected of conspiring to quit their reformed mission lives and returning to their vile heathen, native ways."

Father Margil was temporarily stunned by the harshness of Perez's words, especially in light of the fact that if the neophytes had learned even the slightest Spanish in their time at the mission, which he did not doubt, as teaching of the Spanish language was held within the mission system as being an essential indoctrination into the Church and Spanish culture, the two native men would have undoubtedly overheard the words, as Father Perez did not even lower his voice as they passed by.

Margil watched the two men shuffle towards a building that he guessed was designated for unmarried men. The men appeared uncomfortable in the loose shirts and pants the mission had provided them. After they had cleaned themselves, they would be on their way to evening prayers and supper.

Father Margil fought off his doubts and smiled at Father Perez. "Perhaps it would be better to say that the native people of this land we have come to label as New Spain are only ignorant of our ways and have only to learn. We are all children in the eyes of the Lord, after all."

Perez sneered in response. "These *children*, Father Margil, as you call them, are capable of conjuring the devil." Perez paused and considered Margil's naivety. He began to laugh. "I would imagine you are relatively new to this New World, are you not, Father Margil? And you probably still believe in all of embellished good we are supposed to do here? And you likely also don't believe that your faith can be at all shaken by this place?"

A pronounced feeling of anger was building within Father Margil. Father Perez may have endured hardship at his previous mission posting in Peru, at his own doing or not, but it was no excuse to condescend to a fellow man of the Church, or anyone. It was rare that Father Margil felt the evil fingers of wrath. At such times, he feared he would one day relinquish his faith and succumb to the wickedness he felt surging inside of his body and soul. At such times, images of his father's cruelty and his mother's screams resurfaced.

Once again, however, he was able to regain his focus and avoid losing his self-composure. He shielded Father Perez's blatant attempt to insult him by considering the precarious position of the man in front of him, who was a man of the Lord, even if he had a foul temperament. When he did this, he saw Father Perez as a man who had lost himself in his own fear. Whatever happened in Peru, it left its mark on Father Perez. Furthermore, considering that his predecessor as head priest of the Mission of San Diego de Alcala, Father Jayme, had been dragged from his living quarters in the middle of the night and brutally slaughtered by a group of area natives, it was perhaps only human of Father Perez to be slightly distrustful of his neophytes. With time, Father Margil was certain that the priest would regain the full and beautiful light of God and would feel it move through him again. *When that glorious day occurred, Father Perez would no longer doubt his love for all of mankind.*

"I have not had the honor and pleasure of such a long stay in this wonderful land of our Lord as you have, Father Perez; but I hope that I am fortunate enough to stay here for the rest of my days," Father Margil graciously offered. "It is no doubt challenging to a man of God to fulfill his duties as we have pledged to do here in the New World, but I hope to always remain God's servant and to keep my faith."

Father Perez began to laugh louder, his narrow face elongating itself.

The words had escaped Father Margil's mouth without much consideration, and as he had spoken, he heard an inner voice highlighting the possibly hypocritical nature of his statement. *Was he not, after all, already committing an act that although without doubt was justified in the eyes of the Lord, could also be considered to be dishonest?* Father Margil did not doubt the divine intention of his endeavor to deliver the gold to Monterey, but with each passing day of the journey, he began to feel unwelcome thoughts that he was straying from his priestly oaths.

It may not be as glorious of a calling as I had hoped, but if I do not do this, a far greater darkness could occur in this land that is calling— no begging — for the word of our Lord to endure. "Whatever may await me here, Father Perez, will not deter my faith," he said aloud.

Father Perez halted his laughing and moved closer. He stared searchingly into Father Margil's eyes. Father Margil hoped to see kindness, love, and compassion behind the steel gaze of Perez, but disappointment ensnared him as he witnessed the opposite.

"*Just wait,*" Father Perez said. Perez turned and began a languid pace towards the mission's cathedral, and Father Margil stood watching him go.

19.

Year of our Lord 2009.

A PLATE OF GLISTENING roasted chicken, wild rice, and a grilled artichoke was set on the table in front of Gibson. Rachel had a sizeable bowl of Caesar salad topped with grilled prawns in front of her and they shared a flash of mutual anticipation.

The restaurant's courtyard where they sat had a couple of large oak trees; their massive branches managed to enclose the area yet allowed the bright sunshine to peer down into it. A fountain gently gurgled in one corner and an assortment of tall plants and simple stone sculptures littered the periphery of the courtyard. Fewer than ten black wrought-iron tables with two to four chairs attached to each surrounded them. Strategically placed yet hidden speakers were located throughout the courtyard, and the likes of Edith Piaf, Maurice Chevalier, and Charles Aznavour serenaded them.

A group of four gabby and elaborately dressed women sat at one table; Gibson noted that they had already finished two bottles of wine and had not even glanced at the menus in front of them, and at another table, a man roughly his age was seated with a woman who looked to be half his age, staring dreamily into one another's eyes as they swirled glasses of red wine.

Gibson cut away a slice of the succulent chicken before him. It was steaming with aromas of sage, rosemary, and thyme. It tasted as it looked — delicious.

∝∞

John Gibson tilted his head back to feel the warmth of the sun on his face. It was odd how drastic the weather change had been. He imagined the temperature difference between the coast and the valley was at least twenty degrees. The added valley sunshine coupled with the lack of moisture in the air led to another ten degrees of perceived heat increase.

Just as he was about to inquire if Rachel would like to split a dessert or even two if the dessert menu proved tempting enough, his phone vibrated against his hip. He reached to grab it. When he saw the name on the caller identification, though, a quick look at Rachel conveyed that he needed to take the call. It was a friend, Sebastian Parker, from a past case later labeled the Haika 4 case.

"Bonjour, Sebastian. *Comment ça va?"* Gibson said as he excused himself from the table and exited the restaurant's courtyard through a wooden doorway. Parker had tried to teach him a few words in French in their time together. Most of the words Gibson had forgotten before he even had an opportunity to speak them; such was the dilemma of an aging mind too tired to put much effort into learning a new language, but he managed to recollect some random words and phrases.

"Ah, *salut, mon vieux. Quoi de neuf?"* Parker's asked over the cell phone. His voice sounded joyous and relaxed.

Gibson considered the words for a moment before responding that his limit of French greetings had been met. "Okay, you've got me there, young man."

"Young man? Unfortunately, I'm not so young anymore."

"Compared to me you are."

"C'est vrai … but when compared to a vintage aged bottle of wine, I suppose I am still a young Beaujolais." Through the phone, Gibson could feel Parker's sly smirk that he had gotten to know so well.

"So please say that you learned something from me about enjoying the pleasures of life more and that I have not caught you at work on a weekend."

"Actually, Parker, you'd be proud of me, as you caught me as I was wrapping up a delightful lunch with a … *friend* … after a little wine tasting on a splendid day in Carmel Valley," Gibson cheerfully responded, leaving out that he was also following a job-related hunch on his visit.

"*Très bien*! I'm glad to hear that you are continuing your progression towards becoming a *bon vivant*. Wait, wait … the way you just said friend makes me think that it's not really a friend at all, but probably more like a *lady friend*."

The comment made Gibson's face turn red. "I suppose one could call her that," he evenly replied, wondering how Rachel would feel being referred to as his lady friend. Instinctively he turned around and peered over the patio's fence at Rachel. She was sitting at the table with a ray of sunshine falling upon her shoulders as she sipped from a coffee cup, looking as lovely as he had ever seen her. She noticed him and smiled, mouthing to him that it was okay for him to be on the phone.

"Ha! You old *dog*!" Parker exclaimed.

"And how is Alaitz?" Gibson asked, changing the subject. In their time together, Parker initially only hinted at the severity of his feelings for Alaitz; however, Gibson had always suspected there was more than what was revealed.

"Oh, she's good. She's working for a non-profit organization that is promoting the central organization of products made in the Basque Country, on both sides of the French and Spanish border."

Gibson was pleased to hear that the two were together. "I can imagine that it's not an easy task."

Parker laughed. "Indeed it's not. But she likes it."

Gibson considered how he only saw Alaitz once, and had never actually spoken to her. It was after Parker was shot in an alleyway of Petit Bayonne. Gibson feared his young partner would die from the gunshot wound, but Parker's mind and body proved determined to continue their enjoyment of life, and he survived the would-be assassin's bullet. Gibson walked out of Bayonne's main hospital after the surgeons announced that they had stabilized Parker and he would need to be transported to a better equipped medical facility in Bordeaux. He noticed a young woman. She was arguing with policemen standing guard at the entrance of the hallway leading to Parker's recovery room. She was not stunningly beautiful, but she had a natural, almost rugged beauty.

Parker later told him that Alaitz refused to leave the hospital until Capitaine Nivelle's men let her into his room to see him after he awoke and had agreed to her visit.

As Parker later described to him, whereas before, Alaitz had never been able to foresee spending her life with him, the prospect of his death changed her mind. When Gibson asked if Parker had seen a light in his near-death experience, Parker's response was that the last memory he had that fateful evening was an image of himself and Alaitz sitting outside of a white stone farmhouse with red trim on a green hillside overlooking the rolling foothills of the Basque Country, with peaks of the Pyrenees Mountains in the distance.

"And how about you?" Gibson inquired.

"Oh, I'm fine. I do some odd jobs here and there for people in the nearby village who seem to have amazingly accepted me, at least they've somewhat accepted my presence, anyway. I think Alaitz had something to do with that, but she'd never tell me if she did. Aside from that, I'm keeping busy with working on our house, which is a couple-hundred-year-old Basque farmhouse."

"You could write a book on your life there; something like the book that the English guy wrote about living in the south of France for a year."

"It's not a bad idea; *A Year in the Basque Country*. But for now, Alaitz has a dream of how she'd like to see this place before we have any kids and I don't see myself having idle moments to write a book any time soon.

"And the way I see it, I've reached heaven on earth, as when I'm sitting outside with Alaitz after she comes home from work and we have an aperitif before dinner, I look out over the Pays Basque and think that this is exactly the last image I remember before the lights went out."

"That sounds pretty nice, Parker." Gibson wondered if Parker was still working on a contractual basis for the CIA. Parker insisted after his recovery that he was resigning from the organization, but the agency may have been very persuasive in requesting Parker's continued assistance. After all, one of the individuals they followed from the murder in San Francisco to France had never been captured: Graciana. Further, the identity of Parker's attacker had never been established, although Parker informed Gibson that Capitaine Nivelle had not withdrawn his relentless pursuit of either. After Parker's attack, however, Graciana and any leads on the shooting simply disappeared into the misty secrets of the Basque world.

"Listen, Gibson. We haven't made any official plans yet, but Alaitz and I are going to get married sometime in the next year and I'd love for you to be here for it," Parker continued.

"Well, of course, I'd love to be there. Just let me know when you set a date and I'll buy tickets and request the time off from work."

"So what are you doing in Carmel Valley going wine tasting and having lunch outdoors with a *lady friend*?" Parker asked.

Gibson thought that Parker had tactfully and strategically changed the subject. "Chiles actually recommended it." No need to mention anything further, Gibson thought.

"*Chiles* … what a dork," Parker responded.

Gibson peered over the patio's fence once again to look for Rachel in the courtyard. She now had a dessert on the table in front of her, and even from a distance, Gibson knew it was her favorite dessert: crème brulée.

"Parker, it's been great chatting with you, but I've left a beautiful woman all alone at a table in public, and although I'm not nearly as worried as I would be if we were in France, where any of a number of men would have long since slithered in with their attempts to charm her, I don't want to keep her waiting."

"*Il n'y a pas de souci, mon ami*," Parker responded. After a prolonged silence, Parker added: "It means no worries, Gibson. I see we really have to get you back over here soon to work on your French. Have fun over there in California in the meantime."

"Okay, Sebastian. *A bientôt* then."

"*A bientôt*, John."

20.

Year of our Lord 1818.

FATHER MARGIL DID NOT LAMENT the caravan's departure from the Mission San Diego de Alcala. It may have represented the last outpost before the difficult stretch of roughly ninety miles before the next mission, but Father Margil did not find the atmosphere of the mission to be either inviting or inspiring. He prayed that their reception at the Mission San Gabriel Arcangel would be more welcoming. In fact, after the test of his fortitude through interacting with Father Perez, he invited the oncoming tribulations that the trail would surely deliver; he was not kept waiting long before the arrival of such tribulations.

After the third day of trekking northward from San Diego de Alcala, Father Margil began to sense unrest building amongst the soldiers and despair mounting amongst the future settlers. Father Margil conceded that it was no easy task to spend the day walking in the sun in the arid and dusty lands of Alta California, but he seized every moment he could by reminding them that the Lord was with them. The hardships of the trail were only reminders of the importance of their journey. *They were bringing Spanish civilization to the primitive reaches of the world; they were bringing the word of God to those unfortunate souls that needed to find salvation; and they were providing assured protection of the Spanish Empire's and thus the Catholic Church's hold on Alta California.* Although, of course, this last purpose of their mission was privy knowledge to Father Margil alone.

The Catholic Church could not allow the further spread of the falsified Orthodox Church to extend into the New World. *It had to be prevented.*

He watched dust rise from every step he took and Father Margil reflected upon the overall plan for the mission system in Alta California. It would be some years before the plan was able to be fully implemented. When completed, there would be a new mission every thirty miles; thus they would be separated by one day's ride on a horse or an average of three days on foot. There were those within the Church that did not wish to see it so spread out in the vast lands of Alta California, and their opposition was a determent to the expansion; however, the efforts of devoted and progressive servants of the Lord such as himself, Father Serra, and others kept the dream alive that one day the mission system would extend along the entirety of Alta California and beyond. His inner reflections on the glory of spreading the Lord's word brought the importance of his mission to mind. It was a sin to be prideful, Father Margil pondered, but *was it a sin to be proud of one's duties if they were centered on ensuring the spread of the word of the Lord?* The subject would be an interesting topic of conversation amongst many he eagerly awaited having with Father Serra.

The reflection on his mission and the greater missions of the Catholic Church also reminded him that he had been negligent in his duty to sprinkle mustard flower seeds. The friars of the Franciscan Order, beginning with Fathers Serra and Portola, and later the friars of his Dominican Order, sprinkled the seeds along the Mission Trail sporadically as they walked the route in order to leave a visible path for future travelers to follow in case maps were inaccurate or not on hand. The weather of Alta California provided an opportune climate for the gestation of the hardy seeds and the bright yellow flowers would be visible in patches along the trail. Father Margil noticed in the near distance that they were approaching a bright stretch of the flowers. He held his hand in the satchel full of seeds he had holstered around his shoulder. *It would be better to wait until after that stretch of the yellow flowers to spread more of the seeds.*

A horse sneezed next to him and he looked at the large animal that had been reined in to trot alongside him. He looked up to see Captain Juan Antonio Echevarria looking down at him.

"I brought a horse for you to ride on," the Captain absently said to him. Echevarria peered at the horizon.

"I consider myself a man of God, Captain Echevarria, and as such, I do as much as I can to limit harm to any living thing."

"But riding a horse is not hurting it," Echevarria responded, his eyes still set on the expanse of land in front of them that was a combination of gentle hills and low plateaus.

Occasionally they reached a point along the trail where if they looked westward, they could again see a glimpse of the ocean. Such occasions were welcomed by both Father Margil and Captain Echevarria, although neither man admitted their appreciation. It was evident to them both that such moments were a blessing for the collective demeanor of the entire cavalcade. Soldiers and civilians alike were overjoyed to reach a summit and see that the sparkling waters of the ocean remained within a hard day's drive in the distance. It was comforting to know that they had not ventured too far into the interior of the unknown lands.

"Has the horse ever told you this, that it is not painful for him to carry you on his back?" Father Margil suddenly responded to Echevarria's question.

The Captain ignored Margil's response. "I'm concerned about the ..." he paused, considering the proper word he wished to use, "... dexterity of our group. And not only the civilians, but my soldiers as well."

"Is this why you stare so intently on the horizon? Are you worried about what awaits us?" Father Margil inquired.

"We have six more days of walking before we reach the Mission of San Gabriel Arcangel; then at least a couple weeks to pass through lands that are reportedly going to make this first stretch of the trail resemble the plains surrounding Madrid." The Captain spoke seriously, without a hint of hesitation.

"They need only remember that we are all a part of the Lord's work by helping to bring His word and civilization to the far ends of the world and their hearts will again be filled. When we set up our camp this evening, I will focus my prayers on this very topic before our dinner."

Captain Echevarria glowered at him from high above on his horse. "I hope you are right, Father."

∞

Diego Alvarez had watched as the "brave" Captain talked to the "good" Father. They both tried to always look so confident and all-knowing. But Diego Alvarez knew how to read people. It was a skill that he had recognized early in his childhood. From the time he was a boy, he knew how to get what he wanted: first from his parents, then from other boys, then from young ladies, and then from men. And something about the look that each of the two men attempted to conceal intrigued him. He was marching close alongside the two of them, without their knowledge, he was certain, as Captain Echevarria never spoke in front of him. In fact, the Captain never spoke within hearing distance of him. *The Captain is scared of me*, Diego said to himself with a sly smile. *As he should be. He knows as I do that the other soldiers would listen to me if I ever asserted myself ...*

Diego Alvarez was not interested in achieving glory for the Spanish Empire or for the Catholic Church. Glancing northward, he thought only of the possibilities that lay beyond the horizon.

How many villages of natives were there in this Alta California? he wondered. Plenty, he was certain; and that meant ample supplies of native women. The desire he felt towards the native women of the New World was unexplainable. It was a burning that he felt throbbing deep in his loins when he watched them. Women were of sordid interest to him and he had discovered pleasure with many a Spanish girl, but something about the native women stirred his blood more than any señorita. Perhaps it was their dark skin, or their savageness, or the way they wouldn't look into the eyes of a Spanish man as he passed by them; whatever it was, it drove Diego mad with lust. On several occasions while he was posted at the San Vincente Mission, he nearly coerced young native women to take a nighttime walk with him away from the watching eyes of the mission, only to have Captain Echevarria abruptly intervene and ruin his plans. Such interference only strengthened his desire.

The natives were also bound to have gold, he trusted. If only it were allowed to be strong and courageous, as had been the conquistadors of old, men such as himself could gain more riches for the Spanish Empire than any peaceful colonization attempts, like the current policy, he thought. In the better times, great and valiant men, such as himself, would be expected to keep sizeable percentages of their plunder for themselves. Pirates were able to continue this noble line of work on the seas, but once on land, the practice was now chastised. He considered how, if he ever were able to get away from Captain Echevarria, he, *Diego Alvarez*, would lead a contingent of soldiers into the unknown and they would pacify the entire savage population of Alta California!

They would march into every village they came across, and once there, demand that they be allowed to have their pick of the finest native matrons the village had to offer. They would demand every piece of gold in the possession of each village. If there would be any refusal, they would begin killing children in front of the eyes of their parents until their demands were met. When they took their pleasure with the women of each village and were assured that they had every scrap of gold, they would force the fiercest-looking young men in each village to join them in their conquest. In this way, he, Diego Alvarez, would become the next great conquistador, alongside the glorious figures of Pizarro and Cortes.

Diego's gaze turned from Captain Echevarria, mounted on his horse as proudly as if he were the great Hernan Cortes, to Father Margil. Echevarria was a man easily read by Diego, as most upper-tier officers were; but holy men continued to represent some challenge. Father Margil was no exception. On the one hand, the Father presented himself as a humble servant of the Lord, but there was something else about him. Diego did not know if the good Father was clever enough to come across as an open book, or an open *Bible* in this case, yet really be a book with secrets hidden away. Irrespective of either, Diego figured there was more to Father Margil than just the man of the Church that he claimed to be. Diego spread two fingers along his wiry mustache and decided to try talking to the Father at the first opportunity that presented itself.

21.

Year of our Lord 2009.

SAMUEL BECKWITH SUBTLY indicated to Victor Mathews, his most trusted Number Two, that he wanted to speak with him exclusively after Zande and Dick left. At the conclusion of their meeting, the four men climbed into their respective cars parked outside the restaurant. Samuel and Victor sat in their cars, Samuel in his Bentley and Victor in his Lexus, waiting for the other two men to leave.

After Zande and Dick drove off, Samuel and Victor stepped out of their cars and Samuel waited for Victor to join him next to a railing overlooking an outcropping of jagged rocks on the shoreline. As Victor approached, both were distracted by the sound of shrieking girls emanating from a large group of Asian tourists taking pictures in the small park area of Lover's Point. "So, what is it you'd like to discuss further?" Victor asked.

"Let's walk," Samuel nodded in the direction of the compacted dirt pathway that snaked its way through the thick carpet of green ice plant clinging to the coast as it passed by the line of houses bordering the roadway. Newer houses were especially prevalent along the road as it passed the Pacific Grove Municipal Golf Course on its way towards Spanish Bay, where not only did the average house size increase, but the acreage of lots did as well, almost like 17-Mile Drive in Pebble Beach, but, not quite, Samuel thought. Even the name of the road changed at that point from Ocean View Boulevard to Sunset Drive.

The PG coast may be nice, but it's still called the "Poor Man's 17-Mile Drive" for a reason. And as much as the PG Municipal Golf Course pretended to be a version of a Pebble Beach course, it's still called the "Poor Man's Pebble Beach," Samuel thought.

"How do you think they are holding together?" Samuel asked after they had taken a few paces along the trail.

"Dick should be fine. He has a big mouth, but I think he's appropriately afraid of you and so occupied constantly trying to kiss my ass that he'll not do anything to jeopardize our situation."

Samuel didn't respond immediately and instead pondered Victor's comments. "I hope you're right. Sometimes I question if we were too hasty in adding him to our team."

Samuel's comment slightly annoyed Victor. He realized that Samuel's questioning of adding Dick to their team was more his questioning of Victor's decision to approach Samuel about doing so in the first place. Victor veiled the irritation he felt growing inside. Samuel was the type of man that just needed to constantly feel in control and self-justified. Instead of revealing his annoyance, he opted for an altered approach to deflect tension between them. "I'm actually more concerned about Zande." It was a risky endeavor, as he knew that mentioning his increasing anxiety over Zande Allen could put Samuel on the defensive. The risk was worth it, though, to Victor, considering that he wanted to remove himself from judgment.

Samuel stopped walking abruptly, so that it took a few steps before Victor stopped as well and turned back to face him. "What makes you say that?" Samuel demanded.

Victor stumbled for a response, worrying that perhaps his brilliant plan had backfired. "Well, what if he's a loose cannon like other crazies down there in Big Sur?"

Samuel began to walk again and Victor fell into stride alongside him. "There's no need to question Zande's loyalty to us. He'll see this thing through." The image of a pair of cigars in his small travel humidor and a flask of cognac in the glove compartment of the Bentley jumped into Samuel's head. "Let's drive down to Asilomar and smoke a couple of cigars."

22.

Year of our Lord 2009.

ZANDE ALLEN DROVE SOUTH from the Monterey Peninsula along Highway 1, first passing the exit for Ocean Street, which led downhill into that pretentious place of Carmel-by-the-Sea, then past the exit for Carmel Valley Road, which led into the once-beautiful area the same pretentious people of Carmel had ruined, then past a road sign that displayed a crooked arrow indicating a winding road, followed by the road conditions for the next seventy-five miles, and then through Carmel Highlands, which consisted of enormous houses clinging to the sides of the steep ridges diving into the ocean. In Zande's view, this represented the furthest encroachment towards his Big Sur. *To hell with these rich bastards,* he said as he spit out of the window in the direction of a line of houses perched precariously along a ridgeline over the Pacific.

Driving past Garrapata State Park, he turned left at the sole entrance to Palo Colorado Road. The road provided access to fifty or so houses either adjacent to it or with steep driveways heading upwards to the unseen hillsides, and also served as an entrance to unnamed dirt roads where a large contingent of his supporters of Return the Sur to Big Sur lived. He never revealed his dream of demolishing the Bixby Bridge, which would demarcate the rest of Big Sur from Garrapata and Palo Colorado Road. It would be an unfortunate loss, as not only did many of his supporters and other good Big Sur folk live off of dirt roads that wound mysteriously out of sight from Highway 1 or Palo Colorado Road, but it also would be a historical and geographical loss.

The mouth of the canyon where Palo Colorado Road intersected with Highway 1 was once the location of the infamous Notley's Landing. Zande's grandfather had relayed stories of the area when Zande was a boy. A cleared and relatively flat stretch of land at the mouth of the canyon had provided an ideal location for a loading facility — a gigantic wooden slide used to drop the huge trunks of redwood trees, harvested from the plentiful groves that lined the canyon eastward into the coastal range and to ships docked at a safe distance from the rocky coastline.

With so many workers in the area for the timber operation, it was only natural that periphery businesses sprouted up, including a rooming house, tavern, and general mercantile store. As the small settlement was a considerable distance from the more civilized area of Monterey, and it was Big Sur after all, which already had a reputation as a wild and untouched region, Notley's Landing quickly gained a reputation for sin, be it in the form of drunkenness, prostitution, illicit trade, gunfights, or even murders.

Zande thought of the many colorful stories he had heard about Notley's Landing as he drove into the canopied canyon of Palo Colorado Road and again considered how unfortunate it was that the canyon was not south of Bixby Bridge with the rest of the true Big Sur lands. However, it was a war and there were always casualties in wars. Besides, the argument could be made that what had become known as Carmel Highlands was actually more a part of Big Sur than Carmel, but the rich bastards from San Francisco, Los Angeles, and wherever the hell else had already ruined it. It was only a matter of time before Palo Colorado was ruined as well.

Zande drove into the darkened interior of the canyon. The canopy provided by the redwoods darkened its floor even on sunny days and Zande flipped on his car lights. The narrow two-lane road that occasionally converged into one lane was consistently damp from the moisture trapped underneath the tree cover. Dark green moss grew in thick patches on the sides of trees and on the wooden fences residents with houses alongside the main road had erected in an attempt to conceal themselves from the world. Water seemed to perpetually drip from somewhere above, even if rain had not been seen for months. Palo Colorado Road was a different world: a dark, damp place that was not friendly to outsiders. Signs stating 'no trespassing' frequently adorned the wooden fences and gave the impression that they were not for show.

The desire for privacy and seclusion was not unrealistic. Even though the road was clearly marked from Highway 1 and even though it was the only paved public road leading off Highway 1 for a stretch of twenty miles, both tourists and Peninsula residents would pass it without a second glance.

Zande thought this was perhaps due to the tunnel-like appearance of a grove of eucalyptus and redwoods at the intersection of the two roads. Passing by the intersection, one would catch a glimpse of the dark and uninviting interior of Palo Colorado Road and have no desire to investigate. Coupled with most motorists reaching speeds of fifty to sixty miles per hour after driving twenty to thirty on the preceding winding stretches of the highway, Palo Colorado was almost protected by design, whether premeditated or not.

Some tourists did manage to penetrate the road's secret, though, primarily because a National Forest campground named Botcher's Gap was located twenty miles inland from the Highway 1 turnoff. On their way, they would pass a few turn-offs to narrow dirt roads marked only with mailboxes. Palo Colorado Road eventually transformed into an unpaved fire access road that twisted into the Santa Lucia Mountains. At the end of the road was a primitive campground and a trailhead for hiking trails leading into the Ventana Wilderness, a two hundred thousand acre tract of untamed land within the rugged coastal mountain range that helped protect Big Sur from the outer world.

It was along this route that Zande turned off onto an unmarked and obscure dirt road only wide enough for one vehicle that led up the face of a steep ridge. The intersection was unmarked, but after climbing beyond sight of the main road, a sign stated that trespassers would be shot. Zande held minimal doubt that his friend, Hawthorne Williams, would happily follow through with the warning on the edge of his property.

Hawthorne, born and raised in the log cabin resting silently on the summit of a peak overlooking the dark outline of Palo Colorado canyon, preferred to be called Hawth. Hawth's parents had been an enlightened product of the Sixties who had left their affluent families on the East Coast and attended college at Berkeley. Their failure to assimilate into mainstream culture after the end of the *movement* led to their abandoning of civilization, as Hawth put it, and they had moved to Palo Colorado in their quest to achieve nirvana in isolation from the world. The combined inheritance they received from their families was enough to buy land from a Palo Colorado resident who lived on the canyon floor yet held deed to fifty acres of property up the mountain on the way to Botcher's Gap.

The old-timer they bought the land from had been hesitant to sell, reciting how it had been in his family since his grandfather had worked in the timber operations and had secured the land before the surrounding area had been designated national forest. But when Hawth's parents made it clear to the grizzled old man that they would provide his asking price in cash and would agree to an arbitrary price on the official paperwork, allowing him to claim a lower amount from the sale of the property for taxation purposes, and agreed with a handshake to never build more than one small house, letting the rest of the property remain as wilderness, he agreed.

Hawth's parents built their house, more of a three-room cabin, on their own and lived off their land as much as they could by forming a small farm, complete with an expansive kitchen garden, chicken house, and herd of sheep. The sheep were always troublesome, even for Hawth, because they seemed to be a favorite meal of mountain lions.

Hawth was home-schooled by his parents, and after their death, continued to live at the cabin, living off of his land and his respectable inheritance. Some years before, Hawth paid for electricity and a phone line to his home, although he waited until his parents' death, as they were insistent that the house be entirely detached from modern civilization.

Zande turned the corner at the last bend around a stately oak tree and saw Hawth's cabin. His parents may have been brilliant academics, but they were certainly not carpenters and Zande wondered how efficient at farming they had been. The house appeared orderly from a distance, but its edges were not properly aligned and the roof appeared slanted at too steep an angle.

Hawth appeared from behind an outbuilding set off on its own. Zande remembered that the small shed housed Hawth's chickens. Hawth's initial expression was unconcealed suspicion, and he had a sawed-off shotgun draped over his shoulder. *True to his word.* Recognizing the vehicle and driver, Hawth set the shotgun down, resting it against the side of the shed.

Zande descended from his Jeep and remarked that Hawth looked pleased to see him. The thought then occurred to Zande that he was perhaps the first person that Hawth had seen in a while. Hawth was known for going weeks, if not months, at a time without leaving his property and he rarely, if ever, invited people to visit. Zande would never consider a casual stop to say "hi." Hawth was a good man, but also lived by himself on top of a mountain in the wilderness and made a point of proving he did not care for people; it was wise to afford such men as much distance as possible. However, after a recent phone call, Hawth had invited Zande to visit and Zande accepted.

Zande shared many characteristics with Hawth, but not all, and Hawth had a way of scaring Zande Allen, who scared most people. But Hawthorne Williams was the undeniable depiction of the very good, honest people of Big Sur that Zande wanted to protect. Hawth, like some of the others, though, was on the extreme fringes of Big Sur folk.

Hawth smiled widely as he approached Zande. He was wearing brown denim pants and a beige button-up shirt and was built like an ox. Both of his garments looked like they had not been washed in a month. He extended his hand and his wide grin revealed a missing molar from his bottom row of teeth. "Hello, Zande. I'm glad you could make it," Hawth said as the two shook hands.

"Hello, Hawth. How's life in the wilderness?"

"That damned lion snatched one of my lambs last night. Those animals are smarter than people give them credit for. I staked it out myself all night the previous three evenings, but last night I wasn't out there and it came into my camp and snatched one."

"People in the cities love to talk about there being no wild animals left in the states, but they've never been into the woods, have they?"

Hawth heartily chuckled in response. His massive shoulders bounced as he laughed, and Zande questioned if Hawth's frame would have developed so stoutly had his parents decided to raise him in a typical residential setting as opposed to the wilds of Big Sur. "Nah, I don't think even people living in California realize we have such things as wild boar and wild turkey."

Zande considered mentioning the sign posted near Highway 1's intersection with Rio Road that indicated a wild boar crossing, but decided against it. Hawth was likely correct in his statement, as even though the sign was there, it probably held no significance, as wild boar sightings along Highway 1 were rare. The wild pigs preferred to roam in the interior valleys.

"I shot a turkey this morning, if you wanted to stick around for dinner," Hawth offered.

"Thank you, Hawth, but I've got to meet someone later down on the coast."

Hawth glared at him momentarily and Zande could not discern if it was a friendly or slightly hostile glare. "Okay, next time, then," he finally said. "Speaking of wild pigs, though, I've got some sausage I can give you when you head out."

"Well, thanks, Hawth. That sounds great."

"Also about pigs, I wanted to let you know, just to get the word out to people like yourself, that I'm going to start taking people into the hills on boar hunting trips. I figure there are a bunch of rich dentists and doctors and lawyers around here for their little golf outings that may want to do something a little more dangerous with their time."

Zande considered Hawth's idea. It was, he had to admit, a good idea; however, he found it odd coming from Hawth, since as far as he knew, Hawth was in no need of money, as he lived cheaply and was sitting on a bountiful inheritance. Hawth could have perfect teeth if he wanted to, but Zande was certain that Hawth avoided any medical treatment and those who provide it. He was also certain of Hawth's disgust of most people, especially wealthy dentists, doctors, and lawyers. Hawth was looking intently at him, awaiting a response. "Well, it sounds like a good idea, Hawth, but …"

"*But what?*" Hawth quickly asked.

Zande considered how to respond in a way that would not come across as condescending. Hawth was undoubtedly smart, but Zande sometimes wondered if the combination of home schooling by idealistic and rebellious parents combined with living alone in such an isolated place had not taken its toll. "But I wouldn't have thought you would want to be around people like that all too much and such an activity would require you to spend a considerable amount of time with them."

Hawth looked skyward, deep in thought. "*Shit*, you're right ..." Zande felt one of Hawth's large hands pound his shoulder. "I'd probably end up shooting the dentists before I could get them to shoot at the pigs!" They both laughed.

"I really should focus on finding my treasure anyway," Hawth added as a distant expression covered his face and he looked off somewhere to the south.

Zande knew Hawth was referring to the legendary Indian treasure supposedly hidden in a cave on Pico Blanco Mountain, roughly ten miles south; some years earlier, Hawth had shared with him that it was his dream to find the treasure.

It was a tale as old as the settlement of Big Sur itself, with the first settlers trading stories that they learned from mission Indians in Carmel of a cave filled with gold somewhere on Pico Blanco. It was not difficult to imagine why the mountain had been held to be sacred by the tribes of the area, as it was one of the most distinguishable peaks in the Santa Lucia Mountains; Pico Blanco was the only mountain in the entire range that had a peak entirely cleared of vegetation and replaced by white limestone that in sunlight gleamed brilliantly, even from vantage points miles away.

Zande knew that Hawth made the twenty-plus round trip hike up and down the summit of Pico Blanco on a weekly basis. He kept a handmade map he had sketched of the mountain and each week he surveyed a different quadrant of his map. "According to the legend, that cave is up there somewhere, Hawth, and I can't think of a better man to find it than you," Zande commented.

Hawth turned away from the general direction of Pico Blanco, which was obscured from their vision by the tangled thick curving branches of a group of oak trees bordering the cleared area on Hawth's property. "Yup, one of these days I'm going to find it. But, of course, you wouldn't ever tell anyone about me being up there?" Hawth cast a suspicious look at Zande.

Zande quickly replied, "Oh, hell no, Hawth. What you do up there is your own business entirely."

Hawth approved of the response and a goofy grin returned to his face. "And you've still got your other hobby, I'm sure," Zande added, referring to Hawth's pastime of searching for pieces of jade along the

Big Sur shoreline that he would sell to a group of young locals, who would then sell the jade pieces on the internet. The pieces he found would demand exorbitant prices due to the rarity of finds of the semi-precious stone along the coast. Hawth didn't need the supplemental income, but the skill of being able to actually find the jade, which he had reputation of being able to do better than anyone else, provided some thrill for him.

"Yup, sure do," Hawth replied with beaming grin. "I only head down in the winter months when it's stormy and also 'cause that's when the tourists aren't around." Zande knew that by 'tourists,' Hawth meant anyone not from Big Sur, meaning that he spoke with contempt about people from Monterey as much as he did about people from Ohio.

"I'm told by my jade guys that some time back, some asshole from Kansas or somewhere posted some website about searching for jade in Big Sur and he had the balls to give people directions to some of the beaches I and others of us true Sur folk go to."

Although searching for jade in Big Sur had always been relatively unknown and safeguarded by a few, the California State Parks Department had designated a stretch of beach on the Big Sur coast as Jade Cove State Beach, sparking the interest of many tourists driving on Highway 1 passing through Big Sur. *Just another way for the State of California and the U.S. Federal Government to maintain its constant attempts to rape Big Sur of everything real and wonderful about the place,* Zande thought. Ironically, though, this particular action had directed Hawth to his Return the Sur to Big Sur group, and Hawth was a major contributor.

The thought of the incident stirred the thick blood of Hawthorne Williams and also jarred a new line of thinking that he wanted to share with Zande Allen.

"Say, Zande, you and your organization … you know all about this computer stuff, right?"

"Sure, Hawth. I use the internet to get the message out and keep in touch with members — those that don't get my personal visits, that is," Zande replied, returning a jab into Hawth's shoulder, although he was careful to punch Hawth less hard than Hawth had punched him.

"You think you could have someone trash that asshole's website in Kansas so it won't tell people about how to get to some of our secret jade beaches?"

Zande considered the request. It wouldn't be overly difficult or even expensive to pay a hacker to disrupt a personal website. The site was likely just of an amateur, anyway, posting with minimal, if any, security. And shutting it down would, after all, benefit the overall goal of Return the Sur to Big Sur. Considering things further, Hawth was also about to give him an envelope with up to twenty thousand dollars, which he had done on annual basis from Zande's first year of operation; it was good to keep Hawth pleased.

"Sure, Hawth. We can arrange for that to happen," Zande responded, receiving the biggest grin he believed he had ever seen sprout on Hawthorne Williams' face in response.

23.

Year of our Lord 2009.

ISIDRO DE LA VEGA STOPPED at Asilomar Beach on his way to Point Lobos to say hello to an old friend. Isidro had first met Sir Tom some years earlier at the Asilomar Conference Center. A national tourism association had organized a conference on how a strong tourism sector can boost a local economy. The ever-successful tourism industry on the Monterey Peninsula proved an excellent example, and the conference grounds was a superb setting.

The Monterey Historical Society was requested to participate and provide a representative to sit on a panel devoted to "preserving historical integrity while promoting tourism." When his time to present arrived, Isidro instantly caught the entire room's attention by stating that the panel had been incorrectly titled, and should have been "sustainable historical tourism."

At the time, Isidro was relatively new to presentations, but he proved to be a gifted presenter. He was relaxed, captivating and yet informative to an audience, without giving an impression of being nervous, boring, or self-absorbed. It was a far different side of him than the Isidro de la Vega on every other occasion, who was more prone to be awkward and tentative in the presence of other people.

The event was not open to the general public, but Sir Tom wandered in randomly, despite the distinct sign near the entrance of the large A-framed wooden conference hall announcing the conference, and without regard to being the only person in the audience not wearing a conference name tag. Sir Tom had been cutting through the Asilomar grounds on his way toward the beach to conduct his daily combing of the beach with his metal detector when the activity outside the entrance of the grand hall caught his attention and he simply walked in and had a seat with the rest of the crowd.

Isidro's fellow presenters, a woman from the Cannery Row Association and a gentleman from the Pebble Beach Company, both more than sufficiently defined how their respective associations were able to profit from historical elements, allowing funding to be available for historical preservation. Isidro, on the other hand, provided a different approach to the subject by suggesting that historical preservation had many faces.

After mentioning the huge financial success of Pebble Beach and Cannery Row, he alluded that too much development can do more harm than good in the name of seeking tourism dollars. Careful not to offend his co-panelist, Isidro mentioned that development along Cannery Row and Fisherman's Wharf had been allowed to perhaps develop a little too unhindered. With a snarling glance from the woman representing the Cannery Row Association, he quickly countered that perhaps too much preservation was to blame for the ultrapreserved yet sparingly viewed adobe houses of the Monterey State Park, which had houses and buildings located within walking distance from Fisherman's Wharf, and in spite of no entrance fees, knowledgeable staff, and pristine houses more than a hundred years old, received roughly ninety-five percent less visitors on an annual basis than Fisherman's Wharf or Cannery Row.

A look of bewilderment overwhelmed expressions throughout the hall, but it was Sir Tom, the man who was not even supposed to be in the audience, who broke protocol and interrupted Isidro, shouting out a question instead of waiting for the last ten minutes scheduled for a question and answer period.

"If nobody goes to Monterey's adobes, then they are better preserved, right?" Sir Tom called out.

The question didn't faze Isidro, who responded without pause. "There's more to preservation than just maintenance …"

"*Such as?*" Sir Tom blurted in response.

Isidro noticed heads then beginning to nod in agreement with the line of questioning arising from a voice in the audience. "Allow me to provide an example to illustrate my point. If we take a structure of historical significance, such as a two-hundred-year-old house that on top of its age played some role in our collective cultural history, and lock it up entirely, thereby restricting access to it completely … who would ever learn about it? How would the historical heritage of this particular structure then be passed on to our children?"

"Through books!" a new voice called from the audience.

Isidro smirked knowingly. *"Through books …"* He paused, considering the suggestion thoroughly. "Yes, I would agree that books are an intangible asset with regards to the passing along of historical knowledge to future generations." Isidro paused again, feigning conceding defeat, but then quickly added, "Unfortunately, books aren't as popular with children as they once were. Their imaginations have been hijacked by graphic video and computer games."

"Well, that's it! The *internet* is the answer. You could post the history of your old house and photos on the internet and then it'll be even more accessible to people." This time the answer had not emanated from the audience, but from his fellow panel member representing the Cannery Row Association seated at the other end of the table from him. The panel member, a fierce-looking woman wearing a red business suit that seemed entirely out of place for the usual informal Peninsula attire, leaned back in her chair and glared at Isidro, obviously pleased with herself.

Silence hung in the air of the large hall and everyone eagerly awaited Isidro's next words. "True, the internet is an extremely valuable tool to disseminate information, including information related to significant historical structures. And yes, one can easily post photos of a historical house, for example, on the internet for anyone and everyone to see, and then, in theory, this historical resource is just one click away.

"However, what books and even the internet cannot do is let one enter into one of our Monterey adobes and unmistakably notice as they step through the doorways how much shorter our not-so-distant ancestors of this region were; nor can a book or the internet make one feel how narrow and steep the wooden staircases to the second floor of these structure are; nor can a book or the internet allow one to notice as they walk through such houses that the floors were not always so even.

"Quite simply put, a book or the internet do not and cannot provide an opportunity, even if it is only a brief moment of recognition, to experience what life was truly like here on the Monterey Peninsula two hundred years ago. And if attendance and, quite frankly, appreciation of such historical gems is not prioritized, they will be lost and all people will ever remember of their visit to Monterey is a T-shirt from Cannery Row and a drive along 17-Mile Drive. People don't even walk away knowing that the name of '17-Mile Drive' originated from this being the round-trip distance to Pebble Beach from the former Hotel Del Monte."

Silence once again ensued. Not even the red-suited woman seemed to want to further entice him. The gentleman from the Pebble Beach Company stared directly ahead, not wishing to partake in any component of the ensuing argument. Sensing the awkward silence, Isidro concluded his diatribe. "My concluding point is that perhaps the most effective manner to teach and pass along a true appreciation for history is to allow an opportunity for people to experience it first-hand, even just a touch of it such as walking through a house."

Only one person in the audience clapped. The man stood up from his chair, continuing to clap, and slowly walked out of the hall. It was Sir Tom.

The moderator of the panel quickly intervened after Isidro's comments and announced that there would be no further questions. Isidro didn't bother attempting to reconcile with the red-suited woman and had little intention of trying to gain supporters in the crowd that gawked at him in disbelief as he shared his views on the topic. He made his way through the crowd of onlookers towards the doorway. Isidro noticed that people were not anxious to be polite and move aside, allowing him to pass.

When he emerged into the bright sunny day, he noticed the man who at first antagonized him and later clapped walking on the path through the dunes toward the beach, loosely carrying a metal detector in one hand. Isidro followed after him.

"Hello, sir. I'd like to talk to you if you have a minute," Isidro called to the man when he was within a few paces from him on the pathway.

The man turned with the backdrop of the ocean framing his profile. He was in his early sixties, Isidro assumed, with long silver hair pulled into a tight ponytail behind his head. He was shorter than Isidro, but not a short man by any means. The silver ponytail that on many other men his age in California indicated a former free love and acid-laced past somehow looked more dignified on the man in front of him. Sir Tom was no old hippie, but many would label him eccentric, as Isidro would soon come to learn.

"Well, you came after me to say something; now aren't you going to say something?" the man asked flatly.

"I just wanted to thank you for encouraging me to say what I really wanted to say. I went in there with the intent to say those things, but I wasn't sure I would be able to if the opportunity arose," Isidro responded.

"*As the wind shakes the barley*, you lack confidence in yourself, kid. Don't let people hold you back. God knows there are too many people these days going around gabbing all over the place that don't have a clue what they're talking about." With that, the man turned and returned to walking down the path towards the ocean.

Isidro ran after him. "I'm Isidro de la Vega," he said as he caught up alongside the man and offered his hand.

"I saw your placard on the table. Interesting name," the man commented without reaching for Isidro's hand and without slowing his pace. Isidro slowed to a stop and watched the man advance in front of him, feeling discouraged and bewildered. The man then suddenly turned and held out his hand, smiling widely. Isidro approached him and the two shook hands.

"Thomas Andrews; but I like to be called Tom and I like to be called *Sir Tom* even better." Sir Tom then abruptly withdrew his hand from Isidro's and returned on his way to the beach. "Come and see me on the beach some time, kid!" he called out loudly without turning around.

When driving along Sunset Drive, Isidro would often see Sir Tom's silver ponytail moving slowly along the beach and tidal pools; the same tidal pools that Doc Ricketts had scavenged for oceanic biologic samples for his laboratory and where the early residents of Pacific Grove had searched on a nightly basis, easily finding soccer ball-sized abalone and basketloads of mussels.

Sir Tom continued the tradition, but he wasn't searching for biological specimens or abalone. His search was far grander. He always told Isidro he was searching for *treasure*, as he had lost his own treasure.

Isidro eventually deciphered this cryptic riddle, configuring the connection between Sir Tom's lost treasure and his wife who had died.

Sir Tom kept the treasure he sought fairly tight-lipped as well, but with his thorough knowledge of historic events in the region, it did not take Isidro long to figure out Sir Tom's endeavors. Sir Tom was interested in finding historical artifacts that might wash ashore from the countless known and unknown shipwrecks off the coastline extending from Spanish Bay to Point Pinos. Sir Tom made it clear that he had no desire to profit from finding any actual treasure and that he would donate anything he found to the Monterey Historical Society. Isidro found him to be harmless, pleasant, interesting, and engaging.

"Hello there, young man," Sir Tom said aloud, without looking upward from his hunched position.

"Hello, Sir Tom. Do you have a gold Spanish coin from the 1700s down there?" Isidro asked.

Sir Tom laughed, rising from his knees to greet Isidro with a pile of sand in his hand, which he slowly released through his fingers. When the sand drained from his hand, a dime and two nickels remained in his palm. "Think that will cover my monthly electricity bill?" he asked, chuckling. He tossed the coins into a small basket he wore on his hip, set his metal detector down, and turned to begin walking along the beach, as he usually did after Isidro's arrival. Isidro learned quickly that this was Sir Tom's way of inviting him for a stroll.

"Do you think there's really more sitting out there waiting to be washed ashore?" Isidro gestured toward the ocean, and as he did, he noticed a surfer catching a wave off Asilomar Beach.

"As the wind shakes the barley, young man, there were many shipwrecks in these waters. With the passage of time, a lot has been lost by being washed ashore and then taken by soulless people who keep such things for themselves. But there's no way it's all come in.

The ocean has a way of keeping its secrets. If you listen closely, you can hear some of them at times."

You're right. There'll always be treasure out there to be found," Isidro said. His comment reminded Isidro of the mysterious letter he discovered at the San Antonio Mission. *What occurred nearly two hundred years ago that resulted in a priest committing such an act?*

Sir Tom suddenly stopped walking and turned to stare into Isidro's eyes. His gaze was serious, as serious as Isidro had ever seen it. "No, young man! Treasure is not just out there to be discovered," he replied, pointing out to the ocean. "It's everywhere to be found!" He whirled his hand around wildly in the air. "Even here," he said, jabbing a finger sternly into Isidro's chest. "And it's there, my boy, that's where you'll find the real treasure. When your heart finds the treasure that makes it whole."

A leap of intuitiveness was not required to understand that Sir Tom was referring to finding one's love. "I understand what you're saying; but I must say, it's unfamiliar territory for me," he abashedly admitted.

A moment of silent reflection between the two ensued as they ambled slowly along.

"As the wind shakes the barley, you will! You will one day, young man. I promise you that. There are some in this world that never are allowed to find true love, but I'll tell ya, those bastards don't deserve it!" Sir Tom shook an angry fist to the sky upwards. "But you, you, my boy; I can see the goodness and passion in your soul and I know that you will find true love, or that it will find you."

"How do you know?" Isidro asked, genuinely curious. He didn't so much mind his bachelorhood, but the thought of having a female love in his life was provocative.

"Ah, Sir Tom knows such things. I'm in tune with the universe, and, as the wind shakes the barley, I know things."

"So how would you recommend that I keep myself open enough?" Isidro paused, feeling slightly goofy about what he uttered next. "To … to 'the universe' in order for me to find my true love?"

Normally the subject would thoroughly embarrass Isidro, and if he were discussing it with anyone else, he would have changed the subject of conversation long before. But there was something about Sir Tom's sheer honestly and simplicity that made him comforting. "And why doesn't it happen?" Isidro asked.

Sir Tom came to a stop and turned to look directly at Isidro. "There's no point asking so many *whys* in life, young man. The sooner you learn that, the better off you will be. Now, listen to me; you just stay open to the universe and it will open itself to you. You will never know when this could happen, but you will know it when it does. WHAM!" Sir Tom loudly slapped his hands together to exemplify his point, causing Isidro to jump backwards. "It'll happen! And when it does, you can't let it slip away.

"One day you could be hiking and, as the wind shakes the barley, *it'll happen*. It could be raining and chilly morning and — WHAM!" Sir Tom loudly clapped his hands together, again startling Isidro. "All of a sudden you'll get a sensation that you really want to go hiking. You'll go hiking alone, trekking a trail on a dreary and cold day. You won't know why you're so eager to do it, you'll just feel a predisposition to do it, to be outside in the fog and cold and rain on the hiking trail by yourself. You won't know why, but you'll be doing it!"

The intensity in Sir Tom's voice grew steadily. "So you'll be there, hiking in this dreary weather *and you'll be loving it*! You'll be in your own world, connected to the universe. You'll be trekking along like you're a mountain goat, with a Siddhartha contented grin.

"Then — WHAM!" Sir Tom slapped his hands together again. "She'll be there."

"She'll be there when you take a turn, or you'll pass one another and the flash of her smile and glint of her eyes will startle you to initiate conversation. Or maybe she'll be seated on a log by herself, a gigantic fallen redwood among a whole thick grove of those towering noble giants, and a small creek will be gurgling nearby, and once you see her ..." Sir Tom paused, closing his eyes tightly for a moment while turning away, "... once you see her, you will know; you will know."

"After that point, as the wind shakes the barley, there'll be no going back."

Sir Tom slowed his pace and he inhaled deeply. "And if you lose that person, if you lose that person, my young friend, you'll want that to be the place where you go to die."

Isidro awoke as if from a dream, abruptly realizing he was walking alone. He turned around to see that Sir Tom had stopped walking some ten paces behind him. He returned and Sir Tom's hand clutched his shoulder. "When I know the time is right, I want to go back there. I know it's there that she'll be waiting for me," Sir Tom said to him softly, not bothering to wipe away the tears falling down his cheeks.

Sir Tom then abruptly returned to sweeping the sands of Asilomar with his metal detector.

Isidro didn't quite now what to think of Sir Tom's story, but he was glad to have heard it. As he walked to his car, he smelled the heady scent of cigar smoke just as he rounded a low sand dune extending from the raised wooden walkway that stretched across the entire length of the beach, connecting it to Spanish Bay.

24.

Year of our Lord 2009.

THE FAT CIGARS HAD A RICH aroma that blended faint traces of dried orange peels with subtle spice. They were the kind of cigars that lingered in your mouth for a day after smoking them, but unlike cheaper versions from places such as Panama, these were the *real deal,* grown and produced on the sun-drenched island of Cuba. Samuel P. Beckwith bought them from a friend who managed to acquire the little beauties through his business dealings in Central America. The cigars were top of the line, fit for a smoke by Fidel himself, although perhaps it would be a smoking experience from a hospital bed for him these days. It was like smoking money; it produced a sensation of tasting luxury in your mouth as you smoked them.

Samuel turned his head to glance at Victor Mathews, who looked entirely uncomfortable seated on the sand, as Samuel had insisted they do. "What do you think of the cigar, Victor?"

Victor squirmed a little before responding. "The cigar is lovely. But sitting here in the sand is going to ruin my slacks," he said as he fidgeted, brushing a few grains of sand off his pant leg.

Samuel passed him his gold-plated flask with his initials engraved on the front of it, prominently raised in large white gold lettering: SPB. Victor grabbed the flask absently and took a drink from it. It was cognac and Victor glanced at the flask as he swallowed, nodding in approval. "Wow, that's good stuff. I never thought cognac would taste so good from a flask."

Victor held the flask above his head as if toasting to heaven. "Just as you said it would, the *Stevenson Plan* is working out just as planned," Victor gleefully called out to the hazy sky above.

Samuel rammed a balled fist with as much might as he could muster into Victor's shoulder, which was followed by a sharp cry of pain from Victor. "Have you lost your goddamn mind?" Samuel said in a forced whisper before turning his head to look in every direction to see if anyone might have overhead Victor's ridiculous and ill-conceived outburst.

A hunched white-haired woman was walking a perfectly manicured poodle down the beach's wooden walkway; they were safely out of range of her hearing aid. A couple of young teenagers were wading in the shallow waters on shore in front of them, looking awkward as they held hands; the steady crashing of the waves around them would have blocked out everything else. A shaggy-haired hippie was throwing a tennis ball to a yellow Labrador along the beach not far from them. The canine enthusiastically dove into the water of the ocean to retrieve the tennis ball and return it to its master every time. Samuel figured the hippie would be too wacked-out to have understood the context of anything he might have overheard. A slightly crazy-looking old man with a silver ponytail was down the beach not far from them, but he had on a pair of earphones connected to the clunky metal detector he was sweeping over the sands of the beach.

Samuel thought he had heard someone walking behind them just moments before, but when he turned around, there was no one to be seen. When he was sure that there was not a soul present who could have overheard Victor's ill-timed remark, he turned back to confront him.

"That was idiotic, Victor," Samuel said menacingly.

"I know, I know. I'm sorry, Samuel. I just lost my head for a moment," Victor apologetically responded.

Samuel narrowed his vision on Victor. *He is my Number Two, after all, and if I didn't have him, I wouldn't have been able to pull off this thing.* "Ah, forget about it. Just keep your cool from now on, okay? I need you with me one hundred percent on this thing. Those other two — they're good guys and I believe in them, but I could get by without either of them; I can't finish this without you."

Samuel's comment made Victor blush. Even after his many outstanding accomplishments in life, he still adored a compliment of his talents as much as a ten-year-old receiving praise from his parents for bringing home a good report card.

At the same moment that Victor Mathews felt elation, Samuel Beckwith considered the context of the words he had just spoken. *If it comes to it, I could get by without the others, all of them,* he heard his own voice say inside of his head. He grabbed his flask from Victor and took a long swig of cognac from it while admiring the horizon; it was still blocked by a thick layer of dark fog hanging over the water.

"How about we get together for a round of golf this week?" Victor suggested.

"Sure, but I'll get us a tee time on my course," Samuel responded, referring to *his* golf course, the famed Cypress Point Club, which his grandfather had founded.

"Wonderful. Now let's finish that flask and get out of here; I feel like we are a couple of guys *slumming it* on this beach," Victor responded.

The Stevenson Plan, Isidro said to himself. He thought of how strange a reference he had overheard one of the very nicely dressed men exclaim as he had raised a very expensive looking gold flask into the air.

As he walked by behind them, Isidro noticed that the flask was engraved on the front with letters. The men were smoking fat cigars and looked out of place. He passed behind them by rounding a low sand dune and then climbing off the beach onto the wooden walkway that led back to the road. Isidro was not one to pry into the business of others, but something was altogether bizarre about the men seated on the beach in the midafternoon with their nice clothes, rotund cigars, and expensive flask.

He brushed aside the questions swirling in his head and dismissed them. It was time to play tour guide to this Gibson and his friend, who he was to momentarily be meeting outside of Point Lobos.

Part II

25.

Year of our Lord 1818.

THE CARMEL MISSION may as well have been on the other side of the continent they were treading upon, or so the caravan collectively viewed it as they continued northward across the dry lands of Alta California. The couple of days' reprieve they were awarded when they reached the Mission San Gabriel Arcangel was welcome, but Father Margil sensed that the general spirit of the convoy might have remained stronger if they had bypassed San Gabriel Arcangel and proceeded directly onward toward the Santa Barbara Mission. The stopover at San Gabriel Arcangel embedded relief in the souls of the caravan, soldiers and non-soldier alike; and Father Margil supposed most of them would have accepted an offer to remain at San Gabriel on a more permanent basis.

The prospect of reaching the Mission Santa Barbara after ninety miles on the trail was daunting; the prospect of the one hundred eighty miles afterward that remained to the Mission San Carlos Borromeo de Carmelo was beyond imagining. Father Margil took every opportunity he could to plant seeds in the minds of the caravan to begin viewing their trek in smaller segments rather than the entire route at once, his logic being that perhaps the route would be perceived as less grandiose.

Even Father Margil would admit, although only to himself and potentially Echevarria if the Captain inquired on his opinion, that the expanse of the trail between San Diego de Alcala and San Gabriel Arcangel was precarious. The route had been especially deceiving, as after the first few days of walking, majestic snow-capped mountains began to appear as noble towers around the deep valleys and basins they trailed across. This proved deceitful in the scrubby foothills of the mountains and the valley floors, as both areas were dry and filled with desert vegetation, yet the vision of the gleaming white snow around them allowed one to easily believe it would be an area ripe with freshwater streams and rivers. On the contrary, flowing water proved to be extremely sparse, so much so that members of the caravan began to curse the arid land out loud for being so misleading.

As the caravan ascended into a range of foothills at the base of larger mountains near the northern extent of the basin, which Father Margil remarked from his notes and maps indicated that the trail had nearly reached San Gabriel Arcangel, the Father turned to look backwards to the south across the wide basin the expedition had traversed. He wondered if people would ever attempt to settle such a place.

The friars at the Mission San Gabriel Arcangel assured those of the caravan that the next stretch of the trail to Santa Barbara would be more pleasant, as the sun and heat would no longer be so intense and the ground they would step upon would be softer than the hard, arid land they had already crossed. A cooling breeze would blow in from the ocean and there would be more fresh water available along the trail, they promised.

One man in particular began to become a concern to Father Margil. He was a Catalan named Diego Alvarez and Father Margil had increasingly noticed how the man held sway with the other soldiers. It was impossible for anyone to not hear the man, as words spewed from his mouth incessantly; even when Captain Echevarria ordered the man to be quiet, the man's mouth continued to whisper words. But it was the way that the other soldiers keenly honed in on whatever Alvarez would be saying that concerned Father Margil.

As for the man himself, something about him troubled Father Margil. Father Margil held himself to be a true man of God, and he believed there was good in the heart of every man; he also believed that there was no abolishing of wickedness and evil from the world of man, and try as he may, he could not suppress feeling the presence of darker forces whenever he was in the proximity of Diego Alvarez. The man attempted to approach Father Margil with conversation on numerous occasions, and each time, Father Margil noticed how undeniably he felt dishonesty and distrustfulness surrounding the man before him. When confronted on the subject of Alvarez, Captain Echevarria reluctantly conceded sharing concern for the man; however, the Captain assured Margil that he would be able to handle Alvarez and that despite the man's annoying banter, he was largely harmless.

Father Margil prayed that Captain Echevarria was correct in his assessment and prediction. The consequences of what might occur if Diego Alvarez discovered the true contents of the large trunk on the back of the wagon designated for affairs of the Church would surely be devastating. Father Margil prayed that if such an unfortunate situation did arise he would have the strength to do whatever was necessary.

26.

Year of our Lord 1818.

WILLIAM BECKWITH WAITED patiently for Isabella's arrival. He had fallen in love with her at first sight on the day of his arrival and knew that he could never leave Monterey. Beckwith was clever with his arrangements to be granted permission to stay in Monterey. He befriended John Cooper-Molera, and Cooper-Molera, taking an instant liking to the charming young lad, pleaded his case to Governor Fages.

In his interview with Governor Fages on behalf of Beckwith's cause, Cooper-Molera highlighted the young man's talents and capabilities by pointing out that Beckwith had managed to teach himself a considerable grasp of the Spanish language while on the long voyage between Boston and Monterey. Clearly, Cooper-Molera proclaimed, the young man was exceptional and would be a valuable asset in Monterey as a man of enterprise. Cooper-Molera knew this addition to his case for the acceptance of the lad would heighten the young man's favor in the mind of the governor, as the governor often complained of the gluttonous nature of the vast majority of Monterey's residents. They were more interested in indulging in eating and drinking and following such activities with dancing, rather than concerning themselves with how the food and drink had actually been delivered to their tables.

The assistance of John Cooper-Molera was unprecedented as William Beckwith attempted to assimilate himself into Monterey's specialized society. Not only had Cooper-Molera encouraged Fages' decision to allow Beckwith *informal* permission to stay in the settlement, but the man had further provided Beckwith on guidance with finding a home and employment. Cooper-Molera led him to a family who happened to have a spare room in their house that they would be willing to let to the young man, provided the young man was able to find employment. Cooper-Molera instantly satisfied this condition by stating his intention to hire the young Mr. Beckwith as his assistant in his trading and commercial enterprise.

In the span of one day, William Beckwith found the blessed fortune to be allowed to live in a Spanish Crown settlement, had a roof over his head, and had secured gainful employment. And considering the level of success that Cooper-Molera had achieved through his trading and commercial store operations in Monterey, his new position offered not only steady employment, but the opportunity to achieve some degree approaching that of a lucrative career.

As with all young men, William Beckwith's thoughts never veered too far away from thoughts of young ladies. Achieving any career success was for the most part viewed as the means to impress or, at least, satisfy the expectations of fair maidens who were hopeful future wives. William Beckwith was no different.

After being granted permission to remain in Monterey, William Beckwith spared little time in his courtship of Isabella. Remaining mindful of local customs, he again requested the advice of John Cooper-Molera.

Cooper-Molera was less than enthusiastic when Beckwith bluntly inserted the subject into a conversation, but he eventually agreed after sensing the young man's determination. At the time, they were discussing the need to ensure projecting what the residents of the settlement of Monterey might need or desire from merchants such as themselves.

"In order that we are able to provide goods that cannot be produced here, we must be able to consider future demand and indicate to the foreign vessels the sort of items we would like to see brought here for our consideration on future visits," John Cooper-Molera said prophetically as he sauntered through the storeroom of his general mercantile store surveying his current inventory.

"I'd like to court the governor's daughter," Beckwith interjected.

Cooper-Molera stopped his slow gait around the boxes of supplies labeled in Spanish, French, and English. He turned to face Beckwith.

"You wish to court the governor's daughter, Isabella Fages?"

"Yes, indeed I do," Beckwith sternly replied.

"Okay, I'll agree to assist you in this noble venture of yours, provided that you do all that I say and do nothing to disgrace me or dishonor the governor or his daughter. As you will soon come to learn, the people here are very concerned with the affairs of others, and these matters must be handled delicately. The fact that you are a foreigner, not of the proper faith, and that you are seeking the attention of the most sought-after maiden in all of Alta California would make your goal insurmountable in the minds of many. But your first order of business shall be to proclaim your interest in Isabella to the governor himself."

William Beckwith smiled inwardly as he remembered that day's conversation some months earlier. Cooper-Molera continued to be invaluable and provided as much guidance and insight as he could in the delicate affair of Beckwith pursuing the hand of Isabella Fages. The governor agreed to Beckwith's introduction to Isabella under the strict supervision of the governor himself.

Months later, seated in the governor's courtyard surrounded by fragrant flowering plants and small citrus trees, William Beckwith watched as Isabella Fages stepped out from the grand two-floor adobe house. Her eyes instantly met his and she managed to somehow stroll through the courtyard toward him without watching where she was walking, as if she were simply flowing through the air. He felt his heart warm at the very sight of her.

William Beckwith's initial intention was to settle in Monterey; it was now altered into a painfully strong desire to remain in Monterey with Isabella Fages as his wife.

27.

Year of our Lord 2009.

JOHN GIBSON WONDERED what Isidro de la Vega would look like. He had sounded like a polite young man on the phone, but he also sounded as if he could be pretentious.

Gibson turned at the mouth of Carmel Valley and drove south on Highway 1 as he had been instructed. He and Rachel passed a sign for the Carmel Mission and next drove by a sign indicating a curving road for the next seventy-five miles.

"Seventy-five miles of curving road?" Gibson commented. "Usually those signs indicate a dicey section of road ahead that is only a few miles ... *seventy-five* is a lot."

He added, "And Big Sur is down that way?"

"Yes, we'll have to head down there on our next trip since we're not going to have enough time this visit."

Gibson was thrilled to hear Rachel's comment. She made it clear that she fully intended that there would be future shared long weekends.

Rachel continued, "There's a road down there I remember driving on a long time ago that's referred to as the Old Coast Road, although officially it's only the Coast Road; before the construction of Highway 1, this narrow dirt road was the only way to access the Big Sur area."

"So this all happened at like the turn of the twentieth century or something, I take it?" Gibson asked.

"Nope, actually more like the 1940s and fifties, believe it or not. There's still some of the wild spirit remaining in its culture."

He pulled the car over to the side of the coastal highway adjacent to a large wooden sign stating "Point Lobos State Reserve" and turned off the ignition. Thin, tall pine trees surrounded them on both sides of the highway.

"Do you think he's here?" Rachel asked.

Gibson turned to glance at the line of cars parked on either side of the road behind them. "Most likely. This Isidro sounds like the impatient type."

Rachel laughed. "Well, he'd better have some patience. He's taking a couple of us old folks out for a hike."

"Who are you calling *old*?" Gibson jokingly asked.

Rachel burst into laughter, causing Gibson to laugh heartily as well. "What do you think he looks like? Do you think he'll recognize us?" Rachel probed as she regained composure.

"Detective Chiles arranged our meeting with him, and Chiles is extremely thorough about everything. I'm sure that he gave this guy Isidro a solid description of us."

"Well, how could Detective Chiles give an accurate description of *me*, considering I've never met him?" Rachel playfully wondered aloud. Gibson turned and smiled at her. "You have not met him, *yet*. I have no doubt that you shall soon after we return to the city. Aside from you, he's one of my closest acquaintances out here."

Just as Gibson finished his sentence, a navy-colored car pulled off the highway and parked in front of them. A dark-haired and handsome young man stepped out from the vehicle. He turned toward them and nodded in a polite manner. Gibson had no doubt that it was Isidro de la Vega.

Isidro took a few steps forward and held out a hand to Gibson, who had by then left their vehicle. "Hello, I'm Isidro," he said.

"Nice to meet you. I'm John and this is Rachel," Gibson replied as they shook hands, and he motioned towards Rachel, who Isidro then shook hands with.

"Well, David mentioned that you may be interested in a little tour of our Point Lobos," Isidro commented.

Direct … Gibson thought to himself. "We would love it," he answered, with Rachel agreeing with a smile. "We'd also like to take this opportunity to thank you for meeting us out …" Gibson realized that Isidro had already started walking towards the entrance to the reserve.

Gibson and Rachel shared a confused glance before Isidro turned and replied, "You're quite welcome. It'll be my pleasure. But let's get inside the reserve a little and away from this noisy highway before we begin." Isidro continued walking; Gibson and Rachel fell in line behind him.

They passed by an entrance station manned with a ranger charging fees from those who drove into the reserve. Isidro marched ahead of them on the paved road without pausing. The road then forked into two different directions; the two road segments were both lined with the same narrow-trunked pine trees along the highway. Gibson and Rachel once again shared an exchange of confused looks. Isidro walked ahead of them, displaying no indication of slowing his pace in order to walk alongside them. His gait was steady and deliberate.

"Isidro, why is it that you had us park outside the gates and then just walk past the entrance?" Rachel ventured to ask, hoping to instigate conversation.

Isidro turned and grinned slightly. "I apologize. I'm a bit lost today thinking about something else that has been bothering me lately. I don't mean to be rude."

"Oh no, no ... you're not being rude at all. I just was curious about the parking arrangement," Rachel promptly replied.

"Well, we can park outside of any state park and simply walk in without paying and then let all of the countless tourists pay the entrance fees."

Isidro's comment perplexed Rachel. Gibson felt her tension increase and was uncertain of what she would say next. Not being one to hold her tongue, she quickly asked, "But from what I've understood, you work in historical preservation. And, excuse me for asking, but isn't the preservation of nature the same thing? Meaning, shouldn't you want to promote people paying for the preservation of nature as much as them paying for the preservation of historical structures?"

Isidro did not appear in the least bothered by Rachel's direct confrontation. Instead, he slowed his pace, walking in stride next to them. "It's a valid question, I admit. However, like you, I pay state taxes; and I think that both historical and natural resources should be automatically preserved by the government and access provided free of charge."

"However, we can happily return to the vehicles, use more gasoline, pay the ten dollar entrance fee, drive into the reserve, increase congestion and traffic within it, and drive the distance that we would have walked otherwise." Isidro stopped talking and awaited their response.

This is one tough customer, John Gibson thought.

"Point Lobos was named by Spanish sailors as the *Punta de los Lobos Marinos*, which directly translated means the 'Point of the Sea Wolves.'"

"This could be derived from the barking sea lions congregating here, but I believe it is more likely named after the jagged coastline. The coastline of the entire reserve is impressively rugged. Considering the number of shipwrecks we know occurred off the coast here, it is easy to imagine that the Spanish contrived an elaborate name for a place that no doubt stirred some fear in them. The Spanish, after all, have a way of overembellishing names for things." Rachel thought she saw a small smile escape across Isidro's face, but if she did, it quickly disappeared and Isidro's stoic demeanor returned.

"Another elaborate yet not entirely unjustified title given to Point Lobos is 'The Greatest Meeting of Land and Water in the World.' I can also tell you that in the area across from the reserve's entrance, there was once a dairy that was the first producer of Monterey Jack cheese."

"*Monterey Jack* cheese, huh?" Gibson repeated.

"Yes, and don't worry — you're not the first person to not have previously made the connection," Isidro added.

"Point Lobos is significant to this region for a multitude of reasons," he continued.

"For instance, these tall, thin pine trees that grow so prolifically throughout the reserve are named Monterey pine. This species of tree grows all over the world; however, Monterey Bay is only one of four locations where this species of pine tree occurs natively. Once we head up the trail a bit, the Monterey pine forest will be interspersed with some

Monterey cypress trees, which have a similar story, yet this spot is the only spot, aside from across Carmel Bay in Pebble Beach, where the Monterey cypress occurs natively. They stand vigil on the perimeter of Monterey Bay looking like large elegant bonsai trees, but in reality, they are not delicate at all and instead display extreme dexterity against the near-incessant barrage of coastal wind and fog that pounds them throughout their existence."

Isidro paused in his presentation. He found it amusing that being fairly antisocial, he never had a problem with presenting. He turned his attention to the cove protected from the ocean by steep cliffs in front of them. "This is known as Whaler's Cove. I'm sure you can guess why it would have been given this name."

"I think we can figure that one out on our own," Rachel pointedly responded. Gibson wondered if her temperament was still running in high gear.

Isidro casually accepted Rachel's remark. "What is not so obvious is that this cove was a center for fishing activity from the moment the first foreigners arrived. Along with whalers originally from the East Coast of the U.S., this was also a favorite area for Japanese abalone fisherman. They used to skin dive or use primitive underwater suits to gather abalone on the seabed."

A group of four men in scuba gear emerged from underwater and swayed up the shoreline towards them. Once the men reached a parked pick-up truck, they removed their gear and set it in the bed of the truck. They peeled back the hoods of their black wetsuits and grinned at one another, already reminiscing about the experience they had just shared.

"As you can see, the area is still popular for underwater activities," Isidro added, gesturing toward the group of four divers.

Gibson remarked how the four men looked far from athletic, with round stomachs protruding from their waistlines that were not even concealed by the sleekness of their wetsuits.

"It's not the most difficult to dive, but the most difficult to be able to be granted permission to dive. Unlike other dive spots, in order to legally dive here at Point Lobos, one has to first obtain a permit from the State Parks Department. People will literally sit in front of their computers for hours, just waiting for the moment that State Parks releases availability."

"What makes it so special here?" Rachel asked.

Isidro took a deep breath and considered her question. "Well, there's such a mystique about diving here that it has been built up into something entirely different. It's not all that dissimilar to the thousands of people that pine to play on Pebble Beach's main golf course and are willing to pay thousands to do so."

"How do you mean?" Rachel quickly countered.

"What I meant to say is that while diving here at Point Lobos is reportedly spectacular, I have never heard that there is anything about it that is unequaled at other diving spots extending from Monterey to Big Sur. When conditions are clear and calm, diving in our pristine kelp forest is spectacular in numerous locations. This, from what I've been told, is similar to playing golf at the main course of Pebble Beach. Yes, it is a lovely course, but there are many, many other lovely golf courses in this area that are little known outside of Monterey County and have neither the price tag nor inflated demand."

Not a golfer ... that's surprising. I would have figured this stuffy guy for a golfer, Gibson thought. "So, where's the most difficult diving around here, then?" he asked aloud.

"That would likely be a beach that is, as a matter of fact, located just over that hillside of trees behind us," Isidro responded. "There's a beach over there called Monastery Beach, after the all-female monastery that is hidden from the highway in that direction. Due to the number of fatalities that have occurred at this place over the years, it's been given the more ominous name of 'Mortuary Beach.'"

"*Mortuary Beach.* That certainly sounds inviting," Rachel commented.

"From what I've been told, its perilous nature is due to a few factors, including a very steep beach that one has to literally crawl out of the water onto after the end of a dive when already fatigued, but the biggest danger may be its potential for strong currents. There is an underwater canyon that extends across the depths of Monterey Bay, a canyon that is deeper than the Grand Canyon, and a narrow sliver of it reaches right over to that point, creating a potential whirlpool of current activity."

"Deeper than the Grand Canyon?" Rachel asked.

"Quite a bit deeper, actually. That canyon is why many believe we have such a rich biodiversity of marine life," Isidro responded.

Gibson wanted to try and joke with the stern young man. "Maybe sea monsters live down in the canyon and they come up every once in a while to nab a diver or two," he said, smiling at Rachel.

"Actually, there have been numerous reports of people seeing mysterious sea creatures here. My particular favorite is described as a huge man-like creature with one bulbous central eye on its head that Monterey Bay fisherman of old called 'BoBo.'"

Isidro began walking up the trail leading into the pine forest. Gibson and Rachel heard the faint sound of a small laugh emanate from the direction of Isidro. He glanced back at them, a smile on his face. "Let's go to what I think is the most interesting area of Point Lobos." He turned and walked up the steady incline, and Gibson and Rachel followed.

They hiked up a moderately steep stretch of trail that led along the edge of an area of ocean surf a hundred feet below. The trees had grown thicker and created a full canopy overhead. The effect of endlessly hurling coastal winds upon the trees was apparent, as the trees' trunks and limbs were turned and distorted into apparition-like contortions. Gibson noticed the different pine trees now interspersed with the Monterey pine that Isidro mentioned were called Monterey cypress. Occasionally there were also large oak trees that had wildly contorted branches blending into the landscape as well.

"The uniqueness of Point Lobos has never been obscured from attention, and in the days before accurate maps, it's not difficult to imagine that this area would have been quite distinguishable along the coast if one were on a boat in the ocean looking coastward, and could be perceived as an island. It's really a small peninsula, and from sea one cannot easily discern its landfall connection. The fact that it's surrounded by the small hill-like rock outcroppings and this high, jagged ridge we're now treading upon only add to its appearance as an island separated from the surrounding land mass."

As they walked by a stand of gnarled and ancient looking Monterey cypress trees, Rachel ran her hand across the base of one that was covered in bright orange moss. Isidro commented that it was a form of lichen, which was not harmful to the trees; he agreed with her that it gave the trees a ghostly appearance.

Isidro pointed downward at a small beach that was protected from the pounding surf around it, as it was set back from a rock outcropping that made a formidable wall against the water. On the beach were the light-brown bodies of perhaps twenty harbor seals sunning themselves. As soon as they rounded the next bend, the sound made by the pounding waves a couple of hundred feet below, which managed to occasionally produce a salty mist, blended with the sound of barking sea lions.

Isidro came to a halt. "The appearance of an island combined with being very noticeable from the water must have made this an inviting destination to bury treasure here."

"You mean, as in *pirates*?" Gibson asked.

"There were some pirates active along the coast of California during the Spanish and later Mexican periods of California's history, and there are legends that some of them used Point Lobos as a hideout and that they buried treasure here."

"Anyway, the legend even continued into the American period with new rumors of Point Lobos being used for buried treasure from bank robberies by the region's most notorious bandits in the days of the Wild West; then Point Lobos was supposedly used to bury stashes of liquor during Prohibition.

"Thus, as you can see, Point Lobos has had a long history of being labeled as one of those 'X's' on old treasure maps and always has been regarded as a Treasure Island."

A particularly large crash of waves erupted against the shore below them. "As any tour guidebook will inform you, the author Robert Louis Stevenson, or 'RLS' as he's referred to often here, lived for a brief period in Monterey.

"I must admit though, as a historian, I'm frankly annoyed by how much attention is given to the mere matter of a few months of an author living in Monterey. From the amount of attention that visit receives, one would think that RLS was born, raised, and died here."

"But for the purposes of my tour with you today, though, RLS needs to be discussed. You see, I and many others believe that Point Lobos provided the inspiration for *Treasure Island*."

"Wait, I remember reading that Stevenson modeled his Treasure Island after some island in the Caribbean he visited," Rachel commented.

"Yes, that is one view. Others think that the island could have been modeled after one off the coast of Stevenson's native Scotland. Stevenson never indicated his inspiration, but if you ever read that story, I think you'll find it remarkable how many similarities there are between Point Lobos and the island in the tale.

"For example, Stevenson's notes on his visit here remark on his fascination with the twisted and gnarled trunks and branches of our cypress and coast live oak trees. It's undeniable that such trees are described on his Treasure Island. He details that the trees are stretched crooked horizontally along the ground, like bony skeletal arms reaching upward from the earth.

"Stevenson himself succumbed to the legend of Point Lobos being a place of buried treasure. It is well known that at the time of his visit to Monterey, the future famous author was near-penniless, and it was reported by various sources that Stevenson took up his hand at digging for treasure on Point Lobos. Even though I easily grow weary of the overindulgence in the use of Stevenson's name, I find it very probable that the often fog-enclosed Point Lobos provided a perfect backdrop for the mysterious island in his story."

Isidro turned and continued walking upwards along the trail before stopping. When Rachel and Gibson arrived behind him, they realized why he had stopped. They were on the *point* of Point Lobos, the farthest edge of land extending into the rough ocean waters below. To their right extended the Monterey Peninsula, with the manicured fairways of the Pebble Beach golf course gleaming in front of castle-sized houses set amongst the dark green backdrop of the Del Monte Forest encompassing them, followed by the inlet of Carmel Bay with its own heralded beach adorned with cute cottage houses leading into a line of hills that extended into Carmel Valley. To their immediate left were the spectacularly steep cliff sides of Carmel Highlands rising abruptly from the pounding surf, with houses sited dangerously close to the ledges of the cliffs and a jagged coastline of mountainous peaks seemingly sprouting directly from the ocean's edge extending the entire horizon southward. In front of them, the vastness of the Pacific Ocean captured one's view with a gray line of fog miles off over the water, just waiting for the chance to overtake the coast once again.

The ghost-like shapes of the wind-sculpted cypress trees thickly surrounded them, and for a moment Rachel felt a strange sensation. She moved forward slightly and nudged a small rock over the cliff with her foot and watched the stone descend downward and disappear into the tumultuous whirlpool hundreds of feet below them.

"Incredible. I have to admit, this is quite an amazing meeting of land and water," Gibson remarked.

"Yes, it is," Rachel added, moving closer to him to feel his warmth. "Something feels spooky about this place, though. Even these trees remind me of scary trees that come alive in children's stories," she observed in a voice quiet enough that she hoped Isidro would not overhear.

"There have been more shipwrecks right out there than anywhere else along this coast," Isidro said, speaking loudly over the sound of the crashing waves. "Although I've never heard of the trees *coming alive*," he added, grinning. "Shall we move on?"

Once they descended from the hillside, they were in a small meadow. Isidro mentioned that in order to do an entire walking loop of the reserve, they would need another hour and that he did not have time for it. He assured them, however, that they had seen the most exhilarating aspects of the place.

Gibson remarked on the reserve's beauty and uniqueness and thanked Isidro for his time. Rachel agreed. She then asked, "I was wondering," as they returned to a paved roadway, which Isidro said would lead them to the park's entrance, "being a representative for this area, what do think of its overall image?"

Isidro smirked knowingly in response to Rachel's question and continued for a few paces without responding, unable to conceal his eagerness. Gibson and Rachel both noticed the reaction and were pleased that the young man's personality was perhaps not so stern. "I'm actually glad you asked that question, as it concerns something I've been grappling with for many years and has been a topic of presentations I've given. An article recently published in a major U.S. travel magazine included the City of Monterey as one of the top twenty 'prettiest cities' in the U.S."

"Well, that doesn't sound like such a negative distinction," Rachel responded.

"No, indeed, it's not. This list of twenty included other desirable locations such as Savannah, Sedona, and Jackson, Wyoming," Isidro quickly replied. "But there were two things in particular that disturbed me about Monterey's inclusion. The first was the photo and the second was the description."

"It sounds like, in your opinion, they only got the name right." Gibson laughed a little at his own joke. Rachel smiled. Isidro did not.

"I would even take issue with that. I think that due to the historical and geographical connection of all of the little sub-areas here: Monterey, Pacific Grove, Pebble Beach, Carmel-by-the-Sea, Carmel Valley, Carmel Highlands, and Big Sur, one has to take into account Monterey's entire surrounding area; although, of course, each of these places has their unique identities at the same time."

Gibson thought about commenting on how Isidro had just vastly contradicted himself, but decided to let him continue undeterred. He was sounding passionate about his subject again, after all.

"But that's a separate issue. In direct reference to the photo and caption included for Monterey, the photo was of a line of homes, a delightful blend of Victorian style houses alongside one-story former fishing cabins that over time were converted into houses, along an inlet of a rocky coastline with mounds of thick kelp floating in the waters closely offshore," Isidro continued.

"That sounds lovely," Rachel offered. "Of course, if the editors of the magazine were only including one photo shot for each location, they had to pick one of many and I'm sure they would admit that there are few locations where one sole photo is able to provide a comprehensive depiction. from the way you've been talking, I would have thought that you would be pleased that a photo of Cannery Row or Fisherman's Wharf was not included for the Monterey insert."

"In theory, I was impressed with the inclusion of the photo, as I would have indeed expected it to be of one of those two places."

"So what was the problem?" Gibson asked. A squawking group of birds passed over their heads.

"The problem was that the photo was not of Monterey, but of Pacific Grove," Isidro gravely responded.

"How's that?" Gibson asked.

"Well, the limits of Monterey actually stop just after one passes the aquarium, and the photo is clearly of the PG coastline along Ocean View Boulevard."

Rachel recalled having driven earlier that day by the area Isidro referred to. "I can see why you may be annoyed by the misleading photo, Isidro, but I would think you would still be pleased that a nice shot of a location such as that was included."

Isidro remained silent for a moment, letting his eyes fall to watch each step he took. The pine forest on either side of the road was so thick with a dense layer of scrub underbrush that a wall was formed on either side of them. "Yes, I'll concede that it was nice that they did not have a photo of Cannery Row." Rachel felt a rush of pride at the thought of having won a debate with the stubborn young man. "*But*, I stand firm in that it's not a good shot to include in the first place, given the history of the area in the shot."

Rachel winced. "I've always thought of Pacific Grove as a quiet, peaceful, beautiful place on the edge of the Peninsula."

Isidro huffed condescendingly. "Sure, it's a quiet and peaceful place with a quaint downtown, a picturesque coastline, lots of trees, and more butterflies at times than most will ever see anywhere else. It's a place that was founded as a puritanical religious retreat, and it could be argued that it's remained the same after all these years. Its downtown turns out its lights early nightly, and not long ago, a law remained in place ordering that curtains on houses be drawn closed in evenings. For many years, long after its founding, a thick fence with a locked gate surrounded the limits of Pacific Grove, and entrance into it was strictly monitored. It's frankly no surprise it was the last dry city in the state, and to this day, you will not find a bar in its limits that is not merely an appendage of a restaurant; not that I care one way or another, but I do question the city's line on its distinction between church and state. Especially, *especially* considering the event that occurred in the very area where that photo was taken."

Isidro paused for dramatic effect as he often used as a tactic in his presentations. "Well?" Gibson asked.

"*Well*, in that area once stood one of this region's most colorful neighborhoods. It was our Chinatown and it provided a gem of diversity at a time when the area was quickly becoming dominated with Italian and Sicilian immigrants." Isidro could feel he was wavering away from his specified topic once again and quickly scolded himself to return to the subject at hand.

"It was actually a separate village unto its own, in fact comprised of perhaps a hundred families that constructed tiny wooden one-room houses along the shoreline and on piers that extended out over the water. It was unique and self-sufficient and did nothing but provide a fresh seafood market to its white neighbors in Monterey and Pacific Grove. There are stories of curious Monterey and PG residents going there during Chinese New Year festivities, when the place would be alight with exotic fireworks. Onlookers visiting the area would remember boiling pots of rice on outdoor stoves and sweet-smelling incense burners hanging from the wooden rafters on the porches of the shacks. However, with time and with the expansion of Pacific Grove, the village came to be viewed as a blight on the landscape. These were *heathens* living right next to the good PG Christians!"

Rachel and Gibson shared a sly look of amusement. It was by far the most animation they had yet witnessed from Isidro de la Vega.

Isidro sensed their light mockery of him. He paused momentarily in his diatribe to calm himself. As for their fun at his expense, he did not mind. Isidro had never minded what others thought of him. "So, we have these strange darker-skinned people who looked and acted differently and even spoke their own languages most of the time living right next door to the Peninsula's resident Puritans. It was these people, the very people who took delight in the sideshow qualities of the fishing village and frequented its fish market, who eventually burned the village of their peaceful neighbors to the ground, and in the ensuing cleanup, the Pacific Grove administrators were able to ensure that no new fishing village would sprout up again in the same location.

"The residents of the former fishing village moved on, undoubtedly sensing that they were no longer welcome. With that, a colorful piece of this area's history was neatly wiped away. The shame of that event still haunts Pacific Grove.

"There is an annual 'Festival of Lanterns' in PG that is supposed to be a tribute to the former Chinese fishing village." Isidro looked to his right and saw that although the two were still following his explanation, they looked lost with his mentioning of the festival and its applicability to the former fishing village. "You see, the Chinese fisherman loved to fish for squid, and the best time to fish for squid is at night. In order to attract the squid towards a boat, lights are used to lure them closer, and in those days, the lights consisted of candle lanterns, which the PG residents would see at night out on the bay. Thus, they came to associate the lanterns on the water with the fishing village. Even these days, when limited squid fishing is allowed off the coast, the waters are filled with boats casting huge sets of lights down at the water. It's so bright it looks like a Christmas tree out there."

"Wait, back up a bit." Gibson shook his head in confusion. "Was it actually proven that Pacific Grove, or PG, as you referred to it, had anything to do with the fire? Or that anyone from PG even started it?"

"Well I don't believe that the FBI was put on the case or anything," Isidro pointedly remarked, causing Rachel to smile and Gibson to sneer, "but I think there's enough certainty for it to be very safely assumed that PG was behind the fire.

"The people of PG, as much as they may have enjoyed the curiosity of the nearby fishing village and its fish market, also secretly, and then not so secretly, loathed it. But destroying a village and potentially killing innocent people seems a bit extreme. And in my view, PG's curse is that by throwing this festival every year, the scab on its past will never be healed, as the festival will continue to ironically serve as a reminder."

Gibson noticed that they were nearing the entrance to the park. "You'd better get to that second part of your argument about why you didn't like the article."

"Yes, I should move on," Isidro conceded. "My second problem was with the caption beneath the photo. Even though I mentioned how I was impressed that the photo was not of Cannery Row, the caption focused on it, including references to the Monterey Aquarium and Fisherman's Wharf. Of course, as a Monterey County historian, I was, and always am, miffed when a description of Monterey's attractions fails to mention our fantastically preserved historic adobes, or even that Monterey was the first capital of California and for many years, but this even goes further into the heart of what visitors leave here thinking of Monterey."

"You're going to have to explain that one a little further," Gibson commented.

"I figured that I may need to." Isidro took a deep breath and considered how to convey a subject in the span of minutes that would normally take him at least an hour. "I'm talking about the overall image of Monterey; the image that others receive and take with them when they visit here and the image that even the people who live in this area hold for the very place they live. I say this *area*, as, in my opinion, Monterey is a symbolized center of its surrounding environs. I try not to talk about one without the other, as Monterey and its vicinity are so interconnected.

"Monterey, as many other places in California, especially on the coast, gets often lumped into the images of southern California beaches with bathing suits and glowing tans galore. I distinctly remember one particular time when a group had been shuttled to shore from a cruise ship docked in the bay, which happens occasionally, and they had left the cruise ship in sunshine, mistakenly believing that it was hot enough to walk around Monterey in shorts, sandals, and bikini tops. I took the group on a tour and I don't believe I've ever witnessed such agony ... the people were practically frozen."

"So, are you saying you don't like the weather here?" Rachel asked.

"Not at all. Much to the contrary, I love it. Except for a temporary period of my life, it's all I've ever known and I wouldn't want it any other way.

"I'll conclude by saying that there's much more to the Monterey Peninsula than what one will see in a weekend."

After they thanked Isidro again for his time, Rachel and Gibson watched the young man drive away, not quite sure what to think of him.

28.

Year of our Lord 1818.

GOVERNOR PEDRO FAGES' conversation with Father Junipero Serra the evening of the fandango solidified his belief that there was nothing more he could do but await one of two things: either the Russian would return before the gold arrived and all would be lost, as he would then return with gunships and soldiers and easily overrun their meager defenses, or the expedition with the priest would arrive before the Russian's return and all would be saved.

Governor Fages and Father Serra did not agree often, but on the opinion that if not appeased, the Russian would be a catalyst to disaster in Alta California, they did. The threat of Bouchard remained, slyly hiding underneath the fabric of their conversation regarding the Russian, but Serra's reluctance to discuss the issue of its eventuality and outcome confirmed Fages' suspicion that Father Serra shared his apprehension. It was possible the reinforcing contingent of troops arriving in the convoy would sufficiently boost the reserves in Monterey to repel any attack, but nothing was certain.

As soon as the expedition arrived, Serra would deliver the gold to Fages, the Father assured the governor. With little else to discuss, Serra politely took his leave from the fiesta to return to his mission.

At that point, night had fallen like a thick blanket. The only illumination came from the lanterns surrounding Cooper-Molera's courtyard. Governor Fages offered Serra lodgings in his own house for the evening as a courtesy, as the road over the hill could be treacherous in the dark. Father Serra laughed at his suggestion, saying that the Lord would protect him from the hill's infamous evil spirits. Father Serra rose from the table and walked directly through the space that had been cleared for dancing, not minding or not realizing that he disrupted couples dancing to the lively music the musicians were playing. Governor Fages grinned to himself. He felt connected to the stubborn old man of the cloth, even if they were locked in perpetual disagreement on most topics.

With Father Serra departed, Governor Fages' thoughts turned to a different matter. During his conversation with Serra, he could not help but notice Isabella and Beckwith dancing. Fages mentioned to John Cooper-Molera that he wished to speak with the young Beckwith.

William Beckwith approached him graciously, performing a ceremonial bow in front of the governor. "My dear sir, I wish you good evening," Beckwith unhurriedly said in impeccable Spanish.

Fages laughed at the young man's determination. "My, your Spanish has quite improved."

"Thank you, sir."

"I am pleased that you have managed to assimilate yourself so thoroughly and so quickly into our society here in Monterey."

"It is a spectacular place, sir. I desire to be nowhere else. Monterey's greatness is no doubt largely attributable to its great governor."

"There's no need for such ornamental language, young man. Cooper-Molera holds you in high regard, and as he is one of my most trusted advisors, I shall grant you the same consideration."

Fages watched as the effect of his words took hold on William Beckwith. His Spanish was commendable, but it was obvious that he still had further comfort to achieve with it. At times, it took a moment for the young man to consider his words before he spoke or to reflect on what he heard before fully comprehending. The comprehension of Fages' words was unmistakable, though, as he witnessed the young man smiling widely. He once again bowed in front of the governor. "Sir, I thank you for your confidence. I assure you that I will conduct myself with poise and honor and shall live up to my expectations."

Governor Fages grinned at the eager young man in front of him. "I have no doubt that you shall, my young man." Fages' attention was distracted by the sight of Isabella crossing in front of the musicians in her long red dress, which he had bought for her from a French trader.

"I know you seek the hand of my daughter, but such things must be done in accordance with tradition, even here in the New World."

"Yes, sir. I understand," Beckwith obediently responded.

"And if you are successful in your efforts, I hope you are aware that you must renounce your Protestant faith and be baptized a Catholic. There is no other choice if you wish to marry here. Cooper-Molera is a prime example."

"I was born into a Protestant family, sir, without having the choice to decide between a form of Christianity. If I must convert to being a Catholic, I shall do so with no reservations."

Fages commented to himself on the quick mind of the young man seeking his only daughter's hand in marriage. He may not have been his first choice for his daughter, but he certainly would not have been his last, either. "Very good. Continue with your full integration into our society here."

William Beckwith was unable to contain his excitement, and the smile on his face grew even wider.

"However, be mindful of our traditions and do not betray my trust in you," Governor Fages added firmly.

"I shall not betray your trust, sir. Thank you for your confidence." William Beckwith backed away, correctly sensing that the governor had spent enough time with him for the moment. Turning to walk away, Governor Fages was sure that Beckwith's expression conveyed a positive message, as Isabella gleamed in response and the two met in the dancing area. The two did indeed make a handsome couple.

29.

Year of our Lord 1818.

THE GENTLE DAYS OF RELAXATION at the Santa Barbara Mission faded from the shared memory and sentiment of the convoy as quickly as they had appeared a week earlier. The previous stretches of the Mission Trail on their route had been broken into segments of ninety miles between each mission. The next length of the trail, however, the distance between the Mission Santa Barbara and the Mission San Antonio de Padua, was one hundred twenty miles. This was attributable to both the increasingly thin resources of the Church and the fact that there had been little interest in establishing settlements in the expanse between Santa Barbara and San Antonio.

Although it was well-established, there was also the perception that during this stretch of the trail, somehow one felt farther from the ocean than on the other sections of the trail, as the ocean was never in sight.

These considerations weighed heavily upon Father Margil's heart. Santa Barbara had been quite agreeable. The friars running the mission were kind-hearted souls and the converted mission neophytes were equally gentle people. The days had been warm and full of bright sunshine. And the stunning setting of the location itself, a wide sweeping inlet with a towering plateau starting to rise from the moment the ocean touched the land, was of unparalleled beauty; Father Margil believed it possibly the most visually pleasing landscape he had ever encountered. "Very fortunate people will inhabit this place in future years," he joked with the residing friars.

It was not long, though, once the caravan was again en route, that the good spirit he had encountered while in Santa Barbara was overcome with an overriding sense of growing despair. The good people of the group quickly appeared more disillusioned than they had ever before, cursing out loud when they accidentally kicked a rock that stung their feet. They spoke their blasphemies in attempted hushed voices, but they were not muffled enough, as anyone within their general vicinity would hear their sinful mutterings. This bothered Father Margil greatly. If he lost the faith of the people, there would be no one left if the soldiers lost their determination as well. And the soldiers — the soldiers worried him more than the settlers.

One among them, Diego Alvarez, had become dreadfully worrisome, as he began to pace around the wagon designated for Church items, which held the chest of gold for the Russian, whenever the convoy came to a stop for a brief rest. As he would do so, he would keep his eyes on Father Margil, as if searching for a change in the Father's expression that would reveal something to him. Father Margil resented what had occurred in Santa Barbara with the man.

The night before the convoy's return to its journey on the Mission Trail, as provisions were being loaded onto wagons and preparations for the next stretch of one hundred twenty miles were being made, two crates fell from the Church's wagon, temporarily revealing the location of the wooden chest containing the gold destined for Monterey and destined to save Alta California. As fate, *ill-fated* as it may have been, would have it, just as the crates fell, Alvarez was strolling by the wagon.

Father Margil assumed that Alvarez was drunk at the time, as the man was swaying and openly ogling any female in sight, and thus he did not initially allow himself to be suspicious that Alvarez had noticed anything. At the time, Father Margil hurriedly instructed a pair of converted natives of the mission to return the crates to the top of the wagon and resecure them with ropes. Alvarez, however, turned out to be cleverer than Father Margil imagined him. From that moment onward, Father Margil noticed Alvarez circle the Church's wagon at every opportunity. Margil even considered that Alvarez had only made himself appear inebriated in order to be allowed to approach close to the wagon that Father Margil ensured was guarded day and night.

The clever, sly swine, Father Margil remarked to himself as he watched Alvarez once again slink his way around the wagon. As Alvarez completed his tour of the wagon, the man caught Father Margil's glance. Alvarez puckered his lips at him as he spoke softly to himself and returned to wading through the group of seated soldiers, spewing forth his snakelike words as he wound his way between them.

On the fourth day after having departed from the Mission Santa Barbara, an unmistakable feeling of rising revolt reverberated amongst the convoy. The day began with a broken wagon wheel, followed by the sudden death of one of the horses. To both settlers and soldiers, the latter fueled by the incessant rebellious chatter of Diego Alvarez, the two events, combined with the daunting task of the trail remaining ahead of them, equaled testament that they were destined to travel no further and must return to Santa Barbara. Father Margil attempted to appease all by repeatedly stating that after Santa Barbara, they had accomplished half of the trail to Monterey and were now well into the final stretch of their journey. His words fell on deaf and uncooperative ears.

Diego Alvarez pounced on the opportunity of perceived disorder by hopping onto the wheel of one of the wagons so that he could stand above the entire expedition. "Good people, hear me! Why do we continue onward towards what is surely our deaths, when we could return to the beautiful coast of Santa Barbara if we desire? All that awaits us on this road is death and deprivation, I assure you. We do not need to listen to this Father or this Captain," Alvarez said, pointing towards Father Margil. As he turned to look for Captain Echevarria, he was struck by the flat side of an iron sword across his face. The SMACK echoed loudly in the still air as Alvarez tumbled from his perched spot upon the wagon wheel and fell face first on the hard ground beneath him. He looked upward, his face covered in dust, to see the profile of Captain Echevarria mounted on his horse staring down at him.

"Move but an inch, and I'll not use the broad side of my sword with my next swing at you, Alvarez," the Captain threatened from above.

Diego Alvarez did not move. Captain Echevarria ordered Alvarez put in chains, but as they did not have the iron shackles with them normally placed on prisoners, a knot of rope had to suffice for Alvarez's bindings. The Captain called for a period of rest to allow a settling of tensions. He also insisted on having a side discussion with Father Margil. The Captain descended from his horse, and the two men walked slightly ahead of the group, just out of hearing range, but not too far to not notice any potential unrest that might rise in their absence.

"We're losing them," Captain Echevarria said with panic clear in his voice.

Father Margil resisted an urge to respond sarcastically by saying that he was well aware of the situation. "Yes, I'm afraid our people, both the settlers and your soldiers, seem to have succumbed to a significant loss of faith," he replied, shaking his head despairingly.

"We can't lose control. There must be something we can do," the Captain said bravely. He turned to gaze towards the horizon north of them, where a line of mountainous ridges formed a barricade dropped on the land. "I know from the maps that we are meant to follow the trail that direction," he said as he pointed towards the northeast, where there appeared to be a faint break in the mountains through a narrow valley. He estimated the break to be at least forty miles away, another two days' march if they were lucky. Considering the battered condition of the convoy and the consensual undertone of disillusionment stirring through all, he calculated that the break was more realistically four days ahead.

Captain Echevarria's stare turned westward so that he was facing directly north. There was no perceivable break in the line of the mountains in this direction, but the ridges were much closer than eastward. An idea sprouted in his mind. "What if we were to march directly north instead of following the trail to the northeast?"

Up until that moment, Father Margil's eyes had been fixated on the dry pebble-strewn ground at his feet. The Captain's words startled him, as if being awakened from a deep sleep. He hoped he would raise his gaze to witness a flippant look on the face of Captain Echevarria. To his dismay, he did not. The Captain appeared more self-assured and confident than ever. "Are you mad?" Margil commented.

The Captain snapped his head sideways in order to pierce his determined eyes into Father Margil's. "What would you have us do? I just quelled a mutiny back there! I can assure you, if such a spirit arises once, it is sure to return. And I frankly don't see spirit left in these people. If we are to accomplish our mission, then we must consider an alternative!"

Our mission. The words struck Father Margil with the force of the mighty waves he had seen pounding the coastline of Alta California at times. Captain Echevarria was more correct in his proclamation than he could have ever known. And it was true that if he was to fulfill his duty, he needed to reach Monterey with the gold with all haste. A return to the Mission Santa Barbara in order to regroup for a new expedition to Monterey would delay the gold's delivery too long and was therefore not an option. For as ill-conceived as the Captain's plan presented itself, Father Margil could not deflect the reasons behind its creation, rash as they may have been. He realized that he had to think quickly. He tried to remember all that he had heard in the stories the friars of his order shared regarding the trek through Alta California. Gradually, he began to convince himself that such an endeavor might be feasible.

Captain Echevarria stood at attention, awaiting the Father's next words. "It may be possible. I remember from viewing maps of the Mission Trail that north of the Mission Santa Barbara the trail turns slightly eastward in order to remain in flat valleys and avoid transecting the even more rugged terrain of those coastal mountains." Father Margil paused to wipe away dripping sweat from his brow. "But the distance to the Mission San Antonio would be closer if we were able to circumvent those mountains. In this regard, you are correct, my Captain," Father Margil concluded.

"You mean to imply that I am incorrect in another regard?" the Captain eagerly inquired. Father Margil noticed that the Captain's prior mounting tension had diminished rather profusely.

"I do not mean to imply that you are incorrect, sir, only to state that I do not believe you can possibly know what we shall lead our followers into if we take that route."

"*Do you?*" Captain Echevarria asked after a moment's reflection and another glance at the mountains north of them.

Father Margil's eyes wandered over the convoy, soldiers, settlers, horses, and wagons alike. His glance temporarily fell on Diego Alvarez. There were tales from the neophytes of the Mission San Antonio that claimed evil spirits lived in the shadows of those mountains.

Father Margil could have shared this with Captain Echevarria, but with his eyes fixated on the despicable creature that was Diego Alvarez, he simply replied, *"No."*

30.

Year of our Lord 2009.

CHRIS WALKER and his wife Liz were seated at the restaurant's darkly lit bar, which was tucked against the far wall of the crammed room with little regard to aesthetic appeal. Isidro assumed that the apparent lack of interest in the restaurant's general appearance was of no major concern to the owners, and that they relied on the setting and view of the restaurant itself to be its principal selling point. The restaurant, the Sandbar & Grill, which promoted itself as "like dining on a yacht," was known on the Peninsula for having a spectacular setting, offering superb sand dabs, and being a place mostly undiscovered by tourists and amateurs, very much contrary to the restaurants found on Fisherman's Wharf just across Monterey's small marina. The "Sandbar," as locals called it, was set below the municipal pier, often referred to as Monterey's *working wharf*, so that the tables were quite literally directly above the waters of Monterey Bay with seating on a level with the foundations of the pier.

Above the restaurant, at the end of the pier, stood the last remaining vestige of the once vibrant Monterey fishing industry. Isidro often thought of the small grouping of warehouses at the end of the pier as a tombstone. The buildings that had at one time been filled with activity were now nearly vacant, with unloading equipment that had been used to transfer the catch of individual boats scattered about and rusting.

Next to the pier was Monterey's marina, resulting in a boat-level view of docked sailboats and fishing vessels across a narrow channel in front of it. The view from the restaurant consisted of the boats and the pine hills of Monterey sprouting above them.

Chris and Liz loved the Sandbar and would meet Isidro there for dinner, always hoping that Isidro would bring along a date. Isidro often commented that in the Sandbar, it was easy to image being in a different place from Monterey altogether. Chris often countered by stating that after enough of the notoriously stiff Long Island iced teas that the weathered bartender served at the Sandbar, it was easy to imagine being anywhere. This statement would then typically instigate Liz to add that she would be driving home that evening.

Isidro looked beyond the marina and Fisherman's Wharf as he approached the restaurant and saw the familiar "double horizon" that often appeared off the coast of the Peninsula. The double horizon, as Isidro had dubbed it as a teenager, formed when there was one horizon line at the end of one's viewpoint of the ocean and a second line above it marking the top of a dense fog bank forming over the waters of the Pacific.

"So, how was playing tour guide out at Point Lobos?" Chris called loudly as Isidro passed the old bell hanging outside the entrance, which had a tradition of being rung before someone opened the door of the restaurant.

Isidro waited to respond until he seated himself next to them alongside the aged wooden bar counter. "I'm a bit exhausted, to tell you the truth."

"Oh, did our professor give another one of his lectures today?" Chris replied.

"Yes, I suppose I did give the couple a bit of a lecture, but I don't think I went too overboard. They were asking questions, after all."

He then spoke to Liz loud enough for Chris to overhear, "Let me guess, something happened that upset Chris today?"

Liz grinned, embarrassed. "The *weather*," was all she said in response.

"Ah, yeah, that's one of his favorite topics, isn't it?" Isidro said.

"Well how can it not be? I mean, even when it is actually a nice day here, it only lasts for a few hours if we're lucky and then it's back to the chilly or windy or foggy or cloudy day that it is normally. And even on the nice days, by the time you get home from work when you'd be able to enjoy it, most of the time it's already cooled down or windy," Chris replied. He held up a hand to a passing waiter to signal that they were ready to be seated.

"I'm sure that after a harsh winter and hot and humid summer in the Midwest that you would look back to the weather here and consider it not so bad," Isidro responded as they rose from the bar stools and were led by a waiter to a table directly adjacent to the restaurant's floor-to-ceiling glass window.

The arrival of menus distracted Chris, and for a moment the three silently reviewed them. Isidro found the exercise amusing, as Chris and Liz always ordered the same item; perhaps the most non-unique choice on the menu. As per his prediction, they both ordered fish and chips. Isidro ordered locally caught sand dabs with asparagus spears and rice pilaf.

While they waited for their food to be delivered, their topic of conversation turned to local events, as Isidro attempted to provide a list of annual activities throughout the region. The conversation was originally sparked by Chris's complaining that there was nothing to do in the area and that it was a place that was good to be "newly married or nearly dead." Chris's wife took offense to the comment, as they had only been married a few years, and hit him on his shoulder. Chris countered that they were no longer newlyweds.

Isidro truly was tired from all of the talking he had done on his guided tour of Point Lobos, but he refused to allow Chris's comments to go unanswered. Besides, Chris could not be more wrong, Isidro thought.

"Well, let's see, Chris. I guess if you mean that there's nothing to do when you compare the Monterey Peninsula area to, say, San Francisco and its nightlife scene, shopping areas, concerts, sporting venues, restaurants … yes, you're correct in saying that there is less to do down here."

Chris appeared pleased with himself and he took a long drink from the glass of beer he had carried to the table from the bar when they had been seated. His impression turned less than amused as Isidro continued after his feigned acknowledgement of defeat.

"*BUT*, I'm going to take this opportunity to both educate you and highlight your ignorance," Isidro continued as he knowingly smiled across the table at Chris. "Let's start with the beginning of the calendar year and progress forward, shall we?" Chris rolled his eyes, while his wife eagerly nodded her head.

"Each February and March we have the Lenten fish dinners that are held every Friday evening for Lent."

As he spoke, Isidro reflected upon the Friday fish dinners that he attended every year. They were held in a building housing a spacious banquet room capable of seating five hundred people and were arranged by a local Catholic community.

The story of Monterey's fishing industry past was also well-known around the country and globe. The history of the Italians in the area was less intuitive, but no less significant in its influence upon the City of Monterey in particular. There were few descendants of the original Spanish founders of the city, such as his family and a few others, and equally as few remnants of the powerful Mexican families that arrived later. Even the names of the first American families that settled in Monterey were seldom to be found except for as names of streets. One ethnic group able to firmly embed itself in Monterey, however, was the Italians.

The Lenten fish dinners exemplified both worlds of Monterey. On the one hand, the fishing industry was well represented, not solely by the fact that locally caught seafood sourced from Monterey Bay was served each night of the dinners, but also by the fact that it was primarily former Monterey Bay fisherman and their wives that organized and volunteered to work the evenings, doing everything from cooking and serving the fish to seating people, selling wonderful homemade desserts for a dollar apiece, and opening bottles of wine for purchase.

The generation gap was noticeable between the older generation, their children, and their grandchildren. The aging fisherman, who had long ceased their commercial fishing days in Monterey or anywhere, were stout old men that managed to toss out a flirtatious remark to any attractive women who looked over eighteen and passed by them. The wives of these men floated through the lines of the long tables serving plates of fish, normally something breaded and lightly fried, with a side of pasta and garlic bread. These women tended to wear large plastic-rimmed glasses with jewels encrusted inside them and huge gaudy necklaces. Their makeup would be thick and overexaggerated and their hair as poufy as possible.

It was the children of the older generation that comprised the majority of the guests for each Friday dinner. They were middle-aged and arrived with their sizeable number of offspring in tow. And these were the people that were then controlling a vast percentage of Monterey businesses. They became so prolific that in so-called Cannery Row's heyday, the Italian immigrant workers fully immersed themselves and lived along the hillsides above the canneries and adjacent to downtown Monterey. The hillside above downtown became known as "Spaghetti Hill" due to the popular ethnicity of its residents.

The original arrivals of the group quickly became the dominant force in the fishing industry, effectively removing much of their competition. As the fisherman were able to save their wages in the glory days of Monterey's fishing industry, they were able to gradually invest and purchase land and buildings in and on the periphery. With time, the fisherman retired into more professional careers, leading to the establishment of businesses, becoming everything from real estate agents to restaurant owners, bar owners, property managers, bankers, hotel owners, and attorneys. Before long, an overwhelming number of Monterey's businesses were owned and run by those of Italian and Sicilian descent, and it was their names that became the prominent surnames in and around Monterey, not Spanish or Mexican names. Isidro once counted ten surnames of Italian origin that were arguably the most prominent last names in the area.

"In April, there's the Castroville Artichoke Festival."

"Yeah, in the 'artichoke capital of the world' that lovely Castroville has claim to ... makes me want to go just for the sheer excitement that the title produces in the mind," Chris offered sarcastically.

"In May, we have the race out at Laguna Seca racetrack, regarded as one of the legendary racetracks in the world. And this is an event I would see you enjoying, since the track is located in one of the warmest spots in the county, there's plenty of beer consumption involved, and there are cars that drive really fast."

Chris nodded in approval. "I do like Laguna Seca, I have to admit. But perhaps mostly because it's one of the most *non-Peninsula-feeling* things to do around here."

"You truly are impressively difficult at times, my friend," Isidro lamented.

Chris brushed aside the remark and eased backward into his chair. Their entrees were served and Isidro took advantage of the reprieve to reenergize himself for the sure-to-follow second half of the discussion. Besides, he thought, the lightly breaded and pan-fried sand dabs on the plate in front of him looked and smelled delicious. Isidro offered his plate to Chris and Liz, but both refused with a wave of a hand, although Isidro thought Liz secretly wanted to try the light, white flaky fish prevalent in and around Monterey Bay and popular in central coast restaurants. "You know, you guys really should try sand dabs sometime. They are fairly particular to this alcove of the world," Isidro added.

A few moments of silence ensued as the trio enjoyed their food. Chris ordered another beer.

With his plate nearly cleared, Isidro decided to return to their previous discussion. "Also in June is the world famous Blues Festival held on an annual basis, as it has for decades, at the Monterey Fairgrounds, the very place where the infamous Monterey Pop Festival was held in the 1960s."

"Yeah, I admit it's not bad, but it also brings in a lot of old people from the Bay Area," Chris muttered.

Isidro remained determined. "In September, we have the Monterey Jazz Festival, one of the most well-respected jazz festivals in the world."

"I defer to my previous comment concerning the Blues Festival."

"In December, we have my personal favorite, Christmas in the Adobes, where even with the closing of Monterey's wonderfully preserved historic adobe houses, one is able to tour the adobes that used to be open to the public, as well as many that are now privately owned and never open to the public." Isidro paused to cast a menacing stare across the table at Chris. "And if you say one negative thing about old houses being boring, you may actually see me get upset."

Isidro raised his eyebrows in expectation of Chris's response, although he had to force himself to keep from revealing a guilty belief he had concerning the closing of the Monterey adobe tours. Although he was thoroughly heartbroken to see the majestic edifices closed entirely to the public as a result of state budgeting cutbacks, leaving these treasures of Monterey's past dark and lonely, Isidro had not agreed with how they had been previously managed and could not counter any argument that accused inefficiency.

First off, the adobes and other buildings comprising Monterey State Historic Park were kept immaculately and unnecessarily clean, so much so that not a speck of dust would ever be encountered. The same could be said for the various gardens and courtyards of the houses and buildings, which appeared to receive daily weeding and raking. Secondly, each home or building would have a tour guide posted who would stand around idly most days just waiting for a chance encounter with a curious tourist.

"Okay, Isidro. I'll admit that every year you force us to do the 'Christmas in the Adobes' tour, I do actually enjoy it and learn something from the presentations and historical stuff they do in each adobe," Chris admitted.

"I love the flowers," Liz remarked. "My favorites are the pink calla lilies popping out of the ground in August and September every year, and even more profound are the white calla lilies that seem to be everywhere each spring." When an awkward silence befell them, she attempted to change the subject. "Why do you think there's not much happening around here in October and November?"

"Honestly, I think it's because, as you guys know after having lived here for some years, that tends to be the time of year when we have what most consider the best weather. Fairly consistently, the Monterey area experiences a two-month period in autumn where the weather is next to paradise for many: warm days, gentle breezes, if any, and very limited clouds or fog. This period also happens to coincidentally occur when we have the least amount of visitors."

"It's no coincidence," Chris commented as he set down his glass. "Those of us that live here deserve those two months of better weather and less tourists."

Isidro cocked his head sideways and nodded. "That may perhaps be one of the most prophetic statements I've ever heard you proclaim, Chris Walker."

31.

Year of our Lord 1818.

S WEAT POURED FROM Father Margil's face. It dripped to the arid
ground in front of him as he forced his legs to continue stepping
forward, taking him upwards on the side of the mountain alongside
the convoy to Monterey — his convoy. For that was how he had come to
view both the settlers and soldiers. The soldiers may have been lost
souls, but they were still children of God and Father Margil felt
personally responsible for getting the group to Monterey.

The decision to cut across the mountainous ridges he agreed to with
Captain Echevarria was initially received by all in the expedition with
vibrant joy. Open smiles, not seen for many days, reverberated
throughout the group. The smiles, however, did not last long. The
promised shortened distance of the new route was viewed by all as a
positive development, but the more difficult terrain of the slopes proved
to severely dampen the collective spirit of the caravan.

After the first day on the new path, when the convoy stopped to set
up camp for the night, Father Margil was certain that Captain Echevarria
was of the same mind that perhaps the altered trek plan had not been a
wonderful idea. Father Margil conceded, though, that like him, the
Captain would not view turning back to the main trail as an option.
Aside from the extra day of treading backwards, it would have a
disheartening impact on the group that might not be later rekindled.

On the previous evening in the camp, Father Margil estimated that
it would be possible to reach the Mission San Antonio de Padua the
next day, if the caravan was able to find a good route through the

mountains and the people were able to push hard. He made his proclamation as they were seated around campfires, and although his revelation was not received with cries of joy, it was also not received with complaint. Only the foul-mouthed and overall vicious man Diego Alvarez, still tied to a rope attached to one of the wagons, made an audible response by loudly spitting after Father Margil spoke.

That had been the night before. The next day proved to challenge one's faith. To his dismay, soldiers sent ahead to find the most suitable pathway through the mountains were unable to find more than game trails along the ridges and through the canyons. If it were not for the wagons, they would have been able to proceed much more fluidly, but with the wagons, consideration had to constantly be given to their requirements. It slowed the day's progress considerably, and Father Margil's heart sank as by midday, he realized his promise of arriving at San Antonio de Padua that day would not come to fruition. At one point, the wagon carrying the goods of the Church had one of its wheels get caught in a ditch, nearly causing the wagon to tilt sideways and spill part of its contents down the hillside. The chest carrying the Russian's gold fell loose on the back of the wagon. Father Margil felt enraged when he noticed that one of the soldiers had moved the rope binding Diego Alvarez's hands to the Church's wagon. Alvarez stood looking curiously at the chest when the accident transpired, and Father Margil ordered him moved to walk alongside one of the other wagons for the remainder of the journey. Alvarez grinned like a jackal as he was moved.

That evening, when Captain Echevarria and Margil concluded that they would need to camp overnight and hope to reach San Antonio de Padua by midday of the next day, Father Margil perceived dismay in the souls of the group. They had lost hope. It was at this moment, the moment that despair was running rife among them, that Diego Alvarez once again decided to test his mutinous appeal.

"Good people, soldiers and settlers alike, hear me!" he yelled from the edge of the wagon where he remained bound. "These two care nothing for your lives and lead you surely to certain death! If we do not fall to our deaths in the steep chasms they lead us past, then we shall fall to the arrows and knives of savages that are probably already surveying our movement into these merciless mountains or die from heat and exhaustion!"

It was Father Margil and not Captain Echevarria that reached Diego Alvarez first. In a blinding moment of rage, the strongest rage that Father Margil had ever succumbed to, he swiftly brought the back of his hand across the side of Alvarez's face. Alvarez winced in pain as his head fell downwards. As he raised his head, Father Margil noticed from the dim campfire light that a line of blood ran down the side of Alvarez's chin from his lip. Most of the settlers and soldiers promptly stood as soon as Alvarez had begun to spew forth his poison, quickly taken by the vile man's words. The unexpected and unimaginable action from Father Margil resulted in the group staring in disbelief at the figures of Father Margil and Diego Alvarez outlined in the soft light emanating from the nearest campfire. For a brief and tense moment, not a word was uttered.

Father Margil felt hate for the first time in his life. He often encountered feelings of firm dislike for certain human beings, but he had never known the ugly and impenetrable sensation of detesting another human being so severely as to actually assign the word *hate*. He had Diego Alvarez to thank for the awful gift, and recognizing this, he detested the man even more.

Captain Echevarria ordered everyone to return to their seated positions and to ignore the claims of the crazy man Alvarez. The group slowly and reluctantly returned to what they had been doing before the outburst. The Captain began walking towards Father Margil and Alvarez.

Diego Alvarez sneered at him with his eyes narrowed and his lips retracted in a way that prominently displayed his incisor teeth. "Maybe I'll tell them about the contents of your chest over there," Alvarez hissed in a threat, with a nod of his head toward the Church's wagon.

How had this little devil figured it out? Father Margil heard his now-panicked voice ask in his head. And by speaking such directed words towards the precious cargo of the Church's wagon, Diego Alvarez became an even greater threat. Before, he had represented a severe and potentially contagious nuisance; now he represented an undeniable threat. *This man must be stopped before he destroys everything.*

The sound of Captain Echevarria's alarmed voice approaching broke Father's Margil's reverie. "Alvarez! I'll have you locked in chains rowing in the belly of a prisoners' vessel for the remainder of your pathetic life!"

Diego Alvarez cowered in the oncoming presence of the Captain. The Captain had an arm raised, ready to pound into Alvarez, but Father Margil quickly stepped in between the Captain and Alvarez. Father Margil spoke calmly but directly. "This man has requested permission to confess his sins to me, *in private*."

Father Margil was unable to discern the expression on the Captain's face since the Captain's back was facing the light of the fire, but Father Margil could feel the Captain's confusion. "This man must be punished accordingly!" Captain Echevarria exclaimed.

"Yes, I agree, and indeed he shall. But in the eyes of the Lord, he must be allowed to confess his sins … his penance shall follow. Now please bring me a torch and untie this man's rope from the wagon. I shall walk with him away from the camp so that he may confess his sins to God in peace."

Captain Echevarria objected profusely. He eventually warily agreed, as long as Father Margil promised to have Alvarez walk in front of him the entire time.

During this discussion, Diego Alvarez remained quiet.

Diego could not imagine what the Father was talking about concerning a "confession," but regardless he awaited the opportunity to speak to the Father directly concerning whatever the chest on the Church's wagon contained. Alvarez had only guessed at the contents of the chest, but the Father's reaction confirmed his suspicion of the contents being of great value. If he was able to speak to Father Margil in private, he felt confident that the Father would be able to secure his freedom from the Captain once they arrived in Monterey, as well as pay him a sum of the chest's contents in return for his silence — a sizeable sum. For in observing the Father and Captain's discussion, Diego Alvarez also discovered that the Father was keeping the contents of the chest secret, even from Captain Echevarria.

If the secret was that important to the Father, he would do anything to safeguard it, Alvarez gleefully told himself.

Moments later, Father Margil walked behind Alvarez, firmly holding a length of rope that bound Alvarez's hands. Captain Echevarria had tied the knots so forcefully that they dug into the skin of Alvarez's wrists. The two men walked slowly away from the camp, and the people of the caravan watched the light of Father Margil's torch disappear into the still night.

"Where are we going, you old fool?" Alvarez asked Father Margil once they were beyond the ears of the others.

"I don't know where either of us are going," Father Margil absently responded.

"What are you talking about?" Alvarez demanded, turning to face the Father in the dim light of the torch.

Father Margil avoided looking directly at Diego Alvarez. "Just walk a little further and we can talk. In the meantime, I would suggest you try, even if it is for the first time in your life, to quietly reflect on your own mortality." Father Margil was sure he had overstepped Alvarez's vocabulary, but it mattered little. *The man had sealed his own fate.*

Alvarez continued to attempt conversation with Father Margil as they walked into the night, but the Father ignored his words and focused on the benevolence of his assignment. He was leading Alvarez in the same direction the caravan had traversed earlier that day and he knew they were walking along a steep face of a mountain. He recalled a particular spot they had passed not long before stopping for the evening. It was distinguishable as a sheer wall of rock bordering the path on one side, and the other side was a steep vertical drop; a fall from which no person would survive. Although he remained confident that he was doing what he must and that he no other choice, his compassion for mankind was not completely obscured; it was with some sadness that he eventually recognized they had reached their destination. He asked Diego Alvarez to stop walking.

"What is this all about?" Alvarez yelled at him.

"Justice," Father Margil responded calmly and then he quickly lunged forward in Alvarez's direction, holding the torch in front of him.

Alvarez reacted by swiftly moving backward, only to find no more ground beneath his feet.

Father Margil felt the rope he still held burning in his hands as it followed Diego Alvarez into the darkness. He opened his hand, letting go of the rope. Father Margil heard a muted thud far below followed by the sounds of loose rocks falling down the side of the cliff; then all was silent.

In what Captain Echevarria estimated to be roughly an hour after Father Margil had set off into the darkness with a torch and Diego Alvarez, the light from a torch was seen rounding the bend of the hillside adjacent to the flattened meadow where the expedition had set up their camp. Soon thereafter, the outline of Father Margil appeared from out of the darkness. *Father Margil returned alone.*

Late on the afternoon following the incident with Diego Alvarez, the expedition arrived in a sweeping and fertile valley. The white elongated buildings of the Mission San Antonio de Padua shone brilliantly on the horizon as Father Margil's caravan slowly descended from the Santa Lucia Mountains into the San Antonio Valley. A low line of hills bordered the opposite side of the valley, but they may as well been anthills to the members of the caravan after the rugged and unforgiving coastal mountains they had just traversed.

A contingent of mission natives, which had been tasked to search and find the expected arriving convoy, spotted the group and led them to the Mission of San Antonio de Padua. No member of the party was without blistered feet and an array of cuts ruthlessly administered by the thorny tangle of plants that had vastly overgrown the *trail* they had followed through the mountains. Each of them, even Father Margil himself, blinked rapidly at first glimpse of the mission to verify that they were not hallucinating.

The previous evening, Father Margil relayed that *tragically* Diego Alvarez had foolishly walked too far ahead of the light of the torch and fallen off the side of a steep cliff to his doom. Father Margil added that the accident occurred after Alvarez had confessed his sins to God, the addition of which provided some comfort to the settlers and soldiers, as it was perceived as God's will.

No one questioned Father Margil's story regarding the demise of Diego Alvarez. Father Margil hoped this due to a shared perception that a man of such obvious ill-will would surely meet such an end, but he cringed at the thought that a lack of curiosity was mainly due to a heightened sense of despair blended with exhaustion, a mix that would snatch the passion out of any person. One day, Father Margil feared the questions would arise.

32.

Year of our Lord 2009.

THE JELLYFISH REMINDED John Gibson and Rachel of alien creatures from a movie. Gibson found the manner in which the jellyfish distorted their already otherworldly-like bodies as they casually floated in the water to be both comforting and relaxing. Aside from the fact that an apparently endless barrage of children seemed to ram into their knees as they wandered through the exhibits of the Monterey Aquarium, Gibson and Rachel agreed that they enjoyed their visit to Monterey's most popular tourist destination.

"These jellyfish are really fascinating," Rachel commented as they emerged from a darkened segment of the aquarium devoted to the exhibition of the unique invertebrate species of the sea.

"They are," Gibson responded as he moved to quickly dodge a little boy about to run straight into his midsection. "Whew! Close call," he uttered with raised hands and a heightened sense of relief as he and Rachel watched one of a group of other boys enter the darkened interior of the jellyfish exhibit.

"Let's check out the seahorse exhibit before we go," Rachel commented. "And don't worry … I'm glad that the little boy didn't disable you as well …" she said as she ran a finger across his chest and walked towards the stairwell leading down to the main floor.

Gibson followed her, unable to conceal a smirk. "What do ya say after we check out the seahorses we grab lunch and then take our time *checking out* of the room?"

Rachel halfway turned to look at him as she took one step downward on the stairwell. "Hmm, I like the sound of that."

Annoying yet majestic sea gulls stood patiently, perched on the edge of the restaurant's pier foundations, keeping a diligent eye for any food dropped from the tables of the restaurant. A trio of black cormorants stood nearby on the crumbling foundation of a former cannery and took turns diving into the ocean just off shore.

They were sitting outside at a round wooden table at their hotel's bistro. The restaurant was tucked into a corner of the hotel's elaborately tiered deck and patio complex over the bay.

A tray comprised of a mixed seafood assortment was set between them by their waiter. The platter consisted of shrimp, shredded Dungeness crab, mussels, oysters, and calamari … all sourced from the waters lapping gently against the rocky shore twenty feet beneath them.

"I could certainly get used to life down here," Rachel commented as she delicately placed a small calamari into her mouth. "Life in San Francisco is definitely not bad considered to other big cities, but being down here is a vivid reminder that San Francisco, as lovely as it is, is a *big city*. And I do love the quaintness of this place; like for example how the aquarium has that whistle they blow every day at noon as a reminder of the former cannery days — I think that's pretty unique."

A squadron of pelicans passing over the water in bombing formation caught their attention and they watched the pod skim across the kelp beds scouring for prey. "You do look quite relaxed down here, I must say," Gibson commented.

"You mean to say that I don't normally look relaxed?" Rachel quickly countered.

Gibson kicked himself. "Actually, I meant to say that you always seem at ease with the world even in the city, but that you look even more relaxed down here." It had been a long time since he had felt an overwhelming urge to keep a woman interested in him.

Rachel smiled adoringly at him and lightly stabbed a shrimp from the platter in between them. "It's okay, John. I know what you meant." Rachel let the shrimp on the end of her fork dangle in front of her mouth for a moment, building temptation. "And you don't need to worry so much, as I'm very interested in you and really like what we have together." She nibbled half of the shrimp in her mouth and slowly chewed it as she allowed her eyes to linger across the table at him. "Although I think your being a little self-conscious is touching."

John Gibson blushed. Rachel leaned forward and fed him the other half of the shrimp on her fork. *I could get used to this*, Gibson thought. However, as he did, another thought intervened. Just moments before, he had noted a small fishing vessel carousing by on the other side of the thick piles of kelp floating on the water's surface.

The glimpse of the fishing vessel reproduced images he had considered before. *A small fishing boat would be able to fairly easily slip away from San Francisco Bay and tug out into the wide ocean to relative obscurity.* He loathed admitting it to himself, but he knew it was time to get back to work. The importance of his career may have been lessened, but it was his job, and a major federal crime had occurred. And John Gibson firmly believed that it was a crime he could solve.

After lunch was finished, they began the drive north to San Francisco. For a moment, Rachel Dowling expected action on John's earlier *suggested hint* as they packed their luggage in the hotel room, but sensing a slight unease emanating from him, she decided to not press the issue.

There was no denying it — Agent Gibson was back on the case and his mind was focused on his responsibility to solve the crime. In his experience, he had learned that crimes, even the most carefully planned and elaborate, always left a trail lingering behind them for one to follow, if one only knew where to look.

Rachel sensed his growing distraction. "I had a really nice time, John," she commented as they rounded a corner and saw the brilliant image of downtown San Francisco spread in front of them.

"I did, too," Gibson responded. He glanced over at her and smiled. She grabbed his hand and placed it gently on her thigh.

"Listen, I'm going to probably be really busy for a little while, but once the smoke clears, let's go out for dinner at Scoma's." Scoma's, a locals' favorite seafood restaurant hidden down an obscure alleyway and perched on a pier on San Francisco Bay, was a special place to them, not only for the general discreet ambiance of the place and the fantastic food it offered, but because they had gone there on their first date. Gibson made an effort to pick a place that he was told was off the beaten tourist track.

"Oh, I would love that," Rachel gleefully replied, squeezing his hand lightly.

Gibson momentarily contemplated trying to emphasize his growing adoration towards her, but quickly dismissed the thought. There would be time for such things later; it was time to get back to work.

33.

Year of our Lord 2009.

THE SANTA BARBARA MISSION had historically been a central depository for the entire Californian mission system. It was there, from the beginning when the first missions in the new territory were established, that the Church retained all records pertaining to the entire mission network in Alta California. Isidro de la Vega believed that if he were to find any written evidence to help explain the content of the mysterious letter he had discovered at the San Antonio Mission, it would be in Santa Barbara.

His thoughts were conflicted as he made the four hour drive from Monterey to Santa Barbara. Isidro listened to them as they swirled in his head. *What am I doing? I'm a historian and I have no right to keep the discovery of the letter at San Antonio a secret. I should report the letter to the state's Historical Society at once, accompanied with my sincere apologies for having not reported the letter immediately. I could be discredited severely by my peers for having committed this act of selfishness.*

But, on the other hand, don't I deserve the right to investigate the historical significance of this letter before anyone else, as I discovered it? Don't I have the right as a historian to first attempt defining its origins? After all, I have ensured the letter's safekeeping and have secured it in plastic to keep it safe and undamaged until the time that I turn it over to the Historical Society. And furthermore, I may be acting out of some level of selfishness and personal enrichment, but a find and historical investigation such as this is what historians such as myself wait their entire lives to encounter ... and some — most — never have such an opportunity. I owe it to myself and to others in my profession who spend their lives toiling away in the attempt to keep mankind's history preserved and understood to discover the mystery behind this letter!

Isidro suddenly realized he was speeding quite a lot over the posted speed limit on the highway and quickly decelerated his car. Highway 101 was an easy route to veer above and beyond the speed limit, as it stretched across the mostly flat Santa Clara and Salinas valleys, and most of the time, the state Highway Patrol would let vehicles pass that were traveling mildly above the speed limit; but there was a limit to everything.

Seeing the bright yellow of the mustard flowers lining the sides of the highway, remnants of former days when the mission friars had dispersed seeds of the distinguishable flower alongside the Mission Trail, brought a smile to his face. The occasional glimpse of one of the restored bell posts demarcating the former trail also made him smile inwardly as he reaffirmed to himself that the preservation of history was a noble and necessary pursuit.

As he drove, he regarded the elegant Santa Lucia Mountain Range to his right, with the prominent vineyards skirting River Road extending upwards along the steep slopes. To his left, he peered toward the direction of the Pinnacles National Monument, hidden somewhere beyond the reaches of the city of Soledad. Soon he was driving past the oil and gas fields of San Ardo, which was an extremely active production area in the early to mid-1900s, but later receded to near graveyard status, with only idle and rusty rigs dotting the landscape of gently rolling hills, like forgotten tombstones.

Next along the route south, he encountered a stretch of land that could only be described as "vineyard heaven," as the carefully manicured lines of planted grapevines stretched from the edge of the highway in every direction to indiscernible end points somewhere off in the distance. Before long continuing southward, the abandoned 1950s barrack buildings still standing on the expansive Fort Hunter-Liggett stood in stark contrast to the previous image of the vibrant vineyards. And then, suddenly, one left Monterey County and passed into San Luis Obispo County.

The rolling, sun-drenched hills of the Paso Robles domain gradually led into the more prominent peaks standing guard on the periphery of the city of San Luis Obispo. The highway climbed up a steep grade before descending downward at an even steeper angle and passing through the flatter area of the city. After passing through San Luis Obispo, the topography and geologic features seen from the highway changed dramatically. The earth looked drier and features that had before looked like gentle hills then converted into rough canyons. The vibrant smells of sage and juniper filled the car.

As the coast grew nearer, the canyon areas bordering the sides of the highway did as well, and Isidro found himself feeling slightly claustrophobic. The temperature also changed rather dramatically between his departure in Monterey and the oncoming outskirts of Santa Barbara. Leaving Monterey, he had driven through a low dark cloud cover with a temperature in the low fifties. As he rounded another bend closer to Santa Barbara, roughly four hours later, the temperature gauge on his car displayed an outdoor temperature of eighty-three degrees Fahrenheit.

He held the Monterey Peninsula as the most beautiful place on Earth, but if there were to be a designated second place, it would be Santa Barbara. The way that the shelf of a mountainous ridge towered so sharply and closely above the town snugly situated between the ocean and its base provided such a stark variance that one could only gasp in awe when seeing it.

While he drove into the city's limits and noticed the elegant curve of Santa Barbara's bay and the flattened ridge of the mountain idly standing behind the palm-lined streets of the city, images of places he had seen images of, such as Nice and Cape Town, flashed into his head.

It was no wonder that due to its fabulous setting and climate, coupled with its relative proximity to the ever-lucrative television and film industry of Los Angeles, Santa Barbara was a perpetual favorite of glamorous film personalities.

Isidro turned off the highway and entered the city. While stopped at a stoplight, he caught himself staring at a group of four young women crossing the street. All were scantily clad and tanned, strolling down the street with matching uniforms of short jean shorts and tank tops. The outfits were topped off with shoulder-length straight blonde hair and large dark sunglasses.

This was a scene one would never see on the Monterey Peninsula … *It was a different way of life down in Santa Barbara*, he thought.

34.

Year of our Lord 2009.

GENT GIBSON was pleased to have Chiles' collaboration on the case. After dropping off Rachel at her place in the Sunset district the previous evening, Gibson called Chiles to arrange a rendezvous the following morning. They met at the same dingy diner in the Soma district as always. The same waitress as always acknowledged his entrance with a roll of her eyes and eventually made her way over to his table with a pot of coffee in her hand.

"You ready to order?" she said as she filled the white mug on the table without even asking if he wanted a cup of coffee.

"I'm waiting for someone. If you don't mind, I'll wait until he gets here to order anything," Gibson calmly indicated.

The old waitress scowled down at him. "You could have told me that before I walked all the way over here," she huffed in a throaty voice before returning to her station behind the counter, where a couple of old men sat muttering about the weather. Gibson noted on his entry that it was the same two pair of men that were there on his previous visit.

Shortly thereafter, Detective David Chiles entered the front door of the diner. Chiles looked as organized and serious as he normally appeared, but Gibson thought that only a couple of years of stress from the job had begun to wear on Chiles, rapidly transforming him from the once youthful and eager young officer into a hardened veteran.

Gibson rose from his seat and the two men shook hands. The surly waitress behind the counter acknowledged Chiles' entry with another roll of her eyes.

"How did you get that hardass captain of yours to agree to this?" Gibson inquired.

"Oh, well, you know," Chiles lightly pulled at his shirt's collar, "I told him you would agree to make it known that my department was providing assistance should we be successful." Chiles abashedly turned his gaze away from Gibson, hoping that he had not overstepped his bounds.

"No problem, I'll be happy to." Gibson's response provided obvious comfort to Chiles, who noticeably relaxed. "I think it was a clever ploy by you, I must add."

Chiles grinned proudly. "Thank you."

The waitress arrived and poured Chiles a cup of coffee and topped off Gibson's cup without uttering a word to either of them. She took a step back from their booth and smiled forcibly at Gibson. "Now are you ready to order?" she pointedly probed.

Gibson sensed that if they did not order food at that moment they would be going without breakfast. The pending quality of the food from such a place did cross his mind, but it was going to be a long day and some sort of protein intake would be welcome. He shot Chiles a glance, indicating that they should put in an order with the increasingly impatient waitress. Gibson didn't bother to look at the plastic-coated menu on the table in front of him and instead ordered two eggs over easy, bacon, hash browns, and toast. When the waitress turned her penetrating gaze to Chiles, he fumbled with his words for a moment before simply stating that he'd take the same thing.

"Let's get to it," Chiles suggested. "Now, I still don't think that they tried moving the stolen gold out of the city by land, and if they did, they certainly didn't do it right away. It would be too great of a risk to try and get through traffic at that time with the heightened level of alert. As you'll recall, all of the exits out of San Francisco were blocked and any suspicious looking vehicles were inspected." Chiles clearly remembered the effort; it created traffic jams that were unheard of, even for a place famous for its traffic. It was a public relations disaster, as the roadblocks had been unsuccessful and only managed to stir up discontent with the public towards law enforcement officers in the city.

"So one option is that the gold was stashed somewhere in the city immediately after the robbery and later retrieved for transport out of

San Francisco," Gibson continued.

Chiles had a thought. "But couldn't whoever did this have just planned on keeping the gold in the city the entire time and only send it out in small quantities?"

Gibson chewed on Chiles' question for a moment, considering its feasibility. He took another drink of the wretched coffee. "Anything is a possibility, but in these investigations, without the manpower support necessary to conduct a detailed investigation of every possibility, we're best served in focusing our efforts on as few options as possible, or at least on a shared common factor that could be applicable to a few possibilities.

"In this case, I'd say that while a possibility, something about this group tells me that they were not interested in retaining the gold here. To have undergone such an elaborate scheme in order to rob a Federal Reserve Bank, there would seem to be some greater purpose behind it, and greater purposes are usually not carried out piecemeal. This is on top of the fact that distributing their haul into smaller sums would create a much greater risk of traceability. When you steal so much gold from the U.S. Government, you have to be extremely careful about what you try and do with it afterwards.

"Small sales would not be very attractive compared to a few carefully coordinated large disbursements, or perhaps even just one to some shady nook of the world. The group that did this was clever enough to so far have pulled off a miraculous feat, and therefore we have to assume they considered this as well.

"I have a strong feeling that this group wanted it all out of here to wherever right away. And although I do think it possible that they slightly delayed its transport out, I also think that with such a grandiose plan, they would not have stood idle for long." Gibson paused, hoping that he did not sound too much as if he were lecturing the younger man. Chiles had become an accomplished detective himself in a much shorter period than it took for most others.

Two plates of eggs, bacon, and toast suddenly appeared on the table in front of them, delivered by the diner's charming waitress. The waitress asked if they needed anything else and both men shook their heads as they considered the food on the plates. The eggs looked more over hard than over easy, the bacon had been fried too long and appeared more like dried-out pieces of jerky, the hash browns gleamed with grease, and the toast slices were saturated with butter.

Chiles looked up from his plate and his expression returned to a mix of curious and determined. "Do you have any more intuitions on the case?"

Gibson chuckled in response. "I don't know if I would call them 'intuitions,' but I do have some rather strong gut feelings." Gibson picked up his fork and knife. Chiles responded by doing the same. "Although I think they moved the gold out of the city shortly after the heist, I have a feeling they did not move it far. I think the goal was probably just to get it out of San Francisco to another temporary location. Then they would sit on it for a while and wait for the dust to settle, followed by an attempt to move it, likely internationally on the black market."

Gibson went to slice a piece of bacon and was not surprised the knife had difficulty cutting through it. He picked up the strip of bacon with his fingers. Once Chiles saw him, he abandoned his own attempts and joined Gibson by picking up his own. Gibson saluted him with a slight raise of his strip of pork and the two men grinned.

"So you think they took the gold not long after the robbery and are stashing it nearby, but assuredly out of San Francisco?" Chiles inquired after choking down a piece of bacon that he had to quickly follow with a gulp of coffee.

"Yes, I do … kind of like pirates that robbed another ship and then buried their treasure somewhere with a map, making a promise to return to retrieve it at a later date."

Chiles beamed, revealing the boyish grin he often successfully suppressed. *"Pirates and a buried treasure.* This case just keeps getting more exciting and interesting every minute."

"Well, let's keep our 'pirates and buried treasure' expression between us," Gibson casually warned.

"Of course, of course," Chiles responded, his normal stern expression returning. "So what other feelings do you have?"

"Well, first off, let me comment that if I'm right with this theory, then our group is sitting on this *treasure* that they have *buried* somewhere not far from here. And if we can narrow down where it may be, even just a general location, we have a wonderful opportunity to close in on these guys before they are able to return with their *treasure map* to dig up their *chest of gold.*" Gibson started to place a mouthful of hash browns on his fork but quickly abandoned the effort as he peered closer at the fried potatoes and opted instead to start on the eggs.

"Why is that?" Chiles asked as he also began to cut into his eggs.

Gibson finished chewing before responding. "Because we know for a fact that there are more than a couple of individuals involved; a scheme of this depth and magnitude could not have been conducted any other way. And this gives us the human fallacy advantage."

"What do you mean by that?" Chiles inquired.

"It means that people talk and even people that swear to keep secrets tend to blab more than they should; and with a job of this magnitude, the sheer precision of it, someone is going to want to brag."

"So we just need to narrow down a few potential locations and then see if we can get people talking."

"*Exactly,*" Gibson responded.

"But how do we get to that point?" Chiles inquired as he took a forkful of egg.

Gibson considered the question. He needed a map to fully illustrate and develop his theory, but a piece of paper and something to write with would work, assuming Chiles knew his local geography, which Gibson did not doubt. "Do you happen to have a pen on you?"

Chiles set his fork down on the plate and pulled out a pen from his suit jacket pocket. "I always carry one. Learned it from a seasoned veteran such as yourself."

Gibson smiled, accepted the pen handed to him, and silently wished *he* was the seasoned veteran that had imparted such sound advice.

Gibson rose to request any kind of paper from the diner's waitress and she responded with courtesy, surprising Gibson. She handed him a menu that had only received printing on one side and had therefore been discarded.

"Can you draw an outline of the California coastline, say a hundred or a hundred and fifty miles north and south of San Francisco?" Gibson asked Chiles as he returned to his seat in the booth. Chiles eagerly accepted the task. Gibson pushed the remnants of his plate aside, the hash browns untouched, although he had managed to finish the bacon slices while Chiles was sketching.

"Oh, yeah, speaking of the ocean, I did ask my contact at the port authority if anything out of the ordinary occurred on the day of the heist or the day before and after. Unfortunately, he informed me that nothing had," Chiles remarked as he sketched on the paper without looking up from his drawing. "Does this kill your hunch?" he asked, looking up from his drawing.

"No, not at all ... If they did use a boat as transport, I think they would have done everything possible to ensure that whatever they did appeared entirely normal," Gibson quickly responded. "I think we should focus on something very expected and unassuming, like a fishing boat," he added reflectively, more to himself than in response to Chiles.

"Let's focus on this first, though. Please continue with the map." Chiles returned to drawing, suppressing his desire to ask further questions. As Chiles finished the sketch, Gibson considered that he had not called Agent Shapiro in order to check in with him yet. He didn't necessarily mind having to do so, but he was unaccustomed to such protocol. He promised himself to call Shapiro after his meeting with Chiles.

"Okay, now briefly tell me about the different subregions along the coast," Gibson requested. Chiles complied, providing a brief description of the coastline from Mendocino on the north of his map to Cambria on the southern end. After Chiles finished, Gibson reflected on what he had been told as he studied the depiction of the coastline.

Gibson admitted that numerous locations could fit the location of his theory; this included Mendocino and Cambria, but also Half Moon Bay, Santa Cruz and Monterey. Certain elements needed to be present in order for his theory to hold firm. There needed to be a local fishing industry, but there also needed to be a somewhat sizeable population so that a new boat offshore would be relatively unnoticed.

Heading northward along the coast from San Francisco Bay was a remote route, as there was little in the way of settlement along this segment of the coastline. Chiles was also able to add when prompted that fishing vessels departing from the bay often turned southward after they reached the open ocean, and that the coastline north of San Francisco was largely populated by fishing vessels from Northern California harbors such as the Mendocino-Fort Bragg area or even farther north. In Gibson's mind, that ruled out a trip northward, and he concentrated on the southern range of Chiles' map.

"I have a suspicion that we're looking for somewhere with a fairly large percentage of affluence within its population," Gibson mentioned as he continued to stare at the map.

Chiles laughed, but quickly stopped when Gibson raised his eyes from the map with no amusement present. "That doesn't narrow it down at all, actually. As you'll soon come to realize after living here a little longer, there's a lot of money on this stretch of California's coastline," Chiles offered as explanation. "*A lot,*" he added for emphasis.

"The Monterey Peninsula area is certainly one of the more wealthy areas and is probably one of the few areas of the country where people with million dollar homes that drive new BMWs refer to others as 'rich people.' Santa Cruz may be the only exception, as it has a large student and young population, but even then, you have millionaire ex-hippies living there that you would never guess are wealthy from their outward appearance."

Gibson cocked his head. "Oddly enough, what you just absently added is very useful."

"How so?" Chiles queried, genuinely interested in how he had said anything useful when he thought he only added a joke to his previous statement.

"You stated that Santa Cruz is a hippie town … is that true?" Gibson asked.

"Oh yeah, I'm not exaggerating there. It's not uncommon at all to catch a whiff of pot smoke while walking along its downtown streets. And the general attitude and culture there is extremely different from the more conservative side of Monterey Bay."

"Another very interesting and important piece of information," Gibson remarked with a slight smirk.

Chiles looked at him with obvious shock and was speechless. He decided to stop talking and wait for an explanation.

"Okay, I'll save you the anticipation. Although I'm tempted to let you just keep talking. As you'll see in a moment, you are filling in a lot of pieces of the puzzle, whether you realize it or not." Gibson paused to finish the last of his coffee, which had grown slightly cool.

"I think we can rule out Santa Cruz for precisely the reason you said about it being a kind of hippie place. Hippies, even old, rich ones, don't seem to have stealing from the federal treasury on their minds. And I think you've narrowed down where I'd like to focus our efforts: the southern end of Monterey Bay. As you said, it's an affluent and slightly conservative area, which I saw firsthand in the last few days. And by the way, thank you for the introduction to your friend. He gave us a very informative little tour."

Gibson's comment made Chiles laugh lightly. "Yeah, I know, Isidro can be a bit intense at times, but I hope he wasn't too bad," he said.

"He wasn't, in fact; I think maybe the guy just needs to loosen up a bit. But, come to think of it, I want to give him a call; a person knowledgeable and embedded in the local culture and society down there could be invaluable."

"I don't know how into *society* he is, but he's certainly embedded in the Monterey Peninsula. I've tried numerous times throughout our lives to convince him to move up here, but he's never even considered it," Chiles responded.

"Regardless, I have a hunch he'll be very helpful to us," Gibson asserted. "Getting back to it, though, I think this is our target area. There's a local fishing industry, a sizeable population with a considerable amount of rich people, and it's far but not too far from San Francisco. Whoever did this would have not wanted to be in the water for too long, so I already ruled out anywhere farther south."

"But ..." Chiles interrupted.

"Yes?"

"If there is an affluent, potentially conservative population base, why would they be interested in stealing from the federal government?" Chiles asked, hoping he would not be scolded in return.

Gibson leaned back in the booth, the stiff red vinyl of the upholstery cracking behind him as he did. "Because rich people like being rich, and after what's been happening lately with stock markets and businesses they owned, people that were once super rich have been downgraded to just *rich*. And it's the super rich that really adore remaining super rich. What's more, pulling off a heist such as this took a lot of smarts and a lot of money."

Gibson firmly planted a finger on the spot on the map that Chiles had labeled Monterey. "Somehow I think we could find a lot of both of those two things down there."

Part III

35.

Year of our Lord 1818.

WILLIAM BECKWITH'S EVERY THOUGHT was of Isabella. He was a man trapped in the tender folds of love and for the first time in his life, he felt unification between his heart and his mind.

She appeared through the grand house's principal rear doorway leading to its luxurious garden, looking like an angel descended from heaven just for him. Her long brown hair flowed around her face and fell to her bare shoulders, very against the Monterey fashion of the day, as the other maidens in town all wore their hair pulled back tightly behind their heads and their shoulders were more modestly covered. Beckwith loved how Isabella managed to combine her strong spirit with stylistic conformity, as she wore an elegant ruby red dress with elaborate gold tassels and white trim that was opposite to the way she opted to wear her hair and display her gentle neckline, very much an accepted style of the town.

"Good morning, my love," he said as she neared him, unaware that he was calling her his "love" for the first time.

Isabella smiled brightly in response, to the point of glowing. "Good morning, my love," she responded. Beckwith noted how the soft touch of the sun appeared to be captured and then radiate off her tanned skin.

The two young lovers proceeded to engage in the simple oblivious conversation that only new lovers experience before turning towards a more serious tone once mention of Isabella's father arose. "You must not read too much into any disfavor you may perceive from him," Isabella advised.

Beckwith proceeded casually, recognizing that there is often a sacred bond between father and daughter that must be respected. "I'll try not to, then," he offered casually.

Isabella brought her hands to clasp gently around his face. "It is not you, my love, that troubles my father, or," she paused momentarily and blushed slightly, "it is not *you* entirely," she finished, grinning impishly.

"But your father's mere presence commands the respect of hundreds! His reputation is renowned throughout Alta California, and I imagine, easily beyond."

"I'm sure he would be modest in witness of such praise, but I know that he is a man of great influence and that he does not cower in the face of most dangers ..." Isabella's voice trailed away softly with the gentle breeze blowing in from the bay.

William Beckwith watched her with concern. He may have embellished the image of the governor some, but the governor's esteem was well-known to be as strong and powerful as the blow from a bear. He questioned what could bother such a man so profoundly. Beckwith considered and reconsidered inquiring further and concluded that the worst that could happen would be that Isabella would speak no more on the subject. "What troubles him, my love?"

Isabella turned and he felt her intense brown eyes considering his question. "I want to tell you, but I do not want to betray the trust of my father."

"Yes, I understand, Isabella," Beckwith conceded. A moment of silence passed between them. "But I ask only in concern for you; the affairs of the town are secondary to me and whatever is spoken between us rests between you and me."

Isabella turned her face away from Beckwith and locked her gaze upon a tree next to them with red blossoms sprouting between its large leaves. "Do you remember that trading ship at port last week?"

"Of course. Cooper-Molera had me negotiate with the captain of the ship directly, likely as a test to see if I turned out to be capable of the position he has granted me. Apparently I passed, as he continues to employ my services."

Isabella once again turned to look at him as she spoke. "On that ship was a man who reported that Hippolyte de Bouchard is on his way to invade Monterey!" Isabella realized she had foolishly let her emotions take control of her and had allowed her voice to amplify. She placed a hand on his shoulder and peered in every direction, hoping that no one was in their immediate vicinity and had overheard her outburst.

William Beckwith tensed in response. The entire settlement was aware of Bouchard, but no one considered an invasion as an immediate threat; they had no reason to believe otherwise. *"Bouchard?* Coming here?" Isabella raised a single finger in front of her pursed lips, indicating to lower his voice. "That piece of offal," Beckwith continued in a lowered voice. "Your father admits such things to his daughter?" he ventured to inquire.

Isabella lightly and playfully nudged his chest. "Of course not … but his daughter does have a heightened sense of hearing and she overhears his after-dinner conversations, especially his after-dinner discussions with John Cooper-Molera when they drink Madeira or port wines together, as that man seems to be able to get my father to converse more than any other."

"If Bouchard comes, we will beat him back so that he is forced to flee from Monterey Bay," Beckwith proclaimed resolutely.

"My love," Isabella said as she framed his face with her hands once again. "If all of our men had hearts as gallant and pure as yours, I have no doubt that this would be the outcome." Isabella dropped her hands, but the intensity of her regard remained unmoved. "But, unfortunately, this is not the case and I have heard my father admit his lack of confidence in his soldiers many times to John Cooper-Molera."

"What did your father propose we do if Bouchard does attack?" Beckwith asked with utmost curiosity.

"Flee." Isabella quickly responded.

36.

Year of our Lord 1818.

FATHER TOMAS DE LA PENA MET the caravan outside of the main entrance of the Mission San Antonio de Padua. He watched with love and pity as the settlers and soldiers passed by him with a common appearance of having crawled through the underworld on their bellies. He wondered what had possessed the group to make such a grievous error of judgment, abandoning the marked Mission Trail and attempting a trek through the coastal range of mountains. Even the converted neophytes of the local Salinan tribe avoided direct trails through the heart of the mountains whenever possible. Oddly, Father Margil walked near the rear of the group and not near the front as Father De la Pena would have expected from a spiritual leader. Father De la Pena watched Margil closely. Something was wrong.

Father Margil lifted his gaze to greet his brother of God and De la Pena instantly recognized pain and retribution budding in Father Margil's eyes. The two men of the cloth exchanged pleasantries, Father De la Pena welcoming the group to the mission and Father Margil graciously extending his thanks. Afterward, De la Pena inquired as to how long Margil and his expedition would be staying at the mission, receiving an indeterminate answer from Father Margil that seemed to indicate that the group needed a few days to recover before completing the final leg of their quest and arriving at Father Serra's Mission of San Carlos Borromeo de Carmelo.

Father Margil then requested he be left alone in the mission's chapel for a period of time. When De la Pena offered that perhaps Father Margil would prefer to be shown to his quarters where he could rest first, Margil quickly countered that the Lord should never be kept waiting. De la Pena agreed, silently leading Father Margil towards the chapel.

The convoy's departure from the Mission San Antonio de Padua for the Mission of San Carlos Borromeo de Carmelo was delayed longer than anyone in the group would have expected. Even those that had been the most exhausted and downtrodden just days earlier as the group marched overwrought with despair through the merciless mountains were feeling refreshed and ready to complete the final stage of their long journey. The difficulty of the final segment of the Mission Trail would be trivial compared to what they had already overcome, they collectively thought.

Father Margil did not share in the sentiment of joy moving through the group. The importance of his quest did not escape him, but the grief he felt for having committed such a grievous sin overcame him to the point of him temporarily losing his senses. For two full days, he refused to leave the confines of a small room where he was led after his visit to the mission's chapel on the group's arrival.

The head friar of the mission, Father De la Pena, attempted on numerous occasions to converse with him, but Margil merely left the father standing in the doorway of the room without responding to his questions. There was little chance that Father De la Pena would understand, Father Margil repeated to himself as he relaxed his tired body on the flattened mattress of the bed. Even if Father De la Pena was able to grasp the gravity of the objectives of his secret mission, and the dire consequences that were sure to result in the case of Father Margil's failure, he would not be able to understand the necessity that Margil carried in his heart and soul regarding Diego Alvarez.

On the second day after the convoy's arrival, De la Pena invited Father Margil to tour the grounds of the mission so that he could share in the glory of God on earth, as surely His glory was most obvious in such a place, a place where over one thousand of the local indigenous natives had opted to forgo their former ways and turn to a life devoted to hard work, devotion, and prayer.

The grounds of the mission were sprawling; it was one of the largest in the entire Alta California mission system, if not the largest, according to Father De la Pena. An entirely new segment of housing for unmarried female neophytes and male neophytes had recently been constructed on opposite ends of the married neophyte housing. A new building solely dedicated to rendering beef tallow had recently been constructed, and the converted natives proved to be excellent soap and candle makers. It was of lessened surprise that they were equally qualified at the skinning of hides of the mission's cattle and drying it to the liking of the merchants that occasionally arrived from Monterey or Santa Barbara.

Father Margil was tormented and saw none of the prosperous deeds at the Mission San Antonio de Padua. *He had to tell someone of his sin.* Even if it had been a necessary sin, it was still a sin, and although he prayed for forgiveness, he also prayed that he would repent his sin in killing the vile man, Diego Alvarez, as he spoke to the Lord. Yet as he attempted to block out the world around him, he heard his voice repeating inside his head that he needed to tell someone, if for no other reason than to state the dreadful deed out loud.

He considered speaking with Captain Echevarria. Surely, if any person shared contempt for Diego Alvarez as much as Father Margil, it was the captain. And further, the Captain was a soldier, accustomed to facing mankind's potential savagery as much as any man of the cloth. Father Margil doubted little that the captain would retain the crimson secret if revealed to him and Father Margil suspected that the captain already assumed what undeniably occurred when Father Margil and Alvarez had walked off into the night with only Father Margil returning. Yet, even considering this strong sentiment, and even after he and the captain had developed a kinship over the course of their journey together, Margil could not bring himself to speak about Alvarez with Captain Echevarria.

On the evening of the third day after the expedition's arrival at San Antonio, Father Margil requested sheets of parchment and a pen and inkpot from a passing neophyte who Margil noticed typically following closely behind Father De la Pena. The young man promptly did as he was told and soon thereafter, the door to the Father Margil's room was closed; a soft light of a single candle touched the outline of the room's window.

That night, Father Margil sent word through the same young man to notify Captain Echevarria that he was to inform their group of their departure at sunrise the next morning. Father Margil handed the writing tools and sheets of paper back, minus one sheet, to the young man and thanked him.

The next morning, Father Margil's convoy of soldiers, settlers, and precious cargo bound for Monterey passed by the impressive mountainous peak looming westward high above the valley they traversed. It was slightly rounded at its top and had a white-capped ring of snow at its ascent. Father Margil had overheard Father De la Pena mentioning to Captain Echevarria, who was inquiring about the presence of hostile tribes between the San Antonio Mission and the Carmel Mission, that the peak had been named in honor of Father Junipero Serra. Margil grew increasingly uncomfortable in the peak's presence; it followed their progress all through the morning and he perceived that the mountain regarded his every step.

Caught in persistent apprehension, Margil did not notice Captain Echevarria approaching him on his horse. The captain dismounted and began walking alongside Father Margil. "I believe we are all ready to reach our final destination," the captain dryly commented.

Father Margil heard the words, but it took an extra moment for him to realize that he was being spoken to. He then noticed the captain's presence next to him. The captain did not appear to be menacing in any form and instead looked resigned. Father Margil excused himself and asked if the captain would repeat himself.

"I said that I believe we are all ready to reach our final destination."

Father Margil lightly winced at the captain's words, which bore into him. "*Our final destination?*" Margil spoke aloud while gazing off into the distance.

"Well, yes, to the Mission of San Carlos Borromeo de Carmelo and onward to Monterey," the Captain clarified.

"Yes, yes," Father Margil conceded. "It will indeed be a great day to reach our final destination and be done with this cursed trail," Father Margil uttered despairingly.

"*Cursed?*" Echevarria asked.

Father Margil berated himself for having spoken so freely and foolishly. Thankfully, there had been no tone of accusation in the captain's voice and Margil concluded that the man was only trying to engage him in polite discourse. "*Taxing,* I meant to say," Father Margil forced a smile.

"Yes, indeed it has been taxing. Hopefully with a little effort on the part of our group, we will reach the mouth of the Carmel River by tomorrow afternoon and then we shall all rejoice in the past trials and tribulations of our voyage together."

Father Margil suddenly had the thought that the captain was acting more friendly and talkative than normal, and a growing suspicion of the conversation's intentions steadily rose within him. "Yes, it will be a glorious day and we should all thank the Lord for delivering us. If you will excuse me, though, I must return to the Church's wagon to gather some mustard seed, as now that we have returned to the Mission Trail, I must reengage my obligation to spread seeds in the wake of our passage for future travelers to follow."

Captain Echevarria obliged with a nod of his head, and within seconds, he had returned to his mount on the horse and was riding towards the front of the convoy. Father Margil was glad to see the captain ride away from him, as their conversation was increasing his anxiety.

He had lied, however, about his intentions. The supply of mustard seed he had brought on their journey had run out before their decision to detour from the Mission Trail and begin their passage through the mountains.

37.

Year of our Lord 1818.

FATHER MARGIL LEARNED instantly that Father Junipero Serra was an exceptional man in the narrow category of exceptional men. Unlike the friars at the previous missions that the caravan had reached, at the Mission of San Carlos Borromeo de Carmelo, Father Serra did not wait for the convoy to arrive. Instead, once word reached the mission that the group had entered the valley, Serra walked eastward until he found them and could thereby walk with them on the final steps of their journey.

Father Serra, the founder of the Alta California mission system and its leading light, opened his arms widely as he approached the group that was walking alongside the bank of the small river in the center of the valley. He kept his arms raised as he approached them, as if wanting to embrace everyone at once. Father Serra was shorter than Margil expected, and balder. But benevolence emanated from the man, and with a wide grin, Father Serra welcomed the expedition. He ensured them that it was only a few miles further to the mission in the direction behind him, towards the ocean, which they could not see yet.

The caravan came to a complete halt in the presence of Father Junipero Serra. The previous day's walk, the evening camp, and their final trek through the sunny valley lined thickly with impressive stately oak trees had been uneventful up until the moment of Father Serra's arrival. Seeing Father Serra, though, brought joy to them, as it was then that they finally grasped that their journey through the wilds of Alta California was at an end.

Father Serra moved through the group, greeting each and every soul with the ease and comfort one normally perceives only among family or very close and old friends. When he reached Father Margil, the two friars stood in front of one another momentarily before speaking. Margil saw something familiar in Father Serra; they were two men devoted to God and to doing God's work on earth, but Father Margil perceived that, like him, Father Serra was also pragmatic. It was Serra, after all, that had arranged for the gold to be delivered to Monterey in the first place. The two men of God nodded in appreciation of one another. Serra was elated that Father Margil had arrived with the precious cargo intact, which he would have sensed to be otherwise immediately had Margil not met his gaze fully. Margil was delighted to comprehend through Father Serra's mannerisms that their arrival was not too late. There was still time to get the gold to Monterey to appease the Russian.

As the expedition returned to marching westward, it occurred to Margil that in the presence of Father Serra, he did not feel the overwhelming guilt for his sin as he had in the presence of Father Tomas De la Pena at the San Antonio Mission. This realization did not make him feel morose; on the contrary, it stirred a sensation within him that reinforced his justification of his actions for the good of the Church, the Spanish Empire, Alta California, and for God himself.

"It brings me great pleasure that you and your people have arrived safely here, Father Margil," Father Serra remarked as he and Margil surveyed the grounds of the Carmel Mission together. They slowly strolled through the mission's courtyard and outlying areas, Father Margil noticing that the Carmel Mission was not as sprawling or large as the San Antonio Mission, but that it was more ornate, from its architecture to its adornments in the mission's main courtyard. The Santa Barbara Mission was arguably the most elaborate of all the missions in Alta California, and on his journey Father Margil had seen them all, but the Carmel Mission was not far behind in beauty. Even the Carmel Mission's chapel was more akin to the glittering chapels of Mexico City or even of Spain than to its more rustic and rudimentary contemporaries in the other missions.

"And it brings me great pleasure in return to have at last arrived, Father Serra."

"Were the tribulations of the trail perilous?" Father Serra asked.

"Yes. Indeed they were," Father Margil noticed a few of the to-be-settlers from his group pass by them. "But I consider myself blessed by the Lord himself to have been assigned to lead such a noble and fine group of people, settlers and soldiers alike."

"Did you have any losses?" Father Serra inquired directly.

"Yes. One man perished on the trail; he was one of the soldiers," Father Margil lied. He did not consider Diego Alvarez's death to be a loss.

"Ah, that is unfortunate. But, as we know all too well, this life is not without losses and we can only assume that the soldier's demise was in God's plan."

Father Margil did not respond to Serra's comment. A thought flashed across his mind that he would tell Father Serra the truth of what had happened to Diego Alvarez, right then and there. As quickly as the thought appeared, though, it dissipated, and at that moment, Father Margil resigned that he would never tell a soul of what had occurred in the dark of the mountains that night. He had confessed through the letter he had left at the Mission San Antonio de Padua. Eventually, the letter would be found; but he would never speak of the affair again. He would carry the secret to his grave.

"Were you able to perform the funeral rights for the poor soul?" Margil suddenly heard Father Serra asking. Father Margil shook his head and explained that the man had fallen from a steep cliff and that there had been no possibility to retrieve the body, much less bury it and perform funeral rites. "That is truly unfortunate. We shall say a prayer for the man this very evening before supper," Serra resolutely added.

Father Margil wished to change the subject of conversation. "When shall we go to Monterey to see the governor?" he asked.

"Tomorrow morning. It is not a difficult trip; Monterey is just over those hills," Father Serra commented, pointing northward to a ridge line that appeared to sprout directly from the ocean and then extend into the long valley that the expedition had traversed earlier that day.

"That ridge of hills is actually the beginning of a larger peninsula that juts into the sea," Serra continued, sweeping his arm westward.

"And Monterey is just on the other side, situated at the base of the hills and the edge of the peninsula, similar to how we are located here at the mission."

"I do not wish to be imprudent, Father Serra, but should we not depart this very evening?" Father Margil hesitantly explored.

Father Serra stopped walking and turned to face Father Margil. "I can see that you are a man devoted to your cause. But I can also see the fatigue on your face and on the faces of your settlers and soldiers. I therefore must insist that we rest here this evening and that your group enjoys the pure hospitality of our mission for one evening before entering their new lives in Monterey. Further, although it is not overly difficult, the road is steep and bandits are prone to be near it at night, and we would not want to unnecessarily endanger the precious cargo you have devotedly delivered, would we? And I can assure you that if the Russian were in Monterey, we would be aware of his presence. From the little I know of the Russian people, I have gathered that they are a people determined to make their presence known wherever they venture."

The mission's bell chimed, indicating to the converted neophytes working in the fields surrounding the mission and those working inside it that it was time for evening prayers and the evening meal.

38.

Year of our Lord 2009.

S AMUEL P. BECKWITH FELT CRAMMED in the tiny restaurant. Like many other Carmel restaurants, the patrons assumed that people enjoyed being forced to sit at small, uncomfortable tables while being seated so closely to tables surrounding their own that, if so desired, one could partake in the conversation of others. Samuel had no intention of partaking in anyone else's conversations, most of which he regrettably could not block out and included discussions of a local play or art gallery with a new exhibit. Equally, he had no intention of conveying being agreeable to having others attempt to engage him over dinner.

"What the hell are 'tapas' anyway?" Samuel asked. An elderly man dressed in a tacky suit at the table next to theirs perked up at Samuel's question to his wife, ready to respond if she did not. Part of Samuel hoped that whatever answer his wife would provide would be perceived as incorrect, and with the old man trying to butt in, Samuel would be provided with a perfect opportunity to ridicule the old fool. He could feel his blood already boiling; a little push from someone else would have consequences.

Bridgette had picked a slinky black camisole top with tight white pants for their evening. The camisole was low-cut in the front, revealing her ample cleavage. During the play, she would have to wrap herself in the black shawl that she brought as well, but the warmth of the restaurant provided an excellent opportunity for her to unveil herself.

Just to remind her husband of what he had coming later, she unnecessarily leaned forward slightly across the table before responding. "Tapas, honey, is the Spanish name for little plates of food." She tried her hardest to make her lips appear sensual as she spoke.

Samuel noticed the old man in the dated suit sitting next to them recoil as he overheard the correct answer.

"That's why on this menu, we order a bunch of little plates of food that we will then share," Bridgette continued.

"So, for dinner, we are going to order a bunch of little plates of food and share them?" Samuel repeated, glancing down at the menu before him. He had not picked it up yet, as once they were seated, his wife ordered a bottle of Spanish rosé wine that he had to admit was much better than any rosé from California he had tried.

"Yes, that's the idea. In Spain, people make an evening of it, going from tapas restaurant to tapas restaurant, eating a little here and there and drinking wine customarily at each stop."

"How do you know that?" Samuel inquired.

His wife slightly blushed and hesitated for a moment before responding. "Oh, well, you know, honey — I did some traveling before we met."

Yeah, right, Samuel said to himself. *You probably banged a couple of sleazy Spanish guys while you were at it as well.*

"You know, I'm looking forward to going home tonight after the play …" she added in her most practiced, seductive voice while puckering her lips together and rolling her shoulders backwards so that her chest expanded.

Samuel relaxed and took a sip from his wine glass. After setting his glass back down, he asked, "So, is it a special occasion evening when one goes out for tapas with others?"

"No, not at all; in the larger urban areas, it's a weekly affair," the old man sitting next to them blurted, peering through his thick glasses with a smile.

Samuel's malicious glance fixated pointedly on the old man. "Excuse me, but I'm trying to have a conversion with my wife," Samuel said. "If you don't mind," he added in an icy tone. The old man sheepishly turned away and attempted to begin a conversation with the elderly woman seated across the table from him, who Samuel noticed was nodding her head periodically as if fighting off falling asleep.

Samuel recognized how on edge he was feeling, and he knew it was not just the nosy old man sitting too close to them. It was his crew that was bothering him. He was beginning to obsess about every move that had been made and every move that still needed to be made, and he gradually began to lose confidence in the three others. Samuel began having difficulty at times distinguishing between the numbers he had assigned everyone and their actual names. *I'm Number One, that's what counts most*, he would repeat to himself.

Even his Number Two, even Victor's loyalty was becoming suspicious. Why, for instance, had Victor acted so foolishly on the beach? If anyone had been near them, their plan could have been ruined! And why was Victor suddenly not returning his calls? It was time for another gathering, Samuel decided. But he would arrange for it to appear as a casual meeting, one where the others would all be more relaxed and he would then have a chance to really observe each of them for any signs of betrayal. Number Three, that Zande, might be the exception, as Zande never appeared to relax much, but Samuel had other ways to check on Zande, if needed. Zande, the Big Sur nut, could prove to be his most trusted partner, Samuel considered.

"As I was saying, tapas are really popular in Spain," his wife commented, hoping that she could calm down her husband before he gave the old man next to them a heart attack.

After he chastised the old man, Bridgette watched as her husband retreated somewhere else in his mind. It was as if he were someplace else altogether. It was a regard she had noticed often in him in the previous year and she hoped that he was not having an affair. Samuel had made her sign a prenuptial agreement, after all, and without him, she would not have her life of luxury. Of course, in case that it ever happened, she could always try finding another "Pebble man," but even at her fairly young age, she was near the top end of the age bracket for "Pebble wives."

Samuel glared at the old man next to them, ensuring that he was not about to try to join their conversation again. Although he didn't really care about a conversation on tapas, he did want to show some effort to please his wife, especially with her outfit choice ... "Okay, let's order some tapas, then," he said, smiling, not able to resist lowering his eyes to his wife's cleavage.

Samuel supposed the setting for the theater helped to draw crowds, as it was the only one of its kind on the Peninsula. The Forest Theater of Carmel did have a way of being impressive, even if it was in the obnoxious Carmel way. Glancing around him, Samuel counted perhaps one hundred people seated spaciously along the long wooden benches that served as the fairly quaint theater's seating. His wife, and apparently one or two others, found the rustic and bohemian setting of the theater to be utterly delightful, as people carried in their dinners from Whole Foods, Trader Joe's, or a local Carmel shop such as the Cheese Shop, along with bottles of wine.

Samuel laughed to himself as he watched two elderly couples seated in front of them marveling over the contents of a picnic dinner that had been carted in within a handcrafted wicker picnic basket. On an equally expensive looking handwoven quilt, an assortment of fine cheeses, salami, olives, and finely sliced sourdough bread were laid out on display.

Two large fire pits adorned the sides of the seating areas and torches were lit along the walkway from the theater's entrance to and around the seating area. A blend of Monterey pine, Monterey cypress, and coast live oak trees lined the perimeter of the theater grounds, effectively concealing the theater, which was located in the middle of a residential area.

Carmel relished in not having street lights or address numbers for houses, along with narrow roads, a lack of sidewalks, cottage-like houses, an art scene, and an overall village feel. That was all fine and dandy, Samuel thought; but Pebble Beach had many of the same elements, but with more space between houses! Samuel considered that it was perhaps unfair to compare the two exclusive destinations, as in Pebble Beach, few of the tourists that visited would be able to afford to stay in a visitor-serving capacity overnight and they would be kicked out of the area not long after sunset if they were loitering about; yet in Carmel, there was much more opportunity for the average tourist to find a reasonably affordable hotel for an evening. Samuel quickly removed the thought from his mind. Carmelites were mostly old and crabby dog lovers that loved to complain about how things used to be, he told himself. Maybe Carmel was perpetually jealous of Pebble Beach, as residents of Carmel in its early days desired to install a wall around it to restrict access, but unlike its more illustrious neighbor of Pebble Beach, it was never able to block itself off from the outside world.

"This theater has been around since the early 1900s!" his wife exclaimed, as she always did when they attended a performance there while reading the play's program. "Early famous inhabitants of Carmel such as Mary Austin and Robinson Jeffers used to come here to watch plays often."

The name Mary Austin sounded familiar, but not enough to remember who she was exactly. Samuel remembered Robinson Jeffers was a poet that had built the strange castle-like house with its stone tower across from Carmel Beach. "I guess he needed to take a break every once in a while from building his stone castle," Samuel commented, lightly laughing at his own joke.

Bridgette playfully slapped him on the shoulder. "Oh, stop," she pleaded.

The light slap from his wife had a secondary effect of stirring Samuel's suspicions of his team once again. "I'm thinking about inviting some of my friends to get together for a dinner gathering next week," Samuel commented. He was suddenly unable to not think about his recent endeavor. Most days he was able to put the entire affair aside and not stress about it; his conscious had never been able to control him. At this moment, however, his subconscious was wide awake.

"Oh, yeah?" his wife muttered in a disinterested voice as she slightly turned away from him.

The disinterest did not go unnoticed by Samuel and it temporarily bothered him. But he admitted that he could not blame his wife for not showing amusement at his suggestion. Normally when he stated such a thing, it meant that he was planning to meet a group of male friends somewhere, without her. "*With our wives and girlfriends,*" he added.

The effect on his wife was instantaneous. Bridgette turned back to face him with a glowing smile on her face. "*Really?*"

"Yup, wives and girlfriends included." Samuel considered his "girlfriends" comment as he spoke it aloud the second time. Victor would of course bring his wife, but Dick was divorced and Zande, well, who knew with Zande. Samuel figured that Zande probably had a plethora of woodsy chicks in Big Sur. Dick would likely have difficulty finding a date. Even though he was moderately successful, he was not wealthy enough to make his balding head or bulging gut disappear and, furthermore, his personality was not exactly what anyone would describe as being remotely engaging.

"That sounds super, honey," Bridgette said. "You go off with your guys so much; it'll be great for me to get to know them a little more."

Samuel thought of how Zande was the type that would love *to get to know* his attractive wife much better. Samuel noted to himself to be sure and not let her sit next to Zande wherever the dinner gathering ended up.

"Do you have any thoughts on where we could go? I'm thinking of inviting three of my friends, so we'd be looking at a group of eight." *Or seven, if Dick can't find a date*, Samuel added to himself, trying his best to not chuckle at his own inner-monologue pleasantry. "I'd like it to be somewhere kind of special but not too touristy, not too quiet but not too noisy, not too crowded but not empty, and not too expensive, as I'm going to offer to foot the bill, but not too cheap, either."

His wife beamed from the invitation to participate in the planning of the dinner.

Bridgette twisted her face in concentration. Her expression then quickly eased as a wide smile appeared. "I've got it: the Cachagua General Store."

Samuel agreed. It was a cozy space, but it was the type of place where a small group would go unnoticed; and it offered all of the other elements that Samuel wanted. It would be perfect.

As if introduced through stage direction, while Samuel and his wife finalized their decision for the dinner gathering, the lights on the stage dimmed and a man wearing a sixteenth century English nobleman's costume took his place at center stage.

39.

Year of our Lord 2009.

GAZING UPON SAN FRANCISCO BAY, John Gibson wondered if he had discovered his new home. Born and raised in the mountains of North Carolina, after attending college at the University of North Carolina's Asheville campus, he applied to the Federal Bureau of Investigation and promptly found himself in the Washington, DC metro area, where he remained for the next thirty years. DC grew on him, but he never loved living there.

It was still fairly cloudy in San Francisco, but Gibson had quickly acquired an understanding of the city's frequent fog inundation, and from the appearance of the rapidly retreating cloud cover, he figured it would not be long before the famous California sun would break through the clouds and drench the city in sunshine for a few hours, only to have the fog return in full force later to reclaim the city. He listened to the barking of the annoying yet captivating sea lions and watched boats meandering out into the bay with the ominous outline of Alcatraz Island in the distance.

Detective Chiles arrived precisely on time for their meeting, casually approaching and standing by Gibson on the wooden pier's railing over the gently lapping waters below.

Chiles commented, "Quite a unique place, isn't it?"

Gibson turned to face Chiles. "Yes, it certainly is." Gibson took in one more glimpse of the view. "Well, let's get to work."

Chiles smiled in response. "Love to," he said. "There's a guy I've come across before who works down here at the docks who may be able to help us. He's kind of a dock keeper; I guess you would call him that. He pretty much knows which boats are coming and going off these piers at any given time, and if he noticed anything strange around the time of the heist, he would let us know. He tipped me off once about a year ago when a body washed up among the sea lions down here. It was related to a narcotics turf war ongoing here in the City between the Ukrainians and the Filipinos."

"Interesting," Gibson commented. "You said the body was floating with the sea lions?"

"Yeah, it was. It was floating in the water and wedged up against one of those platforms where the sea lions converge next to Pier 39. By the time I arrived on the scene, Japanese tourists were already having a heyday taking pictures of the body. And it was interesting, as the sea lions wanted nothing to do with it. The platform where the body was wedged was completely empty and the rest of them were entirely full of those big, smelly guys."

"So where is this dock keeper?"

Chiles stepped backward from the pier's railing. "He's out there," he pointed leftward to a marina with hundreds of boats tethered to piers. "At the end of the line of piers, he has a tiny station where he's posted most of the time."

"Okay, let's go." Gibson responded and the two walked toward the marina.

They found the dock keeper, just as Chiles had predicted. He was a small Chinese man with thick glasses and he wore a faded San Francisco Giants baseball cap. He was seated on a wooden stool outside of his single-room wooden station. The man did not appear at all alarmed by their approach; instead, he greeted them warmly.

"You lost?" the dock keeper called to them.

"Nope, we're here to ask you a couple of questions, if you wouldn't mind," Chiles answered as they approached closer.

The dock keeper squinted at the pair and then broke into a wide grin. "Oh, I remember you! You are the detective who came when I called about that body!" The dock keeper jumped off his stool and stood. "I haven't had any bodies floating around lately, though."

"We're not here about any bodies today," Chiles assured the man as he shook the dock keeper's hand. Chiles presented Gibson and the little dock keeper was noticeably impressed to have an FBI agent requesting his assistance. "We're wondering if you noticed anything peculiar or out of the ordinary last week."

"Ah … you mean related to that federal building's robbery?" the dock keeper quipped.

"Yes," Chiles clarified.

"Would you have any record of which boats went out that day?" Gibson inquired.

"Not really," the dock keeper responded in disappointment. "When I'm here, I do notice most of the boats which are docked, those departing and arriving — but there's no requirement for the boat owners to report to me when they are coming and going. Some do when they are going to be out for extended periods or if they are going to be away for awhile and would like me to keep an eye on their boat, but day to day … nope." The dock keeper shook his head.

"Did anyone report that they were leaving for an extended period the day of the robbery?" Chiles asked.

The dock keeper again shook his head.

A thought occurred to Gibson. "How about the next day or even a few days afterward?"

The dock keeper peered at him, recollecting. "You know, now that you mention it, one boat did return a couple of days later that I found odd."

"What did you find odd about it?" Chiles asked.

"Because the boat is only used for fishing, yet it returned late afternoon one day." From the expression he noticed on the faces of Chiles and Gibson, the dock keeper provided a further explanation.

"Fishing boats go out in the early hours of the morning and return before noon at the latest, on the same day. To have one return that late in the afternoon was out of the ordinary," the dock keeper turned to look directly at Detective Chiles.

"Tell us more about this boat," Chiles prodded as he exchanged a glance of achievement with Gibson.

Cachagua was an interesting destination, Samuel Beckwith reflected as he turned off of Carmel Valley Road onto Cachagua Road, a narrow roadway rising gradually into a tunnel created by the gnarly oak trees enclosing it. Carmel Valley Road itself turned into an entirely different road immediately past the limits of Carmel Valley Village — the "village," as locals referred to it. Carmel Valley Road stretched through the narrow Carmel Valley all the way to its end near the Carmel River's meeting with the Pacific Ocean, near the Carmel Mission.

Once the road passed the village, there was a dangerous immediate single-lane bend in the road, and passing this point, the valley transformed itself entirely. Whereas before, driving on the road afforded sweeping vistas of the Carmel Valley, after the turn, the valley narrowed dramatically, and the previously wide-open views were limited to occasional breaks in the thick overhanging canopy of oak trees for some fifteen miles.

Driving along this stretch of road, there was an occasional gated property, demarking the gigantic territory of some hidden country haven, or a dirt driveway with a "private property" and "no trespassing" sign located next to a solitary mailbox, but it was mostly just trees and tight curves in the road — a lot of curves. Samuel glanced quickly at his wife and observed that, as usual, she was not doing well with the curves and had a distinctly greenish tint to her complexion. Samuel suggested she crack the passenger door's window open to get some fresh air on her face; she slowly but gratefully responded.

Samuel didn't let his eyes wander from the road for too long, though; aside from the treacherous curves was the possibility that around a bend would be a lost and frustrated tourist taking the curves too quickly or a valley local driving a big-ass truck too fast after a few beers.

"Are you all right over there?" Samuel asked Bridgette. He wanted an excuse to start a conversation, as he could feel anxiety brewing within him to a dangerous level and wanted to appear as cool as a cucumber to the group.

His wife didn't reply with words, opting instead to force a smile with her eyes still closed. Accepting that he was not going to achieve his goal if Bridgette was feeling so poorly, Samuel tried to take in the view and settle himself down on his own. The road continued to rise steadily along a ridgeline until it opened up completely and wound itself delicately around a hillside. There was a fantastic overlook rightward to a forested valley, but Samuel didn't dare remove his eyes from the road. After reaching the clearing, the road narrowed even further and there was no guardrail between the edge of the cliff and a five hundred foot drop just beyond it.

He noticed that Bridgette also kept her eyes focused forward, with one of her hands gently massaging her forehead. *She must really love coming way out here for dinner*, he thought, as she got carsick every time they made the drive yet continued to offer it as a venue option whenever he asked for her recommendation.

The Cachagua area went unnoticed for decades and gradually obtained a reputation as a distant outpost where only the most hardy could live. Aside from having a sparse and small population, and the fact that the nearest modern services were arduous drives in only two directions, Cachagua thrived in its reputation of being off-limits to outsiders. The only reasons for anyone to take one of two turnoffs to enter the place was to drive through it on the backcountry mountainous road that led through the Ventana Wilderness to a Buddhist retreat center hidden snugly in the forest, and the center received limited visitors, or to access remote, rustic National Forest campgrounds that were not well known. Cachagua also experienced colder than average winters, and if there was a populated area of the county that had the best opportunity of seeing snow on the ground in winter, it was Cachagua.

As Carmel Valley experienced its explosion of popularity and property values began to skyrocket, a few stately mansions began to also dot the woods and hills of Cachagua, but unlike in Carmel Valley, Cachagua residents displayed more dexterity, and the explosion that was Carmel Valley did not occur in Cachagua. Instead it remained a dominantly local's place, even with a smattering of affluent outsiders moving in. There were still trailer park communities in Cachagua, something not seen and not imagined as even possible in adjoining Carmel Valley. Curious tourists were often warned, however, to steer clear of the trailer parks, as rumors of paranoid meth communities being embedded within them swirled.

Passing by one of the trailer parks, Samuel noticed the thick chain-link fence surrounding the place; most of the windows of the trailers were covered with blankets, boards, or plastic and there was no sign of life. It looked like a compound to him, and even he, having driven past the same trailer park many times on their trips to the Cachagua General Store for dinner, remained surprised at the existence of such places in Monterey County. The thought solidified his notion that the best of the county lived in Pebble Beach.

"What are you thinking about, honey?" Bridgette asked in a weak voice.

Samuel turned and glanced at her quickly, but not as quickly as he would have done before, as the road had descended from its previously precarious conditions. "I was thinking about you, my sex kitten," he lied. He hoped that his sexual reference would register with her that he was *in the mood* and would want to act on it later in the evening.

"Oh," she smiled and placed a hand lightly on his crotch. "I'll be better later," Bridgette said.

Samuel smiled like a kid who had been promised ice cream after he finished his vegetables.

A clearing in the roadside trees ahead of them signaled that they had arrived at the General Store. Few were even aware of the store's existence, much less its Monday night dinners. The store was in actuality a general store, as its name implied. The wooden exterior of the building appeared to have not been painted in years, as its red paint was not chipped, but falling away in sheets. An extension of the building hid a quaint kitchen and dining area that one evening a week was turned into a restaurant, supplied with food and staff from an organic catering outfit kept busy on weekends with upscale events in and around the Peninsula.

Samuel originally despised the combined idea of driving into the middle of nowhere for dinner and then being served leftovers in what most would label an extended barn with a few crooked tables, wobbly chairs, and tacky decorations. Further, service at the Monday night dinners was frustratingly slow, which was perhaps a given, considering the event's location on top of the fact that the staff were not normal restaurant workers; one could be seated at a table at the store and not even see a waiter look in one's direction for ten minutes at times. Samuel knew, though, that with influence, every situation can be improved for those with means. He usually acted as if he was being forced into driving out to the store for a Monday night dinner when Bridgette recommended it, but he secretly enjoyed it after having set the rules straight on their first visit years before.

Recognizing the lack of attentive service, Samuel ensured they would never be thrust into the crowd of nobodies again. He asked to speak with the manager, and when he did, he mentioned that he had many well-placed friends in the county who often held catered events. At the end of the meal, Samuel tipped every staff member in the establishment with a fifty dollar bill, even those who had not served them in any way. After that visit, their table was always the first served while others gawked and muttered to one another how they did not understand why one table was receiving exceptional service. Samuel had assured that they would receive the service he expected, and the head chef himself came to greet him and his wife at their table personally every evening they attended one of the Monday night dinners.

Reservations by calling the store beforehand were normally required for the dinners, one at six o'clock and the next at eight, especially if one desired to be seated at the earlier of the two seatings. With a maximum capacity of thirty seats, the evenings were consistently packed and booked well in advance. Samuel, however, discovered that he could call the day of, and even if the earlier seating was entirely booked, he would not be declined and was always granted the room's best table, which was slightly secluded from the rest of the room in a sunken area attached to the main dining area.

Samuel parked in the makeshift parking lot, just a partially cleared area in front of the store building, and noticed Victor Mathews and his wife standing next to Zande Allen and a free spirit-looking woman. Zande had a hand clasped firmly on the woman's lower back.

Victor could not have looked more uncomfortable and out of place, dressed in an impeccable blue suit; it would assuredly be the only suit and tie worn in the restaurant. He peered around anxiously during what Samuel imagined was a painful and forced conversation between the two couples. Victor was not the sort to mingle with locals, and he rarely left the safety of his Santa Lucia Preserve. In the clubhouse of the golf course there, Victor could feel comfortable chumming around with others of obscene wealth and their private castles scattered around the private valley. Victor was gently rocking from heel to heel as he stood.

Samuel had only witnessed Victor's wife, Areva, speak on a very limited number of occasions. Areva had, not surprisingly, followed Victor's lead and wore an elegant white dress. As usual, she stood obediently by his side, expressionless. She was an attractive Asian woman, with what Samuel imagined was a tight little body underneath her clothing. *There must be something about her that Victor finds so appealing.* She must come out of her shell and shape-shift into a minx in the sack, he concluded as his eyes salaciously went up and down Areva's figure as they approached the group. He quickly reached down and gave his own wife's ass a squeeze.

Unlike Victor, Zande appeared to be in his element. Zande was dressed in a pair of worn jeans and a faded button-up denim shirt. He had a Budweiser bottle in one hand and a cigarette in the other. Cachagua was more his kind of place: secluded, proud, and weird. It was a place of millionaires who moved in to find tranquility living next to others who had inherited land and houses that served as a sole form of wealth, similar to Zande's own Big Sur. Cachagua's location, deep in the Santa Lucia Mountains, was in many ways a side extension of Big Sur, but any inhabitant from either location would vehemently deny any association between the two locales.

Zande's date looked like she was one of his Big Sur friends, Samuel determined. She wore a flowing maroon skirt with a beige knit top. She had unkempt hair that fell down her back. *Hippie Big Sur chic.*

"Greetings," Samuel said with an outstretched hand.

Zande moved first to shake Samuel's hand. "Good to see you, Samuel," he said, tossing his cigarette to the ground and stepping on it.

"Good to see you as well, Zande. This is my wife, Bridgette," Samuel gestured towards Bridgette standing next to him.

Zande nodded politely and lightly shook her hand. Introductions of the entire group ensued with Zande labeling his date, Kate, as a "friend." Samuel inquired if either Victor or Zande had heard from Dick.

"He'll probably be late, *as usual*," Zande commented.

Also *as usual*, Victor tried to defend Dick. "He probably couldn't get away from his office as early as he would have liked to," Victor commented.

Zande shot Victor a glance conveying his displeasure and recommended that they enter the restaurant and be seated instead of waiting outside for Dick to arrive. The idea was unanimously agreed upon and they moved toward the restaurant.

Near the restaurant's doorway, which looked more like an entrance to a trailer home, there was a group of three people seated along a wooden bench. The sound of music and the smell of food meandered casually through the doorway. The bench was occupied by a younger couple each smoking a cigarette, probably in their mid twenties, Samuel thought, dressed in T-shirts and jeans, and a wiry man in his late sixties wearing a worn brown corduroy suit with various patches sewed on it that Samuel figured was probably a vestige from the 1970s. The corduroy suit man had closely cropped silver hair that looked as if he had cut it himself, and badly, as there were obvious spots where his hair was longer, and it gave the man a perpetual bed-head look. The man's eyes were glassy blue and his thin silver mustache created a stark contrast on his deeply tanned face. It was clear that the young couple had seated themselves for a smoke only to be imposed upon by the wandering odd-looking fellow. Samuel overheard the man explaining how lovely smelling the bundle of fresh mint stalks were that he was offering to the young woman.

The smell of richly flavored food and faint wood smoke engulfed them as they stepped through the narrow doorway into the cozy space of the restaurant, which, even with Samuel's preferred nook area, was still a one-room dining restaurant. The usual music routine was playing, the two musicians sandwiched in one far corner of the room. The act consisted of two old-timers, one playing a guitar and a harmonica while the other played a drum set with his hands, and they played there every Monday night.

The interior of the restaurant offered a more intriguing portrait than the building's exterior. The lightly stained wooden walls almost gave the impression of a log cabin and were covered with an eclectic array of hanging oddities: replicas of old wanted posters for criminals from California's earlier days, photos of quaint European streets, a The Doors' concert poster, a cow skull, and portraits of Native American chiefs. In the center of the room on the far wall was a huge mounted elk head, adorned with multicolored Mardi Gras beads. White Christmas tree lights were strung around the room; roughly a third of the lights were burned out and needed replacement.

The hostess, a woman in her late forties with a tongue ring and a ponytail, instantly recognized Samuel and his wife as they entered at the front of their group, and with a courteous smile, careful to attempt to conceal her tongue art, asked them to follow her to their reserved table.

The other tables in the restaurant, squeezed into the small room, were fully seated, and as they squeezed by the bar area and the two front tables, they passed a group of four people that muttered something with their backs turned as they watched Samuel's party being seated at the only remaining seats. Passing by the disgruntled foursome, Samuel felt a hand nudge his side. As he turned, the bright round and rosy face of an old friend greeted him. The man was a local winery owner who had prophetically purchased land in Cachagua cheaply in the Seventies and had ever since been producing arguably the best Cabernet Sauvignon wines in Monterey County.

The two men exchanged greetings briefly, having to speak loudly as the two-man band had turned up their volume a notch as they collaborated on belting out a tune. Samuel indicated that he needed to cut the conversation short, as they were being seated, and the winemaker quickly reached beneath his stool and thrust an unlabeled bottle into Samuel's gut, promising that it would not disappoint. Samuel thanked him and the group proceeded to the table.

Their server appeared instantaneously with six wine glasses delicately held between her fingers and pulled a wine key out of the back pocket of her tight jeans. She had the bottle opened and dispersed equally in each of the glasses just as the group had settled into their chairs. Lisa was her name and she was young, barely old enough to be serving alcohol; she was designated as their server every time Samuel and his wife arrived.

Lisa religiously sported her tight jeans and a tank top that clung to her body; it was something that Samuel fondly appreciated. This was reflected in the amount of the communal tip he would leave for the staff at the end of the evening, which had likely not gone unnoticed by the workers. It didn't bother him that Lisa could easily be his daughter; if the opportunity presented itself, he would unquestionably have his way with her. From the way she flirted with him, often brushing her taut ass against his side as she brought plates to the table, he was certain she would love every minute of it.

Perhaps sensing Samuel's ambling mind and sexual fantasies, Bridgette slightly adjusted herself and placed a hand across his thigh, allowing her fingers to roughly pass across his manhood as she did.

"Glad to see you're feeling better," Samuel commented to her in a lowered voice.

Samuel raised the wine glass in front of him and the table followed. Samuel merely commented that it was nice to have the group of them together, glasses were clinked, and healthy sips of wine were taken.

"We probably should have waited for Dick to do that," Victor commented as his glance fell on the two empty chairs at the far end of the rectangular table.

"*Screw 'em.* That fat Italian should have been here on time," Zande menacingly added.

Is there more to the tension occurring in full view between Victor and Zande? Samuel asked himself. *Or is Zande displaying so much open animosity towards Dick for a particular reason?* It had been obvious at their initial meetings to discuss the heist that Zande held little respect for Dick. Actually, even from the screening meetings before that, when Samuel organized an outing of the four men to gauge their interactions, Zande Allen did not bother to conceal his less than impressed view of Dick Lombardo. Samuel noted Zande's distaste for Dick; however, he didn't think it would ever escalate into anything he could not handle. Samuel assumed that Zande believed in his cause against the federal government much more strongly than any slight annoyance.

Samuel watched the interplay between Zande and Victor closely. Zande stared directly at Victor; not so much threateningly as tauntingly. Victor nervously took another drink from his wine glass and looked away. *Zande may be crazy, but he would let a federal judge hang him from the gallows before ever doing something as dishonorable as betraying his word. No, there was no need to remotely suspect Zande.*

Victor, however, is acting very strangely, Samuel remarked to himself. *And why is Dick so late, anyway?*

Before Samuel had time to contemplate new possibilities, the commotion of someone forcing their way through the crowd around the darkly stained wooden bar signaled the arrival of Dick Lombardo. A few men scrambled backwards, knocking into the back of Areva's chair, and as they shook their heads and moved back towards the bar, Dick appeared with a woman who Samuel knew was far too attractive to be with the balding and overweight Dick without a reason. She was a thin brunette, considerably younger than Dick, wearing a tight black dress.

"Sorry, sorry we're late," Dick bumbled as he eased himself into an open chair first, and then realizing that he'd left his date still standing, rose again to offer her a chair and then seated himself again.

"Oh, that's okay, Dick. We're getting used to you," Zande commented before Samuel could utter a word.

Dick turned red in embarrassment. He attempted to recover by quickly averting the subject; however, he reacted too quickly and forgot the name of his date. "This is …" Dick turned to glance helplessly at the young woman, who acted as if she was used to such occasions, as she nonchalantly added that her name was Charlotte.

Samuel winced as he noticed Zande's expression immediately brighten. "*Charlotte*, eh?" Zande asked. "Now that's a beautiful name, my dear. How about you tell us all how you two kids met." Zande spoke clearly and loudly, in order that everyone at the table would hear him clearly over the blaring of a James Taylor song being sung by the two-man band. Zande's gaze remained intently focused on the young woman.

The occupants of the table froze in the air of tension rapidly overcoming them. Samuel took advantage of the silence to assert his dominance. "We're glad to have you Dick, and *Charlotte*," he exclaimed loudly, casually peering over at Zande with an insincere smile in an attempt to cool the situation. Dick may be the weakest link in their chain, he thought, but with Zande's persistent antagonism, there would be no possible way to flush out Dick's guilt, if he was indeed guilty.

"We can share stories of how we all met later. But first, let's have some nice wine and enjoy one another's company," Samuel added diplomatically. The tension gradually cleared as Zande relaxed in his chair, Dick's face lost most of its redness, and 'Charlotte' reached for an open bottle of wine that Lisa had snuck onto the table, pouring a glass for herself and Dick. Samuel felt Bridgette's grip around his thigh strengthen and he noticed she was grinning admiringly at him.

Moving beyond the subtle stiffening of his member in his pants, he wondered how in the hell his numbers Three and Four had ever been able to work together and pull off their segment of the plan. Zande, Samuel concluded, must have been in one of his rare generous moods. Zande had probably convinced himself to picture all of the destruction that his cut of the loot would allow in order to tolerate his complete distaste for Dick Lombardo.

Samuel reminded himself to stick to his goal: Sit back and watch them attentively and wait for a sign that one of them was slipping, or already had slipped. If so, it would only be a matter of time before he figured it out. He eased into his chair, trying to relax.

Samuel considered what he would order for dinner. For an appetizer, the roasted quail was his favorite, but for a main course, he was torn between the glazed wild boar, roasted duck, or grilled venison. As he pondered the oncoming culinary delight, he thought back to the gold securely hidden off of Point Lobos. The mere thought of it all just waiting to be retrieved made his erection complete, and his wife noted the final leg of growth with a slight wink of an eye in his direction.

The rest of the table was now calmed and attempting to engage one another. Samuel watched them all like a hawk eying its prey from high above. Everything was turning out just as he planned. *Of course it was.*

"Do you think Isidro will be willing to help?" Agent Gibson asked Detective Chiles. After the revelation they received in their conversation with the dock keeper, the two decided that the best course of action would be for Gibson to head back to Monterey Bay while Chiles remained in San Francisco to follow up on the information the dock keeper had provided them regarding the mysterious fishing boat.

The three of them had walked over to the boat in question, only to find its docking area empty. However, the dock keeper was able to provide a name that he had listed on a dog-eared ledger, and with the slip number attached to a name, it was enough to move on. Fueling their suspicion that the thieves may have indeed used a fishing vessel to make their exit southward, it was more than enough to convince Gibson that it was a solid lead to pursue.

"I'm sure he will; he'll just go about it in his own way. Don't expect him to be all warm and fuzzy at first," Chiles answered.

"That guy gets *warm and fuzzy*?" Gibson jabbed.

Chiles pretended to consider the question momentarily before responding. "Well, now that you mention it, no, I guess he doesn't, really." Chiles laughed lightly.

"*Very funny.* Well, let's give him a call and get it over with."

Chiles pulled out his cell phone and scrolled through his listing of contacts until he reached Isidro and pressed the call button. "Hello, Isidro. How were those pesky tourists I sent your way?" Chiles asked playfully, yet while turned away from Gibson.

"They were fine," Isidro responded.

"Did you give them a history lesson on the Monterey Peninsula?"

"You know I did," Isidro responded in a bland tone.

"You sound less interested than normal in conversation. Did I catch you at a bad time?" Chiles asked.

"Yes, listen ... I'm in Santa Barbara doing research on something and I really don't have time to chit-chat."

A silence followed when neither of them spoke. "David, as I said, I'm busy right now and I apologize if I'm being short; I just am a bit distracted at the moment," Isidro finally broke the silence by saying.

"Okay, understood, but I'm actually calling you on a business issue, rather than a personal one."

"Business issue? As in a *police issue*?"

"Exactly. I want to ask for your assistance with an investigation I'm assigned to that we think has leads in Monterey or its vicinity," Chiles replied.

"*We?*" Isidro asked.

"*We*, meaning Agent Gibson and myself. You remember Agent Gibson, don't you?" Chiles glanced up again at Gibson and received a glance instructing him to tone down his sarcasm with Isidro. Chiles waited, but Isidro didn't immediately respond. "I need to ask you a favor, a professional favor this time, Isidro. Agent Gibson is going to be heading back down to Monterey and I need you to meet him and show him around and answer any questions he may have on the Peninsula."

"Now I really am just a tour guide?" Isidro asked as if he were offended.

"No, no, no ... Not at all. But you are an expert on the area, past and present, and you would be more of a valuable initial resource for Agent Gibson down there than even the Monterey Police Department."

"You mean he's not even requesting assistance from the police department? You expect me to fill in for a policeman? That's utterly preposterous."

"Isidro, Isidro, you're overreacting. Of course he'll let the local police force know of his presence," Chiles responded. "But what is paramount in situations such as these is that a knowledgeable person such as yourself be consulted. Someone like you can make all the difference in an investigation."

"David. We're old friends. But are you honestly asking me to become involved in a situation where I could get shot?"

"Of course not! We're still at the preliminary investigation stage ... I promise that you will be in no danger whatsoever." Chiles suffered through another lengthy pause.

"Okay. I need to be back in Monterey to speak at a Daughters of the American West dinner this evening. I can probably secure a seat for Agent Gibson if you think he'd be interested."

Chiles inhaled and exhaled heavily in relief. "Thank you, Isidro. I owe you one, again. I'm sure he'll be delighted to join you for the dinner."

"Tell him I'll meet him in the garden of the Stevenson House at five thirty. We'll walk to the dinner from there," Isidro said and then disconnected the call, leaving Chiles to stare at his own phone in amusement.

He turned to fully face Gibson. "Well, he agrees. He wants to meet you in the courtyard of the Stevenson House down there today at five thirty. He said he has an engagement tonight with a group called the Daughters of the American West, but that he'll secure you a place to join."

"The *daughters* of the what?" Gibson asked.

Chiles held up a hand. "Get down there to meet your regional expert and I'm sure he'll explain it in thorough detail. I'll tell you this, though: Not too many men or outsiders have been allowed to join or even witness one of their gatherings, so you should show your appreciation."

"*Great, another closed society,*" Gibson moaned.

After returning to his apartment to pack a small travel bag, Agent John Gibson made two phone calls explaining his intended whereabouts for the proceeding few days to Rachel Dowling and Agent Shapiro. Rachel was understanding, although she teased him and reminded him of his pledge to treat them to dinner after his return. Gibson regretted that his call to Shapiro might not go over swimmingly, but, to his surprise, it did. Shapiro was considerate and appreciative for Gibson's call and he did not grill Gibson on what lead he was following. Gibson found the call to be slightly bizarre, but he quickly dismissed the idea that anything strange was afoot, instead telling himself that Shapiro likely was following his own leads.

After surpassing the gridlock traffic driving out of San Francisco, Gibson was able to cruise down the Highway 101 corridor on his way to the Monterey Peninsula. Once he had passed the sprawling limits of San Jose, Gibson noted how the landscape surrounding the highway dramatically changed and it no longer felt as if he was driving through metropolitan areas, as was the case from San Francisco through San Jose. South of San Jose, the highway stretched through a wide, flat plain bordered by endless lines of mountains. The mountains were nowhere near the most impressive ridgelines he'd seen, but they were nonetheless mountains.

The pungent and unmistakable scent of garlic filled his nostrils as he drove past Gilroy, snapping him from his reverie on topography. He noticed a sign announcing that the City of Gilroy was the 'Garlic Capital of the World.' If the aroma of garlic growing in nearby fields was strong enough to overpower his vehicle's air freshener while driving by, Gibson saw little reason to doubt the validity of the sign's claim.

Leaving the aromatic community of Gilroy behind, the route climbed through hills that were brown with patches of trees and occasional houses until he arrived at the intersection cutting westward towards the Pacific Ocean, leading directly to Highway 1. When he reached the coastal highway and turned southward, before long he noticed the remnants of the former Fort Ord military base with its ghostly landscape of abandoned buildings.

As he rounded a bend of the highway, he was instantly rewarded with a stunning view of the forested hillsides of the Monterey Peninsula jutting dramatically into the Pacific. It was one of the most gorgeous images he had ever encountered, and the breathtaking meeting of ocean and low mountains reminded of his travels to the French Basque Country.

At the time Agent John Gibson arrived in Monterey, Isidro de la Vega was still driving northward from Santa Barbara. He was slightly annoyed that David Chiles had recruited him to assist Agent Gibson, but there were few people that Isidro considered to be his true friends and David Chiles was one of them. And if a friend asked for help, Isidro would not refuse.

Besides, he had nearly completed his research at the Santa Barbara Mission at the time of the call from Chiles. The vault of information lying dormant and secure in the mission was a treasure itself and Isidro could easily spend weeks delving into the historical records preserved in its rooms of archives. However, he had discovered a possible clue, or even a few, that could help him to solve the two-hundred-year-old mystery that, try as he might, he could not remove from the forefront of his thoughts.

It was clear from Father Margil's letter that Isidro had found in the San Antonio Mission that Margil had committed an unconscionable sin in the name of some great purpose that he believed was more important than God's laws themselves. *What could have been that purpose?*

At the time of the letter's writing, Alta California was still largely undiscovered, but it was also a time of great transition. The Spanish Empire had finally become aware of its lethargic ways in colonizing the lands of what would later become California and it plunged itself into a valid attempt at solidifying its presence in the until-then vastly untouched and increasingly threatened region. The Church was deeply engrained in the State at the time, the two entities feeding off one another for their own ultimate goals. And, with Monterey designated as the capital of Spanish California, it was the seat of the governor of the entire territory. Therefore, it was not unimaginable that there had been a situation involving the Church volatile enough to have one of its members resort to actions that had dire consequences.

In his research, Isidro discovered official records of a "Father Dominique Margil," who had indeed been involved with a voyage through Alta California with a contingent of soldiers and settlers. It took a little more searching, but he was able to find an unofficial record of the convoy's cargo, which included a strange and apparently purposefully undisclosed item that was listed as being destined for Monterey and to be for a vital purpose; he believed the inventory he uncovered would never be noticed had one not known to begin the search connecting it with Father Margil. In the official documentation, there was also listing of the accidental death of one of the expedition's soldiers somewhere in the Santa Lucia Mountains near the Mission San Antonio de Padua; this didn't make sense to Isidro, as if the caravan had followed the Mission Trail, it would have led them well eastward from the rugged coastal Santa Lucias. It was fairly clear that whatever had happened to the soldier in the mountains, though, had to do with Father Margil.

From his quick research of the archives, Isidro also uncovered that Father Margil was present during Hippolyte de Bouchard's invasion and sacking of Monterey, but the records regarding Margil's arrival to Monterey were extremely vague, as the inventory on his voyage had been obscured. Isidro considered it ironic that Father Margil had seemingly sensed his demise to be near when he had written the letter at the San Antonio Mission, as not long after Father Margil's arrival in Monterey, he was killed by Bouchard when the pirate invaded Monterey.

40.

Year of our Lord 1818.

FATHER MARGIL WAS KEENLY aware that he would never forget his first glimpse of Monterey Bay. Its sparkling waters dazzled him as he marched alongside Father Serra over the crest of the hill between the Carmel Mission and the town of Monterey. The wide, sweeping arch of the glistening bay was spotted with forest, and Monterey itself, at the crux of the bay's hook, appeared like a settlement in some thick mountainous forest rather than a coastal settlement. Even the central area of the town was considerably inland from the banks of the bay.

As stunning as the view was, Father Margil sensed danger in the beauty he was admiring, as if he was watching dark clouds forming over the waters of the ocean, indicating an oncoming horrendous storm. He considered broaching the subject of his growing uneasiness as they gradually descended the road, which was surrounded by a thick blend of pine and oak trees, but Margil decided not to on account of the air of contentment glowing from Father Serra. Father Margil imagined that Serra took great pride in the work that the Catholic Church provided and Father Margil did not want to diminish another's joy.

Vestiges of the settlement of Monterey began as many did, with a gradual clearing of the forest as one neared the center of town. The trees had been cleared for use in construction or for firewood. A wagon, pulled by a pair of horses, clamored behind Fathers Serra and Margil on the rough road as they continued downward into Monterey.

Eventually, remote houses began to appear set back into the woods from the road until they became more numerous and then became organized into orderly alignments on the periphery of Monterey's limited road network. The Fathers walked by a small assortment of buildings with a central garden and spacious courtyard that Father Serra remarked was owned by a man named John Cooper-Molera, who ran the sole general mercantile in the town. Father Serra added that the courtyard of the general store was a usual destination of vice and degenerate behavior.

Their destination was the house of the Governor of Alta California, Pedro Fages. Despite the animosity between Governor Fages and Father Serra being widely known throughout New Spain, and even by some in *Old Spain*, the governor was held as a capable and considerate man, worthy of the trust of the Church. It was a delicate balance, as Father Margil was forewarned in Mexico City at the onset of his voyage. The Church desired to engage the cooperation of Governor Fages, and by doing so, not upset Father Serra. Father Margil reminded himself to be vigilant in his words and actions, as there would be no greater shame than to fail at his mission after so much loss, simply due to a lack of diplomacy.

A large two-story white adobe house appeared before them and Father Margil assumed correctly that it was the home of Governor Fages. One of the governor's house servants, an indigenous girl with darkly toned skin and long black hair pulled into a knot behind her head, greeted them at the main entrance. She asked them to enter and Father Serra asked the four converted natives that had accompanied them over the hill to uncover the chest on the back of the wagon and carry it into the house.

The governor's home was at a meeting of four roads: one veering westward towards the bay, which was mostly lined with houses; one southward that appeared to climb into a hillside, with only a couple of homes visible on its banks; one northward that was bordered with houses like the route westward; and the eastward route, which they descended. Of all of the routes, it was apparent that the route westward towards the bay and ocean was the most important of the governor's views. From the balcony of the second floor, one would be able to gaze all the way to the first building encountered coming ashore after docking in Monterey Bay:

the Custom House. From that balcony, the governor would be able to see any ship in the distance long before it dropped its anchor into the bay.

Father Margil considered the people he witnessed walking, riding horses, or driving wagons through the streets. These were not the rough-looking types he had seen living on the periphery of other settlements in Alta California. The people of Monterey dressed as nicely as those of the upper classes in Mexico City or even in Spain.

The Fathers followed the young woman into the house, opulently furnished with both European and Asian pieces. Father Margil was awestruck at the brilliant display of furnishings in the governor's home and even more so when he discovered later that the governor's home was not even the most lavishly decorated in the town!

They were left seated on a plush ruby red sofa with gold trim in a grand room that Father Margil assumed was the house's primary space for gathering outside of the adjoining dining room, which he could see through another narrow doorway. Governor Fages entered from a side room; Father Serra later informed Margil that it was Fages' private study room.

The governor was a tall man who looked to be in very good form for a man of his age. Father Margil was surprised by the expression the governor's face displayed, as he had imagined that the governor would be delighted at the arrival of the all-important chest of gold.

"Father Serra. I'm pleased to see you," Governor Fages said as he approached to shake hands.

"You should really be shaking the hand of my brother, Father Margil," Father Serra said, motioning to Margil. "He's the real reason for this successful completion of our enterprise."

The governor warmly shook Father Margil's hand. "I cannot convey to you how grateful I am for your endeavors and devotion to this cause," Governor Fages remarked.

"But something still troubles you; this I can see," Father Serra commented.

The governor quickly turned to face Father Serra, prepared to meet any challenge the old priest desired to confront him with. But instead of seeing antagonism in Serra's eyes, as Fages had become accustomed to, there was no fight in Father Serra's dark brown eyes. There was only concern and perhaps compassion.

"I must apologize. You are indeed correct that something is troubling me." The governor paused as if to consider what he would say next. "But where are my manners? Please, let us be seated so that we may converse like gentlemen."

The governor raised a hand towards the young woman that had shown the two friars into the house. "Would you two gentleman care to join me in a nice glass of wine? Surely this occasion calls for it."

"With all due respect, Governor, I'm more interested in discussing whatever issue is at hand rather than going through the normal formalities; and I'm sure I can speak for Father Margil by stating that he has endured more than we can imagine in delivering that chest and that he deserves to know the absolute truth of our current predicament."

Governor Fages raised his hand again toward the young woman who had begun to approach and shook his head. "Quite right you are, Father Serra. Your determination is as fierce as ever, but I appreciate your candor. Please, though, let us be seated while we discuss this concern of mine. And I can assure you that it is something which affects us all."

The three men seated themselves facing one another. Father Margil felt uneasy. Father Serra's comment regarding what he had "endured" in order to deliver the gold struck him deeply. *Can Father Serra see my sin?*

"What I have to tell you, gentlemen, must stay between us. Only the head of my soldiers is aware of what I'm about to tell you." Governor Fages slightly lied, as John Cooper-Molera, in his usual manner of chiding the governor, had achieved having the governor convey the news to him, but Governor Fages saw no reason to inform the friars of Cooper-Molera's awareness of the situation.

"I wish I could tell you that I'm agitated because of Rezanov's return, and having not been provided with our 'gift' he had been promised, he stormed off and vowed to overrun all of Alta California with his compatriots." The two friars shared a look of panic: *Had the gold arrived too late?*

Governor Fages noticed the exchange and quickly added, "No, no, Fathers. That is not the case, but only a poor choice of introduction. What I have to tell you, though, is far more grievous and dangerous for our settlement here, and it has nothing to do with the Russian. There's been no sign of him, and for all we know, he's still content with the small fortune we will be providing on his return to Monterey." He paused for a moment as if to consider the weight of the words he was about to speak. "No, my Fathers, our present trouble lies elsewhere, as I've been informed that we are soon to be invaded by Hippolyte de Bouchard.

"It's long been feared that he would set his sights on Monterey, and now, much to our misfortune, it would appear that he has done just this," Governor Fages added.

"How could you possibly know?" Father Serra inquired.

"A French ship departed our bay mere days ago that had previously been at port in the Sandwich Islands. There have been rumors of Bouchard's interest in Monterey for many months, but the captain of this vessel was kind enough to inform me that Bouchard was in the islands recruiting a contingent of natives to serve as mercenaries for what Bouchard boldly proclaimed to be his *sacking of Monterey*," Governor Fages answered.

"Surely, with your soldiers and cannon, you would be able to repel such an attempt," Father Serra remarked.

The governor did not immediately respond. He considered commenting on how Serra had made it known throughout their relationship that he held little regard for the soldiers of the Spanish Crown and now that an imminent threat was facing them, he was acknowledging the usefulness of such a military presence; but Governor Fages did not trust that he held the strength to undertake a debate with the stubborn old Serra. "I am supremely confident that we can mount an adequate defense if Bouchard attempts an attack," he said.

The air in the room remained still as the three men evaluated one another in apprehension.

"Yet you do not believe you would be able to stop him?" Father Serra finally broke the silence.

"I requested additional troops from the Crown at the moment of my arrival at this post and have repeated this request perpetually, only to receive refusal after refusal, " Governor Fages said as his eyes meandered toward the open dual doorway leading to the garden behind the house.

"That is not exactly an answer, Governor Fages," Father Serra remarked.

Governor Fages snapped his head back towards Serra and retorted, "No, we will not be able to repel Bouchard if and when he arrives. We do not have adequate defenses here; I've stated as much numerous times in my reports to Mexico City and Madrid. We never have had adequate defenses and it's merely good fortune that we've managed to avoid attack until now."

Father Serra nodded in agreement. He did not agree or devote much thought to unsavory military concerns; but he could not deny that understanding the nature of mankind required thorough consideration of the dark element of human nature known as warfare. And there was no denying the threat that Bouchard represented. "What shall you do?" Serra asked.

"We shall mount as much of a defense as we are able with the troops at the garrison. With any luck, we'll be able to significantly damage at least one of the three ships I expect him to bring to attack us. If he makes it ashore, however, I have little doubt that his hired mercenaries would overrun our defenses." Governor Fages noticed his daughter walking in the garden through one of the house's rear windows. "That is why tomorrow morning, I'm issuing orders that the town is to be evacuated except for the majority of our detachment of soldiers, who will rest here to confront Bouchard."

"Surely you do not intend to abandon all that you and these people have built?" Father Margil incredulously asked, receiving a glance of disapproval from Father Serra. "And there is the allotment of soldiers that accompanied me from Lower California, led by Captain Echevarria, that is at the Carmel Mission and will be arriving here shortly with the new settlers."

"I will not let these people be slaughtered by that tyrant," Governor Fages exclaimed, slamming a fist onto the low table in front of him. The tremor from his fist ramming into the table caused a glass vase filled with freshly cut flowers to tumble and crash onto the wooden floor. "The paltry troops to arrive with Captain Echevarria will be a minimal addition to my meager force!"

Governor Fages apologized to the two friars for having lost his temper, while a house servant arrived to clean the fallen vase. "There is no other way. Bouchard may have the reputation for being a vile and insolent man; but in all other occasions where he raided a coastal settlement, he merely scoured the towns for any riches he could find and quickly departed."

Father Margil noticed that the governor's gaze had fallen directly on him and Margil felt uneasy in the attention. He averted his eyes and again noted the many luxurious items in the room: the plush sofas, the elegant side tables, the marvelous paintings.

Governor Fages followed Margil's eyes around the room and remarked, "Bouchard is a pirate, not a furniture or art collector. He will come here looking for gold and jewels."

The mention of gold caught Margil's attention. *"Gold?"*

"Yes, indeed. Thus, I'm torn about what to do with this precious cargo you delivered, Father Margil."

"We could return it to the Mission," Father Margil suggested.

There was an instant response to his suggestion, although not from Governor Fages. "No, we cannot do that," Father Serra said.

"Why not?" Father Margil pleaded, beginning to comprehend why he had felt uneasy about his arrival in Monterey when he should have felt elation.

"Because Bouchard is also infamous for pillaging missions and church grounds with no prejudice and there is no reason to believe that he will make an exception. In fact, he will undoubtedly move to the Carmel Mission after his invasion of Monterey, as, despicable as he may be, the man is not base, and he will be cognizant of the importance of the Carmel Mission in Alta California," Governor Fages disclosed, facing Father Serra. "In fact, Father Serra, I would humbly advise you to return to your mission immediately and begin preparations for a visit by one Hippolyte de Bouchard."

"My neophytes know of places in the valley and deeper into the Santa Lucia Mountains where we can move our valuables while the pirate is near. These are places that Bouchard would never, nor anyone else, ever be able to find. The Santa Lucias are a mystery and only the natives of this land will ever truly know them," Father Serra confidently replied.

"Good," Governor Fages confirmed.

"And what of the chest?" Father Margil inquired.

"I do not believe it would be prudent to return the chest to the Carmel Mission. Bouchard will invade the mission; in fact, he may even pull his ships to anchor in your bay before ours, Father Serra," Fages predicted.

"I agree. The gold should not return to the mission. As much as I would like to guarantee its safekeeping, the action would leave too much to chance and my very small group of soldiers protecting the mission would be no match for a force of Bouchard's," Serra agreed.

"Then it will accompany me and the rest of the townsmen as we head eastward to the Salinas Rancho. Señor Juan Bautista Castro has always been accommodating and I've already dispatched a rider to inform him of our pending arrival; I expect nothing less than his cooperation and hospitality. It will be a long day's walk, but we'll make it and I can take the gold in my care."

Father Margil dreaded the possibilities forming in his mind. "Would this pirate not be able to follow your trail? And if your soldiers are to remain here, after he has defeated them, he could follow and easily overtake you and then have the gold." The bluntness of his speech surprised all three men, himself most of all.

The governor held a perplexed expression on his face for a long moment before responding, undoubtedly still in shock after having witnessed such criticism from the seemingly quiet man of the cloth. "Yes, I concede you do have a point, Father Margil. However, what would you propose we do: Leave the gold chest here in Monterey while we all abandon it?"

"Precisely," Margil replied. "We'll hide it somewhere; somewhere this pirate would never expect it. He is going to be aware that you were informed of his invasion beforehand, as you and your townspeople will have deserted by the time of his arrival. There will be no reason for him to suspect that you or any of your subjects left anything of great value."

"That just may work," Father Serra contributed.

"*It's brilliant!*" Governor Fages proclaimed. "Come, quickly, gentlemen," Governor Fages suggested as he rose from his seat and motioned for the two friars to follow his lead. "Let us get your men to once again move this chest. I have an idea where we can hide it."

"Where is that, may I ask?" Father Margil asked as he rose.

"Beneath the floorboards of any small house that will not appear extravagant to Bouchard. We will enlist the assistance for my friend, John Cooper-Molera, who should easily guide us to a willing and cooperative soul to help us. Now please, come, Fathers. We have no time to waste!"

Father Serra stopped them by stating, "Governor Fages, I appreciate your efforts, but I must return to my mission. I will happily leave you my men to assist, who can return to the mission later. Father Margil, we should be going now."

Father Margil had no intention of leaving the chest, even if directed to do so by a friar regarded as a living legend. "I believe it is my calling to remain here to ensure the safekeeping of this chest, my brother."

Serra inhaled and exhaled deeply. *"So be it,"* he proclaimed and turned to exit the governor's house and return to his Mission San Carlos Borromeo de Carmelo.

Two days after Governor Fages met with Fathers Serra and Margil, Hippolyte de Bouchard invaded Monterey, the famed capital of Spanish California. Bouchard's force included three well-armed vessels loaded with his hardened crew and complemented with mercenaries hired into his service in the Sandwich Islands.

Just as Governor Fages had predicted, the defenses of Monterey were inadequate to repel a considerable attack by sea. After a period when soldiers in the fort above the town were able to fire their cannon at Bouchard's vessel and retard the advance of Bouchard's forces, the soldiers of the garrison retreated from Monterey in the direction of the corridor to the east bordered by stretches of hills on both sides that would lead them to the rancho lands of Señor Castro in what would later become known as the Salinas Valley.

The troops of the garrison were, however, able to hit one of Bouchard's ships that foolishly veered too near to land. As they retreated, the soldiers cheered their success at having sunk one of Bouchard's vessels, which they could see slowly taking on water as it descended below the ocean. But even though their triumph was an achievement in their brief skirmish with Bouchard, the action would only anger the notoriously arrogant Bouchard, who would consider the loss of one of his ships in his later decisions concerning the fate of Monterey.

The soldiers of Monterey's garrison were instructed by Governor Fages to not attempt an on-land confrontation with Bouchard's forces. Fages ordered that after the garrison provided as much of an artillery barrage at Bouchard's arriving forces as possible, the soldiers were to abandon their defenses and follow the trail the rest of the settlement had taken towards the rancho lands of Castro.

The governor's reasoning for this course of action was multifold and it demonstrated his logistical abilities. First, if the soldiers remained in Monterey for a direct confrontation with Bouchard's men, they would undoubtedly be overtaken before long. The strength of position on the hillside overlooking the bay and town of the fort would lose its strategic value once Bouchard's men were able to deploy into smaller boats for landing onshore; once they were close enough, the fort's cannon would be useless and, further, the numbers of the garrison, near seventy soldiers — including the Captain Echevarria and his contingent of soldiers from Lower California that had arrived shortly after Serra's return to the Carmel Mission — would be no match for the hundreds that Bouchard would be able to land for the attack.

Following the trail through the relatively narrow corridor leading inland from the coast to the rancho lands of Castro would require any advancing force to condense itself as it proceeded through the valley, and thus the retreating forces of Monterey would be able to guard the rear of the column of townspeople, if Bouchard decided to pursue them.

Although Governor Fages ordered the mandatory evacuation of the town, he regretted that without soldiers to enforce his command, there would undoubtedly be some who would not abide by his order. Except for a select few he had chosen to accompany him, all of the soldiers were busy in preparations of the town's defenses at the time of his declaration.

Fages was certain that there would be holdouts who believed they would be free of harm. They would be, on the contrary, directly placed in harm's way; and the most egregious of harm would be coming speedily for them. Bouchard held a reputation as a brutal and unforgiving soul; with a force of base men at his command, there would be no limit to his fury. Captured men would either be killed or given a choice to join Bouchard or become slaves of labor on one of his ships; women would be raped and killed. Bouchard would travel from home to home, entering each house scouring for whatever he could find. The governor, with cooperation from John Cooper-Molera, purposefully left stores of food and other items that Bouchard might find attractive in key locations around town — at the Custom House and at Cooper-Molera's store in particular — in hopes of enticing the pirate to take what was *left* and depart.

Father Margil refused to leave Monterey, proclaiming that it was his duty under God to stand watch over the chest of gold to assure its safekeeping. Governor Fages pleaded with him, but it was useless, as Father Margil remained undeterred. Father Margil stated that he would await the arrival of Bouchard at the Royal Presidio Chapel and plead that the church be spared from destruction.

As Governor Fages shook Father Margil's hand in front of the church, he questioned if he would see the friar alive again. Governor Fages appraised Father Margil's stance to be courageous, but also foolish. The gold chest was safely buried beneath the floorboards of an unassuming home that Bouchard's men would pass through quickly without second thought. The small adobe home belonged to John Cooper-Molera, who planned to provide it for a relative of his wife's upon his arrival from Spain. The chest's location was only known by the governor, Cooper-Molera, and Father Margil; a group of four converted natives from the Carmel Mission had provided the manual labor of lifting the house's floorboards and burying the chest, but they departed for their return to the mission immediately after the task was completed and Governor Fages unequivocally trusted the men's loyalty to Serra, who the natives viewed as some form of paternal spirit on Earth. Thus, there was no plausible reason for Father Margil to remain in Monterey, as everyone agreed that all was in God's hands, but the Father adamantly refused and the governor did not have the luxury of time to dissuade the man.

At a hillside, beyond which Governor Fages realized afterward he would no longer be able to see his proud town from any slight clearing in the forest, the governor brought his horse to a halt and gazed downward at Monterey. *Would it still be there in a few days time, after the brutish Bouchard took it for his own, filling its roads and houses with his equally foul men?*

There was no way of knowing what a man like Bouchard was capable of, much less what he would do once he had overtaken the defenses of the fort and moved his forces on land. Governor Fages felt himself saddened at the thought of how Monterey had been built up from nothing into a thriving and vibrant place in a span of less than fifty years since its founding; the sort of place that would only continue to grow, to improve, and to flourish. *And now all of that may be lost.*

Before despair engulfed him in its wretched grasp, the governor's chain of thought pivoted in an entirely different direction. *Let Bouchard do his worst.*

There had been such a momentous rush to move that he could not be certain that all citizens, including servants, were accounted for in his caravan heading for the long valley inland from Monterey, but it was certain that most of the townspeople were evacuated and would thus be safe from the hands of Bouchard and his devils. *And that, combined with the very spirit of Monterey itself, would be more than enough to rebuild whatever damage Bouchard may bring! Monterey's future would be secure*, he assured himself.

The proud governor took one more prolonged gander at his adopted home and reflected on how the dawn of the new century would bring more changes to Monterey than anything Hippolyte de Bouchard could administer. *Would the Russians triumph in their pursuit of conquest? Would Americans stream uncontrollably over the mountains to the east? Would the Spanish Empire retain its prominence and grasp on Alta California? Would the growing unrest in Mexico have repercussions in Alta California?* These were all questions that Governor Pedro Fages asked himself as he sat astride his horse, feeling a cool breeze on his face blowing in from the Pacific Ocean. It was difficult to foresee what the relatively new century held for Monterey, but regardless, he concluded that Monterey would always be there, notwithstanding what the future might deliver to it.

The column of settlers continued onwards toward the rancho lands of Castro through the narrow valley. Fages observed his Isabella and the young Englishman William Beckwith riding alongside one another. The young man refused to leave his daughter's side from the moment the impending invasion by Bouchard was announced. It pleased Governor Fages to know Isabella would be protected long after his own time had passed.

After the first two miles inland, the layer of thick, grayish clouds overhead disseminated and the sun poured down on them. Governor Fages pondered if Father Margil had been with them whether he would see the cascading sunshine as a sign of divine providence. Regardless of religious connotations, Governor Fages closed his eyes and savored the soft sunshine encompassing him as he strode on top of his majestic horse. There was no denying that having to abandon his town to a degenerate pirate was terrible, but he had done what he could to preserve the town and the lives of its citizens, and he felt confident in his actions. Soon the caravan would arrive near Castro's grand rancho and he would send scouts back to survey from afar Bouchard's activities.

The pirate would likely grow bored with an empty town and give into his frustration with having had his *secret* invasion plans revealed long before his arrival. Bouchard would soon depart from Monterey and they would return to continue building it into the glamorous capital of Alta California that it was destined to become. They need only wait for a couple of days for Bouchard to depart.

Meanwhile, Father Margil stood watch dutifully in front of the cathedral. From the position of the church on a slightly elevated hillside above the expanse of most of the town, Margil had a decent viewpoint to watch first the retreat of the soldiers from the fort southwest of the cathedral and then Bouchard's advance as small boats were dispatched from the three large ships anchored offshore. Margil beheld the cannon battle with fascination and horror, as the guns from the fort fired at Bouchard's ships and the ships returned fire. There were brilliant explosions of earth in and around the fort and huge plumes of water formed in the ocean when cannon shots hit it. Father Margil noticed one shot from the fort that did not hit water, though: it directly hit one of the large ships that had moved in closer than the other two.

Father Margil witnessed the line of soldiers retreating from the fort, moving in the direction that Governor Fages had led the column of his citizens away from Monterey. He watched as the smaller boats from the pirate's ship arrived at the shoreline and then immediately returned to the larger vessels in order to reload with men and repeat the trip. Father Margil fell to his knees and prayed that God would protect the chest of gold that had been delivered to Monterey at such a great cost. Margil did not, however, pray for his own safety; he rose and stood alone in front of the cathedral, awaiting Bouchard's arrival.

Hippolyte de Bouchard eyed Father Margil curiously as he approached the cathedral on horseback. It took Bouchard the better part of the day to progress through the town with a troop of his men to the church; the rest of his men were allowed to roam free and pillage as they pleased only after Bouchard had entered all of the most prominent homes first. After Bouchard strolled through a home identifying any items he especially liked to be taken to his private quarters on his ship, he would then pronounce that a house was *open* to the rest of his men.

Margil unflinchingly returned Bouchard's gaze as he stood sternly and confidently at the front of the cathedral.

"You are either very brave or very foolish to have remained here, priest," Bouchard said as one of his men took his horse's bridle and Bouchard descended from atop the animal. Once standing, Father Margil noted that this man who had instilled fear in the hearts and minds of so many was not an imposing or threatening figure at all; instead, Bouchard was shorter than most men of the age and was of slight build, with a paunchy midsection. Bouchard's Spanish was heavily accented with his native French.

"I am neither brave nor foolish; I am merely a man of God, and his strength is with me," Margil announced. "And you may call me Father Margil, instead of *priest*," he added with reproach.

Bouchard laughed as he approached Margil. He had a slight, sniffling laugh that instantly annoyed Father Margil. "I'll call you whatever I like, *Father Merde*," Bouchard replied, laughing hysterically at his own multilingual joke. The men that had accompanied him also began to laugh at the joke that not all understood.

"What gives you the right to invade this peaceful settlement?" Father Margil insisted over the jeers of Bouchard's men.

"What gives me the right?" Bouchard asked, snapping from his laughing fit with his eyes gleaming fiercely. "I need no right! This is a colony of the Spanish Empire, the same empire that wanted to enslave my countrymen!" Small bubbles of white foam formed at the corners of Bouchard's mouth as he leaned in closer towards Father Margil so that their faces were mere inches apart. Margil could smell a thick scent of brandy on the man's breath.

Bouchard stepped backward from Margil. A thin smile that curled into his cheeks emerged. "After I have thoroughly combed through your church, you will accompany me and my men for the remainder of our visit here."

"Why would you take me from my church? The governor has known of your imminent arrival for days. Preparations were made and everything of intrinsic value has been removed. What is left is left for you and you should take it and leave here, leave with these beasts you have brought," Father Margil motioned to the line of burly men now all standing resolutely behind Bouchard.

"Yes, it is a shame that the coward governor uncovered my plan and ran into the hills. I would love to have met his daughter who I have heard so much about." Bouchard chuckled and winked at Father Margil. "So we shall see if what you say is true. But in my experience, not everything could have been taken away," Bouchard performed an about-face toward his men. "And, who knows, maybe there will even be a confession or two for you to administer." The men laughed greedily in response.

"What do you mean? All of the homes have been deserted here," Father Margil questioned.

"Ah, yes, my good Father, you are apparently ignorant in such affairs. Experience has also proven to me that despite all efforts, some will always persist in remaining behind. Even you should have left; but you have remained. And I assure you there will be others. And hopefully there will be a woman or two hiding in one of the homes. My men, after all, have been at sea for quite some time," Bouchard glanced at his men again, who happily greeted his suggestion with howls of lust.

"You would not dare allow such a thing," Father Margil commented, instantly regretting his own foolishness.

"Oh, do not worry, Father. I would not allow such women to continue living in shame," Bouchard threatened quietly into Margil's ear as he brushed him aside to enter the cathedral. Bouchard raised the back of his hand to indicate to his men to enter behind him. Father Margil's hands were promptly tightly bound with a rope; the sensation of the rope tearing into his skin reminded him of Diego Alvarez.

Bouchard then quickly spun to face Father Margil as he was about to step through the open doorway to the cathedral. "I think I will say a prayer in the first pew before we continue."

Much to the displeasure of Hippolyte de Bouchard, his men did not discover any remaining individuals in Monterey apart from Father Margil. Bouchard ordered a detachment of men to pursue the retreating soldiers of the fort and to capture one or two that would assuredly be lagging behind at the rear of the column; Bouchard considered soldiers of the Spanish Empire to be lazy and undisciplined. His men, however, were unable to track the retreating soldiers through the thickly forested hills bordering the town, and after some time, they grew worried of getting lost and returned to the town, having hopelessly failed their main objective.

The unsuccessful returning party reported to Bouchard as soon as they descended from a hillside into the flatter areas where the town and most of the houses on its edges were located. Father Margil was not ashamed to feel pleasure at the sight of Bouchard's frustration and annoyance that the scouting party was not even able to report on the direction taken by the column of retreating soldiers. Bouchard was so enraged that he backhanded each of the ten men in turn, closely followed by unleashing an obscenity-laced tirade on their incompetence.

Bouchard's ire grew even fiercer when countless companies of his invading force approached the cathedral to report on their findings; there was little for them to report in way of success.

Father Margil made the mistake of grinning slightly as band after band timidly announced their failures to discover anything remaining in the town of significant value that could easily be transported to the two remaining ships off-shore, as the third had by then sunk. Father Margil overheard that sizeable food stocks were uncovered in the Custom House. Bouchard would be able to use this to feed his men. A decent supply of hides of great trading value was also found. And, of course, Bouchard had uncovered cases of brandy somewhere, as he and his men liberally drank from bottles that they passed between themselves. But there had been no discovery that Bouchard truly desired. There had been no gold or riches.

Father Margil postulated that he was not within sight nor of interest to Bouchard, which could not have been more incorrect, as Bouchard kept a keen eye on the friar from the moment of their introduction. Father Margil's mistake was to disregard Bouchard as a dense brigand. Bouchard may have been a brutal privateer, but he was also highly devious and calculated in his actions. When Bouchard observed the slight smile escape across Margil's face, he briskly confronted the priest and slapped him with the back of his hand harder than he had hit his own men previously. Margil's head snapped sideways as it received the sudden blow, and when he straightened himself upwards, a steady line of red blood spewed from his left nostril.

Father Margil would not cower in the face of such a tyrannical man as Hippolyte de Bouchard. He firmly stood his ground, not giving Bouchard the luxury of letting him watch Father Margil wipe away the blood cascading from his nose over his mouth and slowly dripping to the cold stone floor.

"You find this all very amusing, don't you, priest?"

"You, who were raised in the Catholic Church and have turned into this vile thing who freely strikes a man of the Church — you ask me of *amusement*?"

Bouchard, laughing hysterically, backhanded the Father again. "You are foolish, priest! God has no hold on me!" The men flanking him inside the cathedral joined their leader in a chorus of loud laughter that echoed off of the stone walls of the church.

Once again, Father Margil straightened himself, refusing to wipe at the now more intense nose bleed that he guessed indicated a broken nose. "I have witnessed evil in the hearts of men, but you are possibly the foulest and most serene example of such that I have come across yet in this world."

Bouchard paced slowly away in careful reflection. "I think I will take that as a compliment." Bouchard paused and then added, "But I think you are lying to me, priest. I think there is something left in Monterey for me to find." Bouchard looked up to meet the tired gaze of Margil, trying to discern any slight change in the friar's expression. Margil, though, had quickly learned to not underestimate the cognitive ability of the pirate before him.

"Hmm, still stubborn. You men of the cloth … I will never understand you. You are able to spew your lies about God and the Church all over the world with such devotion, yet you are incapable of hiding your true emotions in order to lie about anything else. Well, we shall see how well you are able to lie to me. I shall take you with me to each and every home and building in this place and we shall see if there is truly nothing left for me to find here." Bouchard smirked and nodded his head for his men to follow him as he exited the cathedral.

Father Margil dreaded leaving the cathedral in the company of Hippolyte de Bouchard. He also felt fear. Bouchard had proven to be brighter than he could have ever imagined possible and the pirate was correct in his assessment of Margil's ability, or lack thereof, to fabricate lies. It was true that he had done so concerning Diego Alvarez, but he had been fortunate to not have been pressed on the issue by anyone. Now it was different, though, as Hippolyte de Bouchard's despicable nature demonstrated his acquaintance with the darker elements of mankind. Bouchard also appeared to be able to see through Father Margil's attempt to veil the truth.

As he walked alongside the horse of a man that held a rope binding his hands, Father Margil admitted the undeniable possibility that he might have been wrong to insist on remaining in Monterey in order to confront Bouchard.

Bouchard, on the other hand, felt supremely confident that the priest would eventually reveal something to him. Even if it turned out to be a fully stocked cellar of wine or brandy hidden beneath one of the houses, this would be appreciated. A hoard of gold or jewelry would be even more appreciated, but in order to swell his reputation and ego, Bouchard hoped there would be more than the meager commodities seized from the Custom House.

And further, Bouchard sensed that the priest was hiding something from him. In his many years of interrogating people, an activity that he enjoyed greatly, he acquired the ability to sense when people were not as forthcoming on certain subjects or were deliberately lying to him. Father Margil, for example, had spoken too quickly regarding the absence of riches remaining in the town, Bouchard determined. From the moment that the priest had uttered those words, Bouchard's interest had been undivided on the friar's reactions to certain information. The priest had made a grievous mistake in believing that he was only grinning to himself as the reports from Bouchard's men continued to arrive with news of little to nothing being discovered in the town. *The priest knows something*, Bouchard said to himself as he glanced downward from his horse at the old man who, for the first time, now exhibited despair on his broken face.

Bouchard executed his plan precisely as it had been designed. He and a small band of men went from house to house, building to building, and Bouchard had Father Margil dragged inside each. Fatigue had settled into the friar's aged body and Bouchard's marauders had to nearly carry him into a couple of the homes. Initially, they attempted to literally drag the man behind them, but Bouchard insisted this not be done. He wanted to keep the priest conscious as long as possible.

After entering ten adobe houses to no avail, Bouchard's patience expired. Father Margil stood before him, having been lifted through the doorway by two of Bouchard's men, and Bouchard repeated the same lines he had in the previous ten houses.

"Are you familiar with the inhabitants of this household? Do you know of anything hidden within this home or outside of it?"

Father Margil shook his tired head in response. At their arrival in the first few homes, he attempted to explain to Bouchard that he had only recently arrived in Monterey and that his knowledge of the settlement's inhabitants was extremely limited, but Bouchard disregarded this excuse with a disinterested shrug. Images around Father Margil were now beginning to blur together and he frankly had no idea which house he was standing in.

Bouchard sensed the priest's disorientation and it infuriated him. He took three quick steps across the creaking floorboards of the house and slapped Margil again across his face; this time harder than the previous two times. Father Margil's head jolted backwards and pain shot through his nose, causing his head to feel as if it would explode.

Two things then occurred that sealed Father Margil's fate. The two men holding him up adjusted the friar's weight so that his head snapped forward. The quick movement resulted in blood gushing from Margil's nose and mouth to splatter on the wooden floorboards in front of him. Bouchard had instinctively taken a step backwards from the priest, as he anticipated the movement by his men, and as he stepped away from the floorboards in front of Father Margil, Bouchard noticed that two planks were slightly uneven from the others on either side of them.

Wooden plank floors were still considered quite the luxury in Alta California, with many houses having a floor of packed earth; however, when they were installed, they were normally able to be constructed fairly level. The unevenness of the boards indicated to Bouchard that they might have been recently adjusted.

It was the expression on the priest's face that confirmed his suspicion. Feeling a sense of discovery, Bouchard surveyed closely as Margil wearily focused on the puddle of his own blood on the floor before raising his head. In that instant, Hippolyte de Bouchard discerned from Father Margil what he had been waiting for — *pure despair*.

Father Margil was released, where he collapsed to the floor against a wall of the room while Bouchard ordered his men to raise the planks. Others that had been waiting outside then entered with shovels and Margil watched wounded, broken, and helpless at what he could only picture as sheer catastrophe. All that he and so many others had devoted themselves toward was about to be lost.

But he would not let all be wasted without one final attempt. Father Margil was not a warrior, but he was a warrior of God and his faith was his last opportunity to save everything. He slowly rose from the ground as Bouchard's men lifted the chest with the Russian's gold from its hiding place in the dirt beneath the house's floorboards.

"Señor Bouchard, I beg of you to consider the purpose of this gold in the name of God, for he has not forgotten you," Father Margil pleaded.

"Oh, it's gold, is it? Thank you for letting me know," Bouchard managed to say through his wide, salivating grin.

Father Margil moved closer to Bouchard and fell to his knees. "Please, señor, this gold will save California from becoming home to the barbarous Russians."

Bouchard's narrow eyes opened to the size of plums as he peered into the chest after one of his men had broken the lock with a shovel head. "What do you think I care of California or of the Russians, priest? If the Russians take over, I will only continue to raid their towns and settlements. It matters not to me who I invade and conquer." Bouchard spoke to the pile of gold in front of him instead of to Father Margil. He lifted a handful of the gold coins in one hand and let them casually fall from his hand back into the pile in the chest. Bouchard ordered his men to carry the chest out of the home and ordered that it was not to leave his sight. He rose and began to exit the house.

Father Margil sprang from his knees in the way of Bouchard, grabbing the shorter man's shoulder lapels. "I warn you. This gold is cursed! If you remove it from here, its curse will follow you for the rest of your life! Death accompanies this gold!"

Bouchard, in turn, grabbed Father Margil and spun the friar back towards the interior of the house. At the same time, Bouchard drew his sword from his side and thrust it through Margil's ribcage. Bouchard watched the life quickly drain from the priest's eyes while a fountain of blood began to spew from the man's mouth. Bouchard smiled and removed his sword, pushing the priest backwards. Father Dominique Margil's body fell heavily to the floor, adjacent to the gaping cavity in the center of the room where the gold chest had been removed, the blood from his fatal wound streaming into the hole.

∞

Hippolyte de Bouchard and his men enjoyed a day of relaxation and drink in Monterey after the discovery of the gold chest. When Bouchard ordered the departure from Monterey, he also commanded that the entire town be burned to the ground. Bouchard took great pleasure in watching the flames from the fires consume the settlement from the deck of his ship in Monterey Bay. No place would get away with sinking one of his ships. No place would outsmart him by leaving such precious riches hidden in their wake. *And no priest would ever get in his way.*

41.

Year of our Lord 2009.

AS JOHN GIBSON IMAGINED, Isidro de la Vega was already waiting for him at their designated meeting place in the garden area behind the Stevenson House. Gibson located the house easily enough, as it was very near the hotel in downtown Monterey where he booked a room.

Isidro was seated on a bench underneath a large magnolia tree sprouting huge pink flowers. Isidro didn't notice him approaching, or at least, nothing about his outward appearance revealed that he noticed John Gibson.

"Hello, Isidro. Good to see you again." Gibson called when he was close. Isidro glanced up from the book he was reading, but he didn't respond in words. Instead he rose to meet Gibson. "Thank you again for agreeing to this," Gibson commented.

"Actually, I'm not really sure what I have agreed to … but you're welcome all the same," Isidro replied.

Isidro's response left Gibson feeling momentarily deflated. After all, if the person he was relying on was feeling accosted from the first, then the amount of assistance that person provided would be miniscule. Gibson brushed aside his frustration and attempted to let Isidro feel more comfortable with the situation.

"Listen, Isidro, what I really am requesting from you is that you impart some of your knowledge of the area. I realize that this may not seem like it would be so helpful, but believe me, it will be. To be a detective in a place one knows nothing about, especially such a unique place as this, it's impossible to be on top of anything, and even the smallest thing may lead to solving a case." Gibson deliberately paused and watched carefully for Isidro's reaction to his plea.

When he noticed no change in the young man's expression, not even a slight glimmer in Isidro's eyes, he tried again. "I am aware that my being here is a nuisance to you, but I promise that you can help me and it will be greatly appreciated."

Gibson felt frustration settling in once again, as he still did not notice any sign from Isidro that he was going to be of any assistance. Gibson took in his surroundings: a heavily and beautifully landscaped courtyard with a pleasant blend of planted flowers and plants bordered by majestic oaks, magnolias, and a fig tree. A few benches were scattered alongside a winding dirt pathway that led through the garden. The back of the Stevenson House, with its starkly painted white adobe walls, faced them, and behind was an entrance to the courtyard, which led to a city street. He decided to try a new approach.

"You know, I've noticed a few of these historic adobe houses with gardens around Monterey. Perhaps you could tell me their story?" Gibson waited patiently for Isidro's response.

Although he was trying entice the young man, Gibson did think that Monterey was the kind of place where it was possible to look one direction on one day and think there was nothing special about it, then look in the same direction the next day and think of being in a completely different place that was altogether beautiful and fascinating. For example, Gibson had not really noticed how infused with historic adobe buildings the downtown area of Monterey was until after he had reached his hotel, parked, and walked to meet Isidro.

Isidro resolved that Gibson was playing to his vanity, but he didn't overly mind. He was going to help anyway; now at least he had good reason to include a history lesson. "Yes, there are quite a few." Isidro glanced at his watch. "We have some time before our dinner engagement. I suggest we take a seat and have a discussion before we head over to Casa Amesti."

Gibson agreed with a nod of his head and the two sat on the bench underneath the wide magnolia tree. "So do you live in Monterey, Isidro?" Gibson asked, genuinely interested.

"I was born and raised here in Monterey, up near the crest of those hills, near what's known as Skyline Drive," Isidro said, pointing southward towards the solid mass of a green hillside with waves of fog cascading down its side. "Now I live over the hill in Pacific Grove."

"Wait … don't I recall you speaking fairly *negatively* of Pacific Grove?"

Isidro huffed in response. "Just because I live there doesn't mean I have to turn a blind eye to its past."

"I saw an interesting vehicle while walking over here. It was an old orange Volkswagen bus with a woman my age driving it who had a silver ponytail. I noticed she had one of the dream catchers hanging from her rear-view mirror. The license plate cover read: 'Pacific Grove — Fog Happens' and there was a bumper sticker that said 'I Brake for Butterflies' next to another with a faded picture of The Beatles."

"That sounds pretty accurate for Pacific Grove. It has different weather patterns than Monterey, just around the peninsula from it. Being full of thin Monterey pine trees, when we get winter storms blowing in from the Pacific, it's not at all uncommon for the power to be knocked out."

"She also had this light blue license plate frame that I've seen on other vehicles down here; it has something to do with the Monterey Aquarium?" Gibson queried.

Isidro chuckled lightly. "Those are a symbol of perseverance and pride around the Peninsula. It's an indication that one is an official volunteer at the aquarium. People get their names on a list and will wait for years to fill a vacancy, and honestly, I think they are as concerned about having one of those license plate covers as they are about volunteering.

"But returning to the adobes, around fifteen houses or buildings in the vicinity of downtown Monterey are recognized as historic Monterey adobes. These houses and buildings were built one hundred fifty to two hundred years ago, during the Spanish and subsequent Mexican periods of Monterey's history. There are about ten other adobes that have been converted to modern uses over the decades: a bank, a pastry shop, a restaurant, an office building; and with their gutted interiors, all that is left of major historic significance is the facades of the buildings. We lost a deplorable number of structures around the turn of the last century due to lack of interest in the historic houses and structures, leading to their eventual demise."

A squawking bluebird landed on the ground near Isidro's feet and he shuffled a foot to scare the bird off. The bird screeched loudly and flew to a branch above them in the magnolia tree. "Those birds are the worst thing about coming to this particular courtyard. If you don't keep them away, they will practically land on your shoulder and screech in your face," Isidro said with obvious contempt for the bluebirds. Gibson noted Isidro's reaction and liked to see that the young man was not able to always maintain his own facade of near-persistent aloofness.

Isidro decided to convey a thought that had been troubling him from the moment his phone conversation with Chiles had concluded. "Agent Gibson, I'm more than happy to discuss historical and cultural traits of the Peninsula with you, but I have to be honest, I still don't know how you believe I can be of help to you."

Gibson, for his part, had expected the question to arise again and had planned a response on his drive to Monterey. "Well, considering how you seem to be a book of knowledge about the Monterey Peninsula, perhaps just by talking with you, I may be able to figure something out. And, I think someone once said that history has a tendency to repeat itself."

Gibson was especially proud of the last line he had been waiting to deliver. Isidro grinned in response. "Well played, Gibson," he said. "So where do you want to begin?" Isidro asked.

"Well, we've actually already begun. But I want to next talk boating down here, or more precisely, about any places where fishing boats could be docked."

Isidro nodded his head. As he did, his eyes glanced downwards at his watch. "Sure, that will be easy enough. However, as you know, we have a dinner engagement awaiting us, and we can continue this discussion after it is done."

In the short walk to Casa Amesti, Gibson noted that Isidro's lesson encompassed every step they took.

"The original name for this house was obviously not the Stevenson House; it was 'The French Hotel. As you can imagine, associating the place with a famous author was much more of a potential tourist draw," Isidro remarked.

"In many regards, Stevenson viewed Monterey as a piece of aging royalty that had long since lost its grandeur. He described it with empty and lifeless streets and its people as lazy and prone to gossiping. And yet he is still glorified here. Jack London had a similar stay on the Peninsula and all he receives for it in collective memory is having a dark pub that perpetually smells of stale spilled beer named after him in Carmel, and I doubt that most people realize the bar is named after him.

"This square used to be the location of a tavern, named Simoneau's Tavern, where when he wasn't sick in bed or trying to find treasure, Stevenson spent a good deal of his time," Isidro noted as they walked by a central square that served as a public bus transportation spot.

Isidro came to stop at an edge of the square adjacent to a four-street stop intersection. "This is an interesting spot." He turned around and pointed towards a flag pole in the center of the square. "If you look behind us, you'll see that there are four flags flying: one for Spain, one for Mexico, one for California, and one for the United States of America. These flags represent that progression of history in Monterey."

"Hmm, interesting," Gibson commented.

"From here, one is really in the center of what used to be 'old town' Monterey. The tavern, as I mentioned, was behind us. Back in the vicinity of the Stevenson House are some other notable adobes. Right to our left is the Cooper-Molera Adobe, which was both a house and general store of one of the wealthiest men in Monterey during his time who had married into an affluent Spanish family. Behind the tall wooden gates is a wide courtyard with gardens and a massive stable at its rear," Isidro said as he pointed towards the structure seen rising above the tall wooden fence.

Gibson found it odd how the old-looking house complex was directly bordered by the modern-day establishments of a coffee shop and a grocery store.

"Cooper-Molera had a direct view from his place down Alvarado Street, which, as it is today, was the main street of Monterey. Before the hotel at the end of it was built in the Sixties, one would have an obstructed view all the way into the harbor and would be able to clearly see any arriving trading vessels. Across from Cooper-Molera's is the house where the street's namesake lived, the Alvarado House, which as you can see, is now a bank. Just one street up the hill is the Larkin House, which was the home of Thomas Larkin, who was also very well-off and served as a de facto U.S. Ambassador to Spanish California and a de jure U.S. Ambassador to Mexican California. Not many people know this, but that place houses millions of dollars worth of antiques.

"And where we are going, Casa Amesti, is located right over there, across from the Cooper-Molera Adobe. There are other notable houses right around this general area within a few blocks, but in the absence of time, I would suggest we make our arrival at the function and perhaps afterward we can continue our tour of old town."

"I would like that," Gibson genuinely replied.

"Great."

"So are you going to tell me a little about our dinner hosts?" Gibson asked.

Isidro smiled slyly as he began to cross the street. "*Oh no*. I would not deprive Señora Sobranes of that, as I'm sure she is going to be delighted to thoroughly inform you of the complete history and mission of the Daughters of the American West."

"Oh, Isidro! Welcome, welcome!" Señora Sobranes exclaimed as Isidro and Gibson entered through the wide doorway of Casa Amesti. From its exterior, Gibson noted that it was a noble-looking adobe house, even for Monterey standards. It had the standard second-floor balcony lined with black cast iron railings that Isidro told him was common of the 'Monterey style' of architecture in the early to mid-1880s.

"Thank you, Señora Sobranes. We are happy to be here. May I present John Gibson," Isidro replied.

Señora Sobranes wore an elegant blue dress adorned with gold lining. Gibson guessed she was in her seventies, but she had retained a firm figure and was wearing a healthy yet elegant dose of makeup. "Mr. Gibson, I'm delighted to make your acquaintance," Señora Sobranes remarked as she formally extended a hand for Gibson to touch. "You are no doubt equally as interested in the history of our unique little town as the rest of us."

Gibson touched the señora's hand with his own. "Of course, that's why I'm here," he said, grinning.

"Señora, I have purposefully not told Mr. Gibson about the history of your organization, as I knew that you would take pleasure in doing so yourself. Perhaps you could do so as I make my way through the room greeting your other guests?" Isidro suggested.

Señora Sobranes beamed in response. "Oh, I'd be delighted!" She took Gibson's hand and led him into a spacious room bordering the entranceway of the house. "Casa Amesti is one of the most beautifully preserved of all of the Monterey adobes, as you can see from the furniture in this room, which is all authentic from the settlement's early days."

Gibson noted the room solid wooden furniture pieces and vibrant rugs covering the wooden floors. Señora Sobranes moved his hand so that his arm was hooked around hers, as if he were escorting her through the house. There were numerous groups of finely dressed older woman scattered about the house engaged in their own conversations, all with glasses of white wine in hand. A couple of black-tie attired waiters meandered through the room carrying trays of appetizers. "Isidro mentioned that you have your dinner meetings on a monthly basis. Do you always have them here in this house?" Gibson inquired.

"Oh, heavens, no," Señora Sobranes exclaimed as she used her free hand to slap him lightly on his arm. "We would never limit ourselves. We contribute to numerous foundations and associations and the historical society itself, so we are able to move about the adobes as we please." Judging from the dignified clothing and sparkling diamond jewelry he noticed all of the women wearing, Gibson assumed that by "contributions" Señora Sobranes meant that her group was wealthy enough to pretty much do whatever they wanted.

"Each month our dinner gathering is held in a different adobe or historic building. We even are given access to the houses and buildings that are privately owned. We use the House of the Four Winds, just around the corner, for our annual pre-Lenten *El Baile de Los Cascarones*, or in English, the Cascarone Ball; it's a Spanish tradition dating back to the origins of Monterey. Oh, you must come to our next one. I will be sure that Isidro extends you an invitation. It is a lovely affair, but the guest list is limited, you see."

Gibson noticed that the groups of chatting women would occasionally glance in their direction with looks of curiosity mixed with mild disapproval. He began to feel the weight of Chiles' proclamation that he had been offered an exclusive invitation.

Señora Sobranes stopped in order to share a few words with three women who were comparing tastes of an appetizer they had just been served. She introduced Gibson, who nodded politely, and then she urged him to the rear of the house into a large dining room that had floor to ceiling windows looking outward at the adobe's walled garden area. "This is where we shall dine this evening after young Isidro enlightens us on the current progress of the historical society," she commented. "This is one of my favorite locations for our gatherings. Seated here in this room or out in the garden, I can almost feel like I'm back in the 1800s."

Gibson had thought that he would find Isidro in the dining room, but the young man was nowhere to be seen. "How long has your organization been in existence?"

"Oh, for quite some time," Señora Sobranes replied in a tone that he knew indicated she would not reveal much. She squeezed his arm gently with her frail-looking hands, which now both gripped his arm. Gibson, however, remained undeterred. "I've heard of the Daughters of the American Revolution on the East Coast. Is your group similar to them?"

The expression on Señora Sobranes' face instantly turned from smiling to sour. "Those East Coast snobs can keep their claims to the damned Mayflower and the Founding Fathers. We do consider ourselves to be a special group, but we don't look down on others."

Despite her claim to the contrary, Gibson sensed that Señora Sobranes' remark on being "special" indicated the organization's elitism. "How many members do you have?"

Señora Sobranes again squeezed his arm slightly. "Oh, we will always exist. As time progresses, it becomes increasingly difficult to trace bloodlines back to the original habitants of Monterey, be they Spanish, Mexican, or the odd American, Englishman, or Frenchman that managed to settle here, but we manage, and all of the descendants of the women you will see here this evening will be notified in time of their impending responsibility to be a part of our group."

Years of interrogating witnesses proved to Gibson that Señora Sobranes would be a tough character to crack. She had a way of confidently responding to all of his questions, without actually providing any concrete answers. "So your organization is just based in Monterey?"

"Oh, heavens, no." Again, Señora Sobranes slapped his arm lightly. "We have chapters all over California."

"Just in California?" Gibson asked.

"Why heavens, yes. Places such as Arizona and New Mexico may have also had early Spanish settlements of their own, but those places were entirely separate from California."

"And your name — Sobranes — is there some history to it that you could tell me about?"

"Oh, yes!" Señora Sobranes squeezed his arm the hardest she had yet, beaming from ear to ear with a wide grin. "My descendants were extremely wealthy and influential here. They owned an enormous ranch that extended from the coast inward to the Salinas Valley. If you drive south on Highway 1, just south of Carmel Highlands there is a state park. It was my family that donated the land to the state. The creek that runs through the park is still known as Sobranes Creek. My family even has an adobe named after us. It's on Pacific Street, just down from the Monterey Institute. I wish the adobe tours were still being provided, as I would love for you to see my family's home."

Gibson decided it was time to open up a little. "Hmm, you mean with your family's influence, even *you* are no longer allowed access to your ancestral home?"

Señora Sobranes eyed him keenly without responding. "Let's step outside into the courtyard, shall we?" Gibson agreed with a nod and the two walked through the doorway into the adobe's enclosed courtyard. From the time that he had been seated at the bench behind the Stevenson House with Isidro, the air had turned chilly and the sky overhead was a gray mass of fog that occasionally splintered in dangling fingers to scrape treetops or houses.

The garden area of the house was immaculately maintained with a pathway system circling delicate landscaping. Isidro, who had been strolling in the garden on his own, walked up to Señora Sobranes and John Gibson. "It's quite an astounding place, do you agree?" Isidro asked Gibson.

"Yes, it is indeed," Gibson responded. "I see what you were saying earlier about feeling transported to a different place and time," Gibson said, turning to address the señora. "From back here, it's easy to imagine that we are in some place along the Mediterranean."

"Yes, indeed," Señora Sobranes agreed. "Of all of Monterey's *secret gardens*, which is how some people refer to them, I believe this one to be the most impressive in both elegant beauty and for the fact, as you mentioned, that one feels entirely entranced while here. The garden in the private adobe residence adjacent to Casa Abrego may be the only one that comes close," Señora Sobranes added.

"I agree, but even in that garden there is a gated fence that allows passersby to gaze into the home's courtyard, whereas here there is absolutely no way for anyone on the sidewalks surrounding this garden to see in," Isidro commented.

"Yes, this is truly a special place. I doubt that most people living in Monterey are aware of its existence." Señora Sobranes shivered from the cool air and turned to face Gibson. "If you don't mind, my kind sir, I would like to return to the warmth inside the house."

"Sure. Perhaps you could tell me about the meal we'll be having this evening? Isidro informed me that it will all be locally sourced and is styled after traditional regional cuisine," Gibson said.

Señora Sobranes beamed once again and squeezed his arm gently. "Oh, how delightful that you are able to join us this evening!"

Gibson returned the smile and reentered the house with the giddy elder woman clinging to his arm. Isidro followed, discovering the voice level of the women inside had risen.

"Wow. Now that was a meal," Gibson proclaimed as he walked out of Casa Amesti's front doorway. The Daughters of the American West dinner had proceeded marvelously, capped with a brief presentation by Isidro on Monterey's most influential women throughout its history being extremely well-received by his captivated audience. At one

point, Señora Sobranes leaned towards Gibson and whispered that many of the historical female figures mentioned by Isidro in his presentation had descendants in the room that evening.

"I don't know what some of those dishes were exactly, but they were all delicious," Gibson stated as he and Isidro stepped on the brick sidewalk into the damp, fog-laden air. "I wouldn't mind walking some of it off if you're game."

"Sure. We can use the time to continue our discussion," Isidro responded. "Let's turn to our right, away from central downtown for the moment. There's an intersection of streets just up the way that I would like to show you. And, yes, the ladies always have fantastic dinners and this evening was no exception. What did you think of the abalone appetizer?"

Gibson recalled the starter plate that had been breaded strips of lightly pan-fried abalone. "To be honest, for as much hype as I've heard about abalone, I thought it would be a little more special. It didn't seem all that different to me than calamari steak, maybe just a little more tender."

Isidro lightly chuckled. "I would agree, actually. I have never thought it the most amazing of delicacies either. I think it's the exclusivity of it that makes it so special in the minds of many. Back in the cannery days, there used to be a shop where the proprietor made abalone sandwiches for the fishermen and cannery workers on a daily basis; so, as you can imagine, it was not expensive at all. It's similar to the sardines we had next," Isidro commented, referring to the next course that had been served with four shiny, modestly sized sardines that had been caught in Monterey Bay. The sardines were grilled and glazed in a light tomato sauce. "As you know, sardines used to be overflowing from the waters of the bay and now they are caught in such small numbers that they are served as rare delicacies, such as at the dinner we just attended."

"They were delicious, though, I must say. I also really liked the main dish — the braised veal and sage with sautéed onions."

Isidro chuckled again as he came to a halt at the edge of an intersection of five roads meeting an uneven angles. "That was sautéed fennel, actually."

"Ah," Gibson responded. "I suppose that explains why it only looked like onion, but didn't really taste like it."

"Indeed," Isidro replied. "Now, let me explain where we are currently standing. This was actually one of the liveliest sections of old Monterey. Quite a few prominent citizens had houses up here, such as in that line of historic houses there to our right on Calle Principal."

Gibson's eyes had adjusted to the dimly lit streets after leaving the Casa Amesti and he could see what Isidro referred to as a line of houses that vaguely reminded him of row houses one would see on the East Coast.

"California's first court building was established in that one-story adobe building right across the street. Monterey had its share of notorious bandits back in those days and frontier justice often resulted in hangings, which could have been conducted from the broad branches of any of the oak trees in this vicinity.

"And across from it, there on the other side of Hartnell, that red grand-looking house is known as the Stokes Adobe. Legend has it that the house has served as some sort of a tavern or rooming house from the time of its construction. More interestingly, legend also has it that quite a number of disputes were settled with swords and later guns in its front yard. The trees over there also could have easily provided the court-ordered services I mentioned earlier.

"All of these souls departing within its vicinity apparently resulted in a number of them refusing to leave that old house, and its history is ripe with tales of ghost stories."

Isidro led them across Calle Principal, heading in the direction of Pacific Street. "On our right, we are passing by another group of historic homes that are now privately owned. And on our left is Colton Hall."

Gibson could see an expansive landscaped lawn with a grouping of buildings surrounding one central one that was a two-story structure with large columns in front.

"It was there that the California Constitutional Convention was signed in 1849 by delegates from around California, establishing California as a state of the United States of America. You won't be able to make it out in the darkness, but next to the Hall there's a small brick building that was Monterey's first jail. Behind it is a little yellow house where one of Monterey's most infamous criminals, Tiburcio Vasquez, used to hide out in his mother's home while posses were sent into the hills to find him. Ironically, his mother's house is within sight of the very jail where the posses wished to toss Tiburcio. He outsmarted them by realizing that they would never believe he would hole up in such an obvious place. A little farther back behind us is Monterey High School, where on its grounds not so long ago, people miraculously began digging up old gold coins." Isidro paused as he became aware that he was beginning to rant along with his outburst of local history.

"You're kind of like a walking and talking history book, Isidro," Gibson commented with a laugh. "I don't think I've ever met someone like you."

Isidro wasn't certain if it was a compliment or not, but he blushed slightly anyway. "Sorry, I know I go off at times. I'm such a fan of history that at times I feel like I need to impart as much as I possibly can to others."

"There's no need for an apology. It's nice to meet a person like you," Gibson replied.

At that moment, Gibson noticed someone approaching them on the sidewalk. The figure of a man gradually appeared through the fog-veiled darkness. Gibson was surprised and slightly startled when Isidro called out, "Hello, Sir Tom." Sir Tom abruptly came to a stop in front of them and peered forward in the gentle light emanating from a nearby lamppost. "This is John Gibson. I'm taking him on a little evening tour of Monterey."

Sir Tom moved closer to the pair, first staring at Gibson and then at Isidro. "My young lad! How splendid to cross paths with you on this very fine Monterey evening!" Sir Tom slapped Isidro's shoulder. "As the wind shakes the barley, have you found your treasure yet?"

"No, no. Still looking," Isidro responded.

"Do not waste too much time, lad. Find the treasure that awaits you!" Sir Tom then stepped into the street briefly in order to walk around Isidro and Gibson and continue on his way into the night.

Gibson stood perplexed, waiting for Isidro's explanation. "An old friend of mine; he's a bit on the eccentric side," Isidro offered.

"It would seem 'a bit eccentric' is the appropriate label," Gibson countered. "Would you like to sit down somewhere and have a drink?"

"Sure, I know a place you may like and you wanted to know more about the local boating industry," Isidro recommended.

Isidro and Gibson sat in a concealed courtyard filled with tables, heat lamps, and fire pits, with clear Christmas tree lights lining the mixture of fencing and walls surrounding the enclosed outdoor area. Gibson had a glass of red wine and Isidro a steaming mug of herbal tea.

Isidro informed Gibson of local boating activities, which unlike the former fishing days of old, was mostly limited to diving boats, sailboats, yachts, and vessels for whale watching and deep sea fishing outings. As for specific commercial fishing vessels, all that Isidro could think of docked not in Monterey's harbor, but at Moss Landing, about halfway around the bay to Santa Cruz. Gibson pondered what Isidro told him, without sensing any connection he was looking for.

"Tell me, Gibson. Would you expect who you are after to be particularly wealthy?" Isidro asked.

Gibson set down his wine glass and made sure no one was within hearing distance. A group of young people seated across the courtyard from them were smoking large hookahs. "Oh, definitely. Whoever pulled this off had to have had very considerable means available to them."

"Well, this may easily be nothing, and quite frankly I feel a bit ridiculous even suggesting that it may be related, but something about running into Sir Tom as you and I were walking and some recent research I've been doing just seems too interconnected to not investigate the possibility that it may be."

"Please, I'm anxious to hear what you have to say," Gibson encouraged.

"I overheard something recently, something that was out of place and seemed very odd at the time, but I summarily dismissed it until we just ran into Sir Tom back there. You see, just before I overheard this, I had been talking with Sir Tom on Asilomar Beach over in Pacific Grove."

"Well, what was it?" Gibson inquired.

"There were two men sitting on the beach, two men who were expensively overdressed for the beach. In fact, everything about these two men was out of place. And I don't mean that I believed at the time that they were not local, as they looked exactly like what I think of as a typical profile for the wealthy elite here who live in their multimillion dollar homes in Pebble Beach or one of the exclusive subdivisions surrounding the Peninsula. But I did think they appeared very out of place for the setting. Asilomar is a place for families, surfers, and tourists; not a place where people of such standing spend their time."

"That's perceptive of you, Isidro, but I don't see how you think any of this could possibly be relevant to the case."

"The Stevenson Plan," Isidro said aloud.

"Excuse me?" Gibson asked.

"That's what they were discussing, something they called *the Stevenson Plan*."

"All right, I'm thoroughly confused, Isidro. You're going to have to be a little less cryptic on this one."

"Yes, yes, I know. Give me a moment to think this through a little more before I try to explain," Isidro pleaded. After a few minutes of Isidro deeply concentrating and Gibson finishing his glass of wine, Isidro continued. "Okay, bear with me a little, as this may be a little abstract sounding at first. Remember how I mentioned on our Point Lobos tour a pirate named Hippolyte de Bouchard invading and trying to destroy Monterey?"

Gibson nodded. Although eager to hear the young man's story, he was dubious of Isidro's pending revelation.

"There's a legend that when Hippolyte invaded Monterey, he departed with a treasure. It has equally been dismissed throughout time by historians, as there is no record of any such treasure having been in Monterey at the time of Hippolyte's invasion of Monterey, or of any such treasure existing to begin with. I have always regarded the legend as pure fantasy, but recently I uncovered something that may make me consider it differently, and it did not occur to me until just moments ago."

"What was that?"

"The Spanish Crown was not so interested in its far-off Alta California during Hippolyte's reign of terror along its coastline. It is therefore very difficult to imagine any sizeable fortune of the State having been in Monterey, and this would also explain why there would be no official record of any such treasure having existed or having been stolen by Bouchard. But the Catholic Church was very interested in entrenching itself, and thus the Spanish Empire, firmly into Alta California. Now the Church, which had great power, wealth, and influence during this period, could have easily supplied Monterey with such a treasure, and they could have easily done this secretly and without official record of it having ever occurred. Additionally, Father Junipero Serra was at the Carmel Mission at the time and his influence alone could move mountains."

Gibson felt himself being drawn into the mounting intrigue of Isidro's story, even if it had nothing to do with the case. "So what have you discovered?"

Isidro leaned back into his chair, feeling a wave of embarrassment overcome him. "I discovered something, a letter, a close to two-hundred-year-old letter, at the San Antonio Mission that may refer to such a treasure," Isidro reluctantly admitted. "However, I must humbly request that you not mention this to anyone else, as I have not made my discovery public yet; however, I fully intend to do so."

Isidro's admission resulted in Gibson perceiving the young man in a different light. He doubted Isidro was capable of any criminal activity, but the fact that he was willing to skirt along the line of morality made him a little more interesting.

"When David called me yesterday, I was in Santa Barbara reviewing Church records at the Santa Barbara Mission. I found documented proof that a Father Margil was tasked on a mission in the year 1818 to personally oversee the delivery of some unnamed item of great importance to Father Junipero Serra at the Carmel Mission."

"But why would the Church deliver a 'treasure' to Monterey?"

Isidro sighed. "Well, I don't know the answer to that yet. When Bouchard invaded, he didn't even bother taking his men over the hill to the Carmel Mission. At the time, Serra believed it inevitable that the pirate would, and so during Bouchard's invasion, the Carmel Mission was evacuated, along with anything of value within it. So I don't know exactly how that end of the story would line up ..." Isidro shook his head in frustration, speaking more to himself than Gibson.

"But there are elements leading to a strong theory that there was such a delivery made by the Church to Carmel, and perhaps the gold, if it actually existed, was brought to Monterey for some purpose. The

Governor of Monterey of Alta California at the time, Pedro Fages, and Father Serra disputed often, but with a growing threat, greater than even an invasion by Bouchard, perhaps they decided to collaborate."

"There was a threat greater than a pirate invading?" Gibson asked, surprised.

"Yes, there was — the Russians."

Gibson was now thoroughly confused. *"The Russians?"*

"Yes, very much so. American history books to their discredit do not convey that the Russian Empire in the eighteenth and early nineteenth century posed a serious threat of expanding its reach into California. In fact, they had done so at a place now known as Fort Ross on the coast a ways north of San Francisco. And they had already established their presence in Alaska. There was one man among them that was particularly worrisome to the Church, undoubtedly to Governor Fages as well. His name was Rezanov and history has it that he was a particularly ambitious and determined man who may have succeeded in his goal of colonizing California had he not lost the support of the czar and his court in St. Petersburg, who plainly lost interest in North America. But the Church and Fages would have had no way of knowing that the Russian was losing his home support and would have been considerably threatened by him. I've run across records mentioning him and the Church's fear of him quite a few times in my research of archives in the Santa Barbara Mission."

"They let you search through their historical records any time you like?" Gibson inquired.

Isidro grinned mischievously. *"Not exactly.* Not just anyone would be allowed access by the Franciscans into their archives, and even though I'm granted special privileges due to my status as a state historian, and it certainly helps that I'm Catholic, much remains off-limits to me, and I'm not allowed to copy anything in there; they don't even like it when I take notes." Isidro paused to take a drink of his tea. "But from what I was able to find and have seen, coupled with what I found at the San Antonio Mission, I think it's safe to say that the pieces of a nearly two-hundred-year-old mystery are becoming slowly unveiled."

"How so?"

"Any caravan traveling on the Mission Trail up through California at that time would have stopped at the San Antonio Mission in southern

Monterey County. The letter I discovered in an abandoned room there is signed by one Father Dominique Margil."

"Okay, so maybe that proves that the Church and the Spanish were worried about some Russian encroaching too closely for comfort, and maybe that even helps to indicate some amount of gold involved that could have been in Monterey at the time of the pirate's invasion. But tell me again, Isidro; how does this possibly have anything to do with the case?"

"Patience, Mr. Gibson. *Patience*. All in good time," Isidro commented. He took another drink of tea. "Let's, for argument's sake, suppose that this treasure was in Monterey at the time of Bouchard's invasion and he somehow acquired it."

"Sure," Gibson agreed.

"If all that were true, then the legend of Bouchard having his crew bury it somewhere down the coast from here is much more probable. And if that did in fact occur, then its legend would have been handed down from generation to generation; it's very probable that Robert Louis Stevenson himself was told it while he was here in Monterey and that he went searching for it and later wrote a book about it."

"Wait, wait. I'm confused. Why would a famous writer have been searching for buried pirate treasure?" Gibson asked.

Isidro wagged a finger at Gibson. "You're forgetting what I said earlier. Stevenson was unknown and near penniless while he was in Monterey and he was seeking the favor of a wealthy lady. And since he was a passionate individual with a vivid imagination … it makes sense."

Gibson shook his head in confusion. "Okay, let's put Robert Louis Stevenson aside for a moment and return to the original story," he pleaded before finishing his glass of wine.

"Fine," Isidro conceded. "At which part?" he asked.

"The part explaining why Bouchard would have stolen a treasure from Monterey and then gone and immediately buried it somewhere."

Isidro nodded, pleased with Gibson's question. "Ah, that is actually a very good point, but one for which I do have an explanation. Bouchard suffered the loss of a ship in his onslaught of Monterey. That left him two, with the ship that was sunk having been the fastest of his fleet. He was a notoriously anxious character, and it is possible he feared that he would be pursued by any number of potential competitors along the coast and without his fastest ship would not be able to outrun them. After all, the off-shore coastal waters were pretty hot in those days. He may have even feared being overcome by grander vessels carrying superior firepower, and thus did not wish to risk losing the gold either through his ship sinking or his ship being boarded and taken over. By burying the treasure, Bouchard may have seen an opportunity to continue his pillaging down the coastline, which he in reality did, without worry and then return for the gold at a later time. But that's not what is really important for our understanding of the modern-day implications of this legend."

"So what is really important?"

"*The legend itself.*" Isidro paused for effect, but spoke again before Gibson could ask another question. "I've heard various forms of it, but an element arising often is that only one other crewman amongst Bouchard's men knew the location of where the gold was buried; which coincidentally is very similar to the plot of *Treasure Island*, by the way.

"Bouchard was suspicious of his crew, as I would assume most pirate captains at the time were, but he took it to another level entirely, according to some versions of the legend. These versions talked of him stopping at two locations along the coast south of Monterey and sending small boats onshore with chests. Each of the two locations was supposedly 'island-like' and would have been prominently noticeable from ships off the coastline. Bouchard would personally accompany a small contingent of men with the chest inland, while the rest of the small boat's crew stayed at the shoreline. Bouchard returned later, without any of the group he had taken with him to bury the chests."

"Sounds like a ruthless character," Gibson commented.

"I never paid any attention to those variations of the legend … it seemed so drastic, even for Bouchard, but if there was a treasure involved as considerable as what we've been discussing, there would have been more reason for Bouchard to act so cautiously."

"Well, how would the legend have survived if there were only two men who knew of it?"

"Good question," Isidro acknowledged. "Hippolyte was not long afterward chased from Californian waters for good. I'm sure he cursed not being able to return for the treasure, if it did exist, every day of his life. Legend has it that the only other person who knew of the treasure's location was Bouchard's first lieutenant, and he fled from Bouchard's command during a raid on the coast of Peru.

"As this version of the legend goes, when he was dying, he told the tale to his son. Some of the old-timers I used to interview in the area told me they had heard the son came to Monterey in the mid-1800s to search for Bouchard's buried treasure; although I was always assured that the son never discovered it … Bouchard must have tricked his first lieutenant somehow. The first lieutenant's son attempted to be as secretive about his search as possible, but he purportedly told someone, who told someone else and so forth, that his father told him the gold was buried somewhere on an island near Monterey." Isidro breathed deeply, feeling a sense of accomplishment. "And now we return to Robert Louis Stevenson, as this would have been about the time he was in Monterey."

"Okay, but let's try and narrow this down into some relevancy," Gibson requested.

"This is where the story does get precisely relevant to our present situation; in theory, that is … As I've mentioned, while RLS was in Monterey, he reportedly spent a lot of his time at Simoneau's Tavern conversing with its patrons. He undoubtedly would have used the venue to talk about his misfortunes of sickliness, struggling writing career, and so forth, but most of all his dire financial situation, which might deny him the star-crossed love of his life.

"Now, the son of Bouchard's first lieutenant, if he had indeed ventured to Monterey to search for the lost treasure, would have been rather elderly by the time of Stevenson's visit to Monterey. Maybe he would have even abandoned his search by then and would have taken pity on the sight of a sickly, destitute, and melancholic young man. Maybe the first lieutenant's son told Stevenson the tale of the treasure. Perhaps this inspired Stevenson's pen in later years; but it immediately inspired him to pick up a shovel."

"Do you know where he searched?"

"Yes. As I mentioned on our tour of it, Stevenson went searching for treasure at Point Lobos."

Gibson leaned back in his chair, glancing away from Isidro to see if he could catch the attention of a waitress to bring him another glass of wine.

Isidro sensed correctly that Gibson's attention and patience were waning. "Anyone who is a fan of Robert Louis Stevenson here knows about the legend. It's one that parents and schoolteachers tell kids.

"Kids that go to schools here are practically taught to worship the man and his writing. I've even been told that some of the Peninsula's most well-established older families share an obsession for searching for Stevenson's famed lost treasure."

Gibson adjusted uneasily in his chair. "So, you really think that a reference you overheard to the *Stevenson Plan* could be related to our case and that it would indicate something to do with Point Lobos?" Gibson asked with skepticism cemented in his tone.

Isidro relaxed back into his chair, the tension of having formulated and presented a profound theory gradually easing. "You asked me to share my impressions of local culture; this is what I'm doing."

"Okay, okay, you're right." Gibson exhaled deeply. "Sorry, I'm just wondering how you think this is all connected and how it could possibly be something for me to pursue."

"Well, as I said at the beginning of this discussion, it seems there are a lot of connections and that maybe it could lead to something. And as I said, seeing those two guys at the beach who were so out of place and overhearing them make such a local-sounding reference ... it's intriguing."

"Intriguing, yes, I agree. But this is where law enforcement and historical reference theories may conflict. I mean, how could we even begin to search for two well-dressed men you witnessed being out of place on a beach and discussing something that *may* be related to the case?"

Isidro considered mentioning the gold flask engraved with initials that the pair on the beach were passing between themselves, but dismissed the though, as he would not be able to identify the letters. Then Isidro smiled knowingly. He suddenly remembered seeing the black Bentley parked alongside the road at Asilomar. "Do you have the ability to search for people based on the type of cars they drive?"

"Sure, we have full access to DMV records. But unless you have a license plate number, searching for owners of a certain type of car in an area can be an especially daunting task." Gibson noticed Isidro still grinning, waiting to share something further. "Unless, that is, it is a highly specialized vehicle," Gibson added.

"Even in this land of multimillionaires, I think you would find that not too many people drive Bentleys."

Gibson excitedly slapped Isidro's knee. "Nicely done!"

Isidro felt a rush of appreciation move through him.

"I'll be able to get on that first thing in the morning. But, you know, I was thinking of something you said earlier. If this theory of yours turned out to have any truth, it could make this legend a lot more *real*."

"Yes, I realize that as well," Isidro reluctantly admitted. As he took another sip of his tea, it also occurred to him that if the legend were true — all aspects of it — then the stolen treasure of Monterey was still buried somewhere along the coast south of Monterey. And aside from Point Lobos, there was really only one place immediately south along the coastline that would appear as *an island* onto itself from passing ships in the ocean ...

Agent John Gibson woke the next morning feeling energized. His encounter with Isidro de la Vega the previous evening had far exceeded his expectations. Gibson was confident that Isidro would be able to provide him assistance in his investigation, but he did not truthfully expect to be able to derive an actual lead from the young historian. Gibson planned to first contact the FBI office in San Francisco to request the DMV check for owners of Bentleys in the Monterey Peninsula region, then call Agent Alan Shapiro to keep Shapiro informed of his activities, and then visit the Monterey County Sheriff's office.

"Agent Shapiro. Gibson. Just wanted to give you a quick call to let you know that I've come across a possible lead down here in Monterey," Gibson said to Shapiro over his phone.

"That's great, Gibson. Thank you for keeping me informed," Shapiro responded. Shapiro didn't ask any details about the lead.

"I thought I should let you know that I've already requested a DMV search report through the office that should be completed by mid-morning today."

"Wonderful. I really must run now, though. Keep me informed." The line went blank as Shapiro hung up his phone. Gibson stared perplexed at his cell phone. He questioned if Agent Shapiro was unimpressed with his tactics, but decided it was a blessing to be able to move uninhibited.

On his way out, Gibson stopped at the reception desk and informed the clerk that a very important fax would soon be arriving for him on the hotel's fax machine. Gibson pondered whether or not to alert the clerk to pay special care with the list, but there would be nothing secretive of a listing of Bentley owners, so he concluded that highlighting any importance to the list would only result in undue interest.

The drive to the Monterey County Sheriff's Office from his hotel was brief. The office was housed within a large building complex comprised of various government offices. Gibson was greeted cordially in the office reception room and was told that if he would be seated, the sheriff's Chief Deputy would be able to see him momentarily.

Chief Deputy Harris greeted him shortly thereafter. The Chief Deputy fit the profile of a lifetime policeman: serious demeanor, sturdily built, short haircut, strong, graying mustache. "Agent Gibson, I'm pleased to make your acquaintance," the chief deputy said as he extended a hand to Gibson.

"Thank you for taking the time to meet with me this morning on such short notice," Gibson offered in response.

The chief deputy had Gibson follow him back past the reception area to his office. Once the men were seated, the chief deputy asked how he could be of service to the FBI.

Gibson had run into the age-old confrontation of local law enforcement versus federal law enforcement often throughout his career. In his opinion, the real problem was more over egos than jurisdictions. He therefore made it a standard practice to ensure that he met with local law enforcement officials when he began an investigation in order to ease tensions from the start as much as possible. But it was always a delicate game, as was usually the case when men have guns and authority

"Chief Deputy Harris, again, I thank you for taking time out of your busy schedule to meet with me," Gibson repeated.

The chief deputy eyed Gibson curiously. "Agent Gibson, there's no need for formalities with me. I respect that you've come to discuss something with our office, but let's get straight through the bullshit and get right down to it. I personally have no problem with your presence here; I'm mostly curious to hear what it is you are actually doing. Most of the time, we only get FBI agents down here on the Peninsula for some sort of white-collar crime."

Gibson liked the chief deputy's approach instantly. It was nice to meet a no-nonsense type of person every once in a while. "I can assure you that if my lead plays out, it will be far more interesting than a corporate corruption case," Gibson replied. "I'm looking into the San Francisco Federal Reserve heist and I have reason to believe that there could be a connection here on the Monterey Peninsula."

Chief Deputy Harris didn't grin, but his face did reveal that he was becoming more interested in the conversation. "Are you able to share any further details? Monterey County is a rather large and diverse place, as I'm sure you know."

"I believe one or more of your more prominent citizens may be connected to the robbery. I also believe that they made an escape from San Francisco via a sea vessel and used it as transportation to get here." Gibson hoped the chief deputy would not ask for an explanation to the next assumption he was about to reveal. "And I believe there is a connection to the park of Point Lobos."

"*Point Lobos*?" The chief deputy inquired.

Damn. "Yeah, it's kind of a complicated and drawn-out explanation," Gibson added, hoping it would sufficiently deter any further questioning, "but I have reason to believe that it could have been used as some type of staging location for the heist."

Now the chief deputy smiled, but it was not a joyous smile. "You think there's buried treasure out there or something?" the chief deputy asked loudly, followed by a chuckle.

Gibson remained stern. "There may be," he straightly replied.

The chief deputy calmed himself. "All right, whatever you say, Agent Gibson. So you are hoping to stake out the entire Point Lobos State Reserve on a hunch to see if the bank robbers return for treasure that may be there?"

"No, I wouldn't go that far. I only want to convey to local law enforcement that for the foreseeable future, I would like to be notified of anything strange or out of the ordinary that may occur. In the meantime, I'm also going to be checking out a few of your local citizens."

Chief Deputy Harris lightly chomped his teeth together. "Well, here's the deal, Agent Gibson. Unfortunately for you, you could run into a turf battle down here. You see, Point Lobos is under the law enforcement jurisdiction of State Parks, so you're going to need to go over there and inform the rangers of your theory. After that, you'd better pay a courtesy visit to the Carmel Police Department, as being the closest municipality, they would be interested in being kept informed. Then I would stop in and see the Monterey Police Department. Although they don't have any jurisdiction over there, since the reserve is surrounded by unincorporated county land, they do have the largest available force, funding, and resources to assist with an agency investigation here on the Peninsula. You were right in coming to us first, as that would normally make perfect sense, but Monterey County is an interesting law enforcement dilemma.

"Most of the county's resources are needed over in Salinas and the Salinas Valley as we try to keep the Mexican gang wars in check. We mostly leave the Peninsula to the Monterey City Department. On the surface, one would think that they have their hands full, as everyone knows there's a prominent Sicilian mafia presence in Monterey, but those that are here seem to be content with pushing their influence through *mostly* legitimate business ventures. They also have boats, which sounds like if your theory plays out could become useful."

Gibson nodded in appreciation. "Thank you for your candor and your insight. I was thinking I would have to contact the Coast Guard for possible boat resources."

The deputy chief shrugged his shoulders heavily. "You should get in touch with them as well to let them know what you're thinking, but don't rely on them for much. They are stretched pretty thin, as they cover a long section of the coastline here."

"Good to know."

"I would like to ask you, though, what makes you think that even if there is some connection down here, and it has something to do with Point Lobos, that those involved would make any move right now anyway? I mean, from what I've heard and read about the case, it seems like this group was calculated. Of course, I know our line of work and I know that even if the FBI had some identified leads earlier, they would have never let them be leaked, and thus it's better for the public to assume you guys don't have a clue on the case ... but I'm just wondering what makes you believe there's going to be a move down here unless you-all have done something to stir things up?" After a silence settled between them, the deputy chief added, "If you're able to tell me anything ..."

Gibson shook his head. "I can assure you that I'm not being vague purposefully. I don't believe anything has been 'stirred up' yet, but I do believe that there is a lot of money at stake and that there was more than one individual involved in this heist. I figure there had to be at least three people involved, if not four or five, and possibly even more. That being the case, in my many years on the job, I've seen human nature come to my assistance in more instances than not."

"Meaning?"

"Meaning that while they may have displayed patience before, with a bundle of them and that much money involved, one of them is going to slip somehow, and if we are positioned correctly, we can catch it," Gibson concluded.

"Well, good luck, Agent Gibson."

Gibson thanked him and spent the remainder of the day doing exactly as Deputy Chief Harris had instructed him. He paid a visit to the local California State Parks office, followed by a visit to Point Lobos to meet with the head ranger of the reserve, then to the Carmel Police Department, then a call into the Monterey Bay Coast Guard station, and lastly a trip to the City of Monterey Police Department. The deputy chief correctly predicted that he would find the Monterey force the most helpful. When Gibson asked about the potential jurisdictional dilemma posed by the situation, the Monterey Chief assured him that there would be no conflict, as he would put a call into the State Parks office and they would agree to a typical situation between the two parties, whereby the Monterey force would temporarily provide service to State Parks. Gibson pursued the matter no farther. If that was how things were done on the Peninsula, it was fine with him.

By the time he returned to his hotel, it was after seven and he was exhausted. Gibson considered calling Isidro to see if he would like to join him for dinner, but instead opted for a quick meal alone at the small restaurant in his hotel. After dinner, he returned to his room, took a shower, and called Rachel. He was soundly asleep by nine o'clock.

42.

Year of our Lord 2009.

I T WAS TIME TO MOVE; this Samuel P. Beckwith knew for certain.
The time had arrived to transfer the gold down to Zande's place in Big
Sur. With every passing day, Samuel felt his unease growing.
Something was wrong. Try as he might, he could not shake the feeling that
something was amiss, whether one of his crew was going to betray him or
something else. Even the activities that normally were able to completely
clear his mind, such as having his smoking-hot petite wife go down on
him or reading passages of *Treasure Island* while seated on his balcony
with a fine glass of single-malt scotch, were not able to ease his tension.

Samuel stewed over the possibilities after the group had met in
Cachagua. He reached the conclusion that the problem was his Number
Four. The problem was Dick Lombardo, and the solution to the problem
became increasingly clear: Number Four needed to be removed from the
equation.

Samuel arranged to meet with Zande Allen without the others. He
now firmly believed that Zande, Number Three, was his most trusted
of the group, as Victor Mathews, Number Two, constantly defended
Dick. Action needed to be taken, and Zande would be the man for the
job. Samuel had no intention of cutting out Victor, but he had every
intention of keeping his *revised* plan a secret between only himself and
Zande; Victor would no longer be able to make excuses for the
pathetic Dick after Dick was gone.

To no surprise, Zande wholeheartedly embraced Samuel's new plan.
In fact, Zande even volunteered to end Dick himself. The two men

agreed to return to retrieve the gold on their own. Samuel had arranged for their original escape fishing vessel to be returned to San Francisco Bay and had secured a new boat for their retrieval of the gold. *Everything was covered.*

Samuel and Zande would move the gold themselves, then he would declare to the group that it was time to retrieve the gold. They would wait for a night of thick fog, and when the four returned to Point Lobos, it would be arranged for Zande and Dick to plunge into the water first. Zande would then ensure that only he reemerged.

Victor would then be informed of the altered plan and he would have no choice but to accept it. Dick's body would in all likelihood be discovered the next day, washed up on the shores of Point Lobos. He would be regarded as yet another diver who fell victim to under-estimating conditions and his own physical shape and had foolishly gone diving alone. Samuel had even tracked down Dick's date Charlotte through a local escort service and she was easy to buy off … women like her would do anything for money, even lie later if asked and inform the police that she had been with Dick the night of his disappearance but that he had been adamant that they go on a night dive together. When she refused, afraid to go diving her first time at night, Dick became enraged and said he would go by himself.

With Dick out of the picture, they would then divide the loot amongst the three of them and move it off-shore as they had planned all along. The more Samuel contemplated the new plan, the better he felt about it. *It was all going to work out perfectly.*

The day after Agent John Gibson made his rounds to the various law enforcement entities covering the Monterey Peninsula, his vibrating cell phone woke him from a deep sleep in the middle of the night. Gibson had filled his day conducting background research on the small list faxed to his attention at the hotel of individuals who were Bentley owners on or in direct proximity to the Peninsula. He met Isidro for a casual lunch at a local seafood restaurant, which he found surprisingly very good despite looking from the outside like a colorblind old woman's house.

Gibson shared the list of names of Bentley owners with Isidro, who recognized most of the family surnames on it, but admitted that seeing the names alone of some of the Peninsula's most prominent citizens did not rouse his suspicion in any regard. After lunch, Gibson spent most of the remainder of his day on the phone with a research officer in the SF branch office as the officer thoroughly investigated each name on Gibson's list.

When his phone rang that night, Gibson glanced over the side of the bed to see on the alarm clock that it was just past eleven. Gibson then leaned to turn on the light switch behind the bed and picked up his phone. The phone's display screen indicated that a line from the City of Monterey Police Department was calling him. When he answered, a young man enthusiastically instructed him that the Chief of Police requested his presence at the police station as soon as possible to assist in the interview of a group of apprehended suspects.

Gibson tried to pry more information from the young officer, but he only received the reply that the chief assured that he would be very interested in the suspects being held. Gibson replied that he would be there immediately.

Chief Markowski greeted Gibson at the Monterey Police Station with a firm handshake and a proud grin.

"Sorry to bring you down here in the middle of the night, Agent Gibson, but after our chat yesterday, I have a feeling you're going to believe it was well worth the trip."

"No problem," Gibson replied groggily. "I appreciate your help."

"How about some coffee?" the chief asked him.

Gibson nodded in agreement and the chief politely asked the middle-aged woman seated behind a counter to bring Agent Gibson a cup of coffee.

"You're going to want to be wide awake when you see these guys, and unless we come up with something, I'm not going to be able to hold them much longer. Oh, thank you, Marsha," he said as the woman handed Gibson a steaming mug of coffee.

The combination of the chief's words and the scent of strong coffee overtaking his senses instantly revived Gibson.

The chief asked Gibson to follow him into the station to his office. When there, the chief closed the door behind them. "After you tipped us off about a possible Point Lobos connection the other day, we've been paying special attention to it. We've had the county, State Parks, even the City of Carmel forwarding any calls of concern about it directly to us. We also put one of our small patrol boats in the water over there in Whaler's Cove, hidden behind a rock outcropping so that vessels out at sea wouldn't be able to see it, all with permission from State Parks and the Coast Guard, of course." The chief slowly eased himself into the chair next to Gibson instead of opting to sit at the chair behind his own desk. "Now, here's what happened. Earlier this evening, we were forwarded a call from the County Sheriff's office that a resident in Carmel Highlands noticed a boat off-shore of Point Lobos."

Gibson considered the chief's statement, but then confused, inquired, "Is it illegal to be in a boat at night off of Point Lobos?" He took a long drink from his mug of coffee, enjoying its warmth. He had walked to the police station from his hotel, which took only a few minutes, but the streets of Monterey were encased in a blowing fog. Despite being a short distance, his body was thoroughly chilled by the time he arrived at the station.

"No, not necessarily. But you have people there who take note of everything happening around them and if they don't like what they see, they are going to make noise about it. So some old bird out there saw boat lights off of Point Lobos and promptly reported it."

"But why would she?"

"Because she was bored or lonely or nosy — *who knows*? And, for our purposes, it doesn't matter. It could be the break we were looking for, and any citizen has a right to call the police if they think something is amiss. In this case, the old bird may have thought it was illegal abalone diving, as it has been known to occur over there."

"So your men moved in and arrested them?" Gibson inquired.

"Yes, sir — they sure did! We had a patrol car nearby and the two officers entered the reserve and got over to where our boat was docked without being seen from these guys offshore. The officers then boarded the other vessel at sea and apprehended the suspects. But there has been no arrest made."

"So they were caught moving the gold?" Gibson quickly asked. His expression visibly lost some of its building enthusiasm as he noticed the chief struggling to respond.

"Well, no ... no. In fact, we don't have any reason to actually believe that this group of guys has anything to do with your case and we'd frankly have a hard time even charging them with illegal diving." The chief rose from his chair and walked behind his desk. "We just figured it too particular of a coincidence that you mentioned to keep a special eye on Point Lobos and then discover a foursome of very well-off men supposedly night diving."

Gibson's interest again expanded. "*Well-off*, you say?"

"Oh yes, two of the four fall into the obscenely wealthy category. The other two are probably just your typical Monterey Peninsula area millionaires." The chief chuckled at his own joke.

"So what did you bring them in for?"

Chief Markowski straightened himself. "On the charge of illegally diving in protected waters without a permit. We could have even picked them up during the day for diving off Point Lobos without a permit. We even added suspicion of illegally harvesting protected biological resources on top of that. Between the two suspected charges, it was enough to get them down here for questioning, but it's not going to last for long. As I said, these guys have some serious cash and they are going to definitely have good lawyers. What we've done so far is not stretching things too much; however, as I said, we are not going to be able to hold them much longer."

"Has anyone talked to them yet?" Gibson eagerly asked.

"Nope. We wanted to wait for you to get down here first and advise us on what you would like to do."

Gibson considered the situation carefully. "So you don't believe that these guys could have truthfully been out there just diving for the hell of it?"

"Hell, *rich people*. Who knows?" Chief Markowski replied. "Anyway, my thought is to divide the four of them up, put them into different rooms, and then have each tell their story and we'll see if we get four similar depictions or not."

"*You don't already have them separated*?" Gibson immediately asked.

"Illegal diving doesn't exactly qualify as the most heinous crime in the world. We would have no cause to start treating them like criminals and, as I said, a couple of these guys could probably buy the City of Monterey, so we've got to play our cards carefully on this one. With your presence here now, we could justify questioning them and getting their statements on grounds of suspicion of connection with a federal crime such as the one you are pursuing, but we have to this thing delicately."

"Okay, let's do this, then," Gibson responded.

Chief Markowski ordered the four men to be divided into separate interrogation rooms, two having to be offices, as the station only had two interrogation rooms. "So who do you want to talk to first?"

Gibson reviewed the names of the four men being held. Seeing one name brought a wide smile to his face. He had seen the name earlier in the day and had even discussed the individual with his research officer. It was one of his Bentley owners. *Samuel P. Beckwith.*

Agent Gibson recognized the expression he saw on the face of the man seated in the chair before him. Samuel P. Beckwith had the look of defiance blended with arrogance. Before even muttering a word, Samuel was conveying that he was going to be as uncooperative as possible; he also appeared calm and collected.

"Interrogated for *alleged* illegal diving? Isn't this a little far for such a potential crime?" Samuel confidently inquired.

"This is no interrogation, Mr. Beckwith," Chief Markowski replied. "We simply want to get your statement and then we'll let you on your way."

Samuel eyed Agent Gibson suspiciously. "Aren't introductions in order?"

"Certainly, Mr. Beckwith ... my apologies. This is Agent John Gibson from the Federal Bureau of Investigation."

"You've brought in the FBI for suspected illegal diving?" Samuel commented sarcastically. "Is illegally harvested abalone now funding terrorist activities?"

Gibson realized that he would have to strike directly back at Beckwith. "Actually, it could be perceived of as a federal crime, as you were illegally diving in federally protected waters," he asserted.

Samuel stared silently ahead and pondered his situation. He didn't know what the FBI agent might suspect, but his presence alone was alarming. He inhaled deeply, focusing his attention on remaining calm. "Should I have my attorney present for this conversation?" Samuel smugly inquired.

Chief Markowski promptly intervened. "Oh no, no, Mr. Beckwith. That won't be necessary. We just want to ask you a few questions, *that's all*," the chief said with a slight hint of nervousness apparent in his tone.

Samuel relaxed his shoulders. "Well, then, gentlemen, by all means, let's have a little discussion. But I'll have you know that I have a little lady waiting for me at home who is probably worried sick and is most likely calling my attorney at this very moment, and I can assure you that once he arrives here our little conversation will be terminated."

In that instant, Gibson's suspicion of Samuel's involvement with the San Francisco heist multiplied exponentially. Samuel P. Beckwith was no different than countless other guilty criminals he had pursued throughout his career. "From what I've gathered, it has not been so long since you were brought here for questioning. If you were supposedly on a night dive with your buddies, then I wouldn't imagine that she would be expecting you home any time soon."

Gibson watched patiently for the impact of his words on Beckwith. To his disappointment, Samuel Beckwith only provided increased evidence of his skillful temperament. "As I have not been read my rights by anyone and am merely partaking in this conversation as a courtesy to the City of Monterey Police Department," Samuel paused to raise a hand to gesture towards Chief Markowski, "I believe you may want to consider adjusting your language, Agent Gibson, as Chief Markowski will assuredly confirm that no member of our group was actually caught diving. We were all on deck having a conversation when the police cruiser boat boarded our vessel. And, by the way, Agent Gibson: Have you ever been night diving yourself? If not, I'd highly recommend it." Samuel grinned at the FBI agent before him.

He also considered the evening's activities as he spoke. He admitted to himself that in his hastiness, he had picked a night that offered uneven fog cover, unlike the previous evening, when he and Zande had transferred the gold from its resting spot in full cover of a blanket of fog that even obscured the lights from the boat mere feet away. This evening, though, had been comprised of fog waves cascading in from the ocean to the coast, allowing for breaks in the cover that could not completely obscure their activities.

And it was entirely true that the police had not caught any of them in the water. They had, in fact, only shortly beforehand anchored the boat and were just beginning to get suited up for their dive when the police boat cast its bright spotlight on them. Something concerned Samuel, however. At the moment that the police boat pulled alongside theirs, Samuel realized that Dick Lombardo had gone below deck for some reason, probably to grab one last Twinkie before the dive. Samuel had not bothered to pay much attention to Dick's movements, as he savored knowing that shortly, Zande would drop alongside Dick over the side of the boat and drown him, but he had also not planned on the police arriving. His plan had in all other regards played out just as smoothly and unencumbered as he had envisioned it would, and therefore, there was no reason to suspect anything might turn asunder.

But Samuel realized this was where he had failed himself. By allowing his confidence to inflate itself so severely, he had let himself get sloppy, and that was inexcusable. If Dick had gone below deck and only glanced in the right direction, he would have seen that the diving apparatus vehicle that moved the crates underwater was not there, and any idiot would be able to quickly deduce that something was not right. And if Dick suspected something was amiss, he might still be their downfall if the police and this damned FBI agent got to him.

Samuel took advantage of the police's foolish action of allowing the four of them to be held in the same room at first and talked through a strategy for them to use when individually questioned: They were to say that they had stopped off of Point Lobos only temporarily and they were going to head further south to unprotected waters for their night dive. And, of course, they were sorry for the inconvenience they had caused. If each of them repeated the same line, there would be no chance they would be suspected of anything, but if Dick ruined it, they could be in some degree of trouble.

Gibson outwardly cringed as he turned away from Beckwith toward the chief in order to conceal his emotion. Gibson stared intensely at the chief, saying without words, *You didn't even catch them in the water?*

"Yes, yes, he's quite right, Agent Gibson," Chief Markowski replied. "They were not in the water when my men boarded their vessel."

Gibson had been in enough similar encounters with men such as Samuel Beckwith to realize when there was a time to, at least temporarily, toss in the towel. They were going to get nowhere with Beckwith, but the other three were a different story. And the chief's officers would have by then searched the seized boat and would be able to search the waters near where the group was discovered to see if they could discover anything the group might have gone to retrieve. There was no point in wasting precious time with Beckwith. Gibson pivoted and thanked Beckwith for his time, indicating that he wanted to see the others.

As Samuel watched the two men leave the room, he felt a tremor move through him at the thought of their pending conversation with Dick Lombardo.

Agent Gibson, with Chief Markowski standing by, questioned the other three men. Afterward, the four were released, with the chief thanking each for their cooperation. The chief asked, reluctantly, if Gibson wanted to see the four charged with suspicion of intent to dive illegally, but Gibson perceived no reason for it. If they were involved even marginally with his case, then charging them with anything would only guarantee that they would move quickly to cover themselves. By releasing them, though, they potentially would feel less insecure, possibly guiding them to proceed without caution.

Of course, there was still the chance that the four would be scared out of their minds and would retreat into security mode on their release, but it was a risk worth taking. There was something about the group that Gibson sensed would lead at least one of them to do something stupid; perhaps it was their arrogance.

Each of the men had clean criminal backgrounds except Zande Allen, who was suspected of involvement with a probable militant organization in Big Sur, but it had not been positively linked to any criminal activity. Gibson's general perception of Zande Allen was that he was the most volatile of the four. The man's eyes revealed sheer contempt for Gibson and the chief when they questioned him. Allen was a tough guy, that much was clear, and Gibson pictured him as the most reckless of the group. Allen was nowhere in the same affluence category as Samuel P. Beckwith , but he was still considerably wealthy, having inherited a bundle of sizeable properties in Big Sur through his family name, as Gibson later learned.

The next interview was with Victor Mathews, a retired multi-millionaire from Silicon Valley, who was in the same income bracket as Beckwith. Gibson also discerned that Mathews was the most intelligent of the group. If these were his guys, Mathews' presence would explain how they had pulled off such an elaborate and well-orchestrated robbery of a highly guarded building.

The last to be questioned was Dick Lombardo, and Gibson found Lombardo to be the odd man of the group. He was clearly not a member of the wealthy elite of the other men. The chief later mentioned to Gibson that Lombardo was who he referred to as just another typical Monterey millionaire; Dick Lombardo also didn't seem to fit with the rest of the group. Even physically speaking, Lombardo was not a match for his team, if they indeed were his team members. Lombardo was balding, portly, and had a square, dark mustache in contrast to the other three cleanshaven and in-shape men. Lombardo did not convey the same level of confidence as the others, but his answers to the questions asked were nearly identical to those received from the other three, no doubt from the coaching that had occurred when the four had been left alone together.

But unlike the others, Lombardo exuded a slight shakiness in his tone and his eyes darted nervously back and forth between Agent Gibson and Chief Markowski as they spoke with him. Gibson questioned if there was more to what had happened on the boat that Lombardo was not revealing. *Perhaps he had done something wrong from the beginning ...*

It had passed midnight by the time the four were released, and Gibson told himself that he would pay a visit to Dick Lombardo at his place of work later that morning. With any luck, maybe he would be able to catch Lombardo when he had not been prepared for an interview.

"Should we keep an eye on them?" Chief Markowski asked after the four men departed the police station.

"No, we don't want to further alarm them at this point," Gibson replied. He reflected adding, *I don't want any more mistakes made if these really are our guys*, but decided against it. The chief and his force had surely been helpful. "I'm going to look into a few things and I'll let you know if we need to go to that stage." Gibson also resisted the urge to comment that the chief's overeager personnel might easily trigger suspicion with the group, but again declined airing his opinion.

"Well, what we can do then is get to Point Lobos and start scouring the coastline with underwater metal detectors. If there really is anything out there, we can safely assume it's encased in some sort of metal, correct?" Gibson nodded his head in agreement. "So we'll be able to pick it up," Chief Markowski suggested proudly.

"You have that sort of equipment available?" Gibson inquired, impressed by the apparent resourcefulness of the Monterey Police Department. He had been considering calling Agent Shapiro to request that the same search be conducted, figuring that only federal means would be able to administer such an operation.

"Oh, we have some of our own stuff. You know, we get all sorts of things washing up on our shoreline. And what we don't have, we can quickly contract out to get. There are a handful of guys around here that would love to comb the Point Lobos coastline."

Gibson felt his mood instantly brighten. "Fantastic. How quickly can you get out there?" he asked, knowing that the eagerness of the chief to be involved would undoubtedly result in a very prompt response.

"Hell, we'll be out there later this morning!" the chief cheerily exclaimed.

"Wonderful. Please call me if you turn up anything interesting," Gibson responded.

"Will do. Now go get yourself some sleep."

43.

Year of our Lord 2009.

DICK LOMBARDO WAS NOT difficult for Agent John Gibson to track down. Lombardo worked at an insurance company with offices in a business park off Highway 68. Isidro informed Gibson over a hearty breakfast of scrambled eggs, hash browns, bacon, and toast at an old diner in downtown Monterey that the stretch of road was also referred to as the Monterey-Salinas Highway. Isidro added that there had also been a railway in the past through the relatively narrow corridor connecting the two distinctly different endpoints of the Monterey Peninsula and the Salinas Valley. As he drove toward the insurance company's office, Gibson was not surprised when he noted a few signs off the side of the road demarcating the roadway as a "Scenic Highway," as he found it scenic indeed.

Gibson made his entry just as he had planned, arriving at ten o'clock; it was midmorning at a time when Dick Lombardo would likely be feeling a sense of comfort that nothing unpleasant was awaiting him in the ensuing day. *How wrong he would be for thinking so,* Gibson thought as he stepped through the doors into the building.

A young Hispanic woman seated behind an elegant wooden reception counter framed with two grand arching palm plants cast him a disinterested glance as he entered.

"May I help you?" the young woman asked as her eyebrows rose in matching downturned dual arcs.

Gibson forced a grin. "Yes, thank you. Beautiful morning, isn't it? I'm here to see Dick Lombardo," he said in his calmest tone.

The young woman, who Gibson pictured as quite pretty, minus the raised eyebrows and unattractive scowl on her face, eyed him up and down slowly before responding. "Do you have an appointment?" she demanded.

"No, actually, I do not. But if you were to be so kind and give him a call and let him know I'm here to see him, I have little doubt that he will make time to speak with me."

She looked him up and down slowly once again. "Mr. Lombardo is a very busy man. He never accepts meetings unless they are scheduled beforehand, which, in your case, is not the case." The receptionist smiled widely at him as she finished her sentence.

Damn if I didn't try, Gibson muttered in a hushed breath. "In that case, I'm afraid that I must insist on seeing him," he pointedly said.

The receptionist laughed to herself and looked downward before raising her dark brown eyes in his direction once again. "I don't think you understand, sir … *It's not going to happen.*"

Gibson laughed to himself in turn. Then he also looked downward and returned his gaze to the young lady who was about to push a seasoned agent of the Federal Bureau of Investigation too far. With a flick of his wrist, he whipped his FBI badge from his jacket pocket and had it opened in front of the young woman's face. Her eyes instantly fell on the badge before slowly rising to meet the gaze of a now grinning Agent John Gibson.

"Now I get to inform you that I don't think you understand. I need to speak with Mr. Lombardo, now," Gibson firmly stated.

The receptionist clumsily grabbed for the phone on the counter in front of her, fumbling with it for a few seconds. She spoke with another person, was put on hold, and then gently placed the phone down. As she looked up at him, Agent Gibson knew the young woman was about to lie to him. "I'm sorry. His secretary looked for him, but apparently he's not in the office at the moment," she relayed in an unsteady voice.

Agent Gibson grinned at her and remained silent. Then he said, "Nice try, but I saw his car in the parking lot," he lied with a perfectly straight face. The receptionist's face instantly flushed. "How about we forego the in-between of you calling his secretary and you yourself walk me to his office," Gibson urged in more of a statement than a question.

The young receptionist obeyed, leading Gibson through a doorway requiring a remote sensor key to open. When they reached Dick Lombardo's office, his secretary, seated at a desk outside of his glass office, rose from her desk and attempted to dissuade him by stating that Mr. Lombardo was on a very important conference call and could not be disturbed. Gibson looked around her, seeing into the glass-fronted office that Lombardo was trying to make it appear as if he did not notice the scene occurring outside his office. Gibson stepped around the receptionist and let himself in through the glass door.

Dick Lombardo's face erupted in mocked surprise. "Agent Gibson. Is there something you forgot to ask me last night?'

"I'm sorry to disturb you, Mr. Lombardo, but I do in fact have something else I would like to discuss with you and I can assure you that you will want to hear me out," Gibson proclaimed as he closed the door behind him and sat himself in one of the overstuffed leather chairs in front of Dick's enormous desk.

Dick Lombardo seated himself as well. Gibson noted that some of the tension Lombardo had initially exhibited appeared to be easing, but he still appeared extremely nervous. "I've got some time between meetings, so I guess we can talk now," Dick remarked in as confident of a tone as he could manage.

Gibson leaned forward in his chair in order to emphasize his statement. "As I said before, I promise that you will want to hear me out; it's really in your best interest, Mr. Lombardo." Gibson paused to let his words hang in the air for a few moments before proceeding. "I believe you and your friends are involved in something much bigger than a little illegal diving." Gibson deliberately hesitated again, carefully watching the impact of his words on Dick Lombardo. Dick wiped his brow and readjusted himself in his chair. *Bingo.* "Listen, Dick, this is how these things work: You can either go down with the entire group or you start talking and make your future much more pleasant than theirs."

Dick Lombardo adjusted himself in his chair again. "I … I don't know what you're talking about," he finally managed to utter. Dick then saw images of the night before flashing in front of him, most notably the absence of the dive machinery from the boat's cargo hold below deck. *What were they going to do out there without the equipment anyway?* Dick asked himself. Even later at the police station when he had tried to ask Samuel about it, he had only received an order to *shut up* from Samuel and Zande in unison. He also recalled how Zande had been eyeing him the entirety of the previous evening with even more annoyance than normal; this time it had almost seemed like hatred. *Is it possible that they intended to kill me?* Dick knew that Zande despised him and that Samuel had no real love for him either, but Victor would never let anything happen to him, unless Victor had been kept unaware of whatever Samuel and Zande were up to …

"Don't be dumb, Dick. What I'm offering is only going to be offered once. What you all pulled off was impressive, I'll be the first to admit, but the law has caught up with you and we are going to take you all down," Agent Gibson threatened. "You're still going to be in trouble; no one rips off the federal government and pays nothing for it, but you'll be much better off than your former partners. And there's something more you should know …"

Given the growing eagerness in Lombardo's outward expression, Gibson continued. "The City of Monterey Police Department has been probing Point Lobos with the most advanced equipment available, and they haven't uncovered anything yet." Gibson partially told the truth.

It was true that just before he drove to Dick Lombardo's office building, he had spoken with Chief Markowski, who informed Gibson of the ongoing yet unsuccessful scouring of the coastline. That part of what Gibson revealed to Dick was entirely factual. Gibson's fabricated elaboration of the technical capabilities of the equipment being used for the search was his own creative addition, as he had no clue as to the effectiveness or level of capability of the equipment.

"So if there's nothing out there, as is looking to be the case, I think your friends had already moved it before they took you along for a *boat ride*. And if that is indeed the case, that can only indicate that they had every intention of leaving you out there and making a four-way split even more attractive as a three-way split ..." Gibson allowed his voice to slowly trail off.

Agent Gibson's revelation fell heavily on Dick Lombardo. It occurred to Dick that he could finally get an upper hand on Zande Allen and even outmaneuver Samuel Beckwith. It was a shame that he would also be betraying a friend, as he truly believed that Victor would never have agreed to take part in any activity that would have brought him harm. Then again, it was only because of his relationship with Victor that he had become involved in the affair to begin with; once this point crossed his mind, Dick was able to block thoughts of loyalty to his friend.

From what Agent Gibson was saying to him, it did seem very likely that the others had planned to kill him. *The bastards!*

Dick would show them that they had once again underestimated him. He took a deep breath and looked at Agent Gibson. "Okay," he capitulated, nodding his head in agreement.

"Agent Shapiro, I've got great news to share," Agent Gibson reported over his cell phone. He had just stepped away from the building, informing Dick to remain there until contacted and to absolutely not call or take any calls from Samuel Beckwith, Victor Mathews, or Zande Allen. Gibson lied in order to emphasize his point by warning Dick that his phone was wired, and if he disobeyed his instructions, the FBI would know about it instantly and the rosiness of his pending plea bargain package would diminish immediately.

"Hello, Gibson. Wonderful to hear. Did your Bentley search turn up something?"

Gibson had not informed Shapiro of his Bentley hunch, and thus Shapiro revealed that he had kept more of an eye on his movements than Gibson had believed. "It did, actually, but it was more of a clue confirming a grander lead. I've got a confession down here and the whereabouts of the gold and likely have the other perpetrators marked."

Gibson heard Shapiro lightly chuckle on the other end of the phone line. "You really are something, Gibson. I honestly didn't know what to expect of you when they put you on my squad, but you certainly don't disappoint. And I'm even further impressed that you've done all of this pretty much on your own."

"Thank you, sir. I've had some outstanding help as well. Getting to the matter at hand, my source tells me that they are going to try and move the gold soon from where it's most likely temporarily stashed at a location on the Big Sur coast. I also need someone to get over here and take this guy into custody before his friends get to him. If we're going to get this thing done right, I need to request your immediate assistance. I may work well on my own, but I know when I need help, and I need help now."

"And you'll have it. I know exactly which building you are standing outside of in Ryan Ranch and I've already had men dispatched to arrive there within minutes to meet you."

Shapiro must have had him monitored closely from the beginning after all, Gibson thought. "I beg your pardon, sir, but even if you just dispatched them, it's not exactly an around-the-block drive down here from San Francisco."

"Relax, Agent Gibson; they will be meeting you there in minutes. They only had a short drive from a temporary field office we established in Monterey after you first went down there. And you can feel free to drop the 'sir' when addressing me."

Agent John Gibson didn't know how to feel. He was either impressed with Shapiro's craftiness or annoyed by his secretiveness. Regardless, though, it was no time to let emotions cloud his judgment or actions.

"Sorry to keep you in the dark, Gibson, but I wanted to give you your space. And I can assure you that I only dispatched the unit down there in complete confidence of your abilities," Shapiro added. "Now, you said the coast — can you elaborate?"

"Yes. The suspect named Zande Allen has a cabin on his family's land that apparently is fairly hidden in the woods adjacent to a cove on the coast; the cabin is supposedly a secret that not too many know about," Gibson explained.

"*Outstanding*. That makes complete sense."

"How's that, Agent Shapiro?"

"Because we just traced Samuel Beckwith driving one of his vehicles south on Highway 1. We've kept an eye on Beckwith since your Bentley search matched with his temporary incarceration the other night at the Monterey Police Station. When your support arrives, head down there right away. Your group will have a lock on Beckwith's vehicle and will be able to lead you right to it. I'm going to contact the Coast Guard base down there and I'll have them come in with sea support and we can meet in the middle. I'll get down there myself."

"How will you get down here so quickly?"

"I'm a lot closer than you think," Shapiro answered crisply. "If you need anything from me in the meantime, call me back. The agents I'm sending to you have been informed directly from me that you are calling the shots on this one and they will do exactly as you order. Now, let's go get these sons-a-bitches!"

Two Suburbans equipped with tinted windows and each carrying a pair of sunglasses-and-suit-clad agents pulled into the parking lot where Agent Gibson was standing within seconds after his call with Agent Shapiro ended. The four male agents descended from the oversized SUVs and stood silently at attention, waiting for Gibson's directions.

Gibson surveyed their perimeter, and once he felt secure that no one else was in the vicinity began to speak. "I have one perp in this building behind me, Dick Lombardo. I need one of you to stay with him. He's going to be a key witness in this case and we need him safe. I don't care which of you does it, but someone has to." The four men exchanged nods before one stepped forward and proclaimed himself to be the chosen amongst them. Gibson figured that he was probably the newest to the Bureau. He gave the young man instructions to safely transport Lombardo from the building back to the temporary field office and for the agent to remain with him at all times until instructed otherwise. The young man complied with a nod and entered the building. Gibson imagined that the receptionist would not give him the same attitude he had received earlier.

"You other three are coming with me. I'm told you have a trace on Samuel Beckwith?"

"Yes, sir. We have his vehicle tagged and we are tracking him as we speak," one of the eager young agents promptly responded.

"Great. Let's go," Gibson said, climbing into the passenger seat of one of the vehicles.

It was a long drive to Big Sur for Samuel P. Beckwith, and idling tourists creating traffic hazards by either driving at a snail's pace in fear or pulling over for the perfect photo opportunity at any given moment without warning were not entirely to blame. It was the inner torment of the thoughts swirling inside his head that was primarily to blame. *Was that damned FBI agent on to them? Had Dick figured things out? Would he talk?* There were too many possibilities to consider and it was driving him mad.

Now all that he wanted to do was to get the gold out of the country and get himself lost along with it. There was no way he could trust contacting Victor; Samuel didn't intend to entirely cut Victor out of the deal but he figured that he and Zande would transport the gold off-shore and remain out of the country and see if their absence was noted. If not, they could always send for Victor and Dick. If it were to turn out that way, there might not even be reason to knock off Dick, Samuel considered, although he figured that Zande would still consider his charge to be active and, if that were the case, Samuel would not get in Zande's way.

Samuel and Zande agreed to move the final phase of the plan into effect on their own. Samuel made the calls and all was in place. The thick, dark fog line creating a wall on top of the water less than a mile off the coast could not have been more of a gift from nature if Samuel had ordered it himself.

Once he and Zande had the gold loaded in Zande's speedboat kept docked near the cabin, they would be able to reach the fog line quickly, where they were to rendezvous with three other vessels. As soon as he and Zande had decided to move the gold from its resting place, Samuel had put the plan in motion. The gold would be transported with Samuel and Zande to one boat, then the three vessels would branch out in different directions: one north, one south, and one west. If they were followed, the most obvious suspect boat would be the one heading westward into international waters. The second most obvious would be any boat headed south towards the easily accessible Mexican coastline. The least suspect would be the third boat, the one heading north for the Canadian coast.

Samuel had in fact elaborately planned a way to safely move the gold into untraceable deposits to various global destinations through contacts in Vancouver, British Columbia. Once the gold was moved, he planned to become a quiet citizen of any of a number of South American countries, where he believed he would be safe from suspicion and the reach of the U.S. Government. And, with his fortune restored, he would once again be able to live his royalty-like lifestyle. In fact, he dreamed of how he would be even more socially elevated in his new home. It was a shame, a true shame, that he would have to leave his beloved Pebble Beach, but it was necessary. From the inception of his plan, Samuel had regretfully considered that if there was any suspicion directed their way, any dreams of remaining would be abandoned. He felt pride in the thought that his ancestors would be pleased that even in the face of adversity, he had discovered his *treasure*.

Will I send for my wife? Samuel asked himself. She did, after all, have a way of pleasing him. But it would be far too dangerous, he concluded, and a beautiful woman could always be replaced. He had said nothing to her and left no indication that he would not be returning that day or any other day afterward. He assumed that eventually she would assume that he had run off with some other woman in an attempt to leave her with the mountain of debt that he had run them into since the market crash, which she would later learn about herself, but Samuel had never intended to be so cruel to his wife. He knew that she would be protected from his debt due to the intricate prenuptial agreement that his attorney had drafted back when Samuel was still a multimillionaire. It would not be long before she found an elderly bachelor to saddle up on and live out her days as a pampered Pebble Beach resident.

Samuel turned off the highway to park his vehicle per Zande's instruction. Samuel did not see any road leading into the thick woods at the turn-off point, but he then saw Zande waiting for him, obscured from the road by the tree line. Zande pointed for Samuel to continue driving forward and park in a relatively cleared spot that was not visible from the highway. As Samuel slowly inched the Range Rover forward, Zande moved from his hidden location to close and lock a gated entrance that Samuel had not even noticed before.

Zande informed Samuel to grab from his vehicle whatever he needed, as there was no road leading to the cabin and they would be walking through the woods from that point on.

Samuel followed Zande as they trekked steadily through the woods. *Let the final phase of the Stevenson Plan begin.*

There was little need for Agent Gibson to brief the young agents in the vehicle with him, as all three were nearly as knowledgeable of the situation as he. However, agents Chapman, Douglas, and Banks awaited his instruction. As they drove south on the winding road, Gibson reviewed the aerial photographs of Zande Allen's property that Agent Chapman handed him from the back seat; he began to formulate a plan of attack.

There was clearly a boat docked near the cabin, but Agent Shapiro had assured him that an escape via the water would be closed off. Gibson was curious how Shapiro would be able to move so quickly, but he decided that he should not doubt Shapiro's capability, as Shapiro had repeatedly demonstrated his resourcefulness. The thought then struck Gibson that he didn't even know where Agent Shapiro was when they had talked, meaning he could be anywhere. For all he knew, Shapiro could have notified the Coast Guard earlier in the day of potentially pending action.

Assuming that Allen and Beckwith would be at the cabin, which was a fair assumption, he could utilize two of the young agents and himself to create a perimeter around the cabin. As the three of them closed the perimeter by approaching the cabin, they would have all possible exits covered, with one agent remaining near the roadside with the vehicle on the chance that Allen or Beckwith happened to slip by them. Gibson shared his strategy with the younger agents.

The tracking device that had been secured to Beckwith's Range Rover led them to a gate that was nearly entirely concealed by vegetation. Agent Banks pulled the Suburban off to the side of the highway between the road and the trees. Banks quickly surveyed around the gate and fence line and determined that there was no sign of electronic monitoring. Through the trees, Gibson detected the form of two parked vehicles: a beat-up Jeep and a polished Range Rover.

Gibson instructed Douglas to call Agent Shapiro to provide an update on their location. "Agent Shapiro advises to move in on the cabin when you are ready, Agent Gibson," Douglas conveyed.

All right, time to move. Gibson ordered his crew to put on bulletproof vests and Agent Douglas to remain near the vehicle and provide logistical support with Agent Shapiro. Each man installed their earpieces and tested to see if their radio communications were working. Guns were checked and extra ammunition was taken. *It was time to go.*

The three young agents stood waiting for Agent Gibson, watching him eagerly. "If we can do this without shooting, that's the way we do it, okay?" Gibson imparted to his men. The others nodded in acknowledgment. "However, I want to express that you all use extreme caution. I wouldn't normally expect a man like Samuel Beckwith to put up much resistance, but by his actions, he's displayed that he is in a state of desperation. As we all know, desperate men are unpredictable, so don't downplay the fact that this guy does not have criminal violence in his background. On the other hand, this Zande Allen character is to be considered extremely dangerous."

The faces of the junior agents were tight and nervous. "I wouldn't be surprised if Allen has a bazooka back there." Gibson hoped to add a touch of light humor to relax them to a small extent. The three others lightly snickered.

"Now, I'm sorry I'm not familiar with your backgrounds, but I know that you're reps of the Federal Bureau of Investigation and this is what you're trained for; so let's go in there like professionals and get this thing done," Gibson declared. "Chapman, take the southern approach. Banks, take the northern approach. I'll come in directly from the east."

The three agents climbed over the gate and Chapman and Banks moved to Gibson's flanks. Once they had reached a distance of about thirty yards on either side of him, Gibson spoke into the small microphone attached at his shoulder, telling them they had gone far enough. Each agent waited for his next instruction. "Okay, let's move in and take 'em," Gibson ordered.

Spending a significant amount of time alone in a remote cabin in the woods without electricity had sharpened his senses over the years. Zande felt something or someone approaching the cabin long before his eyes confirmed his suspicion. Peering from behind a half-curtained window, Zande was able to discern the outline of a man slowly approaching through the forest undergrowth towards the cabin. *If there's one, there's sure to be more.*

Zande glanced backward at his M-16 rifle resting on top of a small table and then at Samuel, who was pacing nervously back and forth in front of the cabin's fireplace while talking loudly into a satellite phone. He resolved that the rifle was about to become the much more useful of the two.

Witnessing the now *two* men stealthily encroaching towards his cabin, Zande quickly lost interest in Samuel's damned *Stevenson Plan,* or whatever it was that he called it. It had all sounded good initially, but plans don't always turn out how they are supposed to, Zande mulled, and this one was quickly going to shit. Sure, it would be fantastic to escape with the gold, but then again, the more he thought of it in those fleeting seconds ... Zande Allen wasn't so sure he was prepared to leave his home.

If need be, he was sure he could hide out for the rest of his life in the wilderness of the Big Sur mountains; they would never be able to capture him. The wilderness out there was so remote it had swallowed up entire mining towns that were forgotten, just as he would be. And as for Samuel, well ... he could fend for himself. *The Pebble Beach snob wanted to play bank robber, so now let him keep playing and be a bank robber on the run.*

Zande quickly crossed the room to grab his rifle. He returned to his vantage point adjacent to the window and perched himself on one knee.

Samuel, still blabbing into the phone, watched Zande with curiosity. Zande motioned for Samuel to get down. Finally appreciating the situation, Samuel complied and abruptly ended his phone conversation. "What is it?" he asked Zande in a forced whisper.

"The bastards are moving in on us, *that's what it is*," Zande replied, thoroughly annoyed, without removing his eyes from the two men outside in the woods. The men had halted their approach and had taken positions behind large trees that obscured Zande's vision, but he knew they were there.

"Shit! How the hell did they find us?" Samuel exclaimed in panic.

Zande didn't bother responding. *What did it matter how they had been found at this point?* All that concerned him was dealing with the predicament at hand; namely, that there were men outside his cabin who wanted to take away his freedom. *Damn them if they think they are going to take it from me without a fight!*

"How many are there?" Samuel asked after not receiving a response to his previous question.

"Two that I've spotted so far, but if there are two, I have no doubt that there are more out there," Zande replied in a steady, even tone.

"Shit!" Samuel cried out.

Zande snapped his head towards Samuel, his eyes driving spears through him. "You will stay calm and keep your voice down or I will calm you myself," he threatened.

Samuel accepted the hint and tried to calm himself. He leaned his back against the cold stone outlining the cabin's fireplace.

"There's another rifle on the counter in the next room, my thirty-aught-six. You can make yourself useful by crawling your way in there and getting it and then posting yourself at the other window." Zande nodded his head across the small room at the other window.

"Are you crazy? You want to get into a shoot-out with the police or FBI or whoever it is out there?" Samuel asked.

"*Damn straight*," Zande replied without turning his head. "You got a better idea?"

The initial panic had subsided and Samuel felt his composure returning. This was certainly a wrinkle in his plan, but he knew that if he was able to keep his cool and be smart, an opportunity would present itself. "Well, perhaps they are only covering the front of the cabin so far. We can sneak out that back door through the kitchen and quickly get down to the boat and head out to sea. We can be gone before they ever even know we left. The boats are already waiting out there in position for us."

"I'm not running. Let them come try and take me. This is my land and my Big Sur. I'll die defending it if I have to," Zande boldly retaliated.

In that moment, Samuel saw Zande Allen in a different light. He decided that he no longer needed Zande, and if the fool redneck wanted to get himself killed … so be it. It would create a better diversion for his own escape, Samuel realized. "I'm leaving then, Zande," Samuel announced.

"Fine. Go. Nice knowing you."

Samuel crawled his way through the doorway, entering the cabin's kitchen, and slowly rose to his feet. He saw one last image of Zande Allen, crouching near the window with a look of steel on his face as he peered out into the woods.

Samuel considered saying something to Zande about eventually getting his share of the money to him, but he calculated such an effort would be pointless and he had no time to lose. Even if Zande did make it out of the cabin alive, he would disappear.

Samuel slowly opened the back door of the cabin. Once he had the door cracked open, Samuel assessed his surroundings and saw no noticeable sign of anyone. He could see the rock outcroppings on the coast and the dark blue ocean through the trees. It was a mere hundred yards or so to get past the trees and down to the cove where the speedboat was docked. The gold was already on the boat, and if "the law" had arrived only an hour later, Samuel and Zande would have been gone.

Now Zande was staying, *but Samuel was going*. Waves were pounding the coast and Samuel could smell the salt in the air. It smelled like hope. He stepped away from the door and began walking, forcing himself to keep from running and trying to make as little noise as possible.

∞

Agent Gibson instructed agents Chapman and Banks to cease their advance on the cabin by tilting his head slightly to speak softly into the microphone attached to his vest. He instructed them to take position and wait for his move. This was one of those pinnacle moments in law enforcement that officers rarely encountered. Gibson was certain the two men were in the cabin; he was not so certain whether they would resist arrest.

Gibson guessed that if it were only Beckwith they were advancing towards, he would surrender without a fight. Beckwith was nothing more than a rich white-collar crime guy who had decided to take a walk on the wild side. But the reasons were of no importance to Agent John Gibson; analyzing reasons was somebody else's job.

It was the other guy, Zande Allen, who was the wild card. From what Gibson had viewed in the guy's file and especially after meeting him in person, Gibson had no doubt that Allen would feel an overwhelming urge to fight. Gibson sensed he would rather go down shooting than spend a day locked away in a federal penitentiary.

The damp air in the forest chilled Gibson's face. He flicked off the safety on his gun and hoped his two young agents were up to the task. The log cabin looked little more than a single-room home, possibly having a smaller rear room that he was not able to see from the front. The dark wood of the cabin had patches of bright green moss on it in various places. A solid wooden door in the middle of the front of the cabin had two windows adorning each side. Each window was partially concealed with half-drawn curtains.

Gibson raised the small megaphone he was carrying and spoke evenly into it. "Samuel Beckwith and Zande Allen — This is the FBI. We have you surround—" Before Gibson could finish, a shot whizzed by. Gibson fell to his knees behind the trunk of the gnarled oak tree; the first shot was followed closely by a second that was much more accurate. It grazed the side of a tree within feet from him. Another shot shattered a tree limb above.

Gibson ordered Agents Chapman and Banks to open fire on the cabin, focusing on the leftward front window where he suspected the shots had originated. The young agents obeyed and the peace and calmness of Big Sur was disrupted by the brutal sound of gunfire.

Once the gunfire erupted, Samuel P. Beckwith abandoned his plan of slowly and calmly creeping towards the speedboat. *That crazy-ass Zande probably shot first.* Samuel ran as fast as he could.

Zande Allen was aware he had little chance of surviving. First off, he would be outnumbered and surrounded, without an escape route. But the reason he would not survive was not because he was outgunned, it was because he would never surrender.

Most people with law enforcement officers surrounding them and bullets hissing by as they crashed through the glass of the window next to them would panic, but not Zande. He sat calmly with his back against the log interior of the cabin and waited for a break in the shots so he could return fire.

Their fire did halt, but before Zande began firing, he heard the voice again speaking through some megaphone. "We'll stop our shooting if you come out of the cabin with your hands raised."

Zande was not the type to hysterically respond by yelling something along the lines of: *Come and get me, you bastards!* But this was precisely how he felt. *Better to give them nothing. As far as they know, Samuel is still in here and also has a gun pointed at them.*

He had enough ammunition, fresh water, and homemade deer jerky in the cabin to hold out for days, which he intended to do as long as possible before picking the moment to end it. Even though he had cheated on his taxes for decades, Zande laughed at the thought that he was seeing his tax dollars at work with the federal law enforcement officers pursuing him. He admitted that he would not be able to achieve his lifelong dream of freeing Big Sur by cutting it off from the rest of the world, but he smiled because his death, gunned down by the FBI on his own property after resisting arrest, would be an inspiration to others. It would only be a matter of time before another person like him would emerge and continue the fight to *Return the Sur to Big Sur.*

∞

The agents stopped firing and there was no response from the cabin. The situation called for action, and if he didn't mold it in his own manner, he was going to quickly lose control. Gibson had two young agents on his team and at least one armed, highly dangerous individual, who was perhaps ready to die before being taken. People like that had no qualms about taking a few others with them, and Agent Gibson was not going to watch any other young agents get gunned down as he had unfortunately witnessed in his days with the Bureau. *Screw the public and their perceptions of the FBI using excessive force.* The people that wrote those articles were not facing an armed maniac in a remote forested area shooting to kill them.

Gibson carefully peered around the trunk of the tree towards the cabin. If he could get around to the back of it, he could move in while the other two provided cover fire from the front; he only hoped he would be able to approach unnoticed. Gibson only noticed shots being fired from one window. This indicated that there was only one person firing at them, undoubtedly Zande Allen.

If Samuel Beckwith was in there as well, he wasn't firing a gun. And even if he had one in his hand, perhaps he didn't feel desperate enough to fire at federal agents. Perhaps Allen was even hit and down inside the cabin. It was a theory, and a potentially dangerous one, but it was strong enough for Gibson to move on it.

"Chapman, Banks: I need you two to provide cover fire for me for a few minutes so I can get around to the back. Space out your shots so you don't go through your ammunition too quickly," Gibson ordered.

Agents Chapman and Banks confirmed the order and began firing at the cabin in sporadic shots. Gibson didn't hesitate. From the sound of the first shot, he was on his feet and running through the trees in a wide arc, first outward directly into the woods behind Banks' position and then turning abruptly to approach the rear of the cabin from an angle. When he was within thirty paces of it, he stopped and leaned his back against a thick tree. Whitecaps pounded the shoreline not far through the trees in front of him.

He spun around quickly to view the back of the cabin. There were no windows aside from a small one in a rear door. *Perfect.* He took a deep breath and closed the gap within seconds. When he reached the cabin unscathed, he eased himself to a halt and leaned against the wooden exterior of the cabin adjacent to the back door. He felt his heart pounding in his chest. In the intensity of the moment, he had not even had time to consider that in his dash to the back door of the cabin, he could easily have received a direct shot, as the space was cleared of vegetation and he had been an open target.

He hoped his approach had gone unnoticed. With any luck, the back door would be unlocked. Gibson gently touched the handle and felt it turn slightly. It was unlocked. He weighed the consequences of his next choice of action: One, he bursts through the door with gun raised, ready to fire at will; Two, he opens the door carefully and calls into the interior of the cabin, insisting that whoever was in there drop their weapons before he opens fire; or three, he slowly opens the door and slips inside the cabin and tries to sneak up behind whoever was shooting from the front of it. It was a tough call.

Gibson was nearly positive that only one man remained inside the cabin, at least only one uninjured man, which would leave the rear of the house uncovered. In fact, with the rear doorway unlocked, the thought crossed his mind that the other, Beckwith, had escaped through the back door and fled into the woods, perhaps even down to the coast. But he couldn't worry about that possibility at the moment, if the theory was indeed correct. He didn't have the manpower to sufficiently cover all possibilities and had to do what he could in the situation with what he was offered. In this case, he had a suspect within his grasp, and it was better to act on what was certain.

Gibson spoke quietly into his shoulder microphone, informing the other two agents that he was going to enter the cabin through its back door. He also added for the two agents to be aware that there was a very good possibility that the second man had escaped through the rear of the cabin and could be on the loose within their midst. The two agents were complying effectively with his earlier orders to provide a steady cover fire to mask his movements, but he heard both confirm that they understood his update.

Gibson took a deep breath and noticed the beautiful canopy of trees overhead and the sounds of the ocean nearby. *This was not his day to die.*

Gibson instructed agents Chapman and Banks to cease their fire in thirty seconds. He turned the doorknob gingerly and pushed the door ajar. The door swung open slowly. Gibson quickly surveyed the interior of the house. Bullets from the agents' fire ricocheted throughout the cabin. He noticed an older hunting rifle with a box of bullets next to it on top of the kitchen's narrow counter. The doorway led into a kitchen, which blocked off his view into the interior of the cabin, where he figured the shooter, Allen, was positioned. Gibson would have preferred to be able to see into the other room and catch the shooter off-guard, but the blockage did offer cover for him to step into the cabin without, hopefully, being noticed. With as light of steps as he could manage, he quickly stepped in and positioned himself behind the wall between the kitchen and the rest of the cabin.

The gunshots came to a halt. Gibson heard the sounds of a person in the next room readjusting himself with the pause in firing. The wall behind Gibson appeared to be thick enough to stop a bullet fired in his direction, but he didn't take any chances and brought himself to a crouched position.

"Stop now and you won't be harmed!" Gibson yelled out. He held his gun in front of him, ready for anything.

Silence. It was the worst response that Agent Gibson could have hoped for. Even if Allen opened fire in his direction, the man's location would be narrowed down, just as it would if Allen were to respond vocally.

"Allen, don't do this!" Gibson advised.

That goddamn coward, Zande said to himself as he became fully aware that Samuel Beckwith had abandoned him. Once the shooting began, Zande had ceased to consider Samuel and assumed he was hiding like a baby in the kitchen, even if he had said that he was leaving. Now Zande guessed that Samuel had made a run for the boat. Not that his loss would have made much difference, but at least he would have been able to watch the back of the cabin.

Now he had an FBI agent inside the cabin at his rear and at least two more in the front. The two in the front would surely advance on his position as much as they could now that they had one of theirs in position behind him. *Everything was going to shit in a hurry.*

If I'm going, I'm taking one of you federal bastards with me.

"Okay! I'm putting down my gun!" he yelled towards the kitchen. Zande tossed the M-16 on the ground beside him with enough force to ensure that the sound of the gun hitting the wooden floor would be noticed. After he did, he silently pulled his 9mm from his shoulder holster and set it on the floor next to him.

Gibson heard the sound of metal clank against the floor. *What are the odds that this man still has a gun pointed directly at where he assumes my head is located?*

"I want you to get on your knees; lock your hands behind your head, and face the wall nearest you!" Gibson ordered.

"Yes, sir!" was the response from the voice he knew to be of Zande Allen.

"Allen, is Samuel Beckwith in there with you?" Gibson asked, remaining in his crouched position.

"No, that prissy son-of-a-bitch left me!" Allen called out from the other room.

"Where did he go?" Gibson called back.

"Hell if I know," Allen responded.

Gibson assumed Allen was lying, but he judged that the real threat of the two men was in the room next to him, and if Beckwith had escaped, he would be far less dangerous than Allen. He spoke into his microphone, instructing agents Chapman and Banks to approach the cabin, but to do so cautiously. He then informed Agent Douglas to be vigilant of the fact that Beckwith might be trying to return to his vehicle to escape. Gibson instructed Douglas to be armed and ready. He then told Douglas to contact Agent Shapiro to inform him of the situation.

Gibson silently peered around the corner of the kitchen, observing that Zande Allen was complying with instructions, as he was facing a far wall of the room on his knees with his hands locked behind his head. Without announcing his movements, Gibson rose and stepped into the room. Although Allen appeared to be subdued and calm, Gibson did not underestimate such a man. He kept his gun pointed directly at the back of Allen's head.

Zande Allen saw no other choice. With agents coming in from the front of the cabin and one directly behind him, he had no chance to fight them all off. He would not be able to make his escape across Highway 1 and into the coastal range mountains, where he would etch out his life however he could for the rest of his days. *This was the end.*

In one flawless motion, Zande dropped his hands to the handgun on the floor in front of his knees, rolled to his right, and turned his body in order to have a clear shot at the man standing behind him.

Agent Gibson's suspicion was confirmed and his instincts saved him once again. Before Allen was able to get off a shot, Gibson put three bullets into his upper body, instantly ending the Big Sur native's life.

While the scene at Zande's cabin unfolded, Samuel P. Beckwith ran as fast as he could to the speedboat docked behind a large bowl-like outcropping. The large rocks sheltered the cove from the incessantly pounding surf surrounding it, but Zande had earlier told Samuel that they would need to wait until the tide was lower to maneuver the boat out through a narrow entrance leading into the open ocean.

Lower tide or not, Samuel had no time to stall his flight. Zande could be a fool all he wanted by believing he would prevail in a shootout with whoever was closing in on the cabin. Samuel P. Beckwith focused his thoughts on how best to save himself.

Zande had tied the boat with three lines of thick rope connected to steel spikes pounded into the sides of a rock wall. A narrow pathway led down into the cove alongside the boat. Samuel moved as quickly as he could down the cliff side. In his rush, he slipped on the loose, slippery rocks and fell on his right knee while bracing a far worse fall with his left hand. The rocks cut deeply into his knee, tearing through his pants. The impact of the sudden pressure on his left wrist also sent a shot of pain up his arm. Samuel took a deep breath and tried to compose himself, telling himself to stay calm.

Samuel rose and steadily but carefully made his way downward toward the boat, ignoring the surging pain in his wrist and the open gash on his knee, now seeping a steady trickle of blood down the front of his pant leg. When he arrived alongside the boat, Samuel grimaced through the pain in his left wrist as he united it. The boat rose and then fell a few feet at a continuous pace due to the swirling waters of the cove, but Samuel managed to time his jump perfectly and he landed safely on its deck. He rose proudly and smiled at the sky above. As he did, a surge of water forcefully entered into the cove, knocking the boat into the side of the cliff. Samuel lost his balance and tumbled sideways into the passenger seat. Straightening himself once again, cursing aloud as he did, he noticed that his knee had smeared a line of dark blood on the white vinyl of the chair.

Samuel turned the key he had safely stowed in his pocket at the cabin, starting the boat's engine and gently easing the vessel forward in the direction of the cave-like entrance leading to the open ocean and his freedom. The boat continued to rise and fall as it moved through the turbulent waters. Samuel patiently eased the boat forward, aiming at the cave and attempting to ignore the barrage of whitecaps he could see in glimpses outside it. He judged that even though it would not be easy, there would still be at least a foot of space between where the boat would crest and the cave's ceiling as he passed through it. *It will work … It has to work!*

There was no point in trying to time his entrance through the cave, Samuel concluded, and he didn't hesitate to push the throttle forward and steer the boat inside. The cave only extended for roughly fifty feet. Just fifty more feet separated him from a straight shot into the wide open waters of success.

Halfway through the corridor, however, his escape was snagged as a surge of water filled the corridor more than he had estimated. Samuel collapsed helplessly to the floor as the boat rapidly rose. Samuel knew the glass windows protruding upwards from the boat's front were going to be crushed before he heard them cracking loudly against the stone ceiling. Shards of glass and plastic fell around him. He shielded his eyes with his hands and hoped for the damage to be limited to the windows.

Once the boat descended, Samuel wasted no time and punched the throttle forward as hard as he could. The engine roared as it propelled the boat through the cave's entrance. One side of the boat's back end smashed loudly against the side of the cave as it passed through, but Samuel didn't care. He had made it out, and the boat was clearly going to be capable of powering through the pounding waves in front of him.

In that moment, when Samuel P. Beckwith was smiling to himself, recalling descriptions of people being able to smell and taste the freedom that called them forward, he felt another profound sensation. One moment, as his boat ascended to the top of a high wave, he saw only the horizon in front of him where the dark blue waters of the Pacific were curtained with a thick gray veil of fog. The next moment, as his boat descended down the other side of the wave, he saw a U.S. Coast Guard cutter blocking his view, with a bright red helicopter veering directly towards him. It was over for Samuel P. Beckwith; *his Stevenson Plan had failed*.

44.

Year of our Lord 2009.

ISIDRO DE LA VEGA PROMISED John Gibson that brunch at the Highlands Inn would be *interesting*. It would offer a unique and gorgeous view of what was in Isidro's opinion arguably the most scenic spot in Monterey County, located as it was high above precarious coastal cliffs below and overlooking Point Lobos with the Monterey Peninsula's Pebble Beach frontage in the background. Additionally, Isidro noted that the food would be delicious and that the people-watching experience would be equally memorable.

Isidro had never paid much attention to observing such present-day societal settings, as he was more often than not more interested in the past, but recent events made him begin to reconsider his approach to life; perhaps it was time to start considering his future. He was resigned to go hiking on his trail the next morning and start a conversation with the dark-haired beauty. If not tomorrow, the next time their paths crossed, he promised himself.

When Gibson called him the day before, he promised he would tell Isidro as much as he could, as they had not seen each other for a couple of days. Gibson spotted Isidro seated at a table in the corner of the restaurant.

The two shook hands and Gibson seated himself across from Isidro. A waiter promptly arrived at their table and received Gibson's request for coffee. The waiter appeared surprised that Gibson was not also interested in ordering a Bloody Mary or Mimosa.

"So, you've been busy, I've heard," Isidro commented, surprising them both that he had begun the conversation.

Gibson sighed. "Yes, one could say so," he agreed. Gibson wanted to shed some light on the case to the young man who had assisted his efforts, but it was still going to be a delicate subject to discuss. Gibson decided to get Isidro talking about something else. "I actually am curious about a few historical tidbits on Monterey, continuing with our previous conversation, if you wouldn't mind indulging me."

Isidro's face brightened. "You know I would not mind. I'm glad to see that you have continued interest. What more would you like to know?"

"Well, I was wondering about what happened after that pirate, Bouchard, invaded Monterey. I remember you saying that he never returned to the coast of California, but what happened to Monterey?"

It took no time for Isidro to respond. "It was about the same time that, ironically, also signaled the end of the Russian threat to Alta California. Actually, Russian interest altogether in North America died quickly in the subsequent years, which at least partially explains why the United States of America was able to acquire the lands of Alaska at such a notoriously favorable price."

Isidro continued, "After the invasion, the citizens of Monterey rebuilt the town even better than before. Governor Fages endured for some years after Bouchard's invasion, living long enough to see his daughter marry and establish a prominent family with a young Englishman.

"The city flourished for a few more decades until its importance was eventually lost. The garrison in Monterey was increased significantly and funds were appropriated for vastly improved defenses. No pirate would ever try again to invade the then heavily protected harbor of Monterey."

"Father Junipero Serra lived out the rest of his days at the Carmel Mission; luckily, though, he died just before the secularization of the mission system after California became a Mexican territory in 1821, as he would have likely died from distress after witnessing how awfully the Native Americans of the time were lied to and mistreated."

"Why's that?" Gibson asked.

"With Mexico's secularization of the missions, the Native Americans received nothing of what they had been promised after devoting their lives to Christianity and agriculture as opposed to their traditional ways of life. The expansive mission lands were largely divided into enormous ranchos that were granted to prominent Mexican citizens, a good majority being those that had served in the Mexican army in its fight to kick out the Spanish. This also was a brilliant way to further overcome Spanish influence with Mexican integration.

"Ironically, not long afterward, though, in 1846 to be exact, with the end of the U.S.-Mexican War, formation of the U.S. Land Commission resulted in breaking up most of the large ranchos in California. The Commission is infamous for having proclaimed the dissolution of the ranchos into public lands able to be settled by others based on the fact that the rancho landowners were not able to provide legal documentation proving their claims to their lands, which of course in many cases never existed to begin with."

Gibson took a sip of the coffee placed in front of him by their waiter. The waiter, noticing that Gibson had not even lifted his menu to view it, stood at attention for a brief moment and then, realizing that the pair was not going to order, scurried away to the nearest table with two elderly women wearing more makeup and jewelry between the two of them than Isidro believed he had ever seen. They had tall glasses of champagne in front of them and plates of food that had been barely touched.

At a table next to the older ladies was a pair of young women he guessed to be in their mid-twenties wearing winter boots, pink sweatpants, sweaters with huge loose necks, and matching oversized sunglasses worn on top of their heads. They were drinking sparkling water and arguing over who had ordered the more healthy breakfast plate.

"And what about the other priest supposedly in Monterey at the time?" Gibson asked with smirk.

Isidro squirmed in his chair before responding. "Yes, Father Margil. Frankly, I don't know," he truthfully admitted. "It's a historical mystery that I am going to continue to try and solve, but as I mentioned before, there is very little in the way of historical record of Father Margil."

"But what you found ..." Gibson paused, then continued, "what you found confirms that the man did exist."

"Yes, yes it does. I also drove to the University of California, Davis yesterday and was allowed to conduct a quick carbon test on the parchment. It was not the full analysis that would provide more precise dating, but it was enough to confirm that the letter was from the same general time period as it's dated," Isidro added.

"What do you believe happened to him?"

"It's clear to me that records of Father Margil, for one reason or another, were purposefully obscured, destroyed, or restricted. Whatever he was involved with must have certainly left him unpopular, as it's not often that a man of the cloth completes an important mission on behalf of the Church and receives no recognition for his deeds." Isidro took a sip of his cup of black tea. "Especially if he becomes a martyr, which I believe I will be able to prove one day. Or … that's my theory, in any case," he quickly added.

"*A martyr?*"

"Yes, I believe so. His presence in Monterey at the time of Bouchard's invasion is reasonable to presume, and if his quest had pushed him to such an extreme point before, there is no reason to believe that he would not have attempted to resist the pirate in some way that resulted in his death." Isidro set down his cup and glanced out through the restaurant's gigantic windows at the jutting Monterey Peninsula.

Gibson considered Isidro's statement for a moment before responding. He took another sip of his coffee. "But so far, your theory also assumes that his actions were sanctioned by the Church, does it not?"

Isidro turned back to face John Gibson, smiled, and said nothing.

Gibson chuckled lightly. "And what about Stevenson?"

"Oh, well, eventually his love interest decided that she had endured enough time in Monterey and returned to San Francisco, with him following." Isidro then suggested that they put in an order for brunch.

Isidro ordered the house special, Eggs Benedict: poached egg on whole wheat sourdough English muffin, slices of prosciutto, tomato, and sliced avocado, topped with a Hollandaise sauce infused with locally harvested wild sage. Gibson liked the sound of it and ordered the same. Their conversation turned more personal as Isidro asked what Gibson believed the future held in store for him.

John Gibson didn't need to consider the question for very long. He felt undeniably confident that Rachel Dowling was going to be an ample portion of his future and he intended to pursue and strengthen his relationship with her. Gibson then surmised, "We'll see how things go."

"Do you see yourself staying in San Francisco?" Isidro questioned.

Two plates were set on their table and they began eating.

After a couple of bites, Gibson explored his own wishes further. "I'm not sure. I'd like to spend some more time there and take it from there."

"Well, you see, your problem is that you've made the mistake, forgivable as it may be, of moving to the wrong *Bay Area*. You would be better off relocating down here to the Monterey Bay," Isidro suggested.

"Ah, I see. It's the *better* bay?" Gibson prodded.

"You said it," Isidro confirmed with confidence. "As I told you, that city stole our glory one hundred fifty years ago, and if more people living here were better aware of history, I would not be the only one holding a slight grudge against that place to the north."

Gibson laughed. It was good to see the passion come alive in his new young friend. "And what's next for you, Isidro de la Vega?"

Isidro meticulously arranged a forkful and placed it in his mouth. After he slowly chewed, taking the time to consider his response, he answered Gibson's question. "I've decided that I'm going to visit the California State Historical Society's headquarters this week and show them the letter I found at the San Antonio Mission before I return the letter to the Franciscans at the Santa Barbara Mission."

"Won't that displease the Franciscans if you do that?" Gibson stated after he had finished chewing a mouthful.

"I'm sure it will. I fear it will also result in my privileges being slightly, if not entirely, revoked with the Mission's archives. But after I considered my situation further in the last couple of days, I came to the conclusion that it would be better to ensure that the tale of Father Dominique Margil not be completely lost, locked away as a Church secret for all time. My duty as a Catholic may have led me to allow the secret to be buried, but my sense of duty as a historian will not permit such a thing."

"Good for you, Isidro," Gibson proclaimed proudly. Then, leaning closer, he asked softly, "*and how about any treasure hunting?*"

Isidro leaned backwards in his chair, grinning knowingly. "I don't believe Bouchard's treasure will ever be found, and the only treasure hunting I plan on doing is to follow my friend Sir Tom's advice and keep myself open to discovering my own."

After brunch, Isidro de la Vega said goodbye to John Gibson, promising him that on his next visit to the Monterey Peninsula with Rachel, he would happily arrange another cultural tour and be their personal guide once again. As Isidro drove south on Highway 1, the thought occurred to him that during their entire conversation, Gibson had revealed very little about the investigation and arrest of the distinguished Pebble Beach resident that had become the major topic of local news and social gossip. Isidro questioned if it had been a tactic of Gibson's all along to avoid the subject, but decided that even if it had been, it was of no consequence.

The details of what happened were not so important to him anyway, and the local news headlines highlighted the major points rather effectively: FBI RAID ON BIG SUR CABIN, FATALITY AND ARREST OF PROMINENT PEBBLE BEACH NATIVE. Isidro read in the morning's newspaper that the fatality was a Big Sur native with ties to an underground anti-government organization. Society of the Peninsula would be shocked most of all, though, by the arrest on federal charges of the other man, a highly influential individual with origins to one of the region's founding families. It was sure to be a popular topic of conversation on the Peninsula's famed golf courses and in its many extravagant restaurants for years to come.

John Gibson felt the vibration of his cell phone receiving an incoming call. He pulled out the phone from his jacket pocket and answered it. He didn't enjoy talking on the phone while driving, but he could see from the caller identification that it was a call from his FBI branch building in San Francisco.

"This is Agent Gibson," he answered.

"Hello, Agent Gibson, this is Trish." Trish was the receptionist and assistant for Gibson's domestic terrorism department, which had been his department prior to his most recent reassignment. "Hello, Trish. It's good to hear from you."

Trish continued, "I wanted to let you know that DC has been calling for you over the last few days. It didn't sound too pressing, and I was instructed to not contact you about it as you were on the other case, but today I've gotten a few calls that made me think I should get in touch with you right away."

Gibson took in Trish's words, wondering what could be so important. Of course, the Beckwith case was far from over. Sure, Samuel Beckwith had been apprehended and caught with stolen federal property in his possession, and his two partners who were still alive, Lombardo and Mathews, would likely be prompted to testify against him. In a perfect world, his guilt would be unmistakable, but the world is overshadowed by politics, money, greed, and attorneys. Samuel P. Beckwith possessed the means to all of these factors and Gibson realized that even with his capture, there was always the chance that Beckwith might elect to go to trial and attempt to downplay his role in the heist to ease his pending conviction, if not to try to get off altogether. *Rich guys hated going to jail, after all.*

Beckwith and his attorney, or team of attorneys, as was more likely to be the case, could predictably concoct a story whereby they testified that Zande Allen was the true mastermind of the whole affair. It would just be his own bad luck that Allen had managed to get himself killed and would not be able to defend himself. *It's the only system we have, but damn if it doesn't aggravate me at times,* Gibson thought.

"It's no problem, Trish. I'm actually heading on my way back to the City now and will be back in the office this afternoon," Gibson replied.

"Okay … that's great, because these French guys are really insistent to get in touch with you," Trish revealed.

"*French guys?*"

"Yup, that's right. First it was some sleazy-sounding guy who said he was calling on behalf of some *Capitene* or something, and when I mentioned that you were not available, he started trying to flirt with me over the phone," Trish vented.

The French, Gibson said to himself as he shook his head.

"A couple of hours later, that same French guy called back again for you, even though I told him that you were not available and that I would pass along the message. And then another French guy, a *Capitene* Nivelle, took the line and was being really pushy about me giving him your cell number, and this French guy made the other French guy seem charming."

Nivelle, Gibson swerved slightly on the road. He straightened out the vehicle and firmed his grip on the steering wheel. "Yes, he's a handful. Listen, I'll be back there within a couple of hours. It's getting late over there, so I doubt he will call again today, but if he calls back again, promise him that I'll return his call as soon as I can. That won't be good enough for him, but it should at least get him to stop pestering you."

"Okay, thank you, Agent Gibson. Drive safely and see you soon," Trish replied with relief apparent in her voice.

Nivelle … what could you be calling me for? Gibson admitted to himself that his curiosity was piquing and that he actually looked forward to speaking with Capitaine Nivelle.

Isidro de la Vega passed by the trailhead to his hiking trail, past the turn into the darkened entrance to Palo Colorado Road, and over the famous Bixby Bridge. His drive was slowed by a backup of cars at nearly every turn in the road. Normally he avoided driving south on Highway 1 on weekend afternoons, as even in the off-tourist season, the road was assured to be congested with out-of-town visitors, but today he didn't mind the snail-paced traffic.

Isidro was certain of a conclusion he had reached the day before, as certain of any historical research he had ever conducted, and the drive south gave him time to relish his discovery. It was a shame that he would be the only person to ever know the truth, as he promised himself he would take the secret to his grave, *but at least he would always know it.*

It was irrefutable that if he were to unveil his having solved the mystery of Hippolyte de Bouchard's buried treasure, the same mystery that likely had so enticed Robert Louis Stevenson, some degree of fame would be bestowed upon him. But enough blood had been spilled over whatever treasure might lie buried up there and it deserved its final resting place, Isidro thought. And besides, even with the location of Bouchard's treasure remaining his personal secret, he would still be recognized for having discovered Father Margil's letter and for providing a theory on the Father's journey, granting him more than enough professional respect.

Isidro pulled his car over to the side of the highway as the road began to drop to a lower elevation leading into the narrow, flatter green plain that marked the entrance into Big Sur and stood in contrast to the brown foothills lining its eastern boundary. The valley-like area had served as a pasture for grazing cattle for over a hundred years and groups of cows idled alongside the highway. The white peak of the mysterious Pico Blanco loomed in the background, with Mount Manuel's summit beside it and the backdrop of other peaks to the south.

Isidro gazed at the gigantic volcanic rock, hundreds of feet tall, that protruded just off the coast and was only connected to the mainland by a one-lane road. Waves crashed against the shoreline around the point and at times made the road impassable, similar to Mont Saint-Michel off the coast of France.

A steep route led up the side of the rock to a lighthouse, its adjoining light station buildings, and the two-story home that had been preserved as part of the entire point's dedication as a state historic park long after its requirement to be occupied by lighthouse caretakers and their families had fallen into the pages of history. The elegant Victorian home looked dramatically out of place on top of the point, but Isidro de la Vega smiled as he thought of something else; something else buried up there that was even more out of place …

Point Sur, as it had been so named long ago by the first white settlers to brave the wilds of Big Sur, was really *an island*. It would definitely appear as a very prominent one from any ship sailing by in the turbulent waters of the central Californian coastline.

El Fin